MURDER
AT THE FAIR

BOOKS BY VERITY BRIGHT

MURDER
AT THE FAIR

VERITY BRIGHT

Bookouture

Published by Bookouture in 2021

An imprint of Storyfire Ltd.
Carmelite House
50 Victoria Embankment
London EC4Y 0DZ

www.bookouture.com

ISBN: 978-1-80019-420-5
eBook ISBN: 978-1-80019-419-9

To our readers, without whom Lady Swift, Clifford and Gladstone's adventures would be mere hearsay.

'A little sincerity is a dangerous thing, and a great deal of it is absolutely fatal.' – Oscar Wilde

CHAPTER 1

'Thief!'

Her piercing green eyes scanned the immediate vicinity. Luck was on her side. The villagers of Little Buckford were too busy enjoying the warm spring sunshine and the May Fair to have noticed anything amiss.

'Gladstone!' Lady Eleanor Swift hissed at the bulldog hiding his head under the sage skirt of her favourite two-piece suit. 'Whatever have you stolen now, you little terror?' She gently pulled him out, smoothed her skirt down her long, slender frame and tucked one of several mutinous strands of red curls back under her cloche hat. She knew admonishing him was fruitless. He'd been far too loved and indulged by her late uncle – the dog's previous owner – to ever take a reprimand to heart. Fourteen eventful months after she'd arrived at Henley Hall, she still had no real idea how to manage the bulldog or the estate, but had fallen in love with both.

Gently prising the muddy newspaper-wrapped parcel from the dog's unwilling jaws, she groaned.

'Oh, botheration, that looks suspiciously like someone's lunch.'

'Aye, Lady Swift, that it were.'

'Double botheration!' she whispered in Gladstone's ear. *Of all the people, Ellie!* She spun round, slapping on a smile. 'Ah, Mr Cartwright. Happy May Day.'

The stocky farmer's bushy brows met in a solid line as he tipped his flat cap and glowered at her. 'Don't see what's so happy 'bout it. Your dog has gone chased my pigs out of their enclosure and' – he pointed to the parcel in her hands – 'been stealing food out of my truck as well.'

Eleanor sighed to herself. *A grumpy farmer's the last thing you needed, Ellie.* And Cartwright was always grumpy. Well, with her, anyway. She conceded that it might have something to do with her having accused him of murder only a few days after she arrived at Henley Hall. *Some people*, she thought sadly, *take offence at the smallest of things*.

She furtively cast her eye around for her butler, but to no avail.

'I am sorry Gladstone stole your lunch, Mr Cartwright.' She tried to hide her grimace as she held out the dirt-streaked parcel. 'I shall, of course, replace it immediately.'

The farmer's weathered jaw twitched as he hooked his thumbs through the buttonholes of a faded, yet smart, chequered waistcoat.

'You've a rum impression of local folk, Lady Swift. We might not live in a ruddy great pile of bricks as big as yours, but that doesn't mean we stoop to stealing food off of pigs.'

'I beg your pardon?' She stared down at the parcel in her hand, for the first time noticing beech nuts poking through the soggy paper. 'Oh! So… erm, this isn't your lunch then?'

Sensing a presence behind her, she turned in relief to Clifford, her butler. Along with the other staff, she had inherited him with Henley Hall on her uncle's death the year before. Having been brought up most of her life abroad by bohemian parents, she had little idea how a lady of the manor was supposed to behave. Thankfully, he did, and regularly imparted his knowledge whether she wanted it or not.

'Oh, there you are, Clifford.'

Impeccably turned out in a black suit and tie topped off with a bowler hat, he wore his usual inscrutable expression. However, the overall effect of quiet dignity was rather diminished by the squirming piglet he held. She bit her lip at the unexpected spectacle.

'Mr Clifford.' Cartwright nodded, taking the pig and tucking it under his arm.

Clifford nodded in return. 'I repeat her ladyship's sincere apology, Mr Cartwright. You will find a full sack of roasted beech nuts on the driving seat of your farm truck with a little something alongside for your trouble. The rest of his friends' – he gestured at the piglet – 'are now secured also.'

Cartwright licked his bottom lip. 'That'll do alright, Mr Clifford. Thank you kindly.' He leaned forward and lowered his voice, Eleanor just catching his words. 'None of us envy you trying to keep *that* one in order.' With another glower in Eleanor's direction, he stumped off.

She gestured after the farmer. 'Bit of a cheek, even for him, suggesting you are the only one tasked with controlling Gladstone. I am too.' She raised an eyebrow, daring him to correct her.

Clifford's face remained inscrutable although she was sure the corners of his lips had twitched. 'I really couldn't say, my lady.' He pointed at the village green. 'I believe your presence is required.'

Before Clifford had been her uncle's butler, he was his batman in the army, for many years. Despite the class difference, they'd been more than employer and servant. They'd been friends. On his deathbed, Uncle Byron had tasked Clifford with looking after his beloved niece. He carried out his duty with iron resolve.

Ellie shook her head. 'Now, what's all this about pigs and beech nuts?' Even though she'd been at the Hall the previous May, she'd suffered from a short-lived bout of illness, unusual for her, that meant she'd yet to experience Little Buckford's May Fair.

Clifford raised an eyebrow. 'The derby, of course, my lady.'

'Of course.'

She must have looked a little puzzled as Clifford quickly clarified. 'The pig derby. It was detailed in the advance copy of the programme you received.'

'Oh, that. Yes. Well, I might have inadvertently mislaid it, what with everything else going on at the Hall just now.' The 'everything else' was the annual Henley Hall spring clean, an event that had apparently struck dread into her late uncle, a man who, when alive, had fearlessly faced everything from wild animals to deadly assassins.

'If I might enlighten you? The pig derby is the second-biggest highlight of the fair. A great deal of bets are being placed as we speak.'

She flapped a hand at him. 'Oh, no you don't. I may have grown up abroad, but I know perfectly well that traditional English May Fairs do not commonly involve a herd of unruly pigs belting round a course.'

He bowed. 'Welcome to Buckinghamshire, my lady.'

She laughed. 'Okay, when in Rome and all that. The wriggling specimen you handed to Cartwright looked particularly clean and shiny, I must say.'

'Buttermilk.'

She blinked. 'Am I actually caught in a bizarre dream? Buttermilk, Clifford?'

'They are all rubbed with buttermilk, my lady. They need to look their best today, as is tradition.'

She shook her head. 'I suppose they'll have mini jockeys riding on their backs too?'

'Indeed they will.'

She narrowed her eyes at him. *Is he ribbing you, Ellie?* She checked his face, but as ever, it was quite unreadable.

'The ladies of the village crochet a full complement of riders and saddles, my lady, each carefully measured to fit the noble steed they will be riding. The animals themselves are rewarded by following a line of beech nuts, which guides them round the track. I concede, however, country ways can take a while to master. Perhaps you will therefore allow me to give you a tour of the May Fair before your duties commence?' He gestured at the bustling green again, deftly looping a lead through Gladstone's collar with his other hand. 'Shall we?'

CHAPTER 2

As they walked towards the growing hubbub, Eleanor frowned.

'Tell me, Clifford, what exactly is May Day all about again?'

'It is the welcoming in of summer and all the abundance it is hoped she will favourably bestow upon the area. A most significant date in the village's calendar, and thus it has been since medieval times, 1221 being the first fair recorded in the church records.'

Her jaw fell slack. 'Gracious! Here on this very spot. For seven hundred years?'

'Indeed, every May first. It is a particular distinction that you have been asked to be the guest of honour for the 1921 May Fair to mark this extra special occasion.'

Feeling the unfamiliar warmth of belonging after her years of living and travelling abroad, Eleanor stared at the swarm of villagers dressed in their Sunday best still streaming onto the green. She turned to see he had read her thoughts.

'And I get to be a part of that tradition.'

Clifford coughed. 'Indeed, although the part you are judging is a rather modern addition of your uncle's.'

Fascinated by the centuries-old history of the fair, she delighted in letting Clifford lead her through the myriad striped awnings covering the village green. As she went, she kept an eye out for the rest of her staff. She'd given them the day off as her uncle had always done on the day of the fair, and was trying to keep out of their way so they didn't feel they had to behave.

In fact, she was so busy trying to avoid her staff that she bumped into the back of a square-shouldered, square-chinned man evidently as distracted as she was.

She raised her hands. 'I say, completely my fault. I do apologise.'

The man gave a bow worthy of her butler and shuffled off, his prominent aquiline nose buried back in his grey wool scarf. She stared after him. *Why would someone wear such a heavy overcoat and scarf in such warm weather? Oh, poor chap, he must be feeling ill and you had to knock into him, Ellie! Hardly guest-of-honour behaviour.*

Taking more care as to her surroundings, she caught up with Clifford. Several of the tables under the colourful awnings were festooned with a variety of flower-filled baskets, which made her smile. An enormous basket had been left on the doorstep of Henley Hall that morning. Clifford had explained on May Day it was a tradition for an admirer to leave such a gift anonymously for his sweetheart. He had expressed amazement, however, at the size and expense of the one left for her. She'd been equally surprised that her admirer – Detective Chief Inspector Seldon, for she guessed it was from him – had indulged in such an openly romantic gesture. Not, she thought, in keeping with his usual gruff and rather stiff style, especially since their relationship had cooled somewhat since they'd last met.

As they emerged from under the final awning, she gasped at the sight of the birch maypole dominating the centre of the green. Standing twenty-eight-feet high, multicoloured ribbons fixed to the top cascaded down, their ends fluttering in the light spring breeze. An impish thought struck her.

'Nice to see you out of your morning-suit tails, by the way. Ready for a turn around the maypole, are you?'

Clifford pursed his lips. 'Fortunately, the maypole is singularly the province of the village children.'

'Shame, I rather fancied seeing you cavort around it holding a ribbon.'

He sniffed and pointed further down the green. 'And over there are the morris men, performing a traditional folkdance originating from the fifteenth century, I believe.'

After what felt like a hundred caps had been doffed with a deferential 'Lady Swift. Mr Clifford,' they emerged at the western edge of the village green, where a multitude of stalls were swarming with eager fair-goers. She clapped her hands.

'Look! There's a coconut shy, skittle alley, bows and arrow shoot, and a treasure hunt!'

'There is also quoits and hoopla, my lady, hook-a-duck, guess the weight of the ham, and welly wangling.'

She raised an eyebrow. 'Welly *wangling*, Clifford?' Before he could reply, her eye was caught by the sight of the vicar at another stall hurling a stick at a wooden bust of an elderly woman, a long clay pipe poking from her smiling mouth. As the stick smashed the end of the pipe, the crowd roared while the vicar danced a rather undignified but triumphant jig.

'What the?' Eleanor shook her head. 'That doesn't look quite right, Clifford.'

'It is called "Aunt Sally", my lady, a most traditional game in Buckinghamshire and the Chilterns.'

A moment later, as they rounded the striped awning of the refreshment tent, she followed his urgent gesture to duck inside behind the large flap serving as a door.

She lowered her voice. 'Where are we going? Actually, more pertinently, why does it feel like we are hiding?'

'Because we are, my lady. The route of our tour has been such as to ensure you did not cross paths with the chairman of the May Fair Committee. He is most anxious to see you. When you failed to attend his briefing his displeasure was nothing short of palpable.'

She groaned. 'I was so looking forward to all the fun of the fair itself, I'd completely forgotten about Mr Peterson-Prestonwick and his briefing.'

'Regrettably, Mr *Prestwick-Peterson* puts great importance on his briefings. They are feared throughout the village.'

'So I'm already in trouble with a grumpy farmer and an over-officious chairman. You think I'd know better now I've turned thirty.' She shrunk back as Clifford reached inside his jacket and pulled out a huge, pleated blue rosette. 'Oh, no!'

'Oh, yes, my lady. It is tradition that the guest of honour wears such a rosette.'

'But I'm only awarding the prizes for the raft race.'

He peered at her. 'And starting it, my lady. That is one of the great honours of the May Fair. One which your late uncle, his lordship, carried out with immense aplomb. True, he instigated the raft race, but you have, so to speak, inherited his mantle.' As she reluctantly pinned the rosette to her jacket, Clifford snapped his pocket watch closed. 'Shall we adjourn to the river? The race commences shortly.'

She nodded. 'And let's hope it goes off without incident. The last race I judged, well...' She didn't need to finish her sentence. They both knew how that had ended.

CHAPTER 3

Eleanor had never seen the villagers of Little Buckford so carefree. Even at the jolly Christmas Eve luncheon she'd held for them at Henley Hall, as visitors to another world, the grandeur of the Hall had restrained them. Now she was in their world, and their childlike glee was infectious.

Clifford led her to the southern end of the green, where it seemed most of the village had assembled. She felt utterly at peace and very lucky. It was almost as though she was watching seven hundred years of history unfold before her in a single afternoon.

She sighed contentedly. When she had come to Henley Hall after the news of her uncle's death, she had been convinced she would last only a few weeks and would hurry back to her nomadic and chaotic life in South Africa. But now, looking around, she had to admit, Little Buckford felt like home.

Over Clifford's shoulder, she spotted the chairman of the May Fair with his harassed assistant hurrying behind him. The chairman's flaccid face was set in a long-suffering look.

'Lady Swift, if you could please remember the timetable the committee has painstakingly worked out.' He waved what she assumed was the fair programme in his right hand. 'Kindly position yourself to start the raft race in' – he consulted a pocket watch held in the other – 'seventeen minutes.'

She nodded. 'Of course.'

'Very good.' The chairman strode off with his assistant scurrying behind him.

Eleanor turned to Clifford as she started walking along the towpath, Gladstone ambling along behind them. The river was a tributary of the Thames and normally meandered slowly towards its source like a drunken eel. Today, however, after the recent heavy rains, its swollen waters lapped at the bank and swirled and danced their way through Little Buckford.

'Where exactly do I start the raft race from?'

He pointed upstream. 'The starting podium is actually the pontoon for the old foot ferry. It is no longer needed since a second bridge was built a few years back due to the increase in vehicular traffic. When the rafts are lined up at the start line, you simply blow the whistle you will be handed to herald the beginning of the race.'

'Sounds easy enough. And then I grab my skirts and sprint back downstream to the finish line to judge the winner?' The sound of a sharp sniff made her roll her eyes. 'Alright, stroll elegantly downstream as befits the lady of the manor?'

Before replying, Clifford watched a large branch float past, his pocket watch open.

'The current is approximately two-point-nine miles per hour. The fastest winning time of nineteen minutes and forty seconds was achieved in nineteen eighteen with a current of two-point-four miles per hour. Despite the unusual speed of the river, as the finishing line is roughly half a mile from the start point, I feel that ladylike elegance might easily be maintained.' He closed his watch. 'And you will still arrive in time to judge who is the winner.'

She ruffled Gladstone's ears. 'Wonderful, running in these shoes would be a disaster. Now, where's this podium thing?'

As they rounded the bend of the river, she stopped in surprise at the flotilla making its way downstream towards the start point.

'Clifford, just look at the rafts! They are simply' – she caught her breath then burst into laughter – 'spectacular and ridiculous!'

He followed her gaze. 'Indeed. The closely guarded secrets of many, many hours of concerted creative effort. The winner of the race, and the one to come in last and receive the wooden spoon, are easy to judge. However, my lady, I do not envy you in having to choose which one to award "The Best-Dressed Raft" to.'

'I know. I can't imagine how I'm going to decide.'

In front of them were twenty or so home-made floating platforms, the largest of which held twelve or more crew. Painstakingly cobbled together from what looked like old wooden doors or planks, each one was raised on a variety of buoyancy aids such as wooden barrels. But there the similarity ended as their proud creators had uniquely decorated each craft.

The village cricket team had clearly planned ahead as they had covered the floor of their raft in pristinely mown grass, replete with giant replica stumps. Smart in their whites, they stood on the deck of their creation, holding large hand-whittled paddles in the shape of cricket bats. Next to them, a replica of the local Dog and Badger public house dominated another raft, the crew each sitting on a bar stool holding a pint.

Even the constabulary had entered the race with a smart blue raft bearing a passable but enormous model of a policeman's helmet. Two constables, the second seconded from the nearby town of Chipstone as Little Buckford only had one policeman, sat either side with their legs dangling in the water.

Among the remaining rafts, one in particular caught Eleanor's eye. Shaped like an oversized coffin replete with a giant headstone, which kept falling on top of the hapless man trying to captain it, it lagged some way behind the others.

'Clifford, that's Solemn Jon.' Solemn Jon was the local undertaker, a popular figure despite his morbid role in the village. 'Why is he the only one on board? He's got no chance of winning.'

His gaze followed her pointing finger.

'Unfortunately, my lady, his assistant and intended crew member, Mr Willie Green, fell ill at the last moment. But ever game, Solemn Jon decided he would continue on his own. Perhaps, in hindsight, an unwise decision.' He scanned the rest of the rafts. 'A fine array of crafts, nonetheless. Certainly superior to the previous year.'

She tore her eyes away from the organised chaos on the water. 'You mean these aren't last year's efforts? They make a new raft each year?'

'I believe, my lady, that question will be answered for you at the finish line. Or' – he glanced at the rafts again – 'most likely before, for many do not even last that long.'

She looked across to the opposite bank, deep in thought. Her job, establishing safari routes for Thomas Walker's famous travel company, had left her adept at judging the width of rivers as there was rarely a bridge that would take vehicles and, if there was, it was rarely safe. She'd met Thomas Walker while cycling solo around the world (and, no, she wasn't the first woman to do so as she was tired of telling disbelieving listeners) and he'd immediately offered her the job.

She looked at the opposite bank again. Despite being a strong swimmer and at home on the sea, her parents having been keen sailors, she shuddered at the thought of swimming across the river. There might not be crocodiles, but dark, weed-infested water was worse. Who knew what was lurking in those murky depths? *Thank heavens you don't have to actually ride on a raft, Ellie!*

Clifford coughed gently. 'Perhaps it would be prudent to start the race before the rafts start taking on water in earnest?' He glanced at the river. 'I fear St Winifred's is in a bad way.'

CHAPTER 4

On the podium, Eleanor beamed as she shook Mr Prestwick-Peterson's generously proportioned hand. Then she bent down to accept the whistle from the tiny fair-haired girl of four or five, dressed in a sea of homespun white frills with a matching bonnet.

'Welcome, m'lady,' the girl said shyly. She went up on tiptoe to put the whistle around Eleanor's neck and whispered in her ear, 'You're the most beautiful princess I've ever met.'

'Gracious, I'm not actually…' Eleanor stopped and took in the little girl's awe. She smiled and whispered back, 'If I was judging the dresses at the fair today, I would give you first prize for having the prettiest I've seen.' Smiling at the proud twirl this brought on, she straightened up and waved the whistle. 'Teams? Are you READY?'

The wild waving of home-made paddles from the competitors came back in reply. She waited, allowing the undertaker to line up at the start like the others.

'Right. Then, I declare this raft race officially…'

Unfortunately, given the time it took Solemn Jon to join the others, most of the rafts had now drifted off the start line. She waited until a lot of shouting and splashing from the crews and good-natured heckling from the crowd had realigned them. Raising the whistle again, she blew as hard as she could.

Silence, however, was the only reward for her aching cheeks. She stared at the whistle, then shook it. Aware all eyes were on her, she gave Mr Prestwick-Peterson an embarrassed shrug.

'It appears to have somehow become parted from its pea. But no matter.' She pulled off her gloves, slid the first two fingers of either hand into her mouth, and blew with all her might. A long ear-piercing whistle split the air, one that in the South African bush had warned her assistants of dangerous animals many times. Its effect on the riverbank of Little Buckford was to raise a riotous cheer from the crowd and a frenzy of paddling from the rafts. Behind her, Eleanor caught sight of Clifford, eyes closed, pinching the bridge of his nose.

Oops, Ellie! So much for maintaining your ladylike elegance!

'That went off alright, wouldn't you say?' she said as she accepted his elbow to step from the pontoon-cum-podium.

A gaggle of boys in short trousers ran past. One stopped in front of her.

'Nice whistling, m'lady. I ain't never learned how to do that.'

She laughed. 'Come find me later and I'll teach you.'

He whooped in reply and sprinted on to catch his friends up.

She caught Clifford's disapproving eye. 'I know, I know, but even you have to admit it was a good whistle!'

A commotion caught her attention. A raft she hadn't spotted before, consisting of a couple of hay bales and little else seemed to be taking on water rapidly.

'Penry, you dog! I swear I'll swing for you one day!'

It was Cartwright, the farmer she'd had a run-in with earlier over his pigs' stolen lunch. It seemed his craft wasn't sinking, rather the butcher on another raft was using his paddle to fling water over it. Incensed at the drenching he and his raft were receiving, Cartwright jumped up and waved his paddle at the other man. Much to the delight of the crowd on the bank, they were soon drowning each other in as much water as they could scoop up. Eleanor wasn't surprised. She knew first-hand about the butcher and farmer's long-running feud, having seen it for herself when she'd joined the local amateur dramatic society in an attempt to become more involved in village life.

The two rafts were now perilously close to each other. Cartwright, taking his chance, leaned over and with a lucky strike whacked Penry round the head with a loud crack.

Clifford coughed. 'Perhaps it is time to hasten towards the finish line, my lady?'

'But shouldn't we make sure they don't actually do each other a damage... Oh, gracious!'

Penry had launched himself at Cartwright's raft, only to upend not only his but also the farmer's as he landed heavily on one side.

'Oh, botheration!' Eleanor pointed downstream, where many of the rafts were now floating. 'I'm going to be too late to judge who crosses the finish line first. Permission to forgo a little ladylike decorum, Clifford?'

He sighed. 'Purely in the cause of allowing you to perform your duty as guest of honour, reluctantly granted.'

Leaving the butcher and farmer to fight it out, Eleanor grabbed her skirt and hurried back down the towpath, weaving through the stream of people. She noted with faint annoyance that Clifford was keeping pace merely by lengthening his stride, despite now carrying Gladstone. *Dratted skirts, Ellie! You just can't run properly in them.*

'Mid-point, my lady.' He pointed to a fluttering yellow flag. 'And three rafts down already on account of sinking.'

'And two on account of fighting,' she added. 'I'm beginning to think at this rate that I shall be awarding the prize to the only craft that actually crosses the finishing line. Assuming there is one left to cross it, of course.'

At that moment, the cricket team's raft collided with a half-fallen willow, which released a snowstorm of white woolly catkin seeds that settled on the crew.

'Ah, six down,' Clifford said as the crew abandoned ship.

Just ahead, the river took another sweeping curve, this time to the right. The line of hurrying men and women still ahead of them held onto their bonnets and caps as a warm but stiff breeze whipped round to meet them.

'The going is toughest for the racers from this point on, my lady. There are a series of forceful eddies caused, it is said, by submerged rocks which fell from Old Irving's Tor when the Saxon fort collapsed in 1296.'

Two more rafts lost their crew in the eddies, just as Clifford had predicted. Thus, as Eleanor waited on the thirteenth-century arched stone footbridge that served as the finish line, there were only a handful still being paddled downstream towards her. The first to pass under the bridge and scramble up to assemble before her was the suspiciously swaying crew of the Dog and Badger public house.

She chuckled. 'Suffering a little, er, motion sickness, gentlemen?'

The landlord stepped forward unsteadily. 'Since we're the winning team, m'lady, tonight we might all be suffering from a lot more besides. Right, lads?'

This brought a cheer from the rest of the crew and much unco-ordinated back slapping as Eleanor handed over the winner's trophy.

What was left of the last of the rafts and the now exhausted paddlers made their way under the bridge to more rousing cheers and applause. Swimming behind them came several of the teams whose rafts had sunk, while the remainder sploshed down the towpath to stand laughing and dripping among the crowd.

Having awarded the best-dressed raft trophy to the Little Buckford Dairy entry, Eleanor moved on to the next prize.

'And the wooden spoon,' she announced to the onlookers below, 'goes to the last team to cross the line, which is…'

She frowned as the chairman bustled up to her, shaking his head.

'Apparently, there's still one to come in, Lady Swift. Assuming my assistant here counted properly?' He jerked around to glare at the young man behind him.

'Absolutely I did, Mr Prestwick-Peterson, sir.'

'Oh, I say.' Eleanor pointed. 'Isn't that it now?'

Everyone spun round. Someone started a chant of 'Wooden spoon. Wooden spoon!' The rest of the crowd joined in, but something about the scene brought Eleanor's brows together. She peered down over the bridge to where Clifford looked up at her from the bank, a pair of field glasses hanging from his neck. He shook his head and turned his palm upward as he mouthed, 'Capsized.'

The raft was indeed capsized, she could see that now. But of the crew, there was no sign.

CHAPTER 5

Eleanor gripped the stone capping of the bridge as she leaned forward to get a clearer view of the final raft making its lonely, unmanned journey towards her. As it dipped and spun in the river's turbulence, occasionally an edge of it stuck higher out of the water.

The upturned craft caught in a fast eddy and then jammed hard between two of the submerged rocks Clifford had mentioned. With no sign of the crew, Eleanor looked again over the bridge to call out for Clifford to throw his field glasses up to her, but he had disappeared.

She turned back and clutched her chest.

'Clifford, how do you do that? You were down on the bank only half a second ago.'

Without a word he handed her the glasses.

'And how do you know the exact item I need before I do?' She held up a hand. 'I know, I know, you're a butler.' She peered through the glasses, scanning the swirling river, first upstream and then down, an unsettling feeling in the pit of her stomach. 'There's no sign of anyone in the water or along either towpath for as far as I can see.'

They both leaned over the bridge, scouring the crowd.

'Constable Fry!'

Eleanor waved at one of the soggy policemen from the blue raft, holding the tiny hands of three identical jiggling little boys still in nappies. Gesturing for him to join her on the bridge, she stepped over to Mr Prestwick-Peterson who was chiding his assistant.

'I told you to count them off as they came through, boy!'

'But I did, sir. That's how I was able to let you know there was one lagging behind.'

'But why didn't you tick off the names of the teams as well, you halfwit?'

The young man's neck flushed red. 'Because I was only asked to count the number of rafts, not the number of entrants, *sir*.'

Eleanor intervened. 'And what a good job you did. I might otherwise have awarded the wooden spoon to the wrong raft. Now, something's obviously gone awry and—' But before she could point out that, in her humble opinion, a missing crew was more important than an administrative argument, Clifford cleared his throat.

'Mr Prestwick-Peterson, think of all your planning. If we round up whoever was on that raft as expediently as possible, Lady Swift can complete the prize-giving by awarding the wooden spoon. Otherwise the next event surely cannot start as your programme clearly states?'

The chairman stiffened. 'Well, the order of events certainly cannot deviate from the agreed programme. I could not countenance such a thing.'

'What's the hold up?' yelled a voice.

This prompted a rumble of discontent among the rest of the crowd.

Mr Prestwick-Peterson let out an exasperated sigh. 'I suppose the sooner we find the missing crew, the sooner we can continue.'

'Excellent!' Eleanor gestured towards the restless onlookers. 'May I?'

'Gladly,' responded the chairman.

Leaning over the side of the bridge, she faced the crowd. This was what she was used to. Taking charge in moments of crisis.

'Fellow Little Buckfordites, we have a slight addition to the end of the raft race today. Are you game?'

A hesitant cheer and a small wave of hands came in reply amid the mass of confused frowns.

'Oh, I'm not sure they're ready, Clifford. What do you think?'

Playing along, he shook his head.

She leaned further over the bridge.

'I said, ARE. YOU. GAME?'

This time she had to cover her ears as the roar of agreement set a flock of pigeons in the willows on the opposite bank into startled flight.

'Good. Now, I can't award the wooden spoon because the last team hasn't come through with their raft. I think we should hurry. They may have got into a spot of bother, so please group yourselves into one of four teams.'

As the men among the crowd sorted themselves out, Eleanor turned to Constable Fry, who had appeared on the bridge.

'Constable, can you stay here in case we need you to rush off and find the doctor?'

With a hearty nod that reminded her of a heavy dray horse straining against his reins, the policeman took up position on the centre of the bridge.

As she gathered her skirt to make swifter progress down the bridge, Clifford spoke quietly to her.

'Artfully done, my lady.'

'Thank you, Clifford,' she muttered. 'Though I think when we find the so-called missing persons enjoying a lazy swim or walk to the finish line, I'm going to look very foolish.'

Down on the riverbank, she quickly assessed the situation. Twenty able-bodied men had gathered into four groups. Only one seemed to be having trouble amongst its team members.

'What would make you think you're welcome in this group?' Cartwright said. 'You're the lardy muttonhead who lost me the race by starting it on the water!'

'Wind your tongue in, Cartwright,' Penry said. 'We're here to help, not fight.'

Clifford gestured that Penry might wish to swap with another team as Eleanor instructed the others on which direction and side of the bank they should take.

'Please check every inch, gentlemen. But as swiftly as possible. If you find the missing crew, send a runner and I'll whistle to call everyone back.'

'Who's missing?' a voice called.

A stocky farmhand held up a sodden cardboard model of a headstone.

'Anyone seen Solemn Jon?' Constable Fry bellowed from up on the bridge. A collective shake of heads had him nodding to Eleanor.

'Right,' Eleanor said to her makeshift search parties. 'That makes it easier. We're only looking for one man.' She felt a frisson of anxiety run up her back as she remembered he had been the only person without a teammate. No wonder he'd lagged behind the rest of the rafts. She shook the worry from her mind and concentrated on what needed to be done. 'Ready?' The teams nodded in unison. 'Then let the search begin!'

Joining the team on the opposite bank, Eleanor suggested she scan the middle of the river, as she had the field glasses, and the others concentrate on the river's edge. Gladstone lolloped along, his lead held fast in Clifford's leather-gloved hand, his nose to the ground, looking every part the bloodhound.

'Come on, boy, help us find Solemn Jon!'

'Regrettably, my lady,' Clifford said. 'I fear Master Gladstone is merely searching for forgotten picnic scraps.'

'Most likely.' She lowered her voice. 'Why do I have a horrible feeling of dread about this?'

He looked at her with concern. 'Probably due to the rather unfortunate plethora of deaths you have become involved in since your arrival at Henley Hall.'

'You feel uneasy too, then?'

'I confess that I do. However, let us assume that Solemn Jon simply decided to rest and then take another way back to the village green for some reason.'

'But if he knew he was last, he would also have known that everyone would have been waiting for him to collect the wooden spoon.'

'My lady!' Penry called up ahead, pointing near the bank. 'There's some more of his cardboard tombstones caught in the weed here.'

'Well spotted! Then extra vigilance all, if you will.'

A few minutes later she was dizzy from trying to walk while peering through the glasses. She was no longer blinded every time she looked through them, as a cloud had drifted in front of the sun, but the sudden drop in temperature made her shiver. Clifford had brought up the rear, sharing signals with his opposite number across the river in case they had missed anything. Penry had assigned himself on point and was good-naturedly marshalling the other four men along.

'I thinks Solemn Jon's simply taken himself off to have it out with that Willie Green,' Eleanor heard one of the group say.

'Reckon you're right.' Penry nodded. 'Fancy not turning up for the raft race and leaving poor old Solemn Jon on his own.'

'Willie sent word he was sick,' another voice called. 'Though Solemn Jon told me he didn't believe any of it. And aside from being the worse for the drink, Willie was in fine form in the wee hours this morning when I passed him as I collected the day's milk delivery.'

Penry shook his head. 'A hangover isn't enough of an excuse to leave your teammate in the lurch. Although, knowing how Willie puts it away when he has a mind to, he probably felt as if someone had planted an axe in his skull this morning.'

This brought a round of chuckles as the towpath widened and the men fanned out to peer through the gaps in the hawthorn hedges and up the generations-worn tracks leading into the ancient woods. Most of the oak and beech trees had only just started to grow their leaf coverage, so the searchers could see further up into the woods than normal.

'Oh, dash it!' Eleanor said a few minutes later. 'We're almost back at the pontoon.'

Clifford appeared at her elbow. 'Indeed, my lady. Let us hope one of the downstream teams has found him.'

'But they should have informed us then.' She let the field glasses fall on their strap around her neck. 'Anything at all?' she hollered across the river through cupped hands. Five heads shook in reply.

She bit her lip. 'Let's return then!' She turned to Clifford and lowered her voice again. 'Well, we've done all we can.'

He nodded. 'Take heart, my lady. Perhaps Solemn Jon needed to return home for reasons of decorum.'

'All the entrants have wet trousers, Clifford. Besides, I've noticed that the rules of propriety are not entirely shared by our more down-to-earth village folk.'

'Wet is one thing, my lady.' He avoided her gaze. 'Not… "intact" is quite another.'

She smiled. 'Ah, you mean he might have ripped his clothing somewhere unmentionable and skulked off to make himself decent? That sounds likely now that you mention it. He was floundering badly the few times I caught sight of him.'

The rest of the search party strode on ahead, chattering and laughing, clearly pleased to be returning to the fun of the fair.

Eleanor shivered as Clifford helped Gladstone down to the water's edge for a drink. *Too much weed for my liking, Ellie. You could easily hide a body in there and no one would be any the wiser!* She shook her head. She really needed to stop reading those penny dreadful novels.

Something caught her eye. She bent down and examined it more closely. It was a thin silvery chain with a small oval medallion. She pulled it out of the mud and wiped it clean with her handkerchief. She turned it over in the palm of her hand. It was so worn it was hard to make out the image in the centre and the inscription around the top of the image was equally so. She could only recognise 'St' of the first word, then 'of' of the second and the final letter of the last word was 'a'. Below the image the writing was a little less faded and she could make out a 'P' and 'y' and 'fo' and 'Us'. She frowned for a moment before comprehension dawned.

Of course, Ellie, it's a religious medallion, a lot of people wear them as a good luck charm. She looked again at the inscription. *St someone*

or other. I'm pretty sure the words around the bottom are 'Pray for Us'.
One of the villagers must have lost it when the chain broke, probably
during a May Fair. She slipped the medallion into her pocket. She'd
ask Clifford or the ladies if they might know whose it was later.
Right now, she had other things on her mind.

'Mare's tail.' Clifford pointed to a long swathe of green fronds
as she joined him. They stood proudly above the water with the
appearance of soft fir tresses. 'Which means that section is more than
close to ten feet deep and colder than elsewhere. Whereas the plant
that Master Gladstone has disturbed here is floating pennywort,
which propagates in slow-moving sections.'

Despite her weed phobia, she laughed. 'And the mat of green
dots covering his nose?'

'Duckweed, or water lentils, my lady. Their proliferation
indicates this section is subject to very little pollution and that the
current here is significantly reduced.'

'Alright, Mr Walking Encyclopaedia, even for you that is particularly specific. Why are you such an expert on aquatic plant life?'

'To better trick the fish onto my rod, naturally.'

Fishing? So maybe that's what he does on his Thursdays off, Ellie.
How can you have spent a year with him as your butler and know so
little about the man?

She rejoined him and Gladstone on the path. 'I think you're
probably right. Solemn Jon has simply gone back home, not realising
he is the recipient of the wooden spoon. I'm embarrassed I've sent
us all off on a wild goose chase.'

At his silence, she frowned.

'Clifford? What's the matter?' She followed his gaze to the thick
bank of waving bullrushes a few feet ahead.

'Forgive me, my lady, I was trying to work out why the rushes
have been disturbed. And why so much duckweed has been set

adrift and caught around the branches of the submerged tree out towards the mid-section of the river?'

They both hurried to the nearest spot on the bank. Leaning forward, she parted the fronds of bulrushes.

'Clifford! There's… there's something in the water. Grab my hand!'

She leant further over the water, pushed more of the rushes aside, and then… froze.

CHAPTER 7

Eleanor frowned. 'Tell me again.'

Mrs Butters, her housekeeper, was explaining the mysteries of spring cleaning to her over breakfast in the morning room. Despite the slight chill that the sun had yet to burn off, the French windows were open, giving Eleanor a view of Gladstone's rump stuck in the air in the far flower border. *Is he burying something, Ellie, or digging it up?* She thought vaguely that she ought to check but her housekeeper's voice cut into her thoughts.

'My lady, begin at the top, and work on downwards, 'tis the only way.'

Eleanor looked at the woman whose diminutive height, well-rounded figure and ever-present smile reminded her of how much she'd missed growing up without a motherly aunt or grandmother. With a wrench, she brought her mind back to the discussion.

'Mrs Butters, you know how much I appreciate all the staff's dedicated efforts during the obligatory Henley Hall spring clean. But would it really be too awkward to leave my rooms until later? Or better yet, the end?'

''Tis your house, my lady. And doing your bidding is our duty, and our pleasure. But 'twasn't me who put the schedule together and it would take a braver woman than me to overrule the one that did.'

'Ah, of course.' Eleanor couldn't help but smile. It was ironic that Clifford's meticulous hand had set the Hall into such disarray.

'His lordship, your uncle, wouldn't let us even start cleaning until after the May Fair and then always made sure to be taken up with most important business elsewhere for the first two weeks of May, my lady.'

'It'll take two weeks!' Eleanor groaned inwardly at the thought of the mansion's forty-three rooms in disarray. Three vast floors filled with nothing but mess and disruption. No chance of cosying up in her late uncle's study or in her favourite sitting room, situated in one of the tall towers that flanked the grand entrance.

Clifford's measured voice came from the doorway. 'Or longer if members of the team are continually distracted from their spring-cleaning duties.' He eyed Mrs Butters pointedly.

'Just ensuring her ladyship had everything for breakfast, Mr Clifford.' Mrs Butters bobbed a curtsey to Eleanor and ducked out of the morning room, avoiding his gaze.

'Or if the very precise timetable is interfered with,' he added as he stepped forward to place a silver tray of coffee things on the serving table.

Eleanor tried to keep a straight face. 'Gracious, who would do that? Only a braver woman than me.' She busied herself with her aromatic herby mushroom and sausage omelette, glancing at Clifford and then away as he caught her eye. She cleared her throat.

As he added just the right amount of cream to her coffee, she sighed. 'Sorry, Clifford. I didn't mean to be snippy. I didn't sleep well.'

'Can it be called a bad night's sleep if one didn't sleep at all, my lady?'

'You too?'

He nodded. 'But I do not wish to spoil your breakfast. Not with discourse over the unfortunate events of yesterday. Suffice to say, a good man has sadly left us. Perhaps we should return to how I might lessen your distress over the upheaval the spring cleaning is causing you?'

'Thank you, but that was just more grumpy whingeing on my part to cover up my upset over Solemn Jon's death. Apologies.

And the truth is I spent so much of my childhood living out of a suitcase, and then doing the same on my travels, that I've come to cherish the Hall's order. And I'm very grateful you're so in command of the spring cleaning. I haven't a clue what any of you are doing. Or really quite why.'

'Exactly as it should be, my lady.'

She took a long sip of her coffee. 'I should have followed Uncle Byron's tradition and left for a while to make the cleaning schedule easier for you. Not that I knew he did until Mrs Butters just mentioned it, but my being anywhere else would probably have helped you all, I'm sure.'

'Will there be anything else, my lady?'

'No. I shall stir my sorrow for poor Solemn Jon's passing into my coffee with extra sugar and perhaps that will sweeten my mood.'

Clifford didn't move.

'Really, it's fine,' she said, without looking up. 'Go rally the cleaning troops and please pass on my sincere gratitude and commendations for their efforts.'

Clifford cleared his throat. 'My lady, Doctor Browning told Constable Fry that Solemn Jon had clearly hit his head on falling from his raft. He was likely unconscious before we even reached the finish line ourselves. And when we found him face down in the reeds, he was already long departed.'

She nodded. 'I know there was nothing we could have done, we were too late. But if I'd only known I would have organised the search parties more quickly and—'

'You did everything you could.' His voice was unexpectedly gentle.

'But Solemn Jon lost his life.' She looked up at him. 'When the man who buries the dead dies, Clifford, who is left to bury him?'

*

Four hours later, she was curled up in the library as she had been since breakfast. It was the only room that had yet to be in any way dismantled in the grand spring clean. Despite being over sixty-feet long and rising two floors, it had a cosy, lived-in feeling, which she loved, and she always felt a little closer to her late uncle there.

Clifford had told her this had been her uncle's favourite room at the Hall, aside from his study. She smiled at the confirmed-bachelor touches of stiff leather Chesterfield chairs and settees and the floor-to-ceiling bookcases filled with scientific, mathematical and engineering volumes. The rather masculine air, however, was offset by the thick patterned rugs, many worn cushions, upholstered footstools and shaded lamps throwing a soft yellow glow over the whole scene.

One oak-panelled recess housed a mahogany desk and the other a vast map table. Dotted in the few spaces without books was a selection of curios her uncle had brought back from his travels. Her favourite was a bony figurine of a man sitting beside a dodo; book in his hand, he seemed to be reading aloud to his feathered companion.

The comforting smell of leather-bound volumes and decades of beeswax was also very welcome after the pungency of the cleaning products pervading the rest of the house. She was trying to be helpful and stay out of her staff's way by distracting herself with a copy of William Blake's poems. Clifford often quoted him, but she found it heavy going and her concentration wasn't helped by Gladstone's bulky form crushing her legs. She looked up from the page, horrified to see a spring squall lashing the windows. She heaved herself out from under the bulldog and dashed to the kitchen.

'Ladies!' she shouted, bursting through the door. 'Rain! The mattresses! They'll—'

She paused in confusion as Polly, her young maid, and Mrs Trotman, her no-nonsense cook, stood casually baking. On seeing her, her maid curtsied, while her cook waved a floured hand towards the back door. Confused, she joined Clifford, who was standing on the back step, sheltering from the deluge under the porch. He was studying a meticulously handwritten list in his neat leather pocketbook. She pointed in horror to the already sodden bedding. He nodded and tapped the page. She read aloud, noting the still-drying blue-ink tick beside the entry he'd indicated. 'Feather beds – drenching.'

'Indeed, my lady. Most effective. Joseph came early this morning to say he suspected a squall around this time and that we could then expect an afternoon of hot sunshine. Perfect for the repeated turning of the mattresses that traditionally follows their soaking.'

Surely there's a more modern way than this, Ellie? After all, it's 1921, not 1821! She resolved to look into it later. In the meantime she simply shook her head.

'You know, Clifford, I'd make a terrible maid.'

'Likely, but isn't that why we are each born to our station?' He scanned her face and then noticed the copy of Blake's poems she still clutched. 'Perhaps some tea and lighter reading material might work better, my lady?' He gave a mock shudder. 'Even a penny dreadful could be countenanced in the circumstances.'

She laughed. 'Or a sherry with my favourite sounding board, if it doesn't impose too much on his hectic schedule?'

'I shall see if I can winkle them both out for you, my lady.'

CHAPTER 8

Back in the library, Eleanor gratefully took the sherry Clifford held out to her on a silver tray, and pulled the soft wool rug he'd also provided over her knees.

'It's no use pretending, Clifford. I know you are as upset by Solemn Jon's death as I am.' She ran her hand over Gladstone's head before taking a sip of sherry. 'He was a good man.'

He nodded. 'Unquestionably, my lady. But he was not a young one, and accidents happen. If I might repeat Doctor Browning's assessment that he would not have suffered and would have passed almost instantaneously.'

'I know, but I still can't help thinking we should have got to him sooner and then the outcome might have been very different.'

He tilted his head. 'Perhaps superstition is not so far removed from all of us as we would like to imagine.'

'What do you mean?'

'Well, the villagers believe that throwing the best May Fair is fulfilling their side of the covenant with nature. They show the Spirit of Summer their appreciation and she reciprocates with good weather leading to bountiful harvests, strong-born livestock and minimal illness. Believing one might have succeeded in changing someone else's fate without having prior knowledge that the sad event had even happened could be considered equally… superstitious?'

Ever grateful for his wisdom and peculiar knack of knowing how to make her feel better, she nodded and raised her glass.

'To Solemn Jon. May he rest in well-deserved peace, having helped many who passed through his undertaker's yard. Including Uncle Byron.'

He went to speak but hesitated.

Eleanor continued. 'Solemn Jon was kindness personified. I know I wasn't here when he buried Uncle Byron, but the fact that such a cheerful soul should be called "Solemn Jon" shows in what affection he was held. He will be deeply, deeply missed.'

Clifford nodded. 'The perfect obituary for him, my lady. Perhaps you might attend the funeral?'

'Of course.'

'I shall too. Solemn Jon was held in high esteem, not just in Little Buckford and Chipstone as a master undertaker, but the whole area. He has been the undertaker for the poor, and not so poor, in this part of the Chilterns for a generation. And his father before him.'

She turned her glass in her hand. 'I can't help wondering what happened. I can only assume, as you've said, that he tripped on his raft, fell overboard backwards and then hit his head on that fallen tree. Doctor Browning said he'd sustained a blow to the back of his head. I suppose it may even have been his raft that knocked him unconscious as it tipped him off.'

Clifford nodded. 'Or a falling branch could have been the culprit. It would have subsequently floated downstream, looking as innocent as all the others we passed.'

'Gracious that would have been a very unlucky case of being in the wrong place at the wrong time! Although I do remember my parents telling me I had an aunt who was killed by a falling tree in a thunderstorm.' She ran her hand over the woollen rug across her lap, thinking about her parents who had vanished one night when she was only nine. She had never found out what had happened that night. 'I am always acutely aware of how ridiculously fortunate

I am. Henley Hall. You and the ladies. Superb health, etcetera. My list of blessings really is endless, but on occasions like this, I'm reminded again of just how long it unquestionably is.' She sighed. 'Well, as usual, you have made me feel so much better. Aided with divine sherry, of course.'

'A particularly fine Oloroso can improve any situation, my lady, as his lordship was oft to say.'

'Now I shall be quite content to sit here and enjoy how fortunate I am. In fact, I'll only venture out to change into my house pyjamas disgracefully early, if that won't offend you?'

'Not today, my lady. Although Constable Fry might blush at your unorthodox form of attire.'

'What? Oh, dash it! I've got to go and sign my statement, haven't I?'

'Indeed. But not for several hours. I shall return in time to galvanise you into an appropriate appearance.'

With his customary bow, he left her to decide if her pyjamas were calling loudly enough for her to run the gauntlet of the chaos of her dismantled bedroom, given that she would have to change again soon to go out. After taking her time to savour the last of the sherry, she decided that they were. She had just reached the door when Clifford reappeared. One look at his face told her something was amiss.

'Clifford? What's happened? You went out that door not a moment ago and you've returned looking, well, decidedly queer.'

He cleared his throat. 'Forgive me, my lady. I would have delayed the news until tomorrow in the hope you might sleep better tonight. However, as you must visit the police station, I felt it better that you find out beforehand.'

'Find out what?'

He held out the afternoon copy of the *County Herald*.

She glanced at the page he'd folded open. 'This is the obituaries page, Clifford?' She ran her finger along the top line. 'Golly, there's one for Solemn Jon already.'

'Indeed, my lady. Unfortunately, it is nothing like the sentiments you uttered at our last conversation.'

For a moment there was silence as she read the obituary, punctuated only by her sharp intake of breath at the end. She handed the paper back to Clifford, her brow deeply furrowed.

'You're right. Who would write this?'

Clifford shook his head. 'And what's more disturbing, my lady, is that it declares Solemn Jon's death to have been—'

'Murder!'

CHAPTER 9

''Tis a rummy thing, alright, m'lady,' Sergeant Brice said as he laboriously searched through a sheaf of papers on the reception desk of Chipstone Police Station.

Eleanor sighed, pretending to consult the large wall clock on the otherwise bare pale-grey wall to her left, fearing she knew exactly what he was alluding to.

'I said, m'lady, 'tis a rummy thing.'

'I heard you, Sergeant Brice. And, yes, I agree it is.'

He jerked upright, scattering the papers over the floor by her feet. 'How's that, then? Seeing as I didn't get as far as saying what's rummy?'

She shrugged. 'Because I imagine you were suggesting it is rummy that I am, yet again, standing here within only a matter of months, because… because a man has died.'

He nodded slowly. 'Mind you, don't get me wrong, m'lady. People pass on. 'Tis the way.' He tilted his head up, indicating the heavens. 'One day 'twill be my turn.'

'Gracious, Sergeant, that sounds rather maudlin.'

'Not to my mind. It's quite the comfort. Right now, I'm here doing this.' He gestured round the functional reception area. 'And a few other things in me spare time. Then sometime, there'll be a gentle tap on me shoulder and I'll open me eyes to find meself in that other place, upstairs. We've nothing to worry about, 'tis all sorted for us, see. Our only job is to make the best of each and earn our place in both. Simple.'

She marvelled at his pragmatic approach to death. His words also made her realise the last thing Solemn Jon would have wanted was for anyone to be sad at his parting. As an undertaker, he had spent his working life among the dead, but had been too full of life himself to wish anything but joy on others.

Brice leaned on the counter. 'Still, 'tis odd that a titled lady like yourself gets caught up with quite so many dead'uns.' His rounded cheeks coloured. 'No offence, m'lady.'

'None taken, Sergeant. Honestly, I'm still learning how to be the lady of the manor. Not that people have noticed.'

Brice stared at her a moment and then slapped the counter with his bear paw hand. 'You had me going good and proper there, m'lady. The local folk have seen too much of you out and about to be fooled into thinking you knows how to be a proper lady of the manor.' Catching Eleanor's eye, he cleared his throat hurriedly. 'But you'll get the hang of it soon enough, I'm sure.' Brice cleared his throat again and looked hopelessly at the jumble of papers on the floor. 'Now, 'pologies, but I'm struggling to find the statement what you gave Constable Fry at the river on Sunday.'

Her butler materialised next to her, picked up the papers from the floor, extracted Eleanor's statement from them and handed it to Brice, who took it with an embarrassed nod.

'Er, thank you, Mr Clifford.' He looked around. 'Should be a pen or summat you can use somewhere… aha, there you are, you rascal!' Brice lunged underneath the counter and then stood up triumphantly brandishing a fountain pen. 'He's forever rolling away and skulking in the corners, m'lady. Anyone'd think he wished he'd been born a pencil.'

She hid a smile again and accepted the pen. Picking up the statement, she frowned. 'Hmm, I wonder if there is anything I should be adding to this?'

Brice stared at her blankly.

'You know, in light of the news this afternoon.'

'News, m'lady?'

'The obituary.'

Brice's face clouded over. 'Pah! Don't let a poor joke in bad taste make no difference to what you remember, m'lady.'

Despite her best efforts to appear only vaguely interested, her brows shot up. 'You really think it is a joke? Because I agree, it seems in very poor taste.'

'Yep. But if you knew the man whose name is printed at the bottom of them words, you—' At that moment the door of the police station flew open, smacking against the wall. Brice's eyes narrowed. 'Speak of the devil,' he muttered, nodding in the door's direction.

Eleanor turned to look at the dishevelled figure blinking in the brightness of the harsh light. She stole a glance at Clifford, who mouthed, 'Willie Green.'

'I'm just going to check this through before signing it, Sergeant.' She grabbed the statement and pen and hurried over to a row of four wooden chairs where Clifford was standing, waiting for her. Once sat down, she busied herself apparently poring over the document.

'William Green,' Brice called over to the doorway. 'Not sure what business you've come here on, but it had better not be any more time-wasting nonsense.'

Eleanor peered over the top of the paper to better take in the man who was tugging at his coat pocket that had become hooked over the door handle. She wracked her brain for a more charitable description, but all she could think of was an underfed ferret. With his sharp dark eyes set in hollow sockets, protruding jaw and barely-there upper lip, his face seemed permanently set in a scowl.

'It's *Willie*, Brice.' His voice was reedy, his words slurred. 'As well you know.'

'And it's *Sergeant* Brice. You've spent enough nights in here to know that.'

Willie Green rang his tongue over his bottom lip. 'That's 'cause your lot has no sense of decency in letting a man be. Only this time, I've come all by me own, ain't I?'

'What do you want, Willie?'

'I'll tell you.' There was the sound of tearing cloth as he yanked his coat pocket free. He walked unsteadily to the counter and grabbed it with both hands. 'I want you to do your job for once.'

Brice's mouth set in a thin line. 'Is that a fact?'

'A man's been murdered and what are you doing about it? Nothing! Same as every time.'

Eleanor stiffened. Clifford flicked an imaginary piece of lint from his jacket sleeve.

Brice's jaw tightened. 'We've seen your latest stunt. Bad show, even for you.'

Willie Green frowned and scratched the back of his hand. 'What stunt? I ain't done nothing. But then I never have, you and your lot have just got it in for me.'

Brice sighed and reached under the counter. He slapped a copy of the *County Herald* in front of him. 'Of all the people who you should have been grateful to. Ashamed, that's what you should be. Drunk were you, as usual?'

Willie looked down at the newspaper, went to let go of the counter to pick it up, and then quickly changed his mind. He glared at Brice.

'See what I'm saying? Why are you blathering on about newspapers when you should be chasing a murderer?'

Brice flicked through to the obituary page and pointed to Solemn Jon's. Willie Green peered at it, blinked hard several times, and then knocked the paper to the floor.

Brice stiffened. 'Steady, Willie. There's a cell waiting for you if you don't behave.'

Willie Green pushed himself off the counter and swayed danger-ously. 'Can't read it. Why do they do the print so small?' He jerked up to stare at the policeman. 'What does it say?'

Brice picked up the paper from the floor and read out the obituary.

John James Jon, otherwise known as Solemn Jon, died this day Sunday, 1st May 1921. The deceased was 55 when death called him at the village May Fair. He left behind a widow.

Solemn Jon was well known to the villagers of Little Buckford and the surrounding areas, burying not only com-moners but also them of higher birth. He died in a tragic accident when his raft capsized in the annual raft race. He was much loved by all.

Only them words is not the truth, dear reader. Although it isn't customary to speak ill of the dead, the record must be put straight. For the man known as Solemn Jon was as villainous a scoundrel as ever lived! A man whose evil deeds would shock you if they was to be revealed.

Far from being loved by all, Solemn Jon had many enemies, one who chose to end his life at the May Fair raft race. For Solemn Jon's death was not an accident, dear reader. It was murder!

William Green

Brice slapped the paper down again. 'So, come on. What do you have to say for yourself?'

'I never wrote that.' Willie Green licked his bottom lip and shook his head. 'Not me.'

'It's got your name here, right at the bottom. Now, I said no time wasting, Willie, and I meant it. It's right up your alley to pull a trick like this and then roll round here so you can make a fuss, claiming you know nothing about it. Enough of crying wolf. I'm not biting!'

'Why would I write that, sling me name to it, then say it weren't me? That would mark me as fit for the loony house.'

Brice looked at him with contempt. 'Like I said, a sick joke from a man who should have been grateful his employer put up with him all those years. Or you wrote it drunk and clean forgot. Now clear off and stop wasting police time.'

Willie's jaw tightened and his voice rose. 'Gonna make me?'

'Here we go,' Brice muttered. 'No, Willie, I'm hoping there's still one ounce of your brain that isn't sloshing with booze and you'll be ashamed enough to slink off home and sleep off the skinful you've had.' He folded his arms. 'Go on now, get going afore I lock you up.'

'Lock me up for reporting a crime, would ya?' He turned unsteadily and took in Eleanor and Clifford for the first time. 'Ha! I got witnesses.'

Brice made to move out from behind the counter, but Willie backed away.

'You're no better than the others,' he slurred, before lurching back through the front door and down the steps.

Eleanor approached the policeman. 'Sergeant Brice, my statement. And your pen, thank you.'

Brice shuffled his feet. 'I am sorry you had to witness Willie's antics, m'lady. Most unfortunate. Not something you should have seen.'

Perhaps it was, Ellie.

CHAPTER 10

'Afternoon, Sandford.'

'Good afternoon, Lady Swift. Welcome to Langham Manor.'

The butler of her great friends, Lord and Lady Fenwick-Langham, greeted her with a bow on the top step of the palatial mansion's sweeping stone staircase that led up to the colonnaded stately entrance. Designed along similar lines to a French renaissance chateau, five floors of pink stone rose imposingly up to the long grey roofline of myriad domed tower-tops and chimneys. In her emerald satin T-strap heels, she could see the shiny bald crown of Sandford's head as he bowed.

'Tell me, am I in significant trouble this time?' she whispered.

As a long-standing friend of Clifford's, Sandford always tactfully overlooked her lack of formality. 'I really couldn't say, my lady.'

'Well, let's hope not. Thanks to Clifford's constant chivvying, I'm only ten minutes late, not thirty as usual.' She put a finger to her lips. 'But don't tell him I admitted that.'

He tried to hide a smile, but failed. 'Of course not, my lady. If you would be so good as to follow me, luncheon is being served on the main terrace.'

As she followed Sandford along the silk-wallpapered hallway, her heels clicking on the chequerboard marble floor, they passed endless, opulently appointed rooms decked out in red velvet and gold trimmings. The grandeur of Langham Manor always made her hold her breath. Her home, Henley Hall, cut a rather demure figure in comparison. It was luxurious in its own way, but also cosier and infused with the air of male practicality and comfort her late uncle had instilled.

As she paused under the exquisite glass central dome spanning the crossroads of corridors, she pulled her shawl tighter around her shoulders. There wasn't a heating system built that could warm all of this castle of a home. Even today, when the bright May sun threatened to burn her fair skin, there was a coldness to the air inside the Manor.

As they continued, they passed rows of family portraits, spanning almost four centuries and over a dozen generations of Langhams. *I wonder what it would be like to live in the same house as your grandparents, Ellie? And great, great-grandparents, and however many greats over a dozen generations is?* Quite a few, she imagined.

She sighed. Her family had never lived in the same house for more than a couple of years, let alone a couple of centuries, which was where she'd inherited her previous, but now jaded, wanderlust. Her current desire was to stay firmly put at Henley Hall.

'Augusta, Harold. Please excuse my slight tardiness.' Eleanor hurried forward after Sandford had announced her to the small group spread across the vast stone balustraded terrace and gardens below.

'Ah, Eleanor, my dear girl, there you are.' Lady Langham rose with evident relief, looking every inch the aristocratic matriarch with her tight greying curls framing her steel-blue eyes. Her signature lilac lace jacket over the matching full-length skirt of her dress highlighted her impeccable poise. But for the first time, Eleanor saw a hint of her hostess' sixty years showing in the hairline creases at the corners of her eyes and mouth.

'We are so delighted you agreed to come.' She took Eleanor's hands in hers and smiled, looking her face over carefully. 'Lancelot was unable to be here today, but he sends his… regards.'

Wishing the ground would swallow her up, Eleanor made a show of rearranging the beaded fringing of her green silk shawl.

She'd broken off her romantic relationship with the Langhams' only surviving son four months back at their New Year's Eve Ball. That Eleanor had been the one to call it off, however, had not diminished how welcome the Langhams made her feel. After all, she had saved Lancelot from the hangman the year before, so she was still the darling of their eye.

Lord Fenwick-Langham ambled over. The ends of his enormous grey handlebar moustache quivered as his face split into the broadest of grins, deepening the laughter lines around his blue-green eyes.

'Eleanor, old fruit. How goes all things at Henley Hall?'

'Perfectly fine, thank you. But, if I'm honest, only because Clifford runs the house with formidable military precision. We are currently deep in the midst of spring cleaning.'

Lord Langham shuddered, making his double chin wobble. He glanced at his wife.

'That's a monstrously unpleasant business to get tangled up in, old girl. Surely, the most sensible option would be to beat a retreat at the merest sniff of such goings on? Your uncle always used to clear off to the seaside, I remember. Brighton, wasn't it?'

'Harold!' Lady Langham said.

'Not a bucket-and-spade girl, then, old fruit?' he asked innocently, clearly not registering the reason for his wife's rebuke.

Eleanor's throat closed up at the thought of the seaside town of Brighton she had visited a few months back for her thirtieth birthday. It would never again be the glamorous holiday destination she had set out for on that fateful day. Seeing her husband's body being carried through the hotel lobby when she'd believed him long dead had made sure of that. She swallowed hard and smiled at both of them.

'Do you know… despite everything, I really am a bucket-and-spade girl. I love sand castles, donkey rides and ice cream. And there is a certain magic to the sea, notwithstanding the grey fog of the

English coast in March. Even Clifford loosened his over-starched collar on the odd occasion. Metaphorically speaking, of course.'

Slipping her arm through Eleanor's, Lady Langham lowered her voice. 'Not wishing to dwell on your recent difficulties, my dear, but I really wasn't sure if it was too soon to ask you to come today. I do hope you would have said?'

Eleanor squeezed her hostess' hand. 'Thank you for your kind concern, but I'm fine and have missed seeing you both dreadfully.'

'Ah!' Lord Langham stopped and slapped his forehead. 'Of course, Brighton! Frightful faux pas of mine, old girl. Terribly sorry.'

'Please don't be.' She hurriedly looked for a way to change the conversation. 'And the gardens' – she swept her free arm across the view – 'are quite captivating at this time of year.'

Beyond the ornate balustrade and the wide stone steps was a full acre of intricate rose beds, each framed by a low-cut box hedge. A narrow moat, its surface peppered with the pink tinge of budding water lilies, surrounded a terrace dominated by a large circular marble bench. From there, the backdrop rolled on into majestic blue cedars and oaks lording over the sweeping lush lawns. And beyond lay the fields and wooded slopes of Lord Langham's beloved shooting grounds. Her hostess smiled proudly, having put many hours into overseeing her army of gardeners. Roses were her passion, and it was even known for her to don overalls and prune them herself.

Eleanor slipped her other arm through Lord Langham's. 'I can't tell you how long it seems since I saw you both. It truly is a treat.'

'Likewise, dear girl,' Lady Langham said. 'Now, I believe it's time for luncheon. I do hope the guests behave.'

Whatever Lady Langham's misgivings about her guests, she hadn't let it show in the catering. Even with her highly regarded reputation as a society hostess, Eleanor thought she had gone to extraordinary lengths for such a small gathering. A long cream silk marquee had been erected over a table fit for kings, its two pointed Arabian rooftops running down to scalloped edging, finished in fluttering indigo tassels. Three sections on each side had been folded back and tied at the waist with purple-and-gold ribbons, which matched the sashes adorning each of the damask high-backed chairs.

With the table itself laid for what Eleanor reckoned should be a wedding party at least, given the array of gold-rimmed plates and crystal glasses, she suddenly felt underdressed. She ran a hand down her now seemingly rather plain emerald-sleeved bodice top and satin skirt, acutely aware of their lack of finery.

Lord Langham leaned down and whispered loudly in her ear, 'Don't mind all the extra fuss and frills, my dear. After a couple of champers none of us will notice or remember that we're supposed to behave.'

His wife groaned. 'Harold, dear.'

'It's like the most beautiful fairy-tale banquet,' Eleanor breathed. She smiled at Lady Langham, whose expression gave away that something was amiss. Eleanor tried again. 'And with the weather so congenial, it is such a wonderful idea to take luncheon outside.'

Lord Langham grimaced but held his tongue until his wife gave him a resigned wave of her hand.

'It's that blessed Marchioness Lambourne's fault, old girl,' he explained. 'She's becoming more tricky with her every visit.' He nodded over to the stone-faced, ivory-haired lady with sharp black eyes standing at the far end of the table. Lady Lambourne, Marchioness of Wendlebury, was already complaining to Sandford over the emptiness of her glass. Her sharp Scottish accent added an extra tartness to the acerbity dripping from her tongue.

'Actually, Harold, dear,' Lady Langham said. 'Perhaps we might not pursue that line of discussion?'

Lord Langham seemed not to have heard. 'Now, my dear. Take no notice of the marchioness today. This little circus has arisen out of her repeated grumbling about the house being too stuffy despite the ceilings being nigh on twenty-feet high.' He rolled his eyes. 'We have to invite her, old friend of the family and all that. Personally, she constantly reminds me of the native Scottish thistle she is so fiercely proud of. Prickly year round and thoroughly invasive.'

Eleanor smiled at the irony that Lord Langham, who had earned several medals serving Queen, then King and country across the empire, found the marchioness more difficult to cope with than an uprising. Then again, the marchioness was a formidable woman, totally lacking an ounce of warmth as far as Eleanor could deduce.

Taking a deep breath, Eleanor slapped on her best guest smile and tried to remember the safe topics of conversation Clifford had suggested en route to Langham Manor. Trouble was, they'd all sounded so dreary, she'd tuned out and enjoyed the flowering hedgerows and lines of beech trees rumbling past the windows of the Rolls instead. However, as Lady Langham led her toward the daunting marchioness, Eleanor wished her faithful butler was on hand to repeat his suggestions. And this time she would take note.

'Lady Lambourne. Good afternoon.' She tried to keep her voice neutral.

Eleanor's greeting drew only a cold, 'Aye, it's you, Lady Swift.'

At that moment, another of the guests appeared on the top step in front of them. Eyes like the bluest lagoons, framed by jet-black hair, the striking combination pulled her up short as it always did. With his tall, powerful physique, broad shoulders tapering to a trim waist and rangy stride, he moved with the bewitching grace and confidence of Michelangelo's *David* brought to life. He bowed to the ladies.

'Ah, Lord Rankin,' Lady Langham said. 'You know Lady Swift, of course. And the marchioness.'

With a look of pure disdain, the marchioness turned her back on him and walked away, her ebony cane, the silver handle of which was in the shape of a spaniel, rapping the ground as she went.

Lord Rankin showed no reaction, merely turning to Eleanor.

'Delighted as always,' he said in a deep silky tone. Taking her hand, he brushed the back of it with his lips.

She fought the urge to snatch her hand back. Even though he was impossibly attractive, on the few occasions she'd met him, she'd found his charms most definitely ended at his appearance; his personality being a poor and ignorant second cousin.

'Lord Rankin,' she said stiffly. 'I trust you are keeping well?'

'I make it my business to do so.'

She noticed his lip curled as he ran his eyes over her hair and face and then down her dress.

Excellent, Ellie! He finds you are far from his flavour of tea. Now delighted with her less than Parisian chic outfit, she turned back to Lady Langham.

'I really must say a proper hello to the marchioness.'

With a nod to Lord Rankin, she continued towards the end of the table. As she moved away, she was aware, even though Lord Rankin's attention seemed to be concentrated on his host, his eyes followed her, sending the same unpleasant frisson up her back she'd experienced on the riverbank the day of the May Fair.

CHAPTER 11

Originally ten for lunch, four guests had cancelled at the last minute, leaving Lady Langham no choice but to seat her guests three either side. With Harold to Eleanor's right, however, there was still a gap at the end of their line.

'Sandford?' Lady Langham said, not having to voice her question any further.

'Mr Edwards retired to the blue drawing room to make a telephone call, my lady.' Sandford gestured towards a set of French windows just as a sharp-eyed middle-aged man in a brash green suit emerged. His complexion had the unbecoming hue of one who worked too many hours in a windowless office.

'Edwards, hurry up and park your trousers, old chap,' Harold called over, waving at the empty seat.

Pausing to shake Eleanor's hand, Elijah Edwards took his place at the table. He ran a thumb and forefinger over his thick moustache, which followed the downward curve of his lips. Eleanor couldn't help thinking it gave him the dubious accolade of looking like the world's best-groomed frog.

'Mr Edwards is the owner and editor of the *County Herald*,' Lady Langham said to Eleanor.

'Among other publications,' Mr Edwards added in a gravelly voice.

That's the newspaper that printed Solemn Jon's obituary, Ellie.

Harold dinged his glass with his caviar spoon and then waved it at Sandford. 'Liquid fortitude, Sandford, there's a good man.

Then roll out the noshings.' He beamed around at Eleanor, Rankin opposite, and then the marchioness to his wife's right. 'I'm positively famished, what! Chef's been teasing my nostrils all blessed morning.'

Eleanor's stomach rumbled at the mention of the Langham's fiery French chef and then doubly loudly as Sandford placed three redcurrant-topped butter pastries filled with a delicate salmon mousse in front of her.

'Aye, Lady Swift,' the marchioness called across far too loudly for Eleanor's liking, 'now that you're no' trying to look your best for Lancelot, you'll have an appetite, no doubt.'

The marchioness was an old friend of the Dowager Countess of Goldsworthy. And as Lancelot steadfastly refused to marry the countess' niece, and ward, thus taking her off the old lady's hands, the marchioness took delight in disparaging him at every opportunity. Especially as, no longer being in a relationship with Eleanor, he was once more in a position to marry the countess' niece, but still declined to.

Even though she made sure not to catch his eye, Eleanor was aware of Rankin's piercing gaze boring into her.

'Lady Lambourne,' Lady Langham said wearily. '*Please.*'

Eleanor came to her host's aid. 'Actually, I've always had a hearty appetite, Lady Lambourne. And Chef Manet really is in a class of his own.' She looked at Rankin. 'Do you have a French chef at Rankin Hall, Lord Rankin?'

He snorted. 'The matter of servants is hardly of interest. Or, indeed, worthy of conversation at such a gathering as this. They have duties to perform but no further place at the table.' He pointedly ignored the footman filling up his glass at that very moment.

She bit her tongue and took a sip of her champagne. *The man really is insufferable, Ellie!*

'Well' – Lady Langham looked around the table – 'we are quite the intimate gathering today, aren't we? Such a delight.'

The marchioness' ears pricked up. 'Who was it who was so rude as to let you down, Augusta? Because I would no' ask them again.'

Lady Langham waved a hand. 'Oh, it's never a case of being let down or rudeness, gracious no. Unexpected eventualities and all that. We were to have been joined by the Wendovers and their daughters, Arianna and Isabella. They are to be presented at Queen Charlotte's Ball.'

Lord Langham shook his head. 'Oh, a pomp and frills sort of thing.' He looked over at Rankin. 'The mysteries of having daughters. Bit of a daunting prospect, what?'

Eleanor's lips itched. 'Which part of a daughter's life, if you had a daughter, Lord Rankin, would you take an interest in? Her education, perhaps? Or her career, if she desired one?'

'Career!' Lord Rankin laughed curtly. 'I think not. A woman needs no career. Her nanny takes care of her from birth, then her governess, and then her husband. But I would have arranged a suitable suitor before she came of age. It pays to be prepared.'

Lord Langham shot Eleanor a quick look. 'I'd have to say good luck with that, old man. You might have a fight on your hands in these modern times.'

Rankin's brow creased. 'There would be no fight. Obedience begins in the nursery.'

Eleanor took another sip of champagne to stop her retorting something quite unladylike. Still speechless, she tried to busy herself with the next course of creamy lobster bisque with tarragon croutons.

'Harold, dear,' his wife called over, 'why… why don't you tell us about next week's shoot?'

Lord Langham took a swig of his drink and set his glass down. 'Love to, light of my life, but' – he leaned over the table towards Rankin – 'word of advice first, old man. Some ladies are quite independent nowadays. Take young Eleanor here. Jumped on her bally bicycle one day and beetled off across the world on her own.' He shook his head in wonder. 'Yet she's turned out alright, wouldn't you say?'

Rankin made a show of looking her over, a smug smile playing round his lips. 'I'll let you know at the end of the luncheon.'

Eleanor gave him a withering look and concentrated on chatting with the other guests until she finished her bisque.

Lady Langham then nodded to the footman to serve the duck and beetroot terrine, artfully displayed on a pillow of crisp salad leaves.

'Lord Rankin,' Lady Langham said, 'our condolences, again, on your father's death. His passing in February probably doesn't seem very far away. You must still be grieving.'

The marchioness let out an audible snort. For a moment Lord Rankin lost his poise and looked murderous.

Oblivious, Lord Langham shook his head. 'Bad business, old man, Spanish flu. Did the right thing burying him quickly with only a few of the family there. Don't want a repeat of nineteen eighteen, what!'

'Harold!' Lady Langham tutted. 'I was just about to ask Lord Rankin if he needs any assistance.' She turned back to him. 'I am sure you are managing the estate sufficiently, Lord Rankin, but if we can lend our estate manager, just say the word.'

Rankin nodded. 'Thank you, Lady Langham, but far from necessary. I have taken on a new manager. He is a most able man who knows his place.'

Edwards cleared his throat. 'Your father's funeral made the front page, Lord Rankin, as it should, even though it was a rather less grand affair than expected. I don't know if you saw the edition?'

Eleanor had known nothing of Lord Rankin's father's funeral until after the event. It had been held at the family estate, Rankin Hall, over the border in Oxfordshire. At the time she'd been in Brighton dealing with her husband's death. She was about to ask who his new estate manager was, thinking Clifford would probably know him, when Lord Rankin shook his head curtly.

'I have never read your paper, Mr Edwards, having no interest in the price of wool or dog racing. That is news if you are a commoner. If I want to learn about news of import to a gentleman, I take one of the London papers.'

What is his problem, Ellie? In truth, while Eleanor had accepted her hosts' invitation out of a genuine fondness for them, she'd also had an ulterior motive on learning that Mr Edwards would be there. In the icy silence that followed Rankin's curt remark, she saw an opportunity to help her host and find out what she could from Edwards without feeling guilty. Purposefully turning away from Rankin, she smiled at the newspaper owner.

'Mr Edwards, I must commend you on the way the *County Herald* serves the people of Buckinghamshire. It is an invaluable source for anyone interested in their local community. Certainly, that is the case in Little Buckford and the surrounding hamlets.'

Edwards smoothed his moustache. 'Kind words but old news.' He chuckled at his joke and then glared at Rankin. 'You are right, the *Herald* is an essential part of the community.' He turned back to Eleanor. 'It's quite the responsibility, of course.'

'Of course. And I have to commend your staff on being able to publish the obituary for Solemn Jon the morning after his passing. Such efficiency.'

Is it your imagination, Ellie, or did the marchioness and Rankin both stiffen at the mention of Solemn Jon's name?

Edwards shrugged. 'Nothing to it, actually, seeing as it had been dropped through the door the night before.'

'Really? Is that usual?'

'Perfectly. No point in paying for postage if you live near enough to drop it in personally. Folk round here haven't money to waste, Lady Swift.'

Aware that her hostess was eyeing her oddly, Eleanor tried to make light of her interest. 'I believe it was a Mr Green who wrote the obituary? A local man?'

'Yes, I believe so. He obviously didn't think much of Solemn Jon, though. First scathing obituary I've published in twenty years.'

Eleanor fought a frown. 'But you were happy to publish it all the same?'

Edwards laughed. 'Despite the number of spelling and grammar mistakes the typesetter had to correct before it was fit to print, yes. And I wish there were more like that.'

Ah, Ellie, that explains that! At the police station it had been clear to Eleanor that Willie Green wasn't well educated and had had difficulty reading the very obituary he was supposed to have written. But if Edwards had had the obituary tidied up before printing, then it was more than likely it could have been Willie Green.

Edwards was still talking. 'Never sold so many papers in a single day. Everybody wanted to read it for themselves.' At her disapproving look, he added, 'Lady Swift, I am a businessman. And the only way I am able to serve the people of Buckinghamshire so well, as you yourself put it, is by making enough to cover costs and beyond. There is no room for sentiment in business.'

'Hence it being the province of men,' Rankin said. 'However' – he looked disdainfully at Edwards – 'I can't believe you are discussing *business*' – he emphasised the word with a sneer – 'at the table, again.' He shrugged and turned to his hostess. 'I can only apologise, Lady Langham, for Mr Edwards' lack of breeding. But I suppose it is to be expected.'

For once the marchioness saved her hosts' blushes. Edwards had turned the colour of puce, but before he could utter what Eleanor could only imagine would be some choice remarks quite unsuitable for the luncheon table, the marchioness spoke.

'Another body, Lady Swift? And on your watch too, eh? I read that you had been the guest of honour at the May Fair. But who was this Soldier Johnny?'

Lady Langham shook her head. 'It's "Solemn", Lady Lambourne, not "soldier". Solemn Jon. Really, dear, you should try one of those new hearing aids.'

The marchioness threw her hostess an icy look. 'There's nothing wrong with my hearing, thank you!'

Eleanor nodded to herself. *Well, Ellie, there certainly didn't seem to be anything wrong with her hearing the first time Solemn Jon's name was mentioned!*

'Well, then,' said Lady Langham, 'Solemn Jon is –was – the local undertaker and Mr Green was his assistant.' A sound not dissimilar to escaping steam came from Rankin's end of the table. Lady Langham ignored him and pulled a lace handkerchief from her sleeve. 'Solemn Jon arranged a ceremony for our two sons who never… returned from the war. Something very special in place of a funeral that could never be.'

Lord Langham pushed his chair back and went round to her side, cupping her shoulder tenderly before gesturing to Sandford to pour the Burgundy and hurry the next course of bacon-wrapped beef and liver roulade along.

For a while the table ate in comparative silence until the strain obviously proved too much for the marchioness. 'You mean you let the local undertaker who buries *commoners*, Harold, bury your sons? How cou—'

'Probably best not, old fruit, eh?' Lord Langham's normally jovial tone had been replaced with steel.

Eleanor, feeling guilty at having instigated the topic of conversation, tried to find another, less fraught, one. She plastered on a smile and forced herself to address Rankin.

'Lord Rankin, I understand you have a strong interest in horses?'

He ran a hand through his ebony hair, artfully lifting the front into something of a rakish wave without making it obvious he had intended to. 'I do, Lady Swift. I can fairly say I have one of the best stables in Oxfordshire and beyond. I am also one of the best horsemen in the Home Counties. In fact, I can offer you a treat.'

'Really?' She arched a brow. 'How kind. Perhaps to ride with you?'

He laughed, but it didn't reach his eyes. 'No. To watch me play polo.'

'A delightful invitation but, forgive me, I am more of a doing than a watching sort of girl.'

Harold nodded enthusiastically. 'Regular dynamo, is our Eleanor, Rankin. You'd do better to challenge her to a few rounds of chukkas.'

Rankin looked pityingly at Lord Langham. 'Chukkas? With a woman? Perhaps you have temporarily lost your bearings, sir?'

Eleanor looked at Lady Langham in mute apology. Her attempt at helping the lunch go smoothly had seriously backfired. *Will you ever master the art of polite conversation, Ellie?* Mind you, she'd done her best...

Turning to Rankin, she smiled sweetly. 'Indeed, the Maharaja of Alwar was kind enough to say I played better than many of the men on his own team.'

Lord Langham thumped the table, causing his newly filled glass to topple over into his fig and rosemary syllabub. Ignoring it, he grinned at Rankin.

'I believe, old man, you've met your match.'

CHAPTER 12

St Winifred's resounded with the soft hum of a hundred voices saying their last farewells to a fellow villager. The twelfth-century church was filled to capacity and beyond, those funeral goers unable to find room inside thronged the entrance, straining to hear Reverend Gaskell's words. Even the choir had been squashed into the tiny upper balcony to make space for a few more friends of a deeply mourned member of this tight-knit community.

From the third row of narrow wooden pews, Eleanor looked around her. Despite the comforting aged and solid feel provided by the deep-ribbed carving of the Gothic arch and the centuries-worn stone floor of the nave, none of this seemed real. Only four days ago, Solemn Jon had been an essential fixture of Little Buckford, always laughing, joking and ready to lend a hand. He'd been as much a part of the village's fabric as this very church, and so full of life. Yet that life was taken from him by a cruel accident. *Or was it, Ellie?*

Her thoughts flew to the obituary in the *County Herald.* In bold black ink it had declared someone, possibly someone in this very congregation, had murdered Solemn Jon. She frowned. It made no sense. Why go to the trouble of alerting the world to a man's murder and then deny it? Especially as Willie Green had made it clear in the obituary he thought Solemn Jon deserved what he got. But even though he'd been drunk, there'd been something in his manner that... *That what, Ellie? That made you think that perhaps he was telling the truth? At least, partly?* She sighed. Maybe the police were right, and the man was just a drunken troublemaker.

She scanned the congregation, but it seemed he hadn't bothered to come and pay his respects. *Not that he had any to pay*, she thought.

At the very back of the church, standing among those who couldn't find a seat, was a broad-shouldered man sporting a thick grey woollen scarf. *The man you bumped into at the fair, Ellie! Was he a friend of Solemn Jon's?* She shivered. The other day she'd thought the man overdressed, but she wished she'd worn a thick coat to the funeral. Despite the May sun streaming in through St Winifred's stained-glass windows, the interior of the church was as cold as the grave.

Her eyes settled on a comely middle-aged woman in the centre of the front row. Her head of soft grey curls shook as she tried to hold back her sobs, the fringing of her black wool shawl quivered with her every sniff. Comforting hands reached out and rubbed her arm or squeezed her shoulders. *Solemn Jon's wife*. Eleanor had seen her around but never met her. Most families in Little Buckford and Chipstone were very traditional, and the men and women kept to their age-old roles, so most women were in the home during the day. A wiry grey-brown head with a matching black wool scarf tied at the neck sat up and nuzzled the woman's cheek. She smiled. It was Patrick, Solemn Jon's beloved Irish wolfhound.

Eleanor reached for the handkerchief Clifford had passed to her before disappearing to the back of the church. She knew this would be particularly hard for him, Lord Henley having been buried in St Winifred's churchyard the year before. Clifford felt responsible for the death of the man he'd so loyally served and striven to protect for as long as she had been alive. Stuck out in the wilds of South Africa, she'd been unaware her uncle had even died until she'd received Clifford's telegram on her return to town, too late to fly to England and attend the funeral. Clifford had not only been left to make all the arrangements himself, but to bear the full burden of his grief alone.

The vicar's voice rang through the church. 'As undertaker to our community, he treated the dead with the utmost respect, but also a refreshing compassionate geniality, hence the ironic nickname bestowed on him. So many times, his unwavering positive attitude to death humbled me. As I'm sure you will all join me in saying, it has been nothing but an honour and a joy to know Solemn Jon.'

'Amen!' the congregation chorused emphatically.

Reverend Gaskell lent on his lectern. 'My friends, I have a confession, a selfish one, I admit.' A hush fell like a thick blanket on the crowd. 'I wish Solemn Jon would yet have been here when I pass on, for there is no mortal I would rather have prepared me for the next life than him.'

Eleanor nodded along with everyone else. She'd seen first-hand how Solemn Jon had cared for those who passed through his hands. But in a flash, the collective moment of respect was lost as a reedy voice yelled from the doorway.

'What are you suggesting, Reverend? That I ain't good enough to prepare the dead?'

As one, the congregation spun round to take in the sight of Willie Green swaying in the arched door frame, his face flushed with anger.

'I'm the undertaker now! Least I should be!'

The vicar raised a hand to quell the mutterings that had broken out.

'Be calm, my son. My words were not a judgement against anyone but a genuine tribute to a man who has long been a friend of this village. Please be seated and we shall continue.'

'Why would I want to stay and listen to a load of lies about what a good and honest man he was?' Willie spat, steadying himself against the door frame.

Eleanor's horrified gasp was lost in the sea of others. Then Clifford was by the man's side, adeptly propelling him out the door before he disrupted the service any further.

*

Later, staring down at the mound of flowers obscuring the coffin in the freshly dug grave, Eleanor felt a sense of guilt flooding back, stronger than ever. *If only I'd found Solemn Jon sooner, maybe he would still be with us.*

'Lady Swift,' a soft voice said behind her.

She turned to see Solemn Jon's wife, with the tall Irish wolfhound leaning against her side.

'Oh, gracious, my sincerest of condolences.' Eleanor wished she had a magic wand to take away the pain etched on the woman's face. 'I'm so, so sorry.' She ran her hand over the dog's head. 'You too, Patrick,' she whispered.

'Thank you, m'lady. At least he had the best of send-offs anyone could wish for. So many friends—' Mrs Jon broke off as she buried her face in her handkerchief for a moment. Eleanor said nothing, sensing she wanted to open up to her. Mrs Jon sighed. 'Lady Swift, my John and me, we'd been married thirty-two years. Saturday last, in fact. And then the next day, he was gone. Taken from me.'

Eleanor waited, not sure what to say.

The woman seemed to gather her courage. 'M'lady, after all them years, you understand your man inside and out and my John had been acting strange for a good few months.'

'What sort of strange?'

'Strange like he was worried about summat he couldn't shrug off. We'd have talked it through of a normal thing, that's how we got through any difficulties. But not lately.'

'Did you ask him what was troubling him?'

Mrs Jon hesitated and then nodded. 'He just said as he was more tired than usual and joked that Willie Green was testing the patience of every saint in heaven. But I knew it was more than that. I've loved him since I was seventeen, he couldn't hide anything from me.'

She paused and then seemed to decide something. Glancing around, she lowered her voice.

''Tis terribly forward of me, m'lady, but… but I wanted to ask if you could… find it in your heart to help me.' She looked down at her hands and shuffled her feet.

Eleanor was lost. *Was this poor woman asking for money?* With her husband dead, she might struggle once she'd exhausted their savings. If they had any. Unless, of course, Solemn Jon had died leaving debts behind.

She smiled warmly. 'I would be delighted to help if I can. What exactly is it you need?'

The woman looked into her eyes and Eleanor realised before she spoke it wasn't money she wanted.

'What I need, m'lady, is for you to find the man who killed my husband.'

CHAPTER 13

Much as she appreciated the dedicated efforts of her staff to keep the disruption caused by the spring cleaning to a minimum, Eleanor needed to escape. It was the morning after the funeral, and Mrs Jon's request hung heavily on her mind.

As she had predicted, Clifford had been elusive since then, burying himself in his work as the very private man he was. Though she had respected that without question and made the minimum of demands on him, she had sorely missed a few moments to talk together.

Thus, as they drove through the May Buckinghamshire countryside she was oblivious to the skittish lambs in the fields and the scurrying squirrels in the beech woods while she recounted her conversation with Mrs Jon.

Clifford nodded slowly. 'Quite the conundrum, my lady. On the one hand, one wants to do all one can for the poor woman. On the other, there is no factual evidence that Solemn Jon's death was suspicious, except Mr Green's unsavoury obituary.'

'True, but she insisted she knew Solemn Jon inside and out, and he'd definitely been acting strange for a good few months.'

'What sort of strange?' he said.

'Strange like he was worried about something he couldn't shrug off. And that whatever was worrying him might have been related to, well, his death.'

They continued on towards Oxford, going over what Mrs Jon had told them, but came to no conclusion. Finally, Clifford turned to Eleanor.

'My lady, forget the facts.'

Eleanor blinked. 'Did I hear you right?'

'Indeed, my lady. I will go as far as to say forget reason and logic too.' Her mouth dropped open, but before she could reply, he continued. 'Does your intuition tell you anything?'

She sat back and closed her eyes. A moment later she opened them.

'Yes.'

He slowed to a stop and turned off the engine. 'And what does it tell you, my lady?'

'That she is right.' Eleanor took a deep breath and exhaled. 'Solemn Jon was murdered.'

The bustle of Oxford was exactly the tonic she needed to distract her thoughts. The mix of centuries-old college buildings interspersed with back streets filled with quirky boutiques had fascinated her on her previous visits. It was also home to the office of a certain gentleman she had arranged to meet. Budget cuts had forced Detective Chief Inspector Seldon to split his time between Oxford and London, and luckily it was the former that had him pinned to a desk this week.

She ran her hand over the end of the emerald-green silk scarf he had surprised her with as a gift on her birthday. Her face lit up as she remembered the evening dancing with him afterwards. But her smile quickly faded over the awkward silence that had reigned between them since. She sighed. *There's only one answer when affairs of the heart go awry, Ellie… shopping!*

To start with, her mind was too distracted to concentrate on the winding medieval flagged lanes filled with colourful shops, but soon they drew her in. Every window seemed dressed with tantalising silk and satin wardrobe additions that she simply couldn't live without.

Emerging from the lanes, she headed for the elegant five-storied stone building proudly displaying the name 'Boswells Department Store'. The smell of lovingly crafted leather, perfume, and beeswax polish filled the air as she entered. After one hundred and eighty-three years in business, it was no surprise Boswells afforded the ultimate shopping distraction. She delighted in strolling through the departments, running her fingers over a roll of exquisite fabric or the band of a heavenly hat.

It must have been close to an hour later that she arrived back on the first floor, her mind full of beautiful gowns, impossibly stylish shoes and myriad trinkets. Having purchased scented hand cream and soap plus a hot-water bottle in a soft-knit jacket as a thank you for each of the ladies, she was feeling much better. Adding a pair of shamrock-green gloves and some silk underwear for herself, she settled the bill and set off in search of the last present on her list.

Oxford exuded an air of calm certainty, steeped as it was in centuries of studious learning and being home to many of the world's most prestigious colleges. Eleanor paused in front of the sandy-cream stone frontage of Balliol College that spanned most of Broad Street. Ornate spires and chimneys peppered its roof, the whole edifice dominated by a rectangular central tower befitting the building's grandeur. Peeping through the tall arched oak gates, she glimpsed the immaculate garden of the front quadrangle, flanked by a veritable village of quaint buildings dating back to the fifteenth century.

Eleanor's mission, however, was across the street at Thornton's Bookshop, a mecca for all things literary. She had just the book in mind, having spotted a meticulously handwritten list in a certain pocketbook and noted this one had not been ticked off. That she would have purchased it from the city's most venerated bookseller since 1835, as the door-mounted brass plaque reminded her, would make it even more special a gift. Undaunted by the modest single frontage of the shop, she stepped inside the Aladdin's cave of leather-bound volumes.

'Honestly, I think it sounds deathly,' she said to the sweet-faced young woman behind the counter ten minutes later. 'I mean, *An Essay on Universal History, the Manners, and Spirit of Nations*? It's hardly what I'd curl up with, even if I was cast adrift at sea for months with nothing else for company. But this is a small thank-you gift for a man who devours the works of Voltaire as greedily as I do chocolate. So there we are. I'm just pleased you had a copy.'

'And what would you rather curl up with, miss?'

'Penny dreadfuls,' Eleanor whispered.

The young woman giggled. 'They're very addictive, aren't they? Well, we've the latest crime novel by Herbert George Jenkins, *The Strange Case of Mr Challoner*. It's not exactly a penny dreadful, but I never guessed the guilty party. Or' – she looked around and lowered her voice – 'we've an illustrated set of *Gentleman Jack* and *Black Bess* penny-dreadful serials, if you're interested?'

'Absolutely!'

Eleanor had a spring back in her step as she approached the Town Hall, consulting her uncle's pocket watch as she walked. The building's mullioned windows were softened somewhat by the Tudor-esque decorative tracery and domed balcony. Along the right-hand flank ran Blue Boar Street, which housed the entrance to the city's police station.

Inside, having been to Seldon's office once before, Eleanor started off in the direction she recalled.

'Not so fast, miss,' a male voice called behind her. 'Civilians are not permitted beyond this point unaccompanied.'

She stopped and turned to the young policeman. 'Oh, that's quite alright. I'm here to see—Ah! *That* gentleman.'

Seldon's tall athletic frame approached her. She instantly felt the familiar cloud of butterflies that always surfaced when he was around. Perhaps it was the way his unbuttoned signature blue wool overcoat hung so perfectly from his broad shoulders? Or the smart form-fitting grey suit underneath that highlighted the length of his legs? Or was it his deep voice that seduced her ears? Perhaps it was all three?

'Lady Swift, good morning. I shall be with you in one moment.'

Tearing her gaze from his chestnut curls and soft brown eyes, she busied herself with her gloves. 'No hurry. I shall be fine here, Hugh.' She gasped as he coloured. *What are you thinking, Ellie! Using his first name here, of all places.*

He let out a long breath and turned on his heels. As he strode away, she sighed.

Oh, dear, Ellie, not a good start!

CHAPTER 14

Outside, Seldon led the way along Blue Boar Street, followed by the equally intriguingly named Bear Lane and then on past the immense Oriel College, set back behind regal green lawns. As they emerged onto the bustling high street, she couldn't help feeling it was more of a frogmarch given the length of his long-legged stride. He had, however, gallantly taken her multitude of shopping bags without a word before they'd left the police station.

A moment later he stopped and pushed open a door.

'Queen's Lane Coffee House,' he said as he followed her inside. 'It's one of the most historic coffee houses in the South of England, established in sixteen hundred and something.'

She looked up at the double-width cream-painted frontage, noting the pronounced dip in the centre of the grey-tiled roofline.

She wrinkled her nose. 'More Clifford's sort of place, really, but far enough from your office so your colleagues won't spot you sitting with me.' She turned back to see his rather crestfallen expression. 'Oh, but what I meant was, it's perfectly lovely for us… to, erm, you know…'

Seldon failed to spare her blushes and promptly told the waitress, quaintly turned out in a frilled apron and matching cap, that they would take a table anywhere away from the window.

Once seated, Eleanor felt the need to clear the air. After their one and only 'date' on her thirtieth birthday, when chatter and laughter had flowed like champagne, he had reverted to his formal and rather gruff self.

'It's good of you to take time out to meet me today. And sorry about calling you Hugh back at the station.'

He ran a hand through his hair. 'Please think no more of it. Would... would it be inappropriate for me to call you Eleanor here?'

She blushed. 'Of course not. I'd love it.'

He smiled at her and then glanced down at the menu. 'What would you like?'

'Oh, yes, best get on with it. You're no doubt very busy.' She ran her eyes over the page, seeing nothing as she tried to think of how to phrase what she had come to ask. 'Tell you what, why don't you choose?'

'Two specials, please,' he said to the hovering waitress. 'Shopping?' He nodded at her bags, which he had placed beside his endlessly long legs. 'And whiling away the afternoon over coffee while your butler awaits your return to the Rolls? Do I detect that you are finally sliding into the role of lady of the manor?'

'Well, now that would make you a very poor detective, which I know first-hand that you are not. No, I fear that I shall never fit that mould, despite Clifford's best efforts.'

She jumped at his deep, rich laugh.

'Hats off, I'm impressed at his stamina for continuing to attempt such an insurmountable task.'

She laughed in return. 'As am I.'

He scanned her face. 'You look well. Pleasingly so. How have you been since... since we last met?'

She coloured. *Come on, Ellie! You complain of his manner, but you know you've been distant yourself.*

'You mean at my husband's funeral? It's okay, there's no need to avoid mentioning it, although I appreciate your sensitivity. Sadly, he'd already been gone a long time for me when it all happened.'

In fact, her husband had deserted her shortly after they'd married in South Africa six years previously. He turned out not to be the dashing officer he claimed, and he was shot in front of a firing squad for running guns. At least, that is what she thought until she went on holiday to Brighton and found her husband's dead body in the hotel she was staying at.

'Honestly, for the first month my stock answer was "I'm fine" to save having to discuss it all. But now, genuinely, I am fairly certain that is true.'

'Good news,' he said quietly. 'Very good news.'

'I'm sorry it was so long. I… I needed to… recuperate, as it were.'

Before he could reply, their order arrived.

'Fruit cake! And it smells divine. It's my absolute favourite.'

'I know. Mine too.'

Once the waitress had set everything out on the table and left, Seldon cleared his throat.

'Well, perhaps to business.' He poured her a cup of coffee. 'You asked to meet me for a reason I have yet to fathom.'

'Oh, yes. I didn't intend to drag you away from your office, though. But now I realise it would have been an inappropriate conversation to have there, anyway.'

'What would have been inappropriate is the level of interest my colleagues would have taken in my meeting with you. They are aware our paths have crossed on several occasions. But at least this time, whatever it is you want my help for, it doesn't involve a dead body. A most refreshing change, if I may say so.'

Her grimace made him groan.

'No! There can't really be another body?'

'There really is. Well, there was. Poor chap. Officially he accidentally drowned and is now six feet under in a coffin crafted by his own skilled hand, since he was the local undertaker. He was also a friend to the entire village, the life, and soul of Little Buckford. It was a horrible shock finding him the way I did.'

Seldon reached out towards her, but then coloured and pulled his hand back stiffly. 'You found him? What is it with you and... bodies? Sorry, badly put.'

She let out a laugh, grateful to break the tension. 'Trust me, I wish I knew. I feel terribly guilty that I didn't get to him sooner. And, as I was guest of honour at the May Fair, I'm probably now responsible for heralding a plague of forty years' famine and pestilence or some such.'

He frowned. 'Let's forget this May Fair and just go back a step. This very popular chap who you say had no enemies, died by accident and has subsequently been buried, right?'

She nodded. *Oh, dear, Ellie, you know what's coming.*

Hugh leaned back in his chair and shook his head. 'What possible help do you imagine I could be in those circumstances?'

Come on, Ellie, you've only got one chance.

'Well, to quote Clifford when I've chewed his ear off for too long, there's a lot to be said for brevity, so here goes. Solemn Jon was at the back of the raft race, alone on his craft. When he failed to cross the finish line, I organised a search party, but when we got to him, he was face down in the reeds. The doctor deemed he had fallen from his raft, hit his head and drowned. But the following morning an obituary was published declaring it to be murder.'

Seldon snorted. 'Sounds like a crank. A hoax. We get them all the time.'

She nodded over her coffee cup. 'You'd think so. Certainly the local police do.'

'Ah, Sergeant Brice on the case, is he?'

'No, that's just it, *no one is*. The doctor's verdict was death by misadventure. And Willie Green, the man who signed the obituary declaring it to be murder, has been let off with a warning by the police as they think he's unreliable to say the least. So' – she shrugged – 'the matter has been closed.'

Seldon put down his cup and ran his hand through his tousled curls. 'Why do I have a sinking feeling that you are going to ask me to reopen what sounds like a straightforward accidental death? *Again.*'

She winced. 'I admit we have been here before.' She took her courage in her hands. 'Solemn Jon's wife spoke to me at the funeral. She believes he was murdered because he had been acting out of character lately and… and she asked me to investigate.'

He raised his eyebrows. 'And you agreed?'

'Well… yes. And normally I'd just go charging off and investigate on my own, upsetting the local police and' – she looked into his eyes – '*you*. So this time I decided I'd be more… responsible and ask you to look into the matter instead. I thought you'd be pleased… in a roundabout way.'

His lips settled into a thin line. 'Well, it's an improvement, but' – he rubbed his forehead and sighed – 'I so hoped we wouldn't be having this kind of conversation when we haven't seen each other since… you know. Especially today,' he muttered.

'Why especially today?'

He shook his head. 'It doesn't matter. If meeting your request to cast my eye over the facts will stop you, as you put it, "charging in and upsetting the local police" I'll do it. However, it will have to wait until tomorrow. I am already overstretched for today.'

'Thank you. I do appreciate it.' Relieved, she tried to ease the tension with some gentle teasing. 'But you could look a little happier about it.'

'No, actually, I couldn't. Because by merely saying yes I will be breaking the bounds of my authority yet again. And I am already fearing you will not take kindly to my findings. As usual.' He gestured to the waitress for the bill. 'It seems we can only ever agree about one thing.'

This isn't going the way you hoped at all, Ellie.

'And that is?'

'Fruit cake. Now if you will excuse me, I have to get back to work.'

Once alone, it was Eleanor's turn to groan. *Oh, Ellie, how could you be so thoughtless? You don't see him for months and then when you do, you make it clear it's only to ask him a favour. And one that will probably end up leading to a row between us.* She shook her head. Every time a man was interested in her, she seemed to push him away. *What's wrong with you, Ellie?*

CHAPTER 15

By the time Friday morning came, Eleanor wished even more she hadn't asked Seldon for help. The guilt she felt in not getting to Solemn Jon sooner still haunted her, but it was now overladen with more guilt at having offended the very man she desperately wanted not to.

'I believe Mrs Trotman will require a few minutes to prepare more sausages, my lady,' Clifford said, interrupting her thoughts. He held up the empty breakfast salver.

She frowned. 'But there were plenty when I started.'

'Indeed.' He gave a discreet cough. 'If you'll excuse me speculating, my lady, I hope your trip to the riverbank will go better than your Oxford rendezvous.'

She had confided in him on the way back to the Hall about her uncomfortable meeting with Seldon.

'Dash it, Clifford! My face always betrays my thoughts.' She bit her bottom lip. 'Any advice?'

'Perhaps practising in front of the mirror?' His eyes twinkled.

'You terror, you know perfectly well I meant advice for getting on better with Seldon.'

'Well, impertinence is not a habit I indulge in, my lady. However, if I might quote Oscar Wilde on this occasion, "Arguments are to be avoided: they are always vulgar and often convincing."' With his customary half bow, he picked the salver up and stepped from the room.

She stared after him. *What exactly did that mean, Ellie?*

Gladstone, having given up his forlorn hope that another round of sausages might magically appear, trailed after Eleanor to the second drawing room, situated in the right-hand tower that flanked the front entrance.

Like most other rooms in the Hall, the spring cleaning had turned it upside down. But as she entered, she was too preoccupied to notice the white sheets covering the bespoke Wedgewood blue settees, crafted to fit the curve of the tower. Nor did she see the tall stepladder set ready to take down the central chandelier. Heading straight to the window, which looked out over the horseshoe driveway, she peered out, waiting for her guest. Gladstone lumbered up onto one of the covered settees via a footstool and eyed her grumpily. He hated Henley Hall's annual spring cleaning as much as she did.

All too soon, the crunch of gravel under car tyres told her she had run out of time to work out how to make this meeting go smoother than the last. Clifford appeared in the doorway with her sage-green hat and matching light wool jacket.

'Thank you.' She raised her voice over Gladstone's snores. 'Wish me luck.'

She was just finishing pinning her hat in the hallway mirror when Clifford opened the door to reveal Seldon on the top step.

'Chief Inspector Seldon to see you, my lady,' he announced unnecessarily.

'Ah, Hugh,' Eleanor said. 'Do come in. Almost done here.' She turned back to the mirror but peeped discreetly sideways as he removed his bowler hat and crossed the threshold. The slate grey of what she noted looked like a new suit highlighted his tall athletic frame far too well for her to keep those dratted butterflies at bay. 'There, ready.'

He stared at her for a moment and then cleared his throat.

'Good. I'm afraid I'm rather pushed for time. I'll have to rely on your sense of direction as I've never had cause to visit the delights of Little Buckford's river before.'

Clifford gave a discreet cough. They both turned to find him holding a sleepy bulldog on the end of a lead.

'Oh.'

She'd had no intention of taking Gladstone along. He would only slow things down and Seldon had just made it clear he was in a hurry. There was something in her butler's demeanour, however, that made her take the lead. She looked enquiringly at Seldon.

He spread his hands. 'I had no idea Gladstone had a nose for anything except sausages. But if you think he might be of use, bring him along.'

Seldon's car was the perfect reflection of him, Eleanor thought, as he navigated the steep hill from Henley Hall down into the village. It felt solid and reliable, but the deep growl from the engine suggested there was something surprising lying dormant, waiting to be unleashed. With the day already warming up, they'd wound the windows down and the breeze flicked at Gladstone's ears and Seldon's curls in equal measure. The waving clusters of white flowering hawthorn hedges filled with chattering sparrows, however, merely highlighted that they were motoring to the riverbank in near silence, Eleanor breaking it only to give directions.

'Perfect, thank you,' she said as he pulled up close to the point from which she had led the village to the river. 'It's not far. We just need to walk down to the bridge and cross over to the other side, since the foot ferry is no longer running.'

'Good. Please lead the way.'

Oh, dear, Ellie. This feels horribly awkward.

She slipped Gladstone's lead from his collar and started along the towpath, wishing Seldon would walk beside her, rather than behind. To be fair, the towpath was too narrow to walk side by side with decorum. *Unless you were lovers, Ellie.* She gasped. Where had that come from? She glanced at Seldon, but he was too busy scouring the ground and the opposite bank to have noticed her blushes.

A few minutes later, she stopped and pointed to the thick bank of bullrushes where she had spotted Solemn Jon's body.

'Right.' Seldon turned in a slow circle, taking in everything within the near vicinity. As his eyes drew level with her again, he swallowed. 'Sorry, how thoughtless of me. Would you prefer to go back and wait?'

Touched, she shook her head. 'Thank you, but I'm alright. And do take your time, please… I mean, as much as you can spare, of course.'

She stepped to one side and watched him scouring the towpath and surrounding bank. Finally, he pointed to the bullrushes. 'Can you remember exactly where you were standing when you saw the bod— the deceased?'

She scratched her forehead. 'I'd say, I must have been' – she strode a few yards further on in the pontoon's direction – 'right about here. In fact, it must have been just here because, look, I broke these stems when I almost slipped in at the shock of seeing… the body.'

He glanced at her, a hint of concern on his face, but then stepped close beside her. 'If I may?'

'May what?' Her heart skipped.

'Stand where you are.'

'Oh, of course.' She moved and bent to ruffle Gladstone's ears to hide her embarrassment, her thoughts flashing back to the other version of this gruff, ever-professional policeman, who had, just once, twirled her so delicately on the dance floor.

He pulled a leather notebook from his inside jacket pocket and held his pen out in front of him as if mentally measuring various parts of the path and the river.

'And you said his craft—'

'Raft.'

'His raft was nowhere in sight at the time of you finding him?'

'No, definitely not. It was probably the one that floated down last, but since there was no one in sight, we didn't wait to check. I'd instigated a search party to take either bank by then.'

He nodded. 'So, I can conclude you all knew who was missing because the crew were ticked off as they crossed the finish line?'

She groaned. 'No, that's precisely the reason I feel so bad about how long it took us to find him. The rafts were ticked off, but not the people. Some rafts had lots of crew onboard. The cricket team had a full squad, for example.'

'Then how did you realise it was this chap you call Solemn Jon who was missing?'

'Because one of his cardboard headstones appeared down at the bridge as we were assembling the two search parties.'

'*Cardboard headstones?* Seriously?'

'Welcome to Buckinghamshire,' she said as wryly as Clifford had said to her the day of the May Fair.

'Peculiar.'

'That's Buckinghamshire for you. Pretty much the entire village were there spectating. Or taking part.'

He grimaced. 'That would rather widen the pool of suspects. How long would you say he was missing?'

She stared up at the cloudless blue sky, trying to remember. 'I last noticed him quite a way before the end of the race, maybe ten minutes even. I'm not sure because I was distracted by Penry, the butcher, and Cartwright, one of the farmers, brawling.' She waved a hand. 'Don't ask! Anyway, it was a while longer before we got a search party together as the chairman was obstructive about a search party being sent out.'

'Obstructive? On what grounds?'

She shook her head. 'Oh, we got our wires crossed, nothing more. But maybe, oh, gracious! Maybe you're right. I hadn't thought about him having had a hand in Solemn Jon's murder.'

'Accident,' Seldon corrected firmly. 'At this point, it is still an accident. The chairman's name, please?'

'Mr Peters-Preston. No, that's not it. Peterson-Prestwick?' She shrugged. 'It's some combination of two of those four.' The corners of his lips curled into what she thought was a smile. *Is he laughing at you, Ellie?* 'We can check with Clifford on our return.'

He nodded. 'And how long before the search parties set off?'

'I'd say, two, three minutes tops.'

'I see.' He looked around once more. 'Well, I'd better see this capsized raft. Perhaps we'll find something there?'

CHAPTER 16

As they neared the now righted coffin-shaped raft that was lashed to the bank, she felt the hot prick of tears behind her eyelids. One of the cardboard headstones was half-sticking up, wedged between the planks of the platform, giving the whole thing the appearance of a bizarre grave.

'Oh, gracious,' she mumbled.

'You really could wait here,' Seldon said as he reached the raft's edge under a weeping willow. 'I shan't be long, there's not much to this contraption after all.'

A few minutes later, he rejoined her.

'Well, there's no sign that the craft was tampered with. The buoyancy aids are all still lashed tightly and the platform itself is intact. Aside from this wooden bar and crude tiller affair at the back here, there's nothing else to its, admittedly unfortunate-themed, construction. There's a length of twine and a hook caught round the bar, but apart from that, nothing else.'

'A hook? Isn't that odd?'

He shook his head. 'Unfortunately, fishermen discard old hooks and twine all the time. They're always fouling boats and the like.' He pointed to the ground. 'There are bits of fishing line and the odd hook not only in the river, but on the bank too.'

While he was talking, she took a look at the hook.

'But isn't that dried blood?'

He nodded. 'Fishermen often stab themselves with their own hooks. Sometimes when they're trying to disentangle them. Then they give up and cut the twine. See there?' He pointed into the branches above them. 'There's twine hanging from that branch too. Wretched stuff is everywhere.' He snapped his notebook shut. 'I know it isn't what you want to hear, but there is nothing here to suggest the man was murdered.'

She went to reply, but he held up his hand.

'I'm sorry, but there are no signs of a struggle where the body was found. The doctor's report clearly stated the blow to the head the man received would have probably rendered him unconscious, but not killed him. Therefore he concluded it was a case of accidental death by drowning. The only way to check further would be to get a warrant to dig the poor fellow up only days after he's been buried and do a full autopsy. And then it might prove nothing more than he did indeed receive a blow to the back of the head and subsequently drowned. I'm afraid, as there's no form of evidence that he didn't die by accident, there's no way a judge would issue a warrant.'

Eleanor cast around to salvage something from his visit.

'Clifford noted where Solemn Jon was found, some weed had been disturbed and was further out in the river than he would have expected.' She frowned. 'For some reason I can't quite remember.'

That sounds so lame, Ellie!

'Disturbed by the man's raft capsizing or his falling in, which, given that he was unconscious, would have been ungainly to say the least. Wouldn't you agree one of those was the likely reason?'

She took the hint and started back towards the bridge, managing not to take a last regretful look at the spot where Solemn Jon had died.

'Well, thank you again for coming down.'

Her words were drowned out by Gladstone's furious barking. Repeatedly charging the bank, his stiff front legs lifted off the ground as he spun in wobbly circles.

'Gladstone!' she called. 'Be careful, silly. You know you can't swim.'

'Has he seen something useful?' Seldon's deep voice tickled her ear as he leaned round her to stare at the bulldog.

'I've no idea. Oh!' A flurry of ducks shot out of the reeds. 'No, Gladstone!'

The frenzied bulldog broke into even more furious barking. Lunging forward, his front legs scrabbled in mid-air, while his back feet lost grip on the edge of the bank. With a solid slap, he landed in the water where an eddy whirled him round and whipped him off down the river.

'Hang on, boy!' she called, ripping at the laces on her shoes.

'I thought all dogs could swim,' Seldon shouted as he passed her, shoes and jacket miraculously already off. Pausing momentarily to assess the depth of the water, he threw his arms over his head and dived expertly into the river.

'Hugh!'

A long second later, his head reappeared. She held her breath as he swam over to the surprised bulldog and grabbed him around the waist with one arm. Striking out with the other, he set off back for the bank, fighting the force of water that was trying to drag them both further downstream.

'Here. HERE!'

She hung out over the water, hand grasped round the thick branch of a fallen tree as she balanced in her stockinged feet on the trunk. With much hauling from Eleanor and shoving from Seldon, Gladstone was eventually deposited on the towpath, a lagoon of water forming around him. She dropped to her knees and scooped him into a soggy hug. He looked utterly relaxed and submitted to her fussing quite calmly. Letting go, she rummaged in her algae-covered jacket pocket and passed the sodden policeman a handkerchief.

'Sorry, it's all I've got.' She tried not to stare at his heaving chest in his now almost see-through shirt, nor at his dark trousers clinging to his legs, outlining every inch of how long and trim they were. 'I'll replace your suit. It looked so good on you, Hugh. Oh, heavens, it's new, isn't it?'

Taking the lace handkerchief, he smiled. 'I didn't think you'd noticed, Eleanor.'

By the time they had reached the Hall, much of the water and weed had transferred itself to Seldon's car. They walked up the steps, Seldon carrying the shivering Gladstone in his arms, Eleanor stroking the bulldog's face and murmuring comforting words. Clifford opened the door, three towels draped over his forearm.

Eleanor looked at him oddly. 'Inspector Seldon needs some dry clothes, if we have any, Clifford.'

'Very good, my lady.' Clifford handed her a towel as Seldon placed the bulldog on the ground. Clifford then bent down and wrapped Gladstone in the second. Standing up, he turned to Seldon, offering the last towel. 'Chief Inspector, perhaps you would like to accompany me and I will find you something suitably… dry? I will also see to the seats of your car.' Turning back to Eleanor, his eyes flicked over her soaked jacket, skirt and ripped stockings. 'A most successful trip, I see, my lady.'

CHAPTER 17

'Do the thing, get the reward.' That's what mother used to say, Ellie. And you definitely want the reward of this being over and done with!

Batting away Clifford's insistence that she might be better resting after the emotion of the morning, she reached for her hat and coat straight after lunch. But even before the Rolls turned onto Pastures Lane, he tried again.

'Master Gladstone has received a considerable shock, my lady. Perhaps curling up with you on the chaise longue in the snug might hasten his recovery?'

'You mean him hogging the chaise longue and digging his sharp elbows into me might? Gladstone is fine, as well you know. The ladies are fussing over him. And I realise you're trying to help, but this will be a very quick meeting since I have unwelcome news to impart. Which, actually, is the only reason I devoured four of Mrs Trotman's delicious beef and Stilton tarts for lunch. For extra courage.' She caught his eye. 'One of the reasons, anyway. Besides, I've been meaning to mention that you found Seldon something surprisingly well-fitting with ease. And you miraculously had dry towels waiting when we returned from the river. If I didn't know better, I might think you sent us off with Gladstone knowing he'd jump in after those dratted ducks and Seldon would jump in after him.'

He cleared his throat. 'I certainly do not confess to arranging the incident, my lady. However, if I might permit the observation, when you left the Hall the atmosphere seemed a trifle… strained. And on your return much more… amenable?'

She gasped. 'So it *was* your intention! Honestly, Clifford! What *were* you thinking?'

'I was thinking of Shakespeare, my lady. "Love goes by haps; Some Cupid kills with arrows, some with traps."' His eyes twinkled. 'Nothing cheers a gentleman more than the unexpected and genuine opportunity to impress a lady.'

She shook her head. 'I know Uncle Byron charged you with looking after my welfare and happiness, but this is above and beyond! Suppose Seldon had got into trouble? Or Gladstone?'

'My apologies, but Chief Inspector Seldon is an expert swimmer, as I believe you had the chance to observe. And Master Gladstone, although by no means a strong swimmer, has the advantage that his shape and mass make him all but unsinkable. He has chased ducks and other sundry waterfowl into the river on several occasions when I was tasked by his lordship with taking him for a walk. On each occasion he floated downstream to the bank and clambered out unaided. Indeed, he sees it as something of a game.'

She stared at him in disbelief. 'I may have said this before, Clifford, but you are a monster!'

'Thank you, my lady.' He kept his eyes on the road, but she could see the faintest of smiles on his lips. 'My only real concern was that you might go to Master Gladstone's rescue before the chief inspector had a chance, but it was a risk worth taking. You are, after all, a superlative swimmer yourself, so were in no danger.'

She tried her best to suppress a smile. 'You're lucky I don't tell Seldon you engineered it all. Honestly! Well. I suppose Hu— Seldon and I parted on good terms. Very good terms, actually.' A small groan escaped her as she remembered back to the coffee shop. 'Unless, oh, no, tell me I'm right and he didn't rant on to you about me when it was just the two of you alone?'

Clifford eased the Rolls to a stop in front of a large herd of cows blocking the road and switched the engine off.

'My lady, if you will forgive my giving an opinion, Detective Chief Inspector Seldon is too much of a gentleman to "rant on" about anything to me. I am, after all, your butler.'

She gave him a mock look of reproach. 'It didn't stop the two of you conspiring against me on my birthday in Brighton so he could surprise me with an evening of dancing.'

The corners of his lips twitched as he stared straight ahead, watching yet more cows plod out onto the road. 'The chief inspector and I may have… colluded in a good cause. But conspired? Never.'

'Hmm, well, they seem pretty similar to my mind, but I don't feel up to engaging with you in a battle of semantics. Anyway, I've decided I am absolutely going to decline to help Solemn Jon's wife despite still feeling guilty that I didn't find Solemn Jon sooner. And I know my intuition's telling me something's amiss. But…' She held up a hand. 'I don't have a choice. If I am ever to stop being at odds with Seldon and most of Buckinghamshire's constabulary, I need to learn to yield to the facts, as you and the inspector would say. I shall wrestle with my conscience later. But first I must see Mrs Jon immediately and get it over with. Now, how much longer must we wait?' She leaned out of the window. 'I mean, where's the farmer?'

'Mr Drinkwater will have opened the gate and then taken the shortcut over the hill to drop down to the dairy, ready for the second milking of the day.'

'Of course,' she said, acutely aware of her ignorance of country ways yet again. 'Where these lumbering ladies are clearly headed of their own accord, I see. And at their own pace.'

Once the cows had finished sauntering across the road, Clifford drove on until he pulled up outside a flint cottage. The extensive prevalence of these sharp grey and black stones in the area had been the scourge of agricultural farmers since Roman days. It had, however, provided a low-cost building material for the local population. Tiny gabled windows set in a moss-covered slate roof looked down on a waist-high wall enclosing a well-tended vegetable garden. Rainbow-coloured beds of fragrant herbs were separated by a stone path leading to an open red stable-style door.

Eleanor felt a wash of sorrow as she drew level with a wooden love bench. Clearly crafted by Solemn Jon's expert hand, a beautifully carved heart spanned the centre of the two seats, a scrolling letter 'J' entwined with an 'M'. She sighed, dreading what she had to say more than ever.

Best just be direct, Ellie. You can't change Seldon's, or the local police's view, on what happened, no matter how much you might want to.

Something moist nuzzled her hand. 'Hello, Patrick.' She patted the wolfhound's wiry grey-brown head and stroked his whiskery chin. His deep chestnut-coloured eyes held hers. 'I bet you're a great comfort right now,' she whispered.

'Oh, he'll take that all day long, m'lady,' Mrs Jon said from the doorway. 'But we don't want to take up any more of your time than need be, 'tis so kind of you to come.'

'Not at all. My pleasure.' Eleanor noted the pale, drawn look to the woman's face and wanted to reach out and take her hand. She didn't, fearing it might upset the woman further. Buckinghamshire was a very traditional county. Most folk were quite happy with the way things were, as she'd found out when standing as Little Buckford and Chipstone's first female MP.

'I wanted to call to see how you are. And Mrs Trotman sent a small hamper of her wonderful kitchen creations.' She held up a wicker basket covered in a blue-gingham tea towel.

'Folks is so kind, m'lady, like yourself. And Mrs Trotman is a gem. I'll unpack this quick-like so you can take her basket back.' She half-turned and then hesitated.

'Is everything alright?'

The woman fiddled with the sleeve of her thick grey wool cardigan without replying. *Maybe she's changed her mind about*

*asking you to investigate her husband's death after all, Ellie, and
doesn't know how to say.*

'I'm sorry, m'lady.' Mrs Jon turned back to her. 'I've never had
a titled lady call at my door afore. Is it too forward to ask you to
take a cup of tea with me?'

Eleanor's smile never wavered. 'I thought you'd never ask.'

CHAPTER 18

Stepping over the threshold and down two short steps, she was surprised to see they were immediately in the parlour. Inside, the cottage was even smaller than she had imagined. The dark beamed ceiling was hung with cut bunches of drying lavender, which smelt like summer herself. Two spotless but well-worn armchairs, one blue, the other mustard, sat facing each other by the flint-and-brick fireplace. Between them, a long, low footstool with a lace mat served as a coffee table. Against one of the whitewashed walls stood an old wooden side table, its plain cream cloth covered in jam jars filled with handpicked posies of wildflowers.

Mrs Jon pointed at the array of floral tributes. 'Like I said, folks is so kind.' She patted the top of the blue armchair. ''Taint what you're used to, I know, but please make yourself at home, m'lady. I'll be just a minute.'

In fact, in many ways it was more than Eleanor was used to. She'd been brought up in both mud-floored huts and marble-floored palaces as her parents travelled from country to country, her father being a consultant for implementing educational and social reforms.

As Patrick trotted off on his mistress' heels, she slid into the chair and looked round at the rest of the room. The oil lamps dotted about testified to the lack of natural light. Few houses in Little Buckford had electricity apart from Henley Hall and the vicarage. A small treadle sewing machine shared the only available corner with a tiny roll-top desk draped in a part-finished patchwork quilt. Two unframed canvas paintings of Buckinghamshire's sweeping chalk hills and ancient beech woods hung on either side of the fireplace. Depicting the same view, one captured the verdant green of spring, the other the red and yellows of autumn.

Her eyes fell on several newspaper cuttings in simple wood frames on the mantelpiece. She rose to look more closely.

'His pride and joy,' Mrs Jon said beside her, nodding at Patrick.

'I didn't realise he was a racing dog.' Eleanor scanned the articles mentioning the dog's many wins. 'He seems so placid, and well—'

'Gangly? No need to be polite, m'lady. He's been called many things but "Hat-trick Patrick" has definitely stuck on account of his stealing the crown three years in a row.'

'Hat-trick Patrick.' Eleanor ran her hand along the dog's back. 'You clever old thing.' She straightened up. 'Sorry, what crown exactly?'

Mrs Jon managed a smile. 'I forgot you are new here, m'lady. Why, the Chiltern Hound Trailing Cup. 'Tis the most prestigious race in these parts. Surprised everyone the first time he won, except my John who took Patrick in as a favour, seeing as he was the runt of the litter. But even when he was just a scraggy ball of fur sticking out at all angles, he said that puppy had good bones and a quiet will of iron about him.'

She thought about the woman's situation again. *With Solemn Jon gone, how would she cope financially?* 'So… do you only win a trophy for this cup? Or… or is there a cash prize as well?'

Mrs Jon tutted. ''Tis just a cup and the honour, m'lady. We keeps the cups in the bedroom. The money's made on the betting. Each to their own, but John and me don't believe in such amoral practices.'

She wondered if they disagreed on religious grounds or if it was just a personal thing. She suddenly remembered the medallion she'd picked up on the riverbank. *If he was very religious, Ellie, perhaps it was Solemn Jon's? Perhaps he lost it if he jumped onto the bank after his raft had become entangled in weeds?*

She was wearing the same sage-green jacket she'd been wearing that day, so she pulled it out of her pocket and held it out to Mrs Jon.

'I know it's a little dirty, but I found this on the riverbank where... well, near where we found your husband. I thought it might be his?'

Mrs Jon took the medallion and shook her head.

'My John never wore nothing like this around his neck. Wasn't one for ornamenting himself, if you know what I mean.' She handed it back, looking a little sad. 'But look now, where are my manners! Please, take a seat and let me pour you a nice hot tea. Even on a warm day like today, 'tis cool in here. That's why the door's usually open, lets in a bit of the sunshine heat.'

Eleanor put the medallion back in her pocket and sat again and took the tea with a slice of warmed flapjack balanced on the saucer.

'It feels very cosy, in truth.' She hoped it came out as she meant it and not at all patronising.

The other woman stared wistfully into space. 'Moved in here the day we got married. 'Twas John's parents' house. Thirty-two years we was together. John always said the place was like me. Made just the way he'd dreamed of and everything he looked forward to seeing at the end of the day.'

This brought a lump to Eleanor's throat. 'Thirty-two years is a long time. A wonderfully long time.'

''Twas wonderful for sure, m'lady. But even though I know he's gone, I can't think of things being "was" and "afore". I keep staring at the door expecting him to walk in, swinging the leather satchel I'd pack his lunch in of a morning, his face all lit up at being home.'

'I know. It's... really hard.' *Dash it, Ellie! Why can't you do that thing Clifford does of always knowing exactly what to say?*

'I'm the lucky one, though, to have had all those wonderful years.' Mrs Jon dabbed at her eyes and sniffed. She seemed to hesitate a moment and then gather her resolve. 'Seeing as you're here, m'lady, I'm guessing you had a chance to think about what I asked you? Begging your pardon again for being so forward as to have come looking for your help, 'specially as we never met afore my John's funeral.'

Here goes, Ellie. 'Gracious, it was absolutely fine for you to have asked, but the thing is, Mrs—'

''Tis Maggie, m'lady, but I wouldn't expect a lady like yourself to call me—'

'Maggie, please understand. I want to help you any way I can, which is why I went to an expert. A Detective Inspector, Chief Inspector in fact, who offered to investigate the matter.'

'Oh, that was good of him. And yourself, m'lady. And what did he find, can I ask?'

Eleanor set her cup down with a sigh. 'I'm sorry to say he didn't find any evidence that your husband's death was suspicious. He agreed with the doctor's verdict.' At Maggie's frown, she added, 'But surely it's better if it genuinely was an accident?'

'If it had been, of course. But it wasn't. I know it.' The woman's tone was measured and calm.

Eleanor tried again. 'You said Solemn Jon had been acting out of character. What if whatever was bothering him had him so distracted that he failed to notice his raft was charging towards one of the many fallen trees in the river?'

'I… I don't believe it, m'lady.'

Why did she hesitate, Ellie? She said a moment ago she was sure. Does she know, or suspect, more than she's letting on?

Maggie shook her head as if clearing her thoughts. 'My John was like Patrick here, could swim all day if he needed to. Always said he had frog's legs for a reason.'

'But he hit his head,' Eleanor said gently.

'Was walloped on the head more like it.'

Eleanor tried again. 'Everyone loved Solemn Jon. He was a huge part of the village. Who could possibly have wanted to harm him?'

'I've no real idea, but someone did for him, m'lady. Someone with a heart colder and more deadly than the winter ice the little 'uns skate across the village pond on, for he would never hurt a fly.'

'Did he ever have cross words with anyone?'

Maggie's expression hardened. 'No, but you don't need to row to have folk want you out of the way.'

'Like who?'

'Willie Green for one. And after everything my John did for him. Even planned to leave his undertaking yard to him. That's how good my John was. Tried to see past all of Willie's drinking and troublemaking. And then there's Pendle, shifty bit of work, he is.'

'Sorry, "Pendle" did you say? Who is he? I don't know that name.'

'Course you wouldn't. You're a proper lady. Arthur Pendle runs the Hound Trailing Club. He tried everything to get his hands on Patrick.' She patted the dog's head. 'Course, even though we could always have done with extra, John would never have parted with him. Especially to that Pendle. Treats his dogs badly. Only interested at how much he can make out of them on the betting. And then when they're too old…' She shook her head. 'Patrick's staying by my side until it's his time to go and then he'll go in his bed by the fire like every faithful dog we've ever had.'

Eleanor could imagine the pain of having to part with Gladstone, but then couldn't imagine who would want him. Pretty well any living creature with a pulse could outrun her lazy, stiff-legged bulldog.

'I suppose this Mr Pendle thinks he could win a lot of money if he owned Patrick?'

'That's right.' Her lips set in a thin line. 'Do you know Pendle's such a scoundrel, he had the cheek the day after John died to waltz in through my open door without so much as knocking. He told me I'd have to sell Patrick now, but I sent him away with a flea in his ear.'

Eleanor's brows met. 'That's terrible. Especially with you still trying to deal with what's happened.'

'And that's not the half of it. That Pendle started a fight with my John at the Dog and Badger the night afore the race.'

'They actually fought? I can't imagine Solemn Jon throwing a punch at anyone.'

'That's how riled he was. Pendle threatened if Patrick wasn't for sale, he'd get him another way.'

But even if Solemn Jon and Pendle did fight in the Dog and Badger, there was no sign of a struggle at the scene of Solemn Jon's death, Ellie. Seldon found nothing. And the entire village was at the river that day. Somebody would have seen something.

She took a deep breath. 'Maggie, I wish I could give you a different answer, but I don't think I can possibly find out anything of use for you. I'm honestly not sure myself it wasn't an accident, although I fully respect that you are. The inspector was my best hope, and he is convinced there is no case.'

What about your intuition, Ellie? You know that's telling you a different story.

Maggie shuffled to the edge of her seat, her eyes beseeching. 'But you proved all the police wrong, afore, m'lady. And more than once.'

'Thank you, but really I was just lucky a few times.'

''Tis no case of luck when it happens a third and then a fourth time.' Maggie's tone was deferential but firm.

'Nor a fifth,' Eleanor muttered, staring at her hands. She wanted to shout out the promise she'd made to herself. No more investigations. No more sleepless nights. No more arguing with Hugh. No more... bodies. She shuddered. Too many images she didn't want flashing behind her eyes.

'Almost isn't good enough for my John, m'lady.'

Eleanor jumped. 'Sorry?'

'I said, almost everyone thinks 'twas an accident. But I don't. I've been praying you would come saying you'd help, m'lady, I shan't lie. Still, 'tis no matter, I shall have to do it myself.' A stream of tears ran down her cheeks as her chest heaved. 'I'll never rest until I know the truth. He'd have done the same for me. I can't let it go.'

'Maggie, I do understand but—'

'But nothing, if you will forgive me being so bold, m'lady. I don't mean to be rude, but I have to do right by my John.' She broke off into more sobs. 'Though I've no idea what to do or where to start.' She buried her face in Patrick's whiskers. 'Sometimes I think it might just be best if I ended everything and joined my John.'

Eleanor grasped the woman's wrist. 'Maggie, that's no way to think!'

'No, 'tisn't. 'Tis a sin, but I'll be straight with you, m'lady. If it wasn't for needing to care for this silly old Patrick here that John loved almost as much as me, I might think on it.'

Eleanor slumped down into the passenger seat with a quiet moan and laid her head back, her hand over her eyes. As they drove off, Clifford opened the glovebox, revealing a miniature crystal cut glass and a bottle of sherry. She took the glass without a word and poured herself a measure. After taking a few sips, she breathed out deeply and relaxed her shoulders.

'Thank you, Clifford. I needed that.'

Without taking his eyes off the road, he nodded. 'Indeed, my lady. A little fortification before the start of a new case is always a good idea.'

She sat upright and opened her mouth to protest, and then slumped back in her seat. *How does he always know, Ellie?* Taking another sip, she shook her head.

'You know, Clifford, a hundred years ago they'd have burned you at the stake.'

CHAPTER 19

'Oh, your ladyship. I'm so terribly sorry! Beg pardon, I'm sure.'

Eleanor tried to ignore the pain in her left foot.

'That's alright, Polly. No… no harm done.' She eyed the tangled heap of velvet curtains the young girl had dropped after they'd collided. 'Isn't that rather a lot to carry in one go?'

''Tis no bother, your ladyship.' Her maid knelt down and started raking the curtains into a haphazard pile. 'There's a fierce amount to be done and in much less time than we had planned now and' – she swallowed hard – 'Mr Clifford used his extra-stern voice this morning.'

Eleanor put her hand on the maid's shoulder. 'Leave Mr Clifford to me. I think I may have unwittingly caused you all a lot of stress.'

Polly's eyes widened. 'Can't be right, the mistress apologising to me, can it, your ladyship? Isn't there a rule it only works t'other way?'

Eleanor joined her maid on her knees and refolded the curtains neatly.

'Trouble is, Polly, I'm not sure the mistress has read the rule book.' She gave a mock grimace. 'But don't tell Mr Clifford.'

The young girl placed a hand over her heart. 'Promise, your ladyship.'

She held her arms out. Eleanor deposited the curtains into them.

'Now, Polly, do you know where Mr Clifford is?'

Curtseying awkwardly with the burden across her arms, her maid nodded knowingly. 'He's choking Penelope.'

*

Downstairs, the clank of a metal bucket and hurrying footsteps caught her attention. She slid down the wide oak bannister to land at the feet of her unusually flush-cheeked housekeeper.

'That's one way to polish it, my lady,' Mrs Butters said with a wan smile. 'But 'tis no use, Mr Clifford will have us do it again anyways. And in double-quick time too, after the stiff talk he gave afore he took you into the village earlier.'

'Oh, gracious.' Eleanor bit her lip. 'Where might I find him? Polly confused me rather over what he is doing.'

'Let me call him for you, my lady. You won't want to be venturing down there, goodness no!'

She insisted that Mrs Butters didn't fetch Clifford, her curiosity piqued to find out what on earth Polly could have meant. A few minutes later, Eleanor had to concede her housekeeper had been right as she descended the narrow spiral stone steps into the second cellar, the musty air settling on her lungs mixed with the black smoke curling up from the oil lamp.

Flinching away from the many cobwebs, she steadied herself against the wall and peered around. Clifford was murmuring softly, kneeling in front of an ancient-looking cylindrical tank with what appeared to be a cauldron bolted on to it. On seeing her, he stood up, wiping his hands on a length of cheesecloth.

'You could have sent for me, my lady.'

'True, but then I would have missed the spectacle of my normally immaculate butler on his knees, shirtsleeves rolled up and forearms covered in goodness only knows what and murmuring sweet nothings.' She couldn't hold back her chuckle. 'I'm sorry, Clifford. But whatever I imagined Polly meant, it wasn't this.'

'Ah, Polly.' There was a tinge of weariness in his tone.

'She is the reason I'm here, but please don't be cross with her. And before I try to persuade you to join me for a quick break, I'm

intrigued by what Polly said you were doing. "Choking Penelope",
I believe it was?'

He shook his head but his tone held a hint of amusement.
'"Coaxing". Not choking.'

She raised an eyebrow.

He cleared his throat. 'My lady, may I introduce… Penelope.'
He gestured to the boiler.

Eleanor wrinkled her nose. 'She's not very pretty, Clifford. Really, if
you're going to make up to a girl, you might want to be a little fussier.'

Despite his pursed lips, it was clear he appreciated the impish
humour in her words. 'Penelope is the backup boiler. She was
decommissioned four years ago when his lordship arranged for
several improvements to the Hall's water and heating systems. He
finally tired of her stubborn and devious nature, having named her
after the wife of Odysseus, from Homer's epic.'

She tutted. 'It never ceases to amaze me that men name inani-
mate objects after women. Why do you suppose they do?'

'I imagine it is actually a sign of affection, my lady… or, as
with Penelope, an indication of the similar characteristics they
see in both.'

She laughed. 'Well, I'm sure no one has a boiler or a motor
car called Eleanor, no matter how troublesome or irritating that
machine might be.'

He gave a gentle cough. 'I really couldn't say.'

She arched a brow. 'But if Penelope's been stood down, then
exactly what are you doing to the stubborn old girl?'

'Trying to revive Penelope, my lady. Regrettably, so far no
amount of "murmuring sweet nothings" has proven fruitful.' His
eyes twinkled. 'I hope that is not too much racy information for
your delicate sensibilities?'

She laughed. 'No, but let me guess, you only needed Penelope
back in service to keep up with the extra hot water? Necessary,

perhaps, for the spring cleaning as I have unwittingly forced you to speed up your original schedule?'

His silence was answer enough.

'Well, I braved coming down here to apologise.'

'Apologise, my lady? I am sure that is far from necessary.'

'You mean "appropriate", I know. Anyway, I hadn't appreciated what a gigantic task the spring cleaning is. And I feel terrible that you've all been trying to do it in half the normal time because I've very selfishly been grumbling about the upheaval. So, I'm rescinding my previous grumblings and instead I insist you and the ladies slow down and take as long as is needed. And in exchange, you can help me work out what the drat I'm going to do about this Solemn Jon business. Agreed?'

'If you so desire, my lady, agreed.'

Fifteen minutes later Clifford appeared suited and impeccably starched in the library's doorway bearing a loaded silver tray giving off the tantalising aroma of hot savoury pastries. He sniffed disapprovingly at the sight of Eleanor sprawled on the floor, one arm around Gladstone, the other turning the pages of an ancient album. Then he spotted what it was.

'Ah! His lordship's birthday album, my lady.'

She half-turned to him. 'You mean each of these photographs was taken on Uncle Byron's actual birthday?'

'Indeed. Each year and then placed sequentially to create a chronological timeline.'

'Of his whole life,' she breathed. She paused at a sepia photograph of him in military dress in – she guessed – his late twenties. A handsome soldier stood one step behind him. 'Gracious! Clifford, it's you!'

He pulled a pair of pince-nez from his inside pocket and peered down at the page. 'Mandalay, Burma, my lady. How fitting then that I brought this decanter, along with the coffee.' He gestured towards the cut-glass crystal carafe on the tray. 'There are a few rare photographs of yourself as a child with his lordship. And a few of your parents.'

'And hopefully lots of the two of you together.' She caught his eye. 'If that won't feel too much like me prying into your previous life? I'll put the album straight back if it does.'

He shook his head. 'No, but thank you. And, as per your instructions, the ladies are enjoying a break from the spring cleaning over tea and plum cake and I have been charged with passing on their sincere gratitude.'

'Perfect, thank you.'

Having removed Gladstone's twitching nose from the vicinity of the pastries, Clifford placed a Stilton and pear pastry case onto her plate. She took a mouthful, savouring the salty sharpness of the cheese against the honey sweetness of the fruit. Meanwhile, he pulled back the edge of the linen cloth on the silver tray to reveal her notebook and favourite pen. 'My lady, if you will forgive my presumption, I actually hastened the spring cleaning this morning partly because I concluded I might be called away to assist with your investigation.'

'Thank you. Your presumption is correct. I don't want to be caught up in poor Solemn Jon's death at all, but the thought of trying to do it without your fiendishly methodical approach is quite daunting. Although, admittedly your approach does make me want to knock your head against something particularly solid on occasions.'

He bowed. 'A compliment, if indeed that is what it was, is not needed to secure my assistance. I fear, however, we may do well in this instance to heed Mr Twain's advice: "A man who carries a cat by the tail learns something he can learn in no other way."' She laughed at the image but tailed off at his serious demeanour.

'My lady, despite our discussions after Brighton that no further investigations would occur, it seems that we are, in fact, precisely here again.'

'I know.' She stared at her coffee cup. 'But the circumstances this time are really quite different.'

'How so, if I might enquire?'

'Because Solemn Jon's wife… Oh, Clifford, it was so awful, that poor woman confessed to having had some dark thoughts. I feel that if we can find out the truth of what happened, it will bring her some solace.'

'Perhaps, my lady.'

'Perhaps?'

He cleared his throat. 'Suppose, my lady, the truth, as is so often the case, is not what she imagines? But worse?'

CHAPTER 20

She took another sip of her coffee and eyed him over the rim of her cup.

'I see now why you quoted Mark Twain's advice. I really was very fond of Solemn Jon, even though our paths rarely crossed. There was something about his compassion for everyone, and particularly the deceased, as the reverend said. But I'm still as determined to find out the truth as his wife is to know it, despite what you said. Although, to be honest, I think even she's not been entirely straight with me. She's holding something back, I'm sure, but what…' She shrugged.

Pouring two glasses of a dark-amber tipple from the decanter, he held one out to her on the silver tray. She was delighted to see his eyes smile as he held the other glass up to make a toast.

'To save you committing another transgression against the rules governing mistress and servant, my lady, I have done it for you.'

'Drinking with the mistress is surely against the rules?' Eleanor said, imitating Polly's young voice.

The corners of his mouth twitched at her impersonation of the young maid. 'Indeed, but his lordship made it a tradition that I partook of a toast with him when we were about to embark on a troubling task. It is a particularly fine Burmese rum with notes of wine fruits leading to a silky oak finish.'

She raised her glass.

'To tradition then.'

'And to finding the truth.'

'Whatever it may be,' she muttered. She ran her finger over her notebook that had helped her solve previous cases, then shook her head. 'I feel the need to work through the facts differently this time. If only to pretend that we aren't caught up in another murder case. Now.' She sat back in the chair and frowned. 'Let me see… who might have wanted poor Solemn Jon out of the way?'

'Mr Willie Green obviously springs to mind, my lady, given his open hostility towards him.'

'Yes, he's definitely our prime suspect at the moment. You know, though, Mrs Jon seemed equally suspicious about a chap called Arthur Pendle. Apparently, he breeds and races dogs. I'm sure you've heard of him. But I find it hard to believe a man would murder another for his dog. I mean, I love Gladstone, but…' She glanced at the bulldog who had shuffled unnoticed up to the pastries again, and shrugged.

He nodded. 'Agreed, my lady. In the case of Master Gladstone, it is hard to imagine anyone fighting, or killing, over an animal that serves no useful function and has no value, perceived or otherwise.'

'Clifford!' Eleanor clapped her hands over the bulldog's ears. 'Don't you listen to the nasty man, Gladstone!'

Clifford tutted. 'I do not mean to malign him, my lady. Were he able to talk, Master Gladstone would readily inform you himself that he has no desire to perform any function that does not involve eating, sleeping or stealing pastries.' He deftly whipped the plate away from the bulldog's exploratory tongue. 'However, some animals are worth a great deal both in terms of money and prestige. Patrick could fall into both categories as the undisputed champion of hound trailing.'

'Bit short-sighted though, wouldn't you say?' She lowered her voice and covered Gladstone's ears again. 'Sadly, man's best friend doesn't live that many years and he certainly can't race when he gets older.'

Clifford held up a finger. 'But his legacy could live forever if he was to, say, sire a generation of future champions.'

'Of course! They'd each be worth a mint! Whoever would have thought that a soppy old wolfhound like Patrick could be such a golden goose? We need to find out if this Pendle character was at the May Fair. Would you have recognised him if he were?'

'I know Mr Pendle by sight, although I am not in the habit of indulging in a "flutter on the dogs", as is the colloquial term.'

She laughed. 'Only a "flutter" on the pigs, perhaps? I hope you enjoyed your winnings from the derby, by the way?'

He cleared his throat. 'I placed that bet at the request of another, my lady.'

'Then I hope Mrs Trotman enjoyed her winnings.' She knew her cook liked the occasional bet. She marshalled her thoughts. 'Now, we have two motives – and suspects – for Solemn Jon's murder. Greed in the case of Arthur Pendle and an unfathomable loathing in the case of Willie Green. And, of course, we mustn't forget Mr Preston-Pestilence or whatever his name is.'

Clifford raised an eyebrow. 'You suspect the chairman, Mr *Prestwick-Peterson*, of the May Fair Committee?' His tone suggested she'd just accused King George of murdering Solemn Jon.

She nodded. 'That's right. Old Pesky-Pesterton. And why not? It was Seldon who put me on to him. He delayed the search party, did he not? And why?' Before Clifford could reply, she held up a hand. 'I'll tell you. To give him… time… to… er, no, that doesn't work, does it?'

'I must give you credit for having such an open mind as to suspect all and sundry, my lady. However, as you yourself have, it now seems realised, as the chairman of the May Fair Committee, Mr *Prestwick-Peterson* was much in the thick of it as it were. I imagine he could call on a dozen or more witnesses for an alibi should the need arise for the time before, and after, Solemn Jon met his unfortunate end.'

She grimaced. 'Pity. Still, there you go, we'll cross him off the list I haven't made yet.'

Before she could mentally do so, a cough interrupted her.

'There is also another name we should add to the list we have yet to make, my lady.'

'Oh, really? Whose?'

'That of Mrs Jon.'

She stared at him, wide-eyed. 'Are you serious?'

'As serious as you were about Mr Prestwick-Peterson.'

She thought for a moment. 'But what possible motive could she have? Ah! I know what you are going to say.'

He nodded. 'It is well known that if a husband is murdered, suspicion is automatically thrown on the wife.'

She hid a smile. 'Really, Clifford! I didn't have you down as a misogynist. Shame.'

He rolled his eyes. 'I was about to add, my lady, "And vice versa."'

'Fair enough. But she did approach us.'

'A tactic to draw suspicion away from herself, perhaps? We have experienced similar before, if you remember?'

She nodded. 'I do. Although, at the risk of seeming contrary, along with Mr Breadstick-Pete—'

'*Prestwick-Peterson*, my lady.'

She hid a smile. 'Exactly. I suggest we cross him and Mrs Jon off the list we have yet to make. I have to confess I have no evidence that she wanted her husband dead, beyond a rather suspect belief that the spouse is often the guilty party.'

Clifford nodded.

'Agreed then,' she said quickly. Something nudged her brain. *Ah, the medallion, Ellie.* Asking Clifford to wait a moment, she ran upstairs and came back down clutching it. He looked it over in silence for a moment, before handing it back with a raised brow.

'Sorry, I meant to mention it before,' she said. 'I found it on the riverbank just before we discovered poor Solemn Jon's body. I thought it might belong to him but when I showed it to his wife, she said it wasn't his.'

He nodded. 'I presume it has been lost or discarded by a villager.'

'I thought that as well. Probably isn't important. They're just lucky charms, really, aren't they?'

He shook his head. 'They are more than that to many people, my lady. They not only ward off bad luck, but also help the wearer stay on a straight moral course. May I take another look?'

She handed it back over and this time Clifford examined it with a miniature magnifying glass he produced from a pocket.

'Despite what his wife said, this might indeed belong to Solemn Jon.'

'Really? What makes you think that?'

He showed her the writing along the top of the medallion under the magnifying glass.

'I cannot swear it, for there are a vast number of saints, and the spacing doesn't seem quite right.' He moved the magnifying glass further away and then back in close. 'However, I believe the visible lettering 'St… of… a' may refer to St Joseph of Arimathea.' She stared at him. 'The patron saint of undertakers, my lady. But it might just be a coincidence.'

She shook her head. *Is there a patron saint for everything, Ellie?* She hid a smile. *Perhaps there was one for butlers or naughty bulldogs?* She wondered if it was a good time to tell him about one of the books she'd bought in Oxford and, unable to sleep the evening before, had all but finished in the night. What would he make of *The Strange Case of Mr Challoner* as the culprit turned out to be none other than the family butler! She decided that conversation was for another day. A thought struck her.

'Perhaps, if it doesn't belong to Solemn Jon, it might belong to Willie Green?'

He nodded slowly. 'A very astute thought, my lady. We must ask the gentleman next time we see him.'

She took another sip of her rum, enjoying the fingers of delectable warmth that tickled her throat. 'This really is too divine. For some reason it makes me wonder what Willie Green's drink is.'

'Regrettably, I fear it is likely the quantity not the quality that is uppermost when making his choice.'

'Are you thinking that because of what Sergeant Brice said to him when we were shamefully eavesdropping at the police station?'

'Rather more because Mr Green's unsavoury reputation is known further than even Little Buckford. He unfailingly can be found of an evening working his way round the public houses in the area that haven't yet banned him.'

Eleanor shook her head. 'I can't condemn a man for drowning his sorrows without knowing his story. Who knows what troubling thoughts he is trying to escape? Like most, I imagine he fought in the war, after all. Lots of men came back unrecognisable as the vibrant youth who left.'

'And women, my lady. Even though they may not have fought directly, I feel their contribution is too often overlooked. You yourself served as a nurse for the greater duration of the conflict.'

She waved his praise away. 'True, Clifford. And thank you. But we digress.'

He coughed. 'At the risk of appearing to slander Mr Green, I believe he was exempt from serving during the war on medical grounds of, according to many, a dubious nature. And on more than one occasion I have heard his name mentioned in the same breath as an unfavourable local expression, "troubled britches into troublemaker trousers".'

'Which means?'

'The boy ever caught in trouble grows into the man who causes it.'

'Gracious, that's quite the indictment. But doesn't that just highlight what a good man Solemn Jon was? His wife said he'd always planned to leave his undertaker's yard to Willie Green. Makes sense in one way, as I assume she doesn't have any carpentry or other undertaking skills needed to continue the business, whatever they may be. And even if she did, I know first-hand how reactionary Buckinghamshire is. They weren't ready for a female MP and I'm sure they aren't ready for a female undertaker.'

'I agree on both counts, my lady. Although as I have never been compelled to forcibly eject a man from a funeral before, I find it hard to believe that Solemn Jon employed Mr Green at all.'

'I agree. But that aside, if he murdered Solemn Jon, why would he send that obituary in to be published when the police had written it off as an accident? Highlighting that it was, in fact, murder, would be madness, or—' She stared at him, sensing he'd drawn the same conclusion.

'Or an ingenious ruse to deflect attention from himself. He murders Solemn Jon—'

'And, knowing he'll be the prime suspect if murder is suspected—'

'Writes and signs an obituary declaring it murder—'

'And then plays the drunken fool who can't remember what he did the night before—'

'Causing the police to believe Solemn Jon's death was definitely an accident and Mr Green is simply a harmless if reprehensible crank!'

Eleanor frowned. 'It all seems a little… complicated? Odd? Still.' She clapped her hands. 'Let's to business! We need to ascertain if Pendle was at the May Fair and if Willie Green was really sick that day.'

'And how might we obtain that information, do you propose, my lady?'

Her brows met. 'Strange question. We'll simply ask around the village. Honestly, keep up, Cli—' She slapped her forehead. 'Of course! We can't let anyone know I – we – are investigating, can we?'

'That depends on whether you wish to hold a lit match to Chief Inspector Seldon's inevitable ire for publicly disregarding his professional opinion.'

She groaned. 'You're right. I tell him I won't investigate and ask him to do so instead when he's very busy. Then I proceed not only to ignore his findings but to very publicly pursue the case myself.' She covered her face with her hands and let out a heartfelt groan. 'What on earth am I to do?'

CHAPTER 21

'Might I enquire what our story is, should we be discovered, my lady?'

Eleanor looked up from adjusting the laces of her favourite Oxford flats. 'I don't have a story sorted yet, as you have no doubt guessed. We'll just have to muddle through.'

'As is so often the way.'

She caught the hint of a smile on his face as she straightened up. 'Let's go, we'll come up with something brilliantly spontaneous if need be.'

She shrugged at his raised eyebrow as he moved round to open her door. They'd partly solved the problem of her investigating Solemn Jon's death without Seldon getting wind of it by asking Mrs Butters and Mrs Trotman to make discreet enquiries on her behalf. However, she couldn't exactly ask them to do a spot of breaking and entering while they were at it. She was relieved to discover, once they arrived, that the undertaker's yard was the only business at the end of a long narrow lane.

They'd discussed telling Mrs Jon about their visit to her late husband's yard, but Clifford had reminded her that she believed Mrs Jon might not be telling them everything she knew. In the end, they'd decided it would be better to tell no one about their plans and just hope Mrs Jon, or Seldon, never found out.

At the bottom of the lane, the wide wooden entrance gates to the undertaker's yard lay latched back, as Clifford had predicted, allowing them to pass through unhindered.

'First hurdle surmounted, then, Clifford. No need for breaking and entering.'

'Not yet, my lady.' He patted his inside jacket pocket.

The ancient cobbled yard was adorned with two planters filled with vibrant magenta and white flowering honesty nestled among sky-blue forget-me-nots. A pair of handmade benches sat facing the rolling Chiltern Hills that rose behind the yard. On one bench a plaque was inscribed in Latin. She turned to him questioningly.

Clifford cleared his throat. 'In amore, in aeternum et ultra. "In love, forever and beyond."'

'Oh, golly!' she muttered.

'My lady, perhaps we should be a little more expeditious in our visit?'

She willed her feet to hurry past the simple funeral coach, reflecting sadly that it had last been used to carry the body of the very man whose death they were now investigating.

At the end of the yard were four low thatched flint-and-timber buildings, each bearing two narrow black-painted doors.

'Each of them serves a specific service.' Clifford pointed to the first three in turn. 'Carpentry shop, stone masonry, storage of the funeral coach used for higher society funerals, along with the horses' ceremonial headdresses. Which just leaves the last one where he prepared the deceased.'

Her eyes strayed to the last set of doors where a wreath of dried roses hung. 'In there?'

He nodded. 'Solemn Jon mentioned when I was here to arrange his lordship's…' He took a deep breath. 'When I was here, that that building commands the best view over the eastern side of the Chilterns as they rise to Beechley Ridge.'

She looked at him in confusion.

'He believed everyone deserved to spend their final time at one with the charms of Buckinghamshire's beauty until they were' – he gave a gentle cough – 'forever interred in her soil.'

She held his gaze. 'Clifford, I'm so sorry I wasn't here to help with the arrangements for Uncle Byron. Truly, I am.'

'His lordship is in no doubt about that, my lady. Nor am I.'

She breathed a sigh of relief as he made short work of the lock on the first door with a set of picklocks. She thought ruefully that he had needed to employ them on an unhealthy number of occasions since she'd arrived at Henley Hall. She followed him inside, shutting the door behind her. It felt so much colder than the warm May day they had left outside.

'Oh!' She stared at the long row of coffins of different sizes standing against the far wall. 'Somehow I hadn't registered that carpentry for an undertaker is mostly making these.' She swallowed hard at the sight of the smallest. 'And… and for children too.'

'My lady,' Clifford said gently, 'as I mentioned, we need to be swift. Someone may arrive at any moment.'

She nodded and shone her pocket torch along the workbenches and oak cabinets lining the other walls while Clifford examined the coffins.

After running the torch over the three benches, she scoured the neat piles of wood on the floor. Finding nothing, she moved on to the cabinets. On opening the first drawer, she let out a whistle.

'Gracious, Clifford, Solemn Jon would have given you a run for your money. Everything is arranged exactly so.'

Over by the coffins he sniffed. 'One would expect nothing less from a master craftsman.'

Feeling a tad chided, she continued to work through each drawer. The contents were mostly chisels, saws, hand drills and braces. The last was empty, but the cloth lining the bottom still showed the indentation of tools. Whatever had been there had recently been removed.

She stood up with a sigh. After checking through all the drawers, she had scored nothing except an appreciation for how neat Solemn Jon had been. That, and a gash to her finger from a mortice chisel hiding under a sharpening block. With a quiet tut, Clifford splashed something that smelled like iodine from a silver hip flask onto a pristine handkerchief and held it out to her.

She took it and dabbed her finger.

'Ouch! Thanks.' She looked around again and then back at him. 'Nothing?'

'Nothing, my lady. I even checked through the rolls of cotton and calico shrouding and the barrels of sawdust. Much to the chagrin of my suit jacket's sleeves, I must say.'

She tried to hide a smile. 'I'll add a new clothes brush to my thank-you list for your help.' She turned in a circle, shining the torch into the far corners of the room. 'I know he may have had the door open, but how on earth did Solemn Jon manage such delicate work in this gloom?' She ran her hand over a polished wooden cross, marvelling at the carved intricacies of two tall arum lily stems interlaced as they wound along its length.

'Most carpentry and masonry work is completed outside, my lady. Year round.'

'Oh, gracious! I've never been better reminded to count all my blessings than now. And, as you mentioned masonry, let's try that next.'

But the masonry workshop also yielded nothing. Clifford paused at the door of the third building, housing the fancier of the undertaker's funeral coaches.

'Two down, two to go.'

Inside, the ceiling had been removed to allow for the tall black scrollwork which ran the length of the ornate vehicle's roof.

Standing almost two feet above the body of the coach, high on each corner, was a gleaming brass cup. At funerals one of the long ebony ostrich plumes that sat in a rack against the wall would be placed in each one.

With the coach being a long, elegant glass box mounted on a simple carriage frame, there appeared to be little to search there either. Still, Eleanor was grateful that Clifford shook his head as she stepped towards the coach, nimbly swinging himself up into the seat. Instead, she turned her attention to the few other items in the space. On a small table a white enamel bowl held a store of glycerine soap, sponges and tubs of leather balsam. Halfway along the same wall, a wooden polished oak board had been set with two hooks, a hat shelf and a tiny face mirror. She slipped her hand inside the pockets of the coat on the first hook, feeling far from brave, and decidedly guilty at snooping in a dead man's clothing.

'My lady, I—'

A scraping noise made them both stiffen. Eleanor pointed to the far wall.

Clifford nodded at her and they crept soundlessly outside. In the yard, Clifford put his ear to the closed door of the next workshop along. Gripping the handle, he gestured for her to move back, but her curiosity overcame her nerves and she stepped forward as he wrenched the door open.

'You!'

CHAPTER 22

Willie Green turned from where he stood, back to the door. For a moment his face registered fear, but then his features quickly set themselves into their usual scowl. He removed the cigarette from his mouth and flicked the ash onto the embalming table.

'Strange place for a lady to be creeping 'bout?'

'Not at all.' She strode inside. 'Especially as I'm not "creeping about". I'm… I'm looking for you.'

His dark eyes flashed. 'For me? You've got no business with me. Besides, how did you know I was here?'

Her gaze fell on the open roll of shrouding cloth, overflowing with carpentry tools beside him. 'That, Mr Green, was very obvious.' An unwelcome realisation had dawned the minute she'd seen him. With Solemn Jon gone, his wife deep in her grief, and the villagers staying away out of respect, the undertaker's yard would have been deserted. Perfect for an unscrupulous light-fingered ferret like Willie to see what he could steal!

He caught her glancing at the tools on the table. 'These is mine. Not that it's any of your business.'

'Quite so.'

'I'm not thieving them, whatever you think. If I was pinching tools, I'd have taken the lot. I earned these for all those years on me apprenticeship and then slaving away for no thanks from him.'

'No thanks from who exactly, Mr Green?'

'Solemn Jon, course.' He spat the end of his cigarette onto the floor near her feet.

'Mr Green!' Clifford strode towards him, but Eleanor raised a restraining hand.

'Well, well, Lady Swift's faithful dogsbody!'

She shook her head. 'Permit me to correct you. Clifford is, in fact, my highly appreciated butler, just as he was my late uncle's. It's called respect, something you seem to have had little of for your employer.'

Willie let out a loud scoff. 'Respect? For the likes of him? None of you ever knew the real Solemn Jon. He had you all going, didn't he? Thinking he was nothing short of a saint.' He shook his head and muttered as if to himself. 'Folk say I'm worth nothing, but even I wouldn't do what he did.'

She looked at him quizzically. 'And what did Solemn Jon do that was so terrible, Mr Green?'

He leaned back on the table. 'Don't matter now, does it? He won't pay for it, and if I try and shout 'bout it, I'll probably be run out of me house for being a liar by the entire damn village.'

She held her hand up to stop Clifford from calling him to order again. 'Is that why you placed the obituary? To get back at him?'

'How many times have I got to tell you?' Willie picked up a chisel and dug it blade down onto the tabletop with a bang that made her jump. 'I didn't write no obituary.'

She nodded. 'I did wonder when I read it, actually.'

He looked up sharply. 'Why? 'Cos you toffy types thinks the likes of me can't write, nor read?'

'Not at all. I wondered how you could have written it as you were apparently too ill the day it was posted through the newspaper office's letterbox to even get out of bed. Unless, of course, you wrote it before Solemn Jon died?' She watched his face as her words sunk in, but she could only see confusion in his eyes.

'How could I have written it afore when I didn't write it at all!'

She tried a different tack. 'This medallion.' She drew it from her pocket and dangled it in front of him. 'Is it yours?'

He glanced at it briefly before shaking his head. "Taint mine, I don't wear nothing like that. What would I want it for?'

'I don't know, Mr Green. Perhaps to ward off illness?'

He frowned. 'What are you on about now?'

'Apparently, you were *so* ill the day of the raft race you were still suffering when we met at Chipstone Police Station the day after, if you recall?'

He eyed her suspiciously, then stared up at the ceiling. He looked back down at her and shrugged. 'Don't see that matters neither.'

She frowned, trying to conjure up one redeeming quality in the man.

'Don't you feel even some remorse at missing the raft race? If you'd been there, Solemn Jon would never have got into trouble. And if he had, you'd have been there to help him. Instead—'

'Pah! Why should I care?' He ran his tongue down the inside of his cheek. 'Couldn't help getting sick, could I?'

'So you were unwell? I do hope, at least, someone was at home to assist you through the worst of it?'

'Ain't' got no wife, nor suited butler. We can't all afford a houseful of servants. So, I just lay down and sweated it out Saturday night right through to Monday. Sheets was only fit for the fire when I came out of it.'

Deciding that was too much information, she changed tack again.

'But you see, that was my reason for finding you today.'

He threw her a disparaging look and lit another cigarette, puffing a plume of smoke in her direction.

'Oh, yeah?'

Without turning around, she reached one hand behind her head and took the calling card she knew Clifford would have magically produced.

'I thought you might not be aware that a while back I offered to assist people in the village with Doctor Browning's fees. And the cost of medicines if they were finding the expense prohibitive.' She placed the card on top of the pile of tools. 'My details are on there if you need help. After all, I'd hate for you to miss another important event with a good man in the future.'

She turned on her heels and left him staring at the card.

Outside, she tapped her chin as she walked.

'I have a strong inkling we shall be questioning that man again at some point. But for now, what did you think, Clifford?'

She slid into the Rolls and waited while he closed her door and climbed into the driver's seat.

'I wonder, my lady, if it's possible that Mr Green might not be quite the scoundrel he is universally painted?'

She nodded as they bumped back down the rutted lane.

'I thought the same thing. As he was so quick to point out, if he is such a rogue, why hadn't he emptied Solemn Jon's cabinet of *all* the tools? I'd imagine they'd be worth something even if he didn't want them for himself.'

'Agreed, my lady. I also caught his rather odd remark.'

She frowned. 'What do you think he meant by "but even I wouldn't do what he did"?'

He shook his head. 'I couldn't say. Perhaps he was merely trying to divert attention from himself?'

She sighed. 'Oh, well, we'll just have to try another line of investigation and come back to Willie Green later.' She hid a smile. 'What worries me now though, Clifford, is how you are going to sleep tonight.'

He raised an eyebrow.

'It's no use pretending, you'll be pacing the corridors of Henley Hall into the small hours and we both know it. Willie Green won't pick up that cigarette or sweep that ash off the floor, Clifford. That mess will just lie there.'

From the corner of her eye, she saw him shudder.

CHAPTER 23

'I'd never even heard of "hound trailing", Clifford. Well, not before Mrs Jon mentioned it.' Eleanor screened the sun from her eyes to look across the fields and woods that seemed to stretch unbroken to the horizon. Despite the summer breeze having picked up, the air was still as warm as the sky was cloudlessly blue. They'd come to Lower Beacon to see what they could learn about Arthur Pendle and his dog-racing business and how it might fit into Solemn Jon's murder. If indeed it did.

She looked around again, unable to spot anything resembling a racetrack for dogs. 'How does it work?'

Clifford straightened up from leaning into the boot of the Rolls.

'Hound trailing, my lady? Well, unlike fox hunting, where the horsemen use hounds to chase and catch the fox, there are no horses involved. Or horsemen. Or foxes, in fact.'

'So it's actually nothing like fox hunting?'

'Indeed, my lady. It is purely a ten-mile race between the hounds themselves along a course pre-marked by a runner. The runner lays a trail using a sack soaked with a scent created from a mixture of paraffin and aniseed. Typically, each race takes well under an hour and the hound which wins the most races over the season is crowned the champion, as Solemn Jon's Patrick was.' He closed the boot lid. 'The start line is just the other side of Four Winds Head, that way.' He gestured up the hill in front of them with what looked like a stout stick.

She glanced at him in concern. *He's never needed any kind of walking aid before, Ellie?*

'Feeling alright, Clifford?'

His brows knitted for a moment. 'Never better, thank you, my lady.'

Unconvinced, she started off up the short but sharp climb. At the top, she was rewarded with a breathtaking view. An endless green vista spread before her of rolling hills punctuated only by swathes of vivid bluebells and a cluster of flint cottages.

'Buckinghamshire is surely England's best kept secret, wouldn't you say, Clifford?'

'Indeed, I would, my lady. Both for her scenery and' – he pointed skywards as a pair of red kites swept overhead, barely fifteen feet off the ground – 'her bird life.'

She nodded, then frowned. *He was only a few steps behind you all the way up the hill, Ellie. He certainly didn't need that walking stick!*

'I must say, though, this seems quite the hike to the start line now. Where exactly is it?'

'Down there.'

She squinted past the thick clump of hawthorn and followed his gaze.

'What! Down by that track where we could easily have parked the Rolls?'

'Yes, my lady. Shall we?'

As they neared a roped-off area at the bottom of the hill, she spotted a group of men in a variety of tweed outdoor wear.

'Which one is Pendle?'

He gestured discreetly with his head to a stout, ruddy-faced man sporting a flat cap.

'Mr Pendle will be checking the betting odds that have been set. The wagers being the real business of the day. Ah!'

The man had turned around and was now staring at them intently. He said something to one of the others, left the enclosure, and puffed up the slope.

Clifford quickly set the pointed end of the walking stick in the ground and opened the other to form a seat created from a single strip of leather.

'You need to be seated,' he whispered.

Ah! That's what it was for, Ellie. She did as he bid, watching him pull several brown-paper packages from his bag. He straightened up, raising his voice. 'I believe for the main event of your picnic, Mrs Trotman has provided ham-and-egg pie, with steeped-onion and beetroot chutney, together with mini herby sausages. Will that meet with your approval, my lady?'

So that's Clifford's sneaky plan, Ellie. Pretending you're merely a lady out for a hill walk with her butler. Perfectly normal.

'Oi! This isn't a free spectator sport,' the man bellowed. She turned to face him and was pleased to see he at least had the manners to hesitate and then remove his cap. 'Ah, Lady Swift, I believe?'

She smiled at him. 'Indeed. Charmed I'm sure, Mister?'

'Pendle. Arthur Pendle. Mr Clifford.' He nodded to her butler, who nodded back. He returned his attention to Eleanor. 'No offence, but I don't encourage folk to spy on the race, as it were.' His red cheeks turned a deeper puce. 'Not meaning to be rude, m'lady.'

'That's perfectly alright, Mr Pendle. But spying? Why, I'm doing nothing more subversive than enjoying a rather splendid picnic.' She tried to avoid staring at the strained buttons of his tweed jacket and held up a slice of pie. 'Perhaps you'd care for a bite. It's really very good.'

He licked his lips but shook his head. 'I didn't mean spying like that, I just meant this is a participation event. Only I'm sure it isn't the kind of thing a lady would take part in.'

'Oh, you're holding an event?' She clapped her hands. 'How exciting. You've picked the perfect day for it as well. What wondrous show shall I be missing as I continue my walk shortly?'

Pendle's brow creased as he looked at Clifford, but then his chest puffed out like a bullfrog, threatening to shoot his already abused jacket buttons across the valley.

'I am holding the May Day Hound Trailing race.'

'May Day, you say? How intriguing. Surely though, May Day was precisely one week ago? Wasn't most of the village at the fair that day?'

This brought a black scowl to his face. 'Ay, and a whole day's racing I lost as a result.'

She inclined her head. 'Forgive my nosiness, Mr Pendle, but I have an acute ear for accents. I find them most fascinating. Yet, I can't quite place yours?'

His waistcoat swelled with pride again. 'Yorkshireman, born and bred. Brought hound trailing with me when I moved down here and set up in business.'

'And I see it has caught on. Good for you. It must be many years ago you settled here, otherwise I'm sure I'd have recognised your Yorkshire roots more readily.'

'Late in 1901, it were alright.' He looked around until his eyes fell on a frail-looking woman wrapped in a long-in-the-tooth, thick brown coat despite the warmth of the day. Cupping his hands, he barked, 'Get thee here, double-quick!'

Eleanor bristled at his attitude towards the woman who was now hurrying over. She coughed to bring his attention back to her.

'I'm sure losing a day's racing was worth it to enjoy the May Fair, albeit that it ended rather tragically.'

'Ay, so I've heard as it did.'

'You weren't there?'

'I've no time for wasting at no fair. I'm a businessman, I am. This is my livelihood.' He narrowed his eyes. 'Even if some folk think it isn't a proper sort of 'un.'

'Being still very much the new girl in town, I have to confess to having no clear idea as to what your business involves. However, I have no doubt you're a most upstanding member of the community, Mr Pendle.' She smiled as the woman arrived at his side, her pale eyes almost as colourless as her ghostly face.

Pendle let out a low growl in her direction.

'We've too much to be doing for you to be standing about, woman.'

Eleanor held out her hand to the woman. 'Lady Swift. I don't believe I've had the pleasure?'

Even by lettuce standards, the thin cold hand that shook hers was limp.

'Lovely to meet you, m'lady.' The woman's voice was as weak as her smile. She bobbed a curtsey. 'I'm—'

'My wife,' Pendle snapped. 'And I told thee we're too busy to be standing about gassing.'

Eleanor ignored him. 'So nice to meet you too, Mrs Pendle.' She accepted the steaming cup of Thermos coffee Clifford held out to her. 'Mr Pendle was just telling me you both missed the May Fair? Such a shame.'

The woman's eyes darted to her husband and then back to Eleanor. 'Ay, that we did, m'lady, because—'

'Because I were out training dogs on the hills as there were no racing and you were where you shoulda been, cooking me Sunday lunch, remember?'

'Of course, I remember, Arthur.'

'What time were you training your dogs, Mr Pendle?'

He shrugged. 'Couldn't rightly say. Between two and five most likely.'

Rather convenient, Ellie.

'And was anyone else on the hills training their dogs? Or out for a walk, maybe?'

'No, they was all at that bl— that May Fair.'

Touché, Ellie.

'Clifford? Is this race, this—'

'*Hound trailing*, my lady.'

'Yes, that. Is this what Mrs Jon was talking about when I went to offer my condolences?'

'I believe that would have been likely as her husband's wolf-hound, Patrick, was crowned champion.' He turned to Pendle. 'Three years in a row if memory serves, Mr Pendle?'

'You're right enough,' he said through clenched teeth.

Eleanor gasped. 'Gracious, this Patrick sounds awfully valuable. If he's the long gangly thing that met me at the door, he must have a tremendous secret. I've never seen less of a canine racehorse.' She laughed rather too loudly. 'If that analogy works. Still, I imagine he'd be rather an expensive purchase if you were tempted, Mr Pendle?'

The race owner shrugged.

'That don't bother me, m'lady. I wouldn't touch that scraggy mutt with a bargepole. 'Twere nothing more than him happening into a kennel's worth of luck these past three years. Mind, Solemn Jon was at me night and day to buy Patrick.'

His wife opened her mouth, and then at his look, closed it quickly.

'Well,' Eleanor said with her best smile, 'I think your business sounds most exciting, Mr Pendle. And I'm sure having a harmless flutter on the dogs brings a lot of people enjoyment. What might be the highest bet ever placed in hound trailing here in Buckinghamshire, or the Chilterns?'

'Two hundred and fifty pounds.'

That sort of money could buy Solemn Jon's cottage, Ellie!

Pendle smirked at the look of surprise on her face. 'Got the best reputation, I have, see.'

Clifford inclined his head. 'Unquestionably.'

Eleanor rose. 'Well, the gentleman must have been ecstatic with his extensive winnings.'

'Unless,' Clifford said, 'he bet against Solemn Jon's dog, of course.'

Mrs Pendle nodded until her husband caught the movement and let out a sharp hiss. 'Get thee moving, woman. Race is about to start and there's work still to be done.' He raised his cap. 'Lady Swift. Mr Clifford.' He spun his wife by the shoulders before frogmarching her across the grass.

'What an unpleasant bully,' Eleanor muttered at the man's receding back.

Clifford nodded. 'I find myself concurring most heartily, my lady.'

Disappointed that he was clearing away the picnic, she gripped her plate tighter. 'By the way, this ham-and-egg pie with this chutney is too divine.'

He sniffed. 'It was only intended to add plausibility to our pretence for stopping at this spot. Mrs Trotman is preparing a substantial luncheon for our return as I believe I mentioned at breakfast.'

'Top-hole. Well, I'd best finish these off too. To spare you carrying them.' She paused, her hand midway to the sausages. She sniffed repeatedly, nose in the air. 'Whatever is that strong oily smell?'

'Afternoon, Mr Clifford, sir.' A voice came from behind them. 'Oh, and your ladyship, beg pardon.' A straw-haired youth appeared, dropping a sack to the ground.

Clifford nodded to the lad and turned to Eleanor.

'My lady, this is young Eric Brimpton.'

Her eyes fell on the sack he'd dropped. 'Are you one of the runners who's just laid the trail for the hounds to follow shortly?'

'Done it since I was eleven, I have, m'lady, every Sunday, April to October.'

'How very diligent. Mr Pendle must heartily appreciate your dedication, I'm sure.'

Eric looked across to where Pendle was deep in conversation with a man with stiff grey hair, a thick sculpted beard, and an expensive-looking waistcoat.

'Can't say as he's ever said so, m'lady.'

'Well, I'm sorry you lost a day's money over the race being cancelled on the day of the May Fair, Eric, but I suppose that happens every year?'

Eric shook his head. 'Oh, no, m'lady, 'twas the first time in all me years I remember it being called off.' He looked back down the hill. ''Scuse me, m'lady, but I'd best not miss the start of the race.'

CHAPTER 24

'Again, Clifford, I simply don't believe anyone has told us the truth.'

They were in the second dining room, the morning room being out of commission on account of the spring cleaning, and even though it didn't ordinarily catch the sun, today bright rays had found their way in and were invading every corner. She had been trying to distract her rumbling stomach from the amazing smell that had taunted her since she'd passed the kitchen thirty minutes earlier. All she'd had since a light breakfast was a glass of chilled elderflower cordial with garden-fresh mint. And a small-ish slice of pie.

'I certainly concur in the case of Mr Pendle, my lady. His assertion that he never tried to buy Patrick from Solemn Jon while he was alive seems a direct lie.'

She nodded. 'And why, for the first time in memory, young Eric's anyway, did he cancel racing on the day of the May Fair?'

'Especially, my lady, as he would have lost money from doing so.'

'Exactly, Clifford! And yet, according to him, it wasn't to attend the fair.'

'I asked the ladies after our return if they'd seen Mr Pendle at the fair, and they all three answered in the negative. So, unless he was somehow disguised, his assertion that he wasn't there at least seems true.'

'It would have to have been a pretty good disguise!'

'Indeed. Once met, Mr Pendle is not an easy gentleman to forget.'

'Well, we'll have to find out why he did cancel his racing. He strikes me as a particularly slippery eel.'

'And not one who likes to lose money, my lady. I feel he must have had a good reason to cancel his May Day race meet one way or the other.'

'I agree. And his wife seemed such a timid mouse, I'm afraid her word seems about as reliable as a paper boat. And apparently there were no witnesses to him training his dogs. At the very time Solemn Jon died, rather conveniently.' She ruffled Gladstone's ears. 'I'm still struggling in all this to believe Pendle killed Solemn Jon to get his hands on Patrick, even though he did come across as an avaricious bully.'

Clifford gave a discreet cough.

'Oh, botheration, Clifford. I meant to have described him a little more charitably. How would you have said it?'

'To my shame, in a way that would have been unrepeatable in polite company, my lady.'

She laughed and took a sip of her cordial.

'I'm even starting to doubt the newspaper owner, Elijah Edwards. I'm wondering if he wrote those dratted obituaries himself to stir up trouble and increase his wretched paper's circulation.'

Clifford's normally inscrutable expression showed a hint of surprise. 'Something I had not considered. Perhaps, however, I might be so bold as to suggest a reprieve from the subject of Solemn Jon's demise until you have finished eating?'

She nodded vigorously. 'Absolutely, I'm famished!'

Soon the table was laden with various covered silver platters and the most tantalising aroma.

'I say, Clifford, what is it?'

'Pyjama roast, my lady.'

'I definitely misheard that. Again, please?'

He lifted the lid of the largest serving dish with a flourish.

'I don't believe you did, my lady. It is indeed "pyjama roast". Named so by his lordship. It was his favourite meal on returning from his travels. He observed it was everything that reminded him of home.'

She leaned forward and inhaled deeply. 'It's the most delicious looking leg of lamb I have ever smelt. I can see why he craved it.'

'Served with crisp, coarse-grain mustard roast potatoes, celeriac colcannon with hazelnuts, buttered baby leeks, honey basted carrots and roasted garlic cloves.'

'Clifford! I'm positively salivating. Please set to on carving. But why "pyjama roast"? Because of the stripes of the delectable bacon it is wrapped in?'

'No, my lady, because his lordship would always change into his pyjamas for this meal on his arrival back from his travels. No matter if the sun was setting or dawn was just a faint glimmer on the horizon.'

She shook her head and glanced at the portrait of Uncle Byron hanging above the fireplace.

'I do hope if he could hear me, he wouldn't mind my using his name and "true English eccentric" in the same sentence.'

'I can assure you, he doesn't, my lady.'

As Clifford ceremoniously carved the golden-brown lamb joint, she had a thought.

'I say, though, if this is pyjama roast, shouldn't I change and enjoy it snugly wrapped in my nightwear?'

He paused from carving, swallowing hard.

She hid a smile. 'It's alright, Clifford. I was just teasing. I'm sure it's best served with an equally delicious gravy, not drizzled in impropriety.'

'Quite, my lady.'

Halfway through the plateful Clifford had presented her with, she managed to pause in savouring the saltiness of the bacon and the sweetness of the rosemary dusted lamb long enough to point out the window.

'Why is Joseph attacking the most enormous block of ice with some sort of clawed hammer, instead of working his green-fingered magic among the flower beds?'

'It is in fact a pick, my lady. And, as is customary at this stage of the spring-cleaning schedule, Joseph has been charged with creating ice chunks for the distiller.'

She gasped in mock horror. 'So Mrs Trotman is producing more of her wonderful liqueurs! Which is it this time? Her infamous cherry brandy, or her lethal honey whisky? Oh, crumbs, is it that dangerously moreish gin concoction we all woke with very sore heads from the morning after returning from Brighton?'

He gave a rueful wince. 'Thankfully, it is none of those. The distiller is being put to work with nothing more intoxicating than water.'

'How disappointing. But enlighten me as to why.'

'The forty-seven chandeliers of the Hall can only be cleaned with glass-polishing cloths soaked in distilled water, my lady. The central three in the ballroom alone have over nine hundred crystal pendeloques, or pendants, each.'

'Gracious! Then I am all the more grateful for the time taken to prepare this very special luncheon.'

'The ladies always enjoy honouring his lordship's traditions. But at the same time Mrs Trotman mentioned that it seemed a shame not to serve the dish anyway as it is unlikely you will be travelling far for... some time?'

She laughed. 'Very clever, and subtle, Clifford. You can inform Mrs Trotman that if I do travel, it will only be for a holiday. And I'll look forward to coming back to the Hall every day I'm away.'

'Most heartening to hear.' He bowed before topping up her plate.

*

Post-luncheon coffee and cocoa-dusted almonds beside the ornamental fountain on the lawn should have been the perfect end to a perfect meal. But as she sipped from a delicious steaming cup, chocolate melting on her tongue and the warm sun cupping her face, the usually melodic ring of church bells rising from the village below sounded positively mournful. She stared out over the immaculate grounds to where she could glimpse St Winifred's spire in the distance.

Clifford followed her gaze. 'Sometimes I still forget how much of your life was spent abroad from birth, my lady. It is Whit Sunday. The seventh Sunday after Easter. The bell-ringers will be completing a quarter peal which will last close to forty-five minutes.'

'And the reverend's flock will all be there, right now, walking through the churchyard where we said such a reluctant goodbye to Solemn Jon only four days ago.' She shuddered. 'Poor Maggie. I can't stop thinking about her.' Something tugged at her thoughts. 'I didn't see her with Patrick as the racing dogs arrived before we left the hound trail course this morning?'

'With no disrespect to the lady, she is not one to tramp the wilds of the hills in all weathers to keep Patrick in race form. Neither, do I believe, would she be comfortable dealing with the likes of Mr Pendle and his betting friends.'

'I know. She was clearly furious he'd had the audacity to march straight into her cottage uninvited and demand she sell Patrick to him now Solemn Jon is dead. And so soon after his death!'

Their conversation was interrupted by Mrs Butters waving from the top of the path.

Eleanor frowned. 'Who is that young lad trailing after her?'

Clifford beckoned over the housekeeper and her nervous-looking charge.

'Thought it best this young lad had a word, Mr Clifford.' Mrs Butters gestured to the lanky youth Eleanor could now see was around sixteen. His trousers were threadbare and flapped way above his ankles, his angular frame suggesting several recent rapid growth spurts had sadly not been supported by a sufficiently nutritious diet. His roughly chopped blond hair stuck up where he had pulled his cap off on seeing Eleanor.

'Ah, Jack Brown. Thank you, Mrs Butters.'

The housekeeper patted the lad on the shoulder and returned to the house. Clifford turned to Eleanor.

'This is Jack Brown, my lady. I believe he may have some information of use to us. Now then, Jack, please tell her ladyship, did your sharp eyes spot something unusual on the day of the raft race?'

She felt a wash of sympathy for the lad as his lips moved, but no sound came out. 'It's alright, Jack,' she said softly. 'You won't get into trouble for speaking up.'

The young lad's Adam's apple wobbled in his gaunt neck. 'Begging your pardon, m'lady, but 'twas probably nothing unusual, really.'

She smiled. 'Tell me anyway, Jack.'

He hesitated, turning his cap in his hands. Finally, he raised his eyes from his scuffed boots. 'I was walking along the riverbank on t'other side to the crowds.' He shifted his feet. 'I might have hung back a bit to see if there were any fish, like.'

Eleanor glanced at Clifford, wondering why the lad should be so awkward about having been fishing.

'How far back, Jack?' Clifford said.

'Upstream, t'other side of the old foot ferry, Mr Clifford, sir.'

'Ah, the best spot to catch loach, isn't it? Because the current is slower there and the riverbed has a proliferation of gravel at that point?'

The lad nodded.

'So,' Eleanor coaxed, 'you were walking along with your fishing rod. Then what?'

The lad's face coloured. 'Beg pardon, m'lady, but I ain't got a rod of me own. Sometimes the fishermen… leaves bits of their catch or… they get snagged in the reeds, like.'

'Ah, I understand. Still, a fish supper tastes just as good whoever caught it, I'm sure, Jack. Now, please tell me what you saw.'

'Willie Green, m'lady. I sees him alright.' His young face fell. 'Not my place, but he did bad by Solemn Jon, saying he was sick when he were right as rain.'

'What was he doing?' She tried to keep the eagerness from her voice.

'Creeping through that little copse that joins the river path, m'lady. Creeping at full tilt too, mind. 'Tweren't anything wrong with his legs, the speed he was making.'

'Did he see you?'

'No, m'lady. I ducked down behind the rushes soon as I recognised him.'

'And where did Mr Green go?'

'Lost sight of him, m'lady, where the path turns left up over the slope to old Bill's top field. You know where I mean, Mr Clifford, sir?'

'I do, Jack. And you didn't see anyone else?'

The lad hesitated, but then shook his head vehemently.

'Sure?'

'Sure, Mr Clifford, sir.'

'Then her ladyship thanks you for being honest, Jack, because the rewards for honesty are?'

'The highest, sir. Reverend Gaskell said so t'other morning.'

'Good lad.' Clifford reached into his pocket and pulled out some coins, which he dropped into the boy's hand. Then to Eleanor's surprise, he produced a pocketknife and snipped four giant white daisies on long stems and gave him those too. 'Of course, you know exactly the reports I expect to hear from Mrs Butters, Jack? Wholly honourable behaviour.'

'Lawks, Mr Clifford, sir.' Jack's cheeks flushed. 'Wouldn't do nothing else. Never, sir.'

'Then off you go.'

Eleanor marvelled out how the lad doffed his cap while clutching the flowers and breaking into a sprint all in one go. She watched him run back to the house. Clifford turned back to her.

'A local delivery boy, my lady, trying to make the best of his talents. A very reasonable young man, particularly given the financial hardship his family endures.'

'Ah, then the flowers were a nice touch for his mother. I wondered what you were doing.'

'Actually, they are for Polly. She has quite the admirer in young Jack.'

Eleanor's eyes nearly popped out of her head. 'And you allow him to make up to her on the kitchen step?'

'Under Mrs Butters' extremely watchful eye, my lady.' He cleared his throat. 'I am loath to return our conversation to the previous matter, however—'

'However, Willie Green definitely needs another visit. And soon.'

'Indeed, but I believe you have a prior engagement in the morning.'

She shuddered. 'Don't remind me!'

CHAPTER 25

Lord Rankin's disapproving tone cut across the yard. 'Jodhpurs, Lady Swift?'

She tore her eyes away from the immaculate stables, which had received considerably more care than the tired monolithic mansion that rose in a series of grey domed roofs behind her.

'Good morning to you too, Lord Rankin. And yes, jodhpurs.' She gestured down at the smart sage-green trousers she wore. 'I thought you said we would be riding out this morning?'

His lagoon-blue eyes held hers. 'Tell me, is side-saddle now considered beneath the modern woman?'

'Only among us competitive ladies. You threw down quite the gauntlet at the Langham lunch last week, you know. I wished to ensure I am in with every chance of beating you.'

'You really do like to win, don't you?' A hint of appreciation coloured his tone.

'Let's find out, shall we?'

Rankin clicked his fingers at his butler and turned on his heel. 'This way, Lady Swift.'

As she quickened her pace to keep up with his purposeful stride, Eleanor silently cursed the effect his strong physique was having on her. There was no denying that his form-fitting black jacket and cream riding britches tucked into long tan leather boots set off his extraordinary physical attributes. He ran his hand raffishly through his raven hair and smiled condescendingly at her.

'You are in for the treat of a lifetime.'

Stopping and leaning back with his elbows along the top of a half-open stable door, one leg bent up nonchalantly, he looked her over.

Bristled by what she took as a rather brazen attitude, she did the same and immediately regretted it as his lips curled into an arrogant smirk. 'I meant another treat,' he said in a silky tone.

How does this man fit his ego onto his estate, however many thousands of acres it is, Ellie?

'First things, first.' His words cut into her thoughts.

'Of course. Which of your prize horses will I be beating you on today?'

He laughed. 'You actually believe you could handle one of my top racing mares? More to the point, do you really imagine I would allow you to ride one, first time out?'

'Of course. I accepted your unspoken challenge to prove that we women can be as competent as our male counterparts. So, a true sportsman would allow me to ride one of his best horses or the lady might wonder if he was afraid of losing?' She cocked one brow at him. 'And as I am sure you are a true sportsman, Lord Rankin, and not afraid of losing, why would I expect any less?'

A noise not unlike the snort of an irritated stallion escaped him, but his expression quickly smoothed over.

'Was that the challenge I set you? Perhaps it was. Let's see, shall we? But, actually, I was going to say, I want to hear you call me "Evander". No room for the formality of titles when you're leaping hedges and thundering across the gallops.'

'Then call me Eleanor, Evander. And I do love the sound of thundering hooves. Shall we begin?'

Rankin gave a sharp nod, then glared at his butler, who was making his way with a silver tray bearing a bottle of champagne and two crystal flutes.

'Tardiness again, man!' he growled as the butler offered Eleanor a glass of golden bubbles.

'Apologies, your lordship. I am still not quite familiar with—'

'Silence, man!' He waved him away.

'Champagne before a ride?' Eleanor feared the fizz would not settle well with all the jumping Rankin had hinted at.

'Nothing wrong with honouring tradition. Even if it is of one's own making. Henderson!' he barked over his shoulder at his groom.

The sound of hooves at the far end of the yard made her turn round to see a smartly turned-out groom leading two magnificent horses towards them.

The two mares she was presented with were equally impressive. A pure grey with steely determination behind her dark eyes and an aristocratic chestnut with a coat that shone in the morning sun.

Rankin observed Eleanor as she whispered in the ear of each. As the chestnut flinched, she turned to him. 'Fifteen-two hands, a tenacious attitude and a passion for crossing the line first. I'll take the grey.'

'Interesting choice, but as you wish. Henderson, Silver Mystique.' He gestured towards the grey mare. Eleanor took the horse's reins and smiled as it snorted gently onto her neck.

Rankin downed the rest of his champagne. 'Henderson, fetch Arion. Now!'

Eleanor waved the groom aside and slid her toe into the stirrup, checking her grip on the raised rear cantle of the saddle.

'Us girls can do this just fine, can't we?' she whispered into the mare's ear, smiling at the soft snort that came in reply. With a nimble bounce, she swung herself up and her right leg over.

'Excitable and stubborn,' Rankin said.

She smiled sweetly. 'Oh, I think Silver Mystique must have some other qualities besides.'

She refused the whip the groom offered her and turned her horse before setting off on a gentle trot, aware that Rankin was watching her every move.

A few moments later, as she finished shortening the stirrups to be better prepared for jumping, Rankin appeared beside her on a tall ebony thoroughbred with an imperious stare.

'Gracious, Evander, what an absolutely exquisite beast.'

'He is the best, Eleanor. I accept nothing less. And' – he leaned across and adjusted her hold on the reins – 'I always get what I desire. The horses have been warmed up, so' – he spurred his horse into a fast trot and on through the open gate, calling behind him – 'let the challenge begin.'

She loosened her reins back off and followed him out of the yard. As they crossed the drive, she was sure she saw a flash of yellow among the trees where the drive swept left. She frowned. The only yellow car she'd seen in the area was Lady Lambourne's Rolls. *Why would she be here, Ellie? It was obvious at the Langhams' lunch that she hates Rankin. Unless it has something to do with his father, she was a close friend of the family.* Shrugging, she dismissed it as none of her business and hurried to catch Rankin up.

The immediate ground they cantered across was a combination of firm emerald grass peppered with magnificent oak and cedar trees. Eleanor swiftly found her horse's rhythm and began to enjoy herself. She'd failed to mention that she'd been taught to ride by the Bedouin tribesmen of Arabia, famed for their horses and riding skills. Soon, the rush of the ground beneath her mount's thundering hooves mirrored her quickened heart rate as she drew level with Rankin.

He eyed her appreciatively. 'I thought you preferred bicycles?'

'Only because they're less complicated and don't need food. It was hard enough feeding myself most days crossing the world, let alone trying to find enough for a horse as well.' She urged Silver Mystique ahead to hide the smile that had sprung to her face.

The rise and fall of the hills and the blur of the ground below intoxicated her as they flew across the first set of fields. Leaping over a small stream, the horses charged past a beech copse and on up a steeper slope. As they raced along the top of the chalky ridge, she caught a glimpse of Rankin Hall below to her right.

A few minutes later, Rankin slowed and pointed forwards, riding one-handed effortlessly. 'The oaks are the start line. Up over the ridge. Sixteen hedges, eight there, eight back. One and a half miles dead each way. If you can handle it, of course?'

'Let the best woman win!' she called back. Running her hand along her mount's neck, she leaned forward and whispered in the horse's ear. 'I'm all yours, Mystique. Let me know what you want.'

At Rankin's shout of 'GO!' her horse's tensed body shot forward into a flying gallop in a split second. Instinctively, crouching up out of the saddle, she rounded her shoulders, focusing straight ahead. In the suspended silence of hooves in the air as they cleared the first hedge, she felt her heart leap from her chest with exhilaration. Landing in perfect synchronisation with Rankin, she cheered silently. Happy that Mystique was clearly as thrilled at the chase as she was, she let her dictate the pace, hoping the horse would show its competitive streak.

She needn't have worried as Mystique kept within a length of Rankin's mount, matching it jump for jump.

'Eighth hedge, girl,' she panted, stealing a sideways look at Rankin, his jaw set hard as he spun Arion and thundered back the way they'd come. She was only half a length behind as she swung Mystique in as tight a turn as she dared for both their safety and set off in pursuit.

With only two hedges left to go, it amazed her that she was still less than a length behind Rankin given he knew his horse and the terrain so well. But then she flinched as he changed hands, allowing her to see he was whipping Arion furiously on his side. Horrified, she let Mystique know to ease up.

Crossing the finish line, several lengths behind Rankin, she felt sickened by the way he had treated his horse. Once dismounted, she took a moment to compose herself. *No point making a scene, Ellie. His father was a friend of Uncle Byron, remember. For his sake, be polite and simply get away as soon as you can.*

'Good try,' he said, jumping out of his saddle. 'For a woman.'

She smiled stiffly. 'Sometimes, Evander, it's not about the winning.'

He folded his arms. 'Ah, now I'm disappointed. And I was actually beginning to think I might enjoy a more spirited filly about the house.'

She smiled coolly. 'It's been an eye-opening ride, Evander. Thank you for the chance to share a special time with this exceptional and courageous beauty. Perhaps we'll meet again at the Fenwick-Langhams?'

He snorted.

'I think not! I have better things to do with my time than waste them in *that* company. No, I accepted their invitation for one reason only.' He stepped forward, his chest almost touching hers. 'Now, I'm not known for my patience. Nor for accepting "no" for an answer.'

Confused, she flapped him backwards two steps. Staring him in the eye, she was uncomfortably reminded just how cold the deepest of blue lagoons can be.

'Whatever are you talking about, Evander?'

He let out an exasperated snort. 'I thought that was obvious.' He looked her up and down, an arrogant smile playing around his lips. 'I mean to take you for my wife.'

Her mouth gaped. *Is he serious, Ellie?* She shook her head in disbelief. Before she could reply, he laughed curtly.

'Come now, why else would I have gone to that travesty of a luncheon at Langham Manor? Ridiculous! A cantankerous old woman from the Highlands and a jumped-up newspaper bumpkin who imagines he's a businessman. Preposterous!'

Confusion showed on her face.

'So… so you only went to see… *me?*'

He rolled his eyes. 'No! I only went so we were *seen* together. The Langhams, for all their inadequacies, carry a good name and represent old money, so our fortuitous re-acquaintance there blossoming so quickly into an engagement will be perfectly plausible. I also made sure it was known it was I who left you a May Day basket on the door of Henley Hall. You seem to be the only one who doesn't know!'

So the May basket was from him, Ellie, not Seldon!

'Evander—'

'I propose August. Three months will be a respectable enough courtship.'

Stuff being civil, Ellie, the man's obviously mad!

'Listen here, Lord Rankin. I don't know if you went out for a ride a while back and fell off and hit your head, but I have no intention of marrying you. Of all the people I—'

'Eleanor!' he barked. She stopped speaking out of sheer disbelief. 'You are thirty years of age, out of your depth trying to run the Henley estate and have no marriage prospects. I saw you with that idiot son of the Langhams, Lancelot, at the tail end of last year. You couldn't even make that relationship work, and he was like a besotted puppy around you. Any woman in your situation would be happy – no, grateful – to have a man like me notice them, let alone desire to marry them.'

Her anger had passed. It was simply all too outlandish to take seriously. She folded her arms and looked at him coldly.

'Evander, as I have already said, I have no intention of marrying you, though I thank you for the offer.'

His expression darkened. 'Don't play games, nor waste my time with coy nonsense, Eleanor.' He took a step towards her again. 'I told you earlier, I always get what I want. I thought you were sharp-witted enough to see that doing it the easy way would be best for you. Not to mention your beloved uncle.'

She frowned. 'What on earth does your preposterous marriage proposal have to do with my late uncle?'

A cruel smile played around his lips. 'Ah, therein lies your answer. After all, a family's reputation never really recovers from a scandal, don't you find?'

She shook her head, wishing she'd never agreed to come. 'Evander, this is all just riddles.'

His eyes narrowed. 'Then let me explain in words simple enough for even a *woman* to understand. You will marry me or I will ensure that the reputation of your beloved Uncle Byron is forever dishonoured and the Henley's family name blackened for all time.' With the agility of a man long in the saddle, he lithely remounted his horse. 'Ask your butler, Eleanor, seeing as you – as your uncle did – seem to think a base servant is trustworthy enough to confide in. He will make it clear that you have no choice. Just mention that I have certain documents in my possession. Documents concerning a transaction your late uncle made on my father's behalf that ended up… well, your butler will furnish you with the rest. Good day.'

Digging his heel into Arion's side, he spun the horse around and cantered off.

CHAPTER 26

'Should I make a detour via Doctor Browning's surgery for some medication, my lady?'

Despite her mood, she laughed. 'I'm not feeling unwell, Clifford, but thank you for your concern.' She shook her head. 'I simply don't know how to start explaining what's wrong without screaming!'

'Ah.' Reaching behind his seat, he passed her an oval green leather case and slowed the already stately pace of the Rolls. She poured herself a slim finger of brandy and gulped it down in one.

'Thank you,' she choked.

'Perhaps a second measure is better sipped, my lady?' His eyes twinkled. 'Might I be so bold as to hazard a guess that your estimation of Lord Rankin did not improve this morning?'

'Well, that depends.'

He raised a questioning brow.

She poured another finger of brandy.

'He certainly doesn't like taking "no" for an answer, that's for sure.'

'Most of us don't, my lady. But as you said yourself, that depends. In this case, on what exactly you were saying "no" to.'

She gulped the brandy down and spluttered. 'Marriage!'

Most people would have detected no noticeable reaction to the news. Her butler's expression remained as inscrutable as ever, but the way his eyebrows – not one, but both – raised slightly told her otherwise.

'Indeed.'

'Indeed and beyond! Out of the blue he simply hurled the offer of marriage at me like I was a giddy, aged spinster who would bite his arm off to accept. It's not as if I'd done anything to lead him to the notion that I hold any amorous feelings for him, dash it.'

Clifford eased the car round a tight bend and up a steep rise. For a few moments he drove in silence before clearing his throat.

'I confess, after reflection, I am not surprised, my lady. Lord Rankin is, many would say, as eligible a bachelor as you will find in these parts. And you yourself, if you will forgive the observation, are one of the most eligible ladies.'

She wrinkled her nose. 'That might be, but I wish you had been there to hear how he proposed. I mean, it was…' Her mouth flapped like a fish hooked from the bottom of a river. 'It was—'

'Romantic?'

'Hardly. He presented it as a fait accompli!'

The corner of Clifford's mouth twitched. 'Then I confess to wishing I had been there to hear your response. I recall the first time you came to stay at the Hall without your parents. I took your compliance of the rules of the house as such a fait accompli. However, I was soon taught otherwise.'

Despite her exasperation, she laughed. 'Beaten by a nine-year-old. Shame on you, Clifford. But, as always, you've made me feel better instantly. Thank you.'

He concentrated on navigating the Rolls through a particularly narrow stretch of country lane before returning to the conversation.

'As you mentioned that Lord Rankin dislikes being told "no", I assume he did not take your refusal well?'

'Yes.' She gritted her teeth. 'I almost took the riding crop he was beating his horse unmercifully with during our race and batted him smartly round the head with it! A race which I let him win to save his horse any further pain, by the way. Seriously, that man's arrogance knows no bounds. You won't believe it, but when I refused he had the audacity to suggest I'd better marry him for Uncle Byron's sake and you of all people would back him up!'

This time even a passing stranger might have noticed the look of concern that passed over her butler's face. Sensing his change of mood, she waited. Having spotted a layby opposite a wide farm gate, he pulled in and cleared his throat again.

'That is concerning, my lady. Deeply so. Without wishing to pry into the finer intricacies of your discourse with Lord Rankin, might I enquire as to his exact words in relation to his late lordship?'

She scrutinised his face. *What's this about, Ellie?*

'Of course.' She closed her eyes and thought for a moment. 'He said something like, "Shame. For you. A family's reputation never really recovers from a scandal, does it?" And then when I complained he was talking in riddles, he told me he had "certain documents" that apparently had to do with a transaction between his father and Uncle Byron. Documents that ended up... well, he didn't say. He rather pointedly advised me to ask you.' *Best leave out the 'base servant' comment, Ellie.*

Clifford nodded slowly. 'Before I explain, my lady, in my capacity of protecting your happiness, as his lordship requested of me in his final moments, can you promise me you will think only of yourself?'

She threw her hands out. 'Now you're talking in riddles too!'

He held her stare. 'Your answer to my question, my lady?'

'Clifford, you know me better than that. I shall do precisely what is right by Uncle Byron's memory – and reputation – and hang the consequences.'

'A noble and heartening sentiment. However, given that the consequence would be you accepting Lord Rankin's marriage proposal, I can assure you categorically, that is not what his lordship would want.'

Her lips set into a firm line. 'Clifford, as I said, I hope you know me well enough by now to have known in advance that that would be my reply. So now you have done your duty by Uncle Byron, please tell me exactly what this is all about.'

He seemed to be about to argue, but one look at her set expression obviously changed his mind.

'Regrettably, as he hinted, it would appear that Lord Rankin has become privy to certain documents that, if revealed publicly, would damage his lordship's reputation irreparably.' Eleanor opened her mouth but said nothing. He took a deep breath. 'Most unfortunately, his lordship was duped into being involved in an illegal financial scheme shortly before he passed away in January of last year.'

She frowned. 'But Uncle Byron was so shrewd. And if you knew about his investing at the time, you would have done that fiendishly meticulous thing you always do with the household accounts of checking everything a hundred times.'

'My lady, his lordship had nothing to do with the scheme himself. He was merely aiding a long-standing family friend. Lord Rankin's father, in fact.'

'Ah! Rankin senior had money troubles?' She remembered the rather dilapidated state of Rankin Hall.

'More respectably referred to as "re pecuniaria".'

She groaned. 'Well, that's one thing Evander Rankin was right about in me. He delighted in noting I'm out of my depth in running the Henley Hall estate. It's only down to you really, that I'm not "re pecuniaria" myself.'

'Thank you, my lady, but you overstate the case. In all seriousness, though, this is a most difficult predicament.'

'That's as might be, Clifford, but Rankin shall not get the better of me or Uncle Byron! Now, kindly elaborate further on this illegal scheme and how Rankin feels he can use it against me and my uncle's good name.'

He started the engine and pulled out of the layby.

'Happily, my lady, but perhaps we should continue the discussion after luncheon in the library?'

She nodded. 'Excellent idea. I need a moment to digest all that you've told me so far. And' – her stomach rumbled – 'rather inelegantly, all this riding has me famished!'

CHAPTER 27

Ensconced in the library after a wonderful meal of Mrs Trotman's speciality ham hock, cider and watercress pie, Eleanor brought the conversation around once more to the topic utmost in her mind. Rankin's proposal of marriage and how he planned to ruin Uncle Byron's good name if she refused.

Clifford composed his thoughts for a moment before replying, while Gladstone composed himself on the chaise longue and promptly fell asleep.

'Well, my lady, to take up the story where we left off, Lord Rankin's father visited his lordship unannounced one evening in a state of considerable agitation. It transpired that the Rankins' family finances were in such a critical position that he had no choice but to ask for help. Naturally, his lordship agreed most readily. The deal was made there and then, and his lordship asked me to drive him to his Oxford bank the following morning. Speed was of the essence or the estate might be lost. Shortly after, his lordship and I were caught up in other business and thought no more of it.'

She scratched her nose. 'But I still don't see how anything illegal occurred. If Uncle Byron transferred funds through his bank to an account held by Rankin's father, what went wrong?' She gasped. 'Unless it was all a ploy by Rankin's father?'

Clifford shook his head. 'With your permission to speak openly, the present Lord Rankin is nothing at all like his father. Lord Rankin's father was a pillar of principles and honesty. Hence his long friendship with your uncle.'

'Then, what?'

'In strict confidence, my lady, Lord Rankin's father had an outstanding debt for estate costs that had accumulated without his knowledge. He only became aware of it when a final demand notice was delivered the day before his visit to Henley Hall. To avoid the scandal of the Rankin estate being seized, he asked your uncle to pay the money directly to those owning the loan. It transpired later, however, that the account his lordship paid the money into was actually being used to finance an illegal scheme.'

She gasped. 'Like the one in all the national papers?'

He nodded. 'Indeed. The actual investigation into the scheme you are referring to started some time ago. However, it still continues to make the news today when ever more unfortunate investors who have lost everything are revealed.'

'I know, it's unthinkable! To set up such a scheme and con people to put their life savings into it by pretending it's got government backing and protection and then to leave them with nothing! I—' She looked at Clifford and the penny dropped. 'You don't mean…?'

He sighed. 'Unfortunately, yes, they are one and the same. The crooked company behind it all targeted, as you say, unsophisticated investors so they could dupe them all the easier. Many lost their savings. And their homes. The public is still baying for the blood of anyone involved.'

'But you said Uncle Byron wasn't involved? He simply—'

He shook his head. 'It later transpired that the account Lord Henley sent the money to was one used by those who ran the scheme. The percentage they each received from the scam was decided by how much money they put into this account in the beginning. Apparently it funded the initial outlay of the scheme, you see.' He stopped pacing. 'It is my belief that someone lied to Lord Rankin's father. There never was a final demand for money owing on his estate.'

She frowned, trying to piece together everything Clifford was telling her.

'But surely Rankin senior would have known the state of his finances?'

Clifford shook his head grimly. 'He hadn't dealt with the estate's finances for a number of years due to ill health. He had left them in the hands of—'

'Evander Rankin!'

He nodded. 'Well deduced, my lady. I believe the present Lord Rankin had been syphoning money out of the estate for years.'

'Perhaps to invest in illegal schemes like this one?'

'Very likely. And when the opportunity came to invest in such a lucrative scam as the one we are currently talking about, he needed to raise more money than he possessed. The reason being, he had by then, I believe, all but bankrupted the estate.'

She frowned. 'But that was his inheritance.'

'I believe Lord Rankin is a man driven purely by greed, my lady. I imagine he desperately hoped, like all gamblers, that this latest scheme would be the one to lay the golden egg and restore his finances and more.'

'What a mess,' she said softly. She stood quietly for a moment, then clapped her hands. 'Right. Time to rally round! We've no need to worry for the minute. Rankin clearly thinks he can blackmail me into marrying him. However, even though I'm not proud of it, I have a way that has rescued me from a few not entirely dissimilar situations, often when travelling alone.'

'Indeed, my lady?'

'Indeed, Clifford. I shall play him at his game by falling back on feminine guile. And' – she stifled a laugh as Clifford's cheeks coloured at the coquettish wiggle she gave – 'better still, feminine wile.'

'You mean to pretend to accept his proposal, my lady?'

'Let's just say, I shall keep him sweet until we can find a permanent solution. My own ego is not so fragile that I cannot see that
Rankin is marrying me purely for my inherited wealth. And I can't
imagine, given what you have told me, that he has managed to turn
the estate's finances around, especially as this illegal scheme was
exposed. Plus, I assume he has obviously also gone into further debt
paying for ridiculously ostentatious stable improvements. So, don't
worry, Clifford, I will do whatever it takes to not have Uncle Byron's
name dragged through the mud. Not by anyone, for anything.'

He bowed deeply. 'Thank you, my lady, most sincerely. From
both his lordship and myself.' Obviously still troubled however,
he ran his hand over his meticulously groomed hair and rubbed
his forehead. 'There is one matter, however, that we have yet to
consider.'

'Oh? Which is?'

'When his lordship tasked me with caring for your happiness,
he apologised most profusely for including one area he felt would
be a particularly uphill endeavour. Without wishing to offend you,
my lady, he was referring to your matters of the heart.'

She laughed. 'But, Clifford, I have no intention of marrying
Rankin. Ever! We'll think of something, we always do.'

'Indeed, but will we think of it in sufficient time to prevent
Chief Inspector Seldon hearing of your "engagement"?'

'What?' She thought for a moment. 'Oh, I see, I hadn't considered that. Thank you, Clifford, but I'll simply explain to Seldon
that Uncle Byron was caught up in an illegal… oh!'

He nodded. 'Precisely. Being a dedicated officer of the law,
Detective Chief Inspector Seldon will have no choice but to have
the matter fully investigated and—'

'And then everything will come to public light and Uncle Byron's
reputation will be lost, anyway. Damnation!'

CHAPTER 28

The following morning Eleanor was happy to let the spring cleaning take precedence over anything else. Mainly because 'anything else' involved investigating Solemn Jon's murder or trying to foil Lord Rankin's attempted blackmail. And her head was too woolly for either.

The reason for her befuddled brain was that the previous evening, she and Clifford had abandoned the unequal task of looking for a solution to both conundrums and turned to chess. Not that she could play, but Clifford had set to with his usual methodicalness to teach her. Meanwhile, she'd also set to with her usual methodicalness to enjoy her late uncle's tradition of consuming port and Stilton biscuits while he did so. Still, she blamed the chess for her delicate state that morning. *The rules are quite insane, Ellie. I'm sure Clifford was making most of them up.*

Outside the morning sun was shining brightly through the French windows and the birds in the garden were singing lustily, while inside the sound of a tornado increased. Or was it a hurricane? Anyway, whatever it was, it was causing her already fragile head to be quite unbearable.

She closed her eyes, wishing it would stop. Instead, it got louder. She opened them again to find her housekeeper standing at the library door.

'Oh, my stars!' With a clatter, Mrs Butters dropped the long cloth wrapped hose she was holding and hurried back out into the corridor. After a terrible whooshing sound that was worse than the original racket, silence returned. Her housekeeper reappeared in the doorway. 'My apologies, my lady, I had no idea you were sitting in here.'

Eleanor smiled weakly. 'No harm done.' She gestured out into the corridor. 'How is our recent addition to the spring-cleaning effort working out?'

''Tis beyond amazing, my lady. I can't thank you enough for being so kind as to purchase a vacuum cleaning machine.' She puffed her chest. 'Never thought the likes of me would be using summat so modern. Those advertisements only started appearing in Mr Clifford's London newspaper about a month ago. I remember because he showed them to me.'

'I know. I asked him to so he could gauge if you might like to try one. It's on a trial purchase in case you don't take to it.'

'Take to it, my lady? I'd take Victor to bed with me and hug the life out of him for all the arm aching he's saved me.'

'Victor?'

Mrs Butters blushed. 'Victor the vacuum.'

'Then I shall have Clifford telephone the company today and let them know we shall definitely be keeping Victor. I'm so pleased it… *he* arrived before the spring clean was finished.'

Her housekeeper beamed. 'As I am, m'lady. And as is old muddy boots, Joseph, who normally gets dragged out of his beloved gardens to lend a hand lifting the carpets. It takes all five of us and the extra help to get them up. Forty-one of them there are. Plus ninety-three rugs and all of them would have needed the life beaten out of them for the spring clean to have been done properly.'

Eleanor smiled. 'You mean to Clifford's satisfaction?'

'Perhaps, m'lady. But us ladies do appreciate he's only doing the best job he knows how. And he honestly doesn't know how to do anything short of perfect.'

'Don't be so bashful, none of you do. Every day it amazes me how so few of you run this vast house to such a high standard.

I'm very grateful and the offer to take on more help permanently still stands.'

'Oh, no, m'lady! Begging your pardon, course.' Mrs Butters pulled a duster from her pocket and waved it for emphasis. 'His lordship liked home to be quiet, probably on account of everything being so noisy and excitable when he travelled.'

Just as well he never bought the staff a vacuum cleaner, Ellie!

Mrs Butters gave a cheeky grin. 'Anyway, Mr Clifford has his hands full with the three of us. Any more women below stairs and I think he'd have a heart attack.'

They were both chuckling over this when Clifford entered the room carrying a silver tray of oven-fresh cherry and almond cake and coffee. Unusually, it also included a large jug of water. He paused on seeing the women together. They both tried to look serious and failed.

'A problem, Mrs Butters?'

'No, Mr Clifford. Quite t'other way round, in fact. Unless there's anything else, I'll be getting back to my new friend.' The housekeeper bobbed Eleanor a curtsey and left.

Eleanor nodded gratefully as Clifford closed the door with his elbow as the tornado started up again.

He placed the tray down and cast a twinkling eye over her.

'Perhaps learning chess during spring-cleaning season doesn't agree with you, my lady?'

She groaned. 'No, but it was dashed good fun.'

He poured her a large tumbler of water and set a dose of headache powder beside it.

'Indeed. You made exceptional progress as a new student. Although it has to be said, the evening concluded without any further headway in our murder investigation, or' – he ran his white-gloved finger round his starched collar – 'the other matter.'

'Trust me, we will find a solution,' she said more confidently than she felt.

'That reminds me, my lady.' From the tray, he retrieved a small oval tin and dropped it into her hand. 'From his lordship's last trip to Burma.'

She opened it and her face lit up.

'Tiger balm! I haven't seen this since I was in Southeast Asia, six – no, seven – years ago. Perfect for my screaming muscles, thank you. I'm still sore from racing Rankin. It's been a while since I raced in earnest.'

Outside, the sound of hoovering had receded into the distance. Clifford poured her a coffee and added a generous slice of moist cake and a delicate silver fork to her side plate. 'My lady, I must add my words of gratitude to those of Mrs Butters'. The vacuum cleaner has expedited the spring clean so significantly that we will be ready with your trunks this afternoon.'

'My trunks? I say, dash it, Clifford! I'm no longer the irritating nine-year-old you no doubt delighted in packing off back to boarding school when you'd had enough of me mucking up your meticulous schedule!'

'My lady, it may, on occasions, have been a slight relief after one of our more protracted contretemps, but it was never a delight. Not once. No, I was referring to your camphor-wood trunks.'

She stared at him blankly.

'They are specialist storage chests made from the tropical Cinnamomum camphora tree. Renowned not only for the medicinal properties of its oil in relieving chest congestion but' – he pointed at the tin of tiger balm – 'the sore parts of one's, ahem, anatomy. And more relevantly, it is also highly effective as an insect repellent, particularly to moths. I wish to ensure your cold-weather attire is perfectly preserved, especially your mother's furs and her velvet coat, which you are so fond of.'

Touched by his thoughtfulness, she smiled.

'You are wonderful, Clifford. Thank you, again. Now, while I indulge in this amazing-smelling creation of Mrs Trotman's, why don't you regale me with a full update on the spring clean? Then I can fully appreciate all the hard work you and the ladies have been putting in.'

'Very good, my lady.' He pulled his leather notebook from his morning-suit pocket and his pince-nez from another.

'Let me see... all the chimneys have been swept clean. The spare mattresses are still airing. Velvet and wool winter curtains have been dusted using the new vacuum cleaner's special attachment, and are currently being washed and packed away. The summer silk and linen curtains once ready will replace them.' He made a note at the bottom of the page and turned to a new one. 'All mahogany furniture has been treated with beeswax and turpentine and two-thirds of the three hundred and seventy-nine china and glass ornaments have been soaked in soap water and polished.'

She shook her head. 'Even with the extra hired help, that's amazing in such a short time!' A thought struck her. 'Have, er, Polly or Gladstone, met the vacuum cleaner yet?'

'Master Gladstone resolutely refuses to countenance being in the same room as Victor, my lady. While Polly.' He sighed. 'Polly is still terrified of the machine after Mrs Trotman told her it would suck her eyeballs out if she stared down the hose while it was on.'

Eleanor laughed so hard she choked on her cake. Clifford eyed her dispassionately.

'Perhaps a turn around the garden will clear your lungs, my lady?'

She nodded, tears running down her face.

'Excellent.' He waved towards the rear lawn. 'And perhaps we could also discover why exactly Henley Hall is overrun with urchins?'

CHAPTER 29

Once outside, they made their way towards the path leading from the tradesmen's entrance to the kitchen. The gangly lad she'd met earlier who was sweet on Polly was hovering near the door with a shorter, less well-dressed boy. *Hardly overrun with urchins, Ellie! There's only two of them!*

She gave a friendly wave, ignoring Clifford's muted tut of disapproval.

'Hello again. Jack, wasn't it?'

The lad swallowed hard. 'Yes, 'tis, m'lady. Ta for remembering.' He stared at his feet.

She looked to Clifford for help. Clifford regarded the two boys sternly.

'Now, boys, do I need to remind you that Henley Hall estate is not a place for unexpected visitors, especially during the staff's working hours?'

They both shook their heads violently.

'No, Mr Clifford, sir,' Jack said, wringing the life out the cap he twisted in his hands. 'I didn't come to see Pol… to visit, sir. 'Tis about what we spoke on afore.' He glanced at his friend. 'We thought as it might be helpful like.'

Eleanor's ears pricked up. *Ellie! Could they really have something useful that might give us a lead in the case? We could so do with that!*

Clifford looked at the newcomer. 'And you are young Matthew, I believe, Mr Mayhew's son?'

'Matthew Mayhew, Mr Clifford, sir,' the smaller lad said in barely more than a whisper. 'But folks call me Mew.'

Clifford nodded. 'What a great timesaver. Now, is it you that has some news?'

The boy took his courage in his hands. 'Sir, yes, sir. 'Bout the race when Solemn Jon died.' His small jaw clenched. 'I wants to help if I can.'

'Wonderful. Are you able to tell her ladyship what you saw or heard?'

As Jack nudged Mew forward, Eleanor gave them both a warm smile. 'Don't be nervous, boys, it's fine. Now, what did you see, Mew?'

'A fisherman, m'lady,' said Mew. 'On the bank where the raft race was. On the day of the fair. Just afore jam 'n fold time.'

'And what was the fisherman doing that caused you to notice him?' She would ask Clifford the meaning of that mysterious term later.

'Not fishing, m'lady.'

Eleanor glanced at Clifford, whose expression made it clear she needed to dig further. 'Could you be more, er... precise, Mew?'

'What's I mean is, m'lady, rummy thing is he had all the fancy stuff. I watched him a good while, hoping he would, you know...' He shuffled his feet.

'No, I don't quite.'

Clifford threw her a knowing look. She nodded discreetly and turned back to the boy. 'Carry on, Mew.'

'Yes, m'lady. Thing is, it took me a while to work out he was pretending, see? Kept casting his line but staring down the river all the while he did. That's no way to catch nothing.'

'Indeed.' Clifford coughed gently. 'And I'm guessing that you watch the fishermen regularly?' As the boy's cheeks paled, Clifford held up a hand. 'It's alright. For the purposes of this talk, your reasons are safe. I shan't ask any more about that.'

'Thank you, Mr Clifford, sir,' Mew muttered as he scuffed the hole in the toe of his shoe on the path.

'Did you recognise the fisherman?' said Eleanor.

'Nope, apologies, m'lady. He was all covered up in fishing hacksters.'

Another local expression, Ellie?

'I see. Well, was he tall like Mr Clifford? Or maybe nearer my height?'

Mew thought about it for a moment. ''Tween the two. And not chicken scrawny like me pa, but not fat neither. 'Tween them two.'

'And did he leave before you?'

The lad shook his head. 'I left. I guessed he was never gonna catch nothing and wents off to find Jack.'

'And where exactly did you see this fisherman?'

Mew screwed up his face. 'I thinks it was… near them reeds where the big tree's fallen in river. It's not dead, we's climbs on it all the time.'

That sounds like the spot we found Solemn Jon, Ellie!

'Is there anything else at all, Mew?' Clifford asked.

'No, Mr Clifford, sir. That's all of it.' His shoulders fell. 'Didn't mean to come with nothing helpful, honest, sir.'

'Quite the opposite, actually.' Clifford reached into his pocket. The boys' eyes lit up as he dropped several coins into each of their hands, adding an extra one into Mew's. 'You said you wanted to help? Well, you can do that by keeping quiet about what you saw and our conversation here today. Understood?'

'Sir, yes, sir,' they chorused.

'Thank you, both. Run along then.'

Eleanor watched the boys sprint away, Jack slowing to let Mew keep up.

'What do you think, Clifford?'

'I think we need to ensure they remain in awe of your position, my lady.'

'Clifford! They're just children.'

'I agree.' He pulled more coins from his pocket. 'However, the lure of remuneration when the family's eldest child is resorting to stealing fish to feed his siblings could be enough for stories to be fabricated.'

'Gracious! So that's why he watches the fishermen. But you know Mew well enough to believe him?'

'I do.' He shook his head. 'He has not grown an inch in the last five or so years.'

'Malnutrition? Maybe I can help his family.'

'Not by turning up with a basket of food, my lady. Mr Mayhew is an independent, and somewhat proud, man.'

'Poor Mew. Clifford, please come up with something I can do.'

He nodded. 'Absolutely.'

'Good. But in the meantime, please explain some of this Buckinghamshire slang. What exactly is "jam and fold time"?'

'A meal comprising a slice of bread, spread with jam and folded in half, my lady. A light tea or supper or the only meal of the day I imagine for the Mayhew children, depending on circumstances. Given the time of day, Mew must have been referring to tea, which is normally consumed around four o'clock, which would fit in with the timing of Solemn Jon's death.'

'Ah! And "fishing hacksters"? I'm mystified.'

'Hat, jacket and trousers. It is common for the village children – and adults, in truth – to run words together. Over the decades many of the words have become the norm.'

She smiled. 'Good old Buckinghamshire.'

Mrs Trotters appeared on the back step of the kitchen and waved at them.

'Ah, my lady. Lunch is almost ready.'

As the cook stood to the side to let them enter, Eleanor turned to Clifford.

'Among our other tasks, we must remember to find out why Pendle cancelled his hound trailing on the day of the May Fair. There's something suspicious there.'

'Trotters will know.'

All eyes, including the cook's, swivelled to the housekeeper, who was busy preparing a tray of polished cutlery and neatly folded napkins. She coloured.

'Begging your pardon interrupting, my lady. What I meant was, Mrs Trotman is up on everything to do with betting around here. She'll know.'

All eyes switched to the cook, who glared at her friend.

'Well, true, I do likes a flutter now and then, but who doesn't?'

Eleanor hid a smile. 'It's okay, Mrs Trotman, I know you're our resident expert, especially after your skill at choosing the winning pig in the derby at the May Fair.'

Any gentle ribbing on Eleanor's part was lost on her cook, who swelled with pride.

'Well, you see, my lady, the trick's in putting the effort in beforehand in studying form, whether it's pigs, horses or dogs. In the case of pigs, of course—'

'Mrs Trotman?' Clifford raised a finger. 'If we could stick to the question in hand?'

'Oh, yes, sorry. Well, old Pendle may've told everyone he cancelled the races on account of the May Fair, but he's never done it afore, has he?'

Eleanor shook her head. 'Not according to young Eric.'

'Ah.' Her cook nodded. 'Agnes Brimpton's lad. Good 'un he is. Agnes said to me only the other d—'

'Mrs Trotman!' For once Clifford's patience seemed to give out before Eleanor's. 'Perhaps, you could answer the question?'

'Right, yes, Mr Clifford. What Agnes told me was that old Pendle's got a rival who's set up racing over the border. Backed by some big names, so she says, and Pendle knew many of his usual crowd wouldn't turn up but go there instead. Helped that there was free beer and food at the other races, so Agnes said. Anyways, apparently, he cancelled his races on that day so as not to look foolish and used the May Fair as an excuse.'

Eleanor nodded slowly. 'The plot thickens…'

In the dining room, she was still trying to work out what her cook's revelation meant in terms of Pendle being a suspect for Solemn Jon's murder.

'So, Clifford, he may have lied to us, but apparently it was only to save face. Assuming, that is, Mrs Trotman's information is correct and it would be easy to check. In which case, Pendle cancelled his racing that day for an entirely innocent reason and not, in fact, to sneak off and do away with Solemn Jon.'

'True, my lady, but there is another side to the shilling. If this business rival is a genuine threat to Mr Pendle's business interests, then how much more desperate might he be to secure Patrick as a star attraction and stud dog?'

She shook her head. 'Blast it, Clifford! Why is nothing ever straightforward? Is Pendle more or less of a suspect now then?'

Before he could reply, the phone rang. While Clifford went to answer, she tried to work it out for herself, but merely ended up even more confused. She greeted Clifford's return with relief.

'Whoever it is on the phone, I'll speak to them. Anything has to be better than…' Her frown deepened. 'What's the matter now?'

CHAPTER 30

Eleanor looked up from trying to concentrate on the week's menus her cook was walking her through. Normally it would have received her full attention, but what with yesterday's news and Gladstone's strident snores from his bed by the range distracting her…

Mrs Trotman obviously sensed it too.

'Perhaps we should go through these another time, my lady? What with… you know.'

Eleanor nodded. 'Perhaps that is a good idea, Mrs Trotman.'

Her cook bobbed a half-curtsey and gathered up the menus. At the door, she met Clifford. They exchanged a look and quickly glanced at Eleanor and then away.

Alone with Clifford, Eleanor grimaced. 'Poor Mrs Trotman, I really couldn't keep my mind on anything she said, what with Gladstone making enough noise to wake the dead.' She looked up at Clifford. 'Bad choice of words.' Burying her face in her hands, she tried to reconcile her warring emotions.

Clifford stood silently for a moment and then cleared his throat. 'The passing of another is always an event to be mourned, my lady. At the same time, it is natural to feel—'

'Elation?'

'Perhaps "relief" is a more appropriate term?'

He's right, Ellie. She sighed. The news from the telephone call had shocked her, and also left her emotions confused.

Evander Rankin was dead. Of that, there was no doubt. Killed in a riding accident. The problem was, his death left her mourning the passing of a life and yet feeling guilty for the sense of relief it also brought.

She frowned. 'How did it happen exactly?'

Clifford hesitated and cleared his throat again. 'When you left Lord Rankin after your race, he rode out for another turn around the estate. Unfortunately, it seems he was thrown from his horse when it stumbled on a molehill. He struck his head on a stone in falling. The gamekeeper found him, but he was already dead.'

She groaned. 'I feel even more guilty now I know it happened almost immediately after I left him. Maybe he was too upset to concentrate properly on riding because I turned him down? Maybe I—'

'My lady!'

She stared at him in shock.

He spread his hands. 'I apologise for interrupting you, but your ever-sympathetic nature is a gift to others, and a burden to you. I cannot accept you blaming yourself for what was, after all, an accident. A number of riders are injured, and, infrequently, killed by being thrown from their horses due to molehills each year. King William III famously died in 1702 in such a fashion. And as to feeling relief at Lord Rankin's passing, that is only to be expected as it has released you from the threat of an unwanted marriage.' His hand strayed to his neat black tie. 'Indeed, I confess to feeling relief myself now his lordship's good name and memory won't be dragged through the gutter.'

She sighed again. 'I suppose so. Still, I shall do the right thing by him, whatever faults he had. When is the funeral?'

'Saturday, my lady.'

'Then I shall attend and pay him my last respects, if only for the family. And then hopefully I will have laid any feelings of lingering guilt to rest.'

*

Later that afternoon, Mrs Butters waylaid Eleanor on her way to the library to spend an hour looking through her uncle's birthday album.

'Oh, my lady, I wanted to tell you that Victor and me have had a most productive time! We've done four of the eight second-floor guest suites in the west wing and all the upholstered furniture is now as fresh as new.' She hesitated. 'Maybe one day you might even invite some folk to come and stay?'

'And put you all to the trouble of endlessly cooking and cleaning up?' Eleanor shook her head. 'Anyway, I don't really know that many people here, having been abroad so much. And I haven't got the hang of being the society hostess by a very long way. Besides, I seem perfectly able to create enough chaos to keep you busy all on my own.'

'Having guests 'twould be no bother at all, my lady.' She gave her a motherly smile. 'Seems a shame sometimes, such a bright and beautiful lady as yourself rattling round a big house like this with only the likes of us. Although Mr Clifford is good company, I know. His lordship, God rest his soul, used to enjoy their rowdy evenings enormously.'

'Rowdy? Clifford? Surely, that can't be right?'

Her housekeeper tapped her nose with her forefinger. She went to speak but blushed as she caught sight of Clifford's silent form behind her elbow. 'Erm, Victor and I'll just go and start on the blue room, if that would suit, Mr Clifford?'

'It would indeed, Mrs Butters,' he said. 'And, in fact, eminently more helpful to the spring-cleaning schedule than whatever you are currently regaling her ladyship about, I'm sure.' There was a twinkle in his eye.

The housekeeper mumbled an apology, collected the various parts of the vacuum cleaner and hurried off as quickly as the cumbersome equipment would let her.

Ellie smiled at Clifford. 'Ah, the afternoon paper and a sherry, a nice distraction from thinking about yet another life so suddenly having departed this earth.'

He coughed. 'Regrettably, my lady, I bring the sherry as a fortification, not a distraction. With apologies for being the harbinger of regrettable news again, but…' He pointed to the open page of the newspaper where it lay on the tray. She picked it up and skimmed the page. A headline came into focus, causing her to cry out.

'What! Another obituary? This time for Rankin!' Scanning down, her jaw dropped. 'Clifford, this one declares the death murder as well!'

He nodded. 'And it is signed "William Green" as well.'

She sat down on one of the hall chairs and read the obituary again. Once she'd finished, she dropped the paper onto a side table and shook her head.

'I don't know whether to believe Rankin's death was murder or not, but I do firmly believe one thing.'

Clifford raised an eyebrow. 'And that is, my lady?'

'Find out who is writing these obituaries and we find out who killed Solemn Jon.'

CHAPTER 31

In a street that looked like it had been cobbled in medieval times and not repaired since, Eleanor was reminded once more of just how lucky she was. The rotten window frames and damp thatched roofs of the houses suggested a less than affluent neighbourhood. She stiffened as a rat scuttled down a wall, clutching something unidentifiable in its mouth. Gladstone shot forward with a deep woof. Restrained by the lead held by Clifford, the dog's front feet lifted off the ground and he was pulled backwards into a seating position. He regarded Clifford with deep disgust.

'Perhaps we should have brought a hungry cat as an icebreaker,' Eleanor said.

'I think a ratting terrier might have been more appropriate, my lady.' He gestured to the size of the hole the rat had disappeared into.

'I agree.' She looked around. 'I must say, this feels like no part of Little Buckford I've ever been to.'

'Indeed, my lady. The village's contingent who possess, perhaps it is most polite to say, "rougher edges" than the majority of the population, or certainly less wealth, tend to converge at her furthest reaches.'

Eleanor was used to dealing with those with 'rougher edges' after her solo travels across the world. She looked around again. *Not dangerous, Ellie, just rundown. No need for concern.*

Clifford stared up at the building in front of them. The four-storey stone edifice stood out sharply from the flint cottages and two-storied dwellings around it.

'I believe this used to be part of the old mill that was demolished, my lady.' He pointed to the far wall of the house that rose directly from the river.

She shivered. It was only half a mile downstream from where they'd found Solemn Jon's body.

Clifford's voice cut into her thoughts. 'I rather fear Mr Green's landlady has taken in lodgers because her husband passed away some time ago. Father Time has clearly been busy ravaging what was once a comfortable enough family home for a wheelwright.'

'I thought you said you didn't know who Willie Green's landlady was?'

'Indeed, I don't, my lady. Not having recourse to visit this part of the village for any of his lordship's business.'

'Then how do you know the landlady's husband was a wheelwright?'

'Only a craftsman would have added such custom-made wooden wheels to a kitchen chair to assist his wife in getting about.'

She followed his gaze. At the right side of the house, an old shawl-clad woman propelled what was indeed a kitchen chair on wooden wheels from a hen house up a rough path. Eleanor noted the small metal pail on her lap and then, in surprise, the large brown rabbit sitting behind it.

The woman spotted them and changed direction to bump her makeshift wheelchair up and over the rough edge of the overgrown grass where the narrow garden met the road. Gladstone ambled forward and put his front paws on her lap. She patted his head and eyed them suspiciously with sharp amber eyes, even more striking, framed as they were, by her long grey tresses and pale face.

'This is private property. Even the likes of us has rights!'

Clifford pulled the bulldog back while Eleanor stepped forward. 'Absolutely and forgive us for not having called out to announce ourselves. We've come to speak to Mr Green, if we may?'

'Pah! You'll not find him at home, not on a day like today.'

Eleanor pointed at the clear blue sky. 'A fresh air man is he?'

'Fresh air! He gets enough of that working all hours outside in the undertaker's yard, don't he? Winter 'n all. Well, he did, I should say now, seeing as Solemn Jon's up and passed over.'

'Such a sad thing to happen. I do hope Mr Green has found another job?'

The woman set her lips in a hard line and stared back at Eleanor without replying.

Eleanor was momentarily stumped. She'd been expecting either a positive response delivered with relief that Willie Green could still pay his rent or a negative tirade that this wasn't a charity house. Clifford stepped forward, his gloved hand brushing Eleanor's jacket pocket as he did so. He beamed a smile at the woman, the like of which Eleanor had never seen on him before.

'Perhaps Mr Green will be returning soon, dear lady?' He positively purred to Eleanor's astonished ears.

'Dear lady!' The woman's cheeks blushed. She patted her hair. ''Tis a long while since anyone called me that, I should say.'

He managed the perfect look of surprise. 'A criminal shame, if I might observe.' He took the pail the woman was struggling to set on the ground and placed it next to her chair. 'But please do not let us take up your time, I'm sure you have a most hectic schedule ahead of you. Lodgers can be a blessing but a burden too with all the work they bring. Am I right, Mrs… erm?'

'Trimble. And too right you are, and no mistake. I've only three staying at the moment. And an empty room going begging. But Willie's on the lookout for someone what needs a roof over their head for me.'

Clifford nodded. 'How lucky you are to have a helpful and attentive lodger amongst your paying guests, dear lady.'

She nodded back and adjusted her shawl. 'Already found me one lodger, he did. Poor man lost his job when his master died. Was cast off, just like Willie. Folk don't take kindly to Willie, but he looks out for those what no one else does. Including me.'

At that moment, the rabbit stood up on its hind legs and stretched out to paw at Eleanor's pocket. She stared down, unable to resist his velvety ears. 'Mrs Trimble, may I?'

She sniffed. 'I shouldn't. Not until you've given him whatever he's after from your pocket unless you want to leave with an angry scratch as long as your arm.'

Mystified, Eleanor reached into her jacket pocket and pulled out a baked apple ring. She cocked her head at Clifford, who looked back impassively. Gladstone shuffled forward and sat at her feet, looking fixedly at the apple ring, willing it to fall into his mouth. Eleanor eyed the greedy bulldog thinking he'd get a shock if she gave it to him. He wasn't a great fan of fruit of any kind unless it was covered in Mrs Trotman's beef dripping.

'Yep, that'll be it, alright,' Mrs Trimble said. 'Apples is his most favourite ever. Only allowed two slices a day, mind. Keeps his inner workings good and proper.'

Eleanor was enchanted as she held the apple ring for the rabbit to chomp through. 'He's simply beautiful and...' She hesitated, not wanting the woman to think she was prying again. 'Excellent company, I imagine?'

'That he is. Rides on me lap all day if he can.'

Eleanor decided to risk it. 'I hope you don't mind my saying, but I was admiring your marvellous chair.'

The woman looked up from stroking the rabbit. 'That right, is it?'

'Goodness, yes. I wondered if perhaps your husband had been a, erm, wheelwright?' She avoided Clifford's eye. As the woman nodded proudly and ran her hand over one of the wheels, Eleanor continued. 'It's simply ingenious. He must have been very skilled and a wonderful man.'

'Luckiest wife in this world, I am. Rollo might've passed over a good while ago now, but he left me the house. For as long as it stands, anyhow.'

Eleanor was intrigued. 'Rollo, that's an unusual name?'

The woman laughed, lighting her face with reminiscent joy. Her eyes shone as she made a circle in the air with a crooked finger. 'Roll-o, like the wheels going round that he made. All folk called him that. Even I never think of him as anything else.'

'What a wonderful memory to have.'

'See this.' The woman thrust her hand out towards Eleanor, tapping an intricate five-coloured banded wooden ring held on her bony finger only by her swollen flame-red knuckle. Gladstone's interest was briefly piqued until he quickly established it wasn't edible.

'Oak it is. A matching pair. He worked them all by his own hand for our wedding. Fitted perfectly then, mind. But we all got to get old. 'Tis the way. And then 'tis our moment to pass. Even the undertaker got taken when his time come round.'

Thankful for a window to steer the conversation back, Eleanor ran her fingers gently along the rabbit's ears. 'Perhaps you might know when Willie will be home?'

'Shouldn't like to say. I don't get involved in what the paying guests get up to. 'Tis best not to ask too much, especially in Willie's case.'

'Well, I wanted to make sure he was better, that was all.'

'Better?'

'Yes, he was so poorly the day of the raft race and a while later when we bumped into him at the pol— elsewhere.' She realised that mentioning the police station might not be a good idea.

Mrs Trimble's amber eyes narrowed. 'That's true. He weren't feeling right. Stayed in bed all day.'

'Really? I thought I saw him in the afternoon at the May Fair.'
That's a pure fib, Ellie, but we're getting nowhere.

The old woman spun her chair around. 'Maybe, I can't remember when he laid in to. My memory's going.'

Eleanor had a shrewd idea the woman's memory wasn't going anywhere, unlike her. She'd almost reached her back door when Eleanor called out, 'Does Mr Green like fishing, Mrs Trimble?'

The old woman shouted over her shoulder. 'Like I said, I don't get involved.' With a spin of her wheels, she bumped into the house and was gone.

As they walked away, Eleanor muttered. 'Did you have the feeling she was covering up for Willie Green, Clifford?'

He considered the question. 'I am torn, my lady. Mrs Trimble seems a decent sort. However, it seems unlikely that a lady clearly in need of money is going to risk upsetting one of her paying guests. Certainly not one who finds other guests for her. She was certainly rather vague about Mr Green's movements on the day of the fair, though.'

'And sent us away with a fly in our ears.'

'A flea, my lady.'

'Yikes, fleas and rats? She'll never let that other room!'

He shook his head and spoke slowly, as if to a child. 'The expression is "leave with a flea in one's ear". And as you pointed out, rats are commonplace in rural locations. I'm sure the inside of the property is as sparkling as Mrs Trimble is able to manage. Her hens were admirably kept, after all.'

'I confess I didn't notice. Bit taken with the rabbit, though. Ah yes! On that note, how did that apple ring end up in my pocket?'

His eyes twinkled. 'I really couldn't say, my lady.'

'Alright, I shan't ask how or why you've mastered that sleight of hand. But how could you possibly have known that she would have a rabbit who adored baked apple rings? Are you actually a wizard?'

'Unfortunately not. Otherwise, we might already have exposed Solemn Jon's killer. I just happened to be carrying a few. Mrs Trotman knows they are a particular favourite of mine and periodically refills my bag with them.'

She laughed. 'Very cute. But I think I prefer the mystique of you being a wizard.' She scanned his face as she ran back over the conversation with Mrs Trimble, seeing a glimpse of the man behind his starched collars and impeccable morning suit. 'That was quite the charm card you pulled there. You made a lady you'd never met before feel very special. It was rather lovely to watch.'

He bowed. 'Thank you, my lady.' At that moment Gladstone let out a warning growl. Clifford gestured across the street. 'Perhaps Mr Green will pull the same "charm card" as you referred to it, on yourself?'

She turned to see Willie Green's scowling face.

She shuddered. *Let's hope not, Ellie. I think his usual charmless self would be preferable!*

CHAPTER 32

'Good morning, Mr Green.'

'Don't see as it is if you're skulking 'bout.' Willie Green yanked his hand from his trouser pocket to point at her. 'You've got no business round here. Anyways, you might get your fancy shoes dirty.'

Clifford wound Gladstone's lead tighter around his hand as the bulldog growled menacingly again.

She shook her head. 'Mr Green, it's a shame you always think I'm trying to cause you trouble whenever we happen to bump into each other.'

'Rot! You ain't never "bumped into me". Following me, that's what you're doing, like a dog after a lick of tripe, hoping for a tasty titbit to try and frame me for summat I never did.' He spat something out of his mouth and reached for a cigarette. 'Likes of you never get punished, even when you done wrong. But me! I get the helmets hammering me out of bed at all hours when I ain't done nothing.'

Eleanor felt a stab of guilt. *You can't help the class you've been born into, or the wealth you've inherited, Ellie, but you can't argue with him either. It's true.*

'The police came to see you?'

'Yeah.' Willie's face flushed. 'Sick of being everyone's whipping boy, I am. 'Taint fair. Why's it always me?'

She sighed. 'I don't know, Mr Green, but I don't believe in grassing people up.'

He shuffled his feet. 'Then it wasn't you who sent the police round?'

'Genuinely, no. I was surprised when you said they had called. But then again, I suppose that having written another attention-seeking obituary, it wouldn't have taken much imagination to expect them to arrive on your doorstep, would it?'

His fists clenched. 'I didn't, I tell you. I never wrote no obituary, not for Solemn Jon and not for that Rankin bloke.' He scratched the back of his neck. 'Why would I bother about a toff like him, anyhow? Couldn't give a tuppence. Never even met him.'

Mmm, Ellie, a little too quick to protest his innocence, perhaps?

'I've no idea, Mr Green. But the obituary had your name at the bottom. Anyway, what did the police threaten you with? Wasting their time?'

'Yeah. And publishing malicious gossip. But they should be hassling that newspaper bloke. He printed them, not me. Why can't you believe me?'

Eleanor scanned his face. 'Do you know, Mr Green, I might just be beginning to. About the obituaries, at least. But it's hard when you lied about being ill on the day of the raft race.' She held up a hand as he opened his mouth. 'You were seen, you see. And not in pyjamas, nor wrapped in sheets only "fit for the fire", as you described to me previously. And you didn't take me up on my offer to help pay for any medicine you may need. The offer still stands by the way.'

His scowl deepened. 'I don't need no charity! Or medicine. You and your lackey here've been following me like a dam—'

'Mr Green!' Clifford stepped forward. 'You yourself informed us only a moment ago that the police have threatened you with arrest for something you insist you haven't done. On either occasion, in fact. Refusing to cooperate with us, the only people who are willing to listen to your side of the story, makes you seem doubly guilty. And foolish.'

Eleanor nodded. 'We are your only hope of getting the police off your back. So care to tell the truth this time?'

He glared at them both, and then all the fight seemed to go out of him. He stared at his hands.

'Alright, I went to see my girl.' He shot Eleanor a look. 'Yeah, Willie Green's got a girl who's sweet on him even though the village thinks I'm not worth walking on the same street as the rest of 'em.'

Eleanor wasn't certain what to say. The thought of any girl falling for Willie Green was difficult to countenance.

'I'm… I'm sure she's very pretty.'

'Too pretty and too good for the likes of me, Gracie is,' he muttered to himself, but Eleanor's sharp ears caught the words. She pretended not to have heard.

'Do her parents also think you are not worthy?'

'Yeah.' Willie looked up, some of his belligerent attitude return-ing. 'Won't even hear my name without spitting buckets of feathers. So I got to blooming well sneak round when they ain't there.'

'Ah! So you feigned illness on that Sunday so you could meet your girlfriend while her parents and the rest of the village were out at the May Fair? And what time was that?'

He hesitated. ''Bout one o'clock.' His scowl momentarily turned to a frown again. 'Didn't mean not to be there for Solemn Jon, but it was the only chance I had to see her.'

This is all very well, Ellie, but we need proof. He's lied before.

'Mr Green, who is your girlfriend?'

'I ain't telling you that! She'll be so deep in the mire with her old man if he finds out she met me for the afternoon, I'll never see her again. Besides, I know you think I'm no better than scum, but I'm looking out for her reputation like a decent bloke. Not that we do anything we shouldn't but folks won't believe that, like they don't believe nothing I say.'

'Did you take the river route to go and meet her?'

He hesitated. 'Don't be daft! Be a right fool if I had. Whole village was there, weren't they, watching the race?' He gave her a leering look. 'Mind, riverbank seems to work alright for some as is making eyes at each other.'

Eleanor stiffened. 'Are you referring to me, Mr Green? If so, I think you may need to visit an optician.'

'Nope. Didn't need no spectacles to see you and that tall bloke with the fancy suit, both on your knees in the mud. And you dabbing at his wet shirt and all,' he ended with a dirty chuckle.

Gladstone growled from behind her. Willie heaved himself away from the wall, hands still in his pockets. 'Don't feel good being watched, does it?' He sauntered off a few steps, whistling, then turned back. 'But I'll tell you summat for nothing. Whoever's writing them obituaries knows a thing or two. Rankin was murdered all right.' His eyes lit up and anger suffused his face 'And good riddance to him! Just like Solemn Jon, he got what he deserved!'

CHAPTER 33

It was all too clear to Eleanor even before Clifford had opened the front door that something was amiss. Uncharacteristically, she could hear raised voices coming from within the Hall. She winced as the argument reached a crescendo.

'Don't bring me into this, Butters. I told you he needed a rest!'

Clifford followed her inside. They both stopped dead at the devastation strewn across the grand entrance hall.

'Oh, my stars!' Mrs Butters muttered. Polly let out a squeak and leapt behind Mrs Trotman.

'Perhaps—' Eleanor started and then clamped her mouth shut, realising in a situation like this, Clifford didn't need his authority usurped by her. She stood silently while he surveyed the chaos.

With a disapproving sniff at the dishevelled and dusty state of the ladies' aprons and caps, he scrutinised the mounds of dirt on the deep-pile Wilton runner, punctuated by an army of footprints and the scattered parts of the dismantled vacuum cleaner. A fire poker stuck out of the hole in the main body where the hose should have been attached, sooty fingerprints covering the casing.

The hall table lay upside down, surrounded by a mess of dried flowers and a china bowl. The vacuum cleaner's flex was still caught around the table's legs, making Clifford's lips purse. But Eleanor could sense it was the fringed end of the Wilton rug jammed down the vacuum's hosepipe that was causing him the most distress.

'Polly,' Clifford said. 'Dustpans, brushes and the rubbish bin from the scullery. Immediately, please.'

'Yes, Mr Clifford, sir.' The maid skittered off on jittering legs.

'I'm very sorry, Mr Clifford.' Mrs Butters avoided his eye. 'I might have been a bit… over-enthusiastic with Victor.'

'Did you read the instructions that came with the vacuum cleaner, Mrs Butters? Specifically, as regards to how often it needs emptying?'

'I started to, Mr Clifford, but there were that many I thought I could either read them all or get on with the spring cleaning. Not both.'

He pinched the bridge of his nose. 'Before you use it again, please make sure you have read the pertinent instructions as to when it needs emptying, and how. Now see to the table and flowers if you would. Mrs Trotman.' Clifford turned to the cook. 'My small toolbox from the boot room, please, that I might endeavour to wrestle the Wilton from the grip of the hosepipe. And kindly take the rest of the vacuum cleaner with you and Polly so I can try to return it to working order later. I'm sure, ladies, we can have this—'

Have this what, Eleanor never heard as her attention was distracted by a line of dusty dog prints leading from the dismantled vacuum down the hall. She quietly followed them into the kitchen.

'Oh, dear!'

Gladstone stood in the centre of the floor with a shred of vacuum bag hanging from his mouth. Or at least she assumed through the cloud of dust that hung in the air that the ghostly-grey form surrounded by the rest of the bag and its contents was her bulldog. For a moment she just stared at the mess in horror. Gladstone looked around him, satisfaction at a job well done written all over his face.

Quick, Ellie, do something before— A groan came from behind her. *Too late!* She turned around to see Clifford in the doorway.

'Ah! You're here. I was just going to—'

A shriek came from behind him as Polly arrived, followed by Mrs Butters and Mrs Trotman. Clifford closed his eyes and seemed to be counting. After he'd reached ten, or at least Ellie assumed so, he opened them.

'Ladies, I—'

Gladstone sneezed violently and shook himself, releasing another cloud of dust that wafted onto Clifford's spotless white shirt. There was a collective gasp from Eleanor and the ladies. Then they erupted into laughter.

Despite himself, the corners of Clifford's mouth twitched.

'If I'm needed, my lady, I will be in the boot room repairing Victor. Mrs Butters. Mrs Trotman. Once you have quite finished, if you would kindly deal with' – he waved at the bulldog – 'this!'

After the kitchen and hall had been cleaned and Gladstone bathed, much to his fury, serenity was restored and Clifford joined Eleanor on the terrace for a much-needed catch up on the case. The blue sky was dotted with fluffy white clouds that occasionally obscured the late afternoon sun and caused Ellie to wish she'd put on a thicker jacket. She thought of changing but it was too nice to finally be able to wear lighter clothing after what had seemed a particularly long winter.

'It seems to me, my lady,' said Clifford, 'that the most important matter to address is not whether Mr Green wrote Lord Rankin's obituary, but whether the obituary's claim that the death was indeed, murder, is correct.'

She nodded. 'Not forgetting Willie Green also claimed it was murder.'

'True. However, Mr Green's insistence that Lord Rankin was murdered sounds more like bluff and bluster each time I replay the conversation in my mind. Especially as he clearly stated that he'd never even met him.'

'Hmm, I know what you mean. In truth, I came to the same conclusion at first. But his anger at Rankin seemed at odds with his insistence that he didn't know the man. And why would he say that Rankin got what he deserved?'

Clifford's brow furrowed. 'Indeed, my lady, you are right. But if I remember, his exact words were, "Just like Solemn Jon, he got what he deserved!"'

She frowned. 'Yes. So?'

'Well, that statement can be interpreted in two ways. Firstly, for some reason we are unable to fathom at the moment, they both deserved to die to Mr Green's mind.'

'Or?'

'Or that they both died if not in the same manner, certainly by the same hand, in Mr Green's opinion.'

She nodded slowly. 'I think you're right. Willie Green may have been suggesting that they were both murdered for the same reason—'

'Or by the same person.'

'Or both. And my intuition is whispering that too. And you know how that has got me out of trouble before.'

'Yes, my lady, but only after it had got you into trouble trying to extract yourself from the situation it got you into in the first place.'

She laughed. 'Okay, a few times, maybe. But moving on, either way, he freely admitted to spying on me. I was very taken aback. Why would he do that?'

'Possibly because he feels you are doing the same to him, my lady? Or, if he is the murderer, in order to keep abreast of what you may have uncovered and from whom, I suggest.'

She grimaced. 'Yes, you're right. My stealthy meetings with suspects and witnesses to date have not been conducted in quite the clandestine fashion I intended. Speaking of suspects, we really are woefully short of them at the moment, you know. Anyway, as I said, I will attend Lord Rankin's funeral, so I should be able to find out more details about his death and perhaps unearth a suspect or two. In the meantime, I think we should find out more about Pendle's movements the day of the murder and follow up on what Mew told us about the mysterious fisherman. See if we can link him with Willie Green. Oh, and, of course, what Mew told us tallies with what his friend Jack mentioned. Remember, Jack said he saw Willie Green creeping through the woods?' She frowned. 'Though not in any kind of fishing clothing… what was it Mew called them again?'

'Hacksters, my lady.'

'Yes, those. But I suppose Willie Green could have hidden them somewhere and put them on later.'

'Although it seems his arriving out of disguise might rather have negated his efforts to later conceal his appearance, since Jack was able to identify him creeping through the woods. Although that doesn't necessarily mean he was the man in that fishing apparel.'

'Agreed, but it would have been more suspicious if he'd left his landlady's house togged up in fishing gear. Unless he does fish regularly. Dash it, we need to find that out!'

'Perhaps, my lady, you might persuade his girlfriend to impart something pertinent apropos Mr Green's fishing proclivity? And also to corroborate or otherwise his statement that he was indeed with her at the time of Solemn Jon's death?'

She threw her hands out. 'I'd love to, but how exactly when we've no idea who she is? It's no use going back to Willie Green, he clearly won't say.'

He coughed. 'I was thinking we might shamefully pump the most readily reliable source of gossip in the area, my lady.'

'The ladies? You think they'd know? I can't imagine them having any dealings with Willie Green, myself.'

'Not the ladies. Who is not only the font of all gossip in the area, but ever desperate to transmit such news, especially to your good self?'

She clicked her fingers. 'The postmistress at West Radington. Clifford, you clever bean! If anyone knows, she will. Let's—'

The ring of the telephone interrupted her. Clifford stepped inside to answer it and returned a moment later.

'Are you at home to the gentleman who fortunately did not require a new suit after it was so thoroughly patted dry after it was unfortunately… soaked?'

'You terror! Of course I am.'

She hurried to the telephone, noting the hall was back to its usual order and the Wilton rug seemingly undamaged.

'Inspector, I mean, Hugh. How are you?'

'Truthfully, I've been better. At least in a better mood.' Seldon's deep voice sounded even gruffer than usual.

What have you done now, Ellie?

'Oh, dear. Anything I can do to help?'

'Yes!' She heard him take a deep breath. 'Please do explain how it came about that not only have you been investigating a murder I told you did not warrant investigating, but doing so in such a way that I get a call from a disgruntled Sergeant Brice?'

She was stunned. 'Brice? But I haven't been anywhere near Chipstone Police Station since signing my statement regarding the events of the raft race.'

An exasperated sigh came down the line. 'Apparently, a Mr Willie Green visited Sergeant Brice and delighted in telling him that I had been sticking my nose into their business without informing them. His description left Brice in no doubt that the man poking his "officious trunk into the undertaker's death" as he put it, was me. And that I had done so with you as my companion.'

She winced. 'Well, that is true, in a way. You helpfully came to take a look.'

'That is not how it was portrayed, and it is certainly not how Brice has taken the news. I may be a senior police officer, but that doesn't mean I don't need to tread respectfully around the toes of the local constabulary. This has damaged not only my reputation but also Brice's trust in me. Especially as this Willie Green fellow then told Brice that, despite my findings to the contrary, you were investigating Solemn Jon's death and telling everyone it was murder!'

Oh, Ellie, what a mess! 'Hugh, what can I say? It wasn't like that.' Silence. 'Hugh, did you hear me?'

Finally his voice came through, quieter but no less angry. 'I did.' He cleared his throat. 'Look, I… we, oh, blast it! I'd begun to believe that maybe, possibly, there was a chance something could work between us but frankly, if you continue to investigate this undertaker's death, well, I really don't know. Now, I need to go.'

'Wait!' She desperately didn't want the conversation to end this way. 'What was it you meant on the riverbank when you said you didn't want us to fight "especially today"?'

There was a long pause. Just when she thought he wasn't going to reply, he came back on. 'I meant because it was precisely five years to the day my wife died.'

The line clicked off.

'Hugh? Hugh?'

He's never said anything about a wife before, Ellie? She slumped back onto the settle, her head in her hands.

'My lady.' Clifford materialised at her shoulder. 'Is everything alright?'

She pulled her hands from her face. 'Let's just say, I'd rather have had the telling off that you just gave the ladies than the one Seldon just gave me.'

'Ah!'

'Ah, indeed.'

He cleared his throat. 'At least you can be certain of one thing.'

'Which is?'

'That his reprimand only stings so deeply because the gentleman truly means something to you, my lady, which is most heartening.'

'Not when he made it abundantly clear that he is through with even trying to work through the intense irritation I bring him every time our paths cross unless—'

'Unless?'

'Unless I go back on my promise to Solemn Jon's wife and stop investigating her husband's death.' She groaned. 'What on earth am I going to do?'

CHAPTER 34

'Are you sure, my lady?'

'Are you trying to dissuade me, Clifford?'

'Indeed, I am.'

She stared up at the sign above her head.

'Look, I didn't promise Seldon anything on that telephone call yesterday. Or, in fact, when I first asked him to look into Solemn Jon's death. He merely assumed I'd take his professional opinion as correct and leave it at that.' She sighed. 'And I had every intention of doing so. However, even if it was in a moment of weakness, I have promised Mrs Jon I would find out the truth about her husband's death. And I can't go back on my word.'

'Admirably said, my lady. Nevertheless, I am troubled your decision entirely discounts your happiness. Again.'

'I can only do what I believe is right. You said it yourself. Caught between a rock and a hard place is a hideous spot to be and certainly doesn't lead to a good night's sleep. Thank you for the soothing cup of hot milk I discovered outside my door at two o'clock this morning, by the way.'

'My sincere pleasure. But our recent line of enquiry regarding any possible connection between Mr Pendle and the mysterious fisherman was achieved from the discreet confines of Henley Hall. I fear this is altogether too public a place to pursue our investigation for it not to reach the ears of Chief Inspector Seldon. Especially as the postmistress is a known gossip.'

Eleanor faced him squarely. 'There would be no point in our being here if she wasn't, would there? To be fair, your wonderful, if no doubt slightly nefarious contact, turned up trumps. Not only did he inform us that Pendle is a keen fisherman—'

'And therefore would own the requisite fishing gear.'

'Exactly. But also he was able to confirm that Pendle's pocket has been hit hard by this new rival setting up over the border. However, your contact spectacularly failed to provide any information on Willie Green's girlfriend.'

'Regrettably so, my lady.'

'Yes. Which is why we are here.' She turned and marched up the steps and into West Radington Post Office and General Stores, Gladstone huffing behind her.

'Morning?' she called out.

'Oh, no you don't. Be off with you!'

Gladstone spun around trying to locate the source of the voice. Eleanor just shook her head. *Oh, dear. It's one of those days, Ellie!* She looked around the seemingly deserted post office, its functional grey walls largely obscured by metal shelving thinly filled with random foodstuffs and household items. The cigarette machine attached to the wall by the window cut out the greater part of the May sunshine, while four bulging buff-coloured mail sacks sat in the far corner. Gladstone ambled over to the furthest sack and gave it a prod with his snout.

'Ouch! Take your clothes pegs and clear off, you vagabond!'

Ah, that's where she's hiding today, Ellie!

'Mother!' A flustered gaunt woman in her early fifties flew through the faded yellow curtains that led to the rest of the house. She froze in horror on seeing Eleanor.

'Lady Swift! I'm so sorry! It's—'

Eleanor held up her hands. 'It's fine, Miss Green. Please don't worry.' She lowered her voice. 'Is your mother… alright this morning?'

'She is fine. Just… having a moment.' The woman ran her hand through her lank auburn hair. 'A rather long, difficult moment, in fact. But I can't believe it occurred while you were here, m'lady, of all people.'

'Perhaps I should return later?'

But the postmistress was already advancing on the mail sacks. 'Mother?'

'Has the gypsy gone?'

The postmistress peered inside the sack Gladstone had taken up guard by.

'Yes, Mother. It's just me and Lady Swift here now.' She turned to Eleanor and whispered, 'The poor dear thinks the gypsies will put a curse on her. I told her that's nonsense, it's redheads… I mean, it's all nonsense, of course.' She hurriedly turned to hide her embarrassment and pulled open the sack.

A white-haired bird of a woman emerged tentatively. Producing a tin of condensed milk from somewhere in her beige wool dress, she held it out to Eleanor.

'Are we coming for tea?'

The postmistress groaned. 'Oh, Mother!'

Eleanor smiled. 'Not today, I'm afraid. Perhaps another time.'

With a grateful look, the postmistress grabbed her mother's shoulders. 'Now, dear, it's time to sit and feed the birds in the garden.' She steered her off through the curtains.

A few minutes later, she reappeared alone. 'Lady Swift. What can I say? I'm so sorry.'

'Please, it's of absolutely no consequence, Miss Green. I'm just concerned for your mother. Actually, for you. It can't be easy.'

The postmistress smiled weakly. 'No, not some days. But we manage. This has been her home since she was born and so it shall be until… until the end.'

Eleanor nodded. 'Well, if you'll forgive my saying, I think it's absolutely wonderful the way you care for her.'

The postmistress blushed. 'Thank you, m'lady. Now, what can I do for you this morning? Stamps, a telegram, a parcel?'

'Actually, it is rather cheeky of me, but I've come to ask for your help.'

The postmistress' face lit up. 'Of course. Not that I'm an expert on anything.'

'Actually, I believe you are. I'm trying to get in touch with a local young woman, but rather embarrassingly' – she tapped her forehead – 'her name eludes me at the moment and I don't know where she lives.'

'Surely, Mr Clifford must. He knows everything and everyone.'

Eleanor smiled. 'Almost. But no. That's why I've come to you. You are rather a font of local knowledge.'

The postmistress smoothed a hand over her hair, trying to hide how pleased she was. 'Well, I do keep my eyes and ears open, you know. And people do feel they can confide in me. Some find it hard to keep a secret, but not me. So, m'lady, what can you tell me about this girl?'

'I know her father lives in Little Buckford, although for the life of me I can't remember where. Oh, and her first name is Grace.'

The postmistress swelled with visible pride. 'And I thought you had a challenge for me, m'lady! There're only two families with young girl's called Grace who live in Little Buckford itself. Padgett and Felcott.'

'Ah!' Eleanor tapped her chin. 'How to work out which it is then?'

The postmistress nodded sagely. 'Hmm, could be either.'

'I believe someone told me she has a… gentleman friend her father disapproves of?'

'Not Grace Felcott, then. Folk say she's about as handsome as a three-legged horse born backwards, which is why she doesn't have any young gentleman courting her. Course, I wouldn't say such things but folk can't help but be honest sometimes.'

Eleanor bit back a smile. 'So it must be Grace Padgett, was it? I seem to remember that name.'

'I think so, m'lady. Her father doesn't approve of his daughter courting with any young gentleman. He'd lock that girl in a box if it weren't against the law. He's not above taking a shotgun to anyone who's foolish enough to imagine his daughter's virtue is up for the taking without having walked her down the aisle first.'

'Oh, I see.'

The postmistress looked over her shoulder and lowered her voice. 'Mind you, I can't blame him. Why Grace should choose to take an interest in *him*, I can't imagine! He is a rogue and a scoundrel. Between you and me, I thought of telling Grace's father myself on account of his being such a menace, but it's not my place. I'm not a meddler, m'lady.'

Eleanor tried to keep her voice neutral. 'Of course not. So, Grace has taken a shine to... Willie Green. Well, well.'

The postmistress tapped the counter sharply making Gladstone jerk to attention. 'That's as maybe, my lady, but there's no connection 'tween his family and mine. Let me make that very clear.'

Eleanor shook her head. 'I honestly hadn't even noticed you share the same surname, Miss Green. It's a traditional Buckinghamshire name, perhaps?'

'It is. But that's all I'd admit to sharing with that menace.' She gave a dramatic shiver. 'I only hope Grace's got the sense not to go to that place of his. Messing about in the woods would be too shocking altogether. Her mother would never recover if 'twere the case.'

Eleanor frowned. The house they had visited when talking to Willie Green's landlady was nowhere near any woods. 'I didn't realise he owned property. But, of course, I've really only heard his name in association with Solemn Jon.'

'Property! 'Tis a shack. No more than a lean-to, with nowt to lean against, and leaning at all angles, it probably is too. Course, how he came 'bout it will be another sorry tale, no doubt.'

'Perhaps he appreciates a little solitude in nature?'

The postmistress laughed drily. 'He's got other reasons I'd warrant. The beech woods are thickest there on the other side of Old Irving's Tor, so it's well hidden. It's also about halfway from Willie's lodgings and Grace's parents' house in Tyler's End Row, at the far edge of Little Buckford. That's all I'm saying.'

'Well, I'm sure Grace has a sensible head on her shoulders. Thank you for your help.' Eleanor went to go and then turned back. 'Oh, you wouldn't happen to know where I can find Grace, do you, Miss Green?'

The postmistress glanced at the clock above the counter. 'You'd do well to try Winsomes Tea Rooms in Chipstone in about an hour. She started as a waitress there not long back.'

'So helpful, thank you.' Eleanor smiled, feeling a wash of guilt at having misled her, even if it was only in the name of trying to catch a murderer.

'Good luck, m'lady,' said the postmistress. 'Mind, you probably don't need luck, do you? I mean, seeing as you're only going to see Grace to talk about…?'

'Fishing, Miss Green. I want to talk to her about fishing. Good morning.'

CHAPTER 35

'Good thing you thought to pack my stout boots, Clifford.'

Eleanor was leaning against the Rolls for balance as she laced up her walking shoes. A few feet away Clifford adjusted a black pouch strapped against his waistcoated torso before doing up his jacket's buttons. She raised an eyebrow.

'I have learned to expect the unexpected on our investigations, my lady.' Disappearing to the rear of the Rolls, he returned with a lead and a tennis ball. 'Master Gladstone will provide us with the perfect cover if we are discovered off the path should the need arise.' He gestured to the wooden stile leading into the woods. 'Shall we?'

As they entered the trees, Gladstone lolloped on ahead, periodically disappearing off the path, and eventually returning after Eleanor's repeated calling.

'I'm not so sure Mr Wilful here is the perfect cover, you know.' She swung herself over a fallen trunk blocking the vague indent in the forest floor Clifford seemed to be confidently following as a marked path. He lifted the bulldog over the obstacle.

'Master Gladstone will settle into a more measured pace presently, my lady. His exuberance is no match for his desire for Mrs Trotman's special liver treats.'

He patted his pocket and the bulldog's head jerked up.

After a short, but steep, climb, they emerged into a small clearing. A forest of waist-high, broad-leaved ferns had opportunely seized the sunlight and space and stood densely packed. After much grumbling, Gladstone allowed Clifford to put him on the lead.

'In case of adders, my lady. More commonly found basking in March when they have just surfaced from hibernation rather than in May. But Master Gladstone gave his lordship quite the scare on a walk not many years ago at this precise time of year.'

'Surely he wasn't trying to chase a snake? He'd have trouble catching a geriatric slow worm!'

'No, my lady, he was repeatedly licking the reptile the full length of its body.'

She stared at the bulldog, his tongue lolling out like a slice of pink ham. 'Really, I wonder sometimes if he was born with much of a brain at all.'

She looked across the lush thicket of ferns and reached her hand out to one of the tightly furled tips to uncurl it.

'Not advisable, my lady.' Clifford produced a pair of white butler gloves from his pocket and held them out to her. 'We may not be in South Africa, where I know you would be expertly informed on dangerous plants, but the fiddleheads of ferns here can cause a very uncomfortable rash.'

She shook her head. 'Snakes, dangerous plants, murder investigations. Clifford, please remind me why I have chosen to stay in Buckinghamshire?'

'Hopefully, because it has begun to feel like home, my lady.' He gave her a rare smile then pointed down the slope. 'I believe the most likely place a cabin might be concealed is in the next section of woods, just beyond. The rockier outcroppings of the tor itself end abruptly at the indistinct line about three hundred yards further on.'

'Let's go.' She forged ahead, grateful for the gloves as she brushed the ferns aside. 'You know I can't imagine Willie Green bothering to wade through all this greenery to visit his cabin though, can you?'

'Indeed not. He will most likely take the river path, whatever he says. If you remember when we were following the raft race, I observed that the eddies in the final section are caused by the rocks that fell from the Saxon fort. It once stood on that very spot behind us, the river being down the opposite side of the slope.'

She grunted, pulling her ankle from a set of fresh badger diggings. 'One day when murder is a dim and distant memory, do you think you might find the time to take me on a full tour of the area?'

'With sincere pleasure, my lady. With a most substantial picnic, of course.'

A glimmer of something metallic caught her eye.

'Clifford, could this cabin be made of that crinkly iron sheeting, do you suppose?'

'Indeed, it could.' He stepped up beside her and followed her gaze. 'Although, like yourself, I had imagined it to be constructed of wood.' He patted his jacket. 'Fear not, however, we shall have whatever is needed to gain entry.'

He gestured that they should take a slight detour left to drop down onto the path that ran close to the partially obscured cabin below them. Soon they were level with the structure, which was surprisingly more substantial than the postmistress had suggested. Skirting around the outside, they could see it was windowless, the only entry being via a thick wooden door. A small hole, likely where a door handle had once been, had been plugged with what looked like a layer of tar.

Clifford knocked loudly. They waited a few moments.

'It seems no one is at home. Or at least, answering,' he said.

Eleanor stared at the formidable metal chain looped through the door and the cabin's front panel. A solid-looking padlock hung from it.

'Surely there's no picklock made that will open that?'

Clifford shook his head and unbuttoned his jacket. He pulled the concealed pouch's black ribbon and it unrolled to reveal what she could only describe as a burglar's toolkit. Instead of going for the padlock, he took a swift look over his shoulder before running the chain through his gloved fingers.

'Ah, this one.'

He gripped the link and with a sharp jab, forced the wedge-shaped end of a mini crowbar into the hairline gap of the link.

Eleanor gasped as the chain swung apart.

'This is precisely why I feel I should be carrying bail money about my person when I'm with you! Honestly, Clifford, my curiosity eats me up when I see your more un-butler-like skills at work. I hope I find a few clues to what you and Uncle Byron really got up to when I finish going through his birthday album.'

'Suffice to say, you would only approve.' He gestured for her to stand back and slid his gloved hand round the door. Pulling it open a crack, he checked the interior. 'Definitely clear, my lady.'

She took the second, larger torch he slid out from the pouch and clicked it on.

Inside, the space felt damp and much cooler than outside. Something in the air made her wrinkle her nose and Gladstone sneezed violently. Her torch beam fell on two wooden crates.

'I can't see why Willie Green would hide these here unless he obtained them by dishonest means.'

Clifford swung his beam onto the crates.

'I agree, my lady. This seems rather like a smuggler's cave of misappropriated bounty to my mind.'

Eleanor swung her torch around the cabin. 'But not the lair of a murderer?'

While they were talking, Gladstone had disappeared under some old sacking in the far corner. A moment later he backed out, trying to drag an item with him.

'Leave it, boy!' she called, but the bulldog was not to be denied his prize. With a grunt he pulled the item clear of the sacking and out into the middle of the floor.

She shone her torch beam on the object, which in fact she could now see was actually made up of three items. Three items of dark green clothing.

She and Clifford stared at each other.

'Fishing hacksters,' they chorused.

CHAPTER 36

As Clifford eased the Rolls out onto the road, she ran her hand over Gladstone's head where it lay in her lap.

'You did well, boy.' But then her shoulders sagged. 'Dash it, Clifford. Not to pour a barrel of iced water on our breakthrough, but I've got that same intuitive feeling again that something is wrong with our thinking, which makes no sense. Mew saw a mysterious fisherman, whose clothing we've almost certainly just uncovered, pretending to fish right about the time and place Solemn Jon was murdered. Jack saw Willie Green creeping through the woods near the riverbank at around the same time, so it all seems to add up. Willie Green pretends to be ill on the day of the fair, he waits until everyone is at the start of the race, creeps through the woods to his cabin and dons his hacksters. Then he waits on the riverbank until he sees his opportunity and strikes.' She shook her head. 'It all fits, but my gut still tells me something is amiss.'

'Perhaps, my lady, but as well as an opportunity we've also established Mr Green had a motive. We know for certain he harbours an exceptionally ill will against Solemn Jon, albeit I admit for some yet unknown reason.'

'That's it!' Eleanor slapped the dashboard, making Gladstone jerk awake. 'That's exactly why I've got this feeling.'

Clifford took his eyes off the road to stare at her for a moment, then nodded slowly. 'Because Mr Green has repeatedly refused to divulge to us the reason for his enmity, even though Solemn Jon is now dead?'

'Precisely. Willie Green's face positively twisted with something close to hatred or disgust on both occasions. He hinted why, but it was so vague I can't remember his exact words.'

Clifford cleared his throat. 'I believe he said, "Don't matter now, does it? He won't pay for it. And if I try and shout 'bout it, I'll probably be run out of me house for being a liar by the entire, ahem, village."'

She gave an appreciative salute. 'A frighteningly good imitation. And memory too. But is that really his reason for not speaking up? Because he fears the villagers' reactions? Somehow I am largely unconvinced.'

'If I might add, now that I think about it, I am wholly unconvinced, my lady. Mr Green has a reputation for deliberately inciting controversy to court adverse opinion.'

'That does it!' She slapped the dashboard again. 'Turn around, please, Clifford.' Gladstone, who had just nodded off again, regarded her with as much indignation as he could muster through half-closed eyes. She patted him on the head by way of apology. 'Sorry, old chum, but it's time we found out the whole truth.'

Beyond the end of the vegetable garden, Eleanor could see that Mrs Jon was sitting on the wooden love bench staring into space as she cuddled her whiskery wolfhound. Taking a deep breath, Eleanor continued up the path. Patrick let out a short woof as she drew level.

'M'lady,' Maggie said with a start, 'what a surprise.'

'I'm sorry to call unannounced but I need to ask you something about Willie Green, if you are up to it?'

The woman's smile faded. 'Of course. But I haven't much good to say 'bout *him*.'

'I fully understand that, Maggie. But that's why I'm also so intrigued about why Solemn Jon kept Willie on even before, you know, the obituary came out. Was it purely out of compassion for a man who needed a job?'

Maggie nodded. 'My John often said as he wanted to give Willie a proper chance since he didn't hold with the brush folks tarred Willie with from birth. A bad father doesn't automatically mean a bad son, though most folk round here think so. And the truth is, Willie has a good set of hands. He's a natural with wood. And stone too, mind. That's a scarce combination. Especially since the war and that Spanish flu took so many of our menfolk.'

Ah! That partly explains why Solemn Jon put up with Willie Green, Ellie.

Maggie let out an angry snort. 'I'm just pleased my John can't read that awful obituary Willie wrote about him. It broke my heart and would have cut my John to the core after all he tried to do for that troublemaker. Course, all Willie did was deny he ever wrote it.'

Eleanor noted the woman had shrugged defensively as she finished speaking.

'I'm sorry to ask, Maggie, but do you know *why* Willie might have written something so scathing?'

'Because he's a bad 'un, after all!' Maggie's shoulders fell. 'M'lady, I'll tell you what folks don't know. My John told Willie a while back that when the day came for him to pass on, he would leave Willie the undertaking yard, *if* – she held up a finger – '*if* he'd earned it. My John told me he'd made that promise and said as I might have to be the one to decide if he was ever taken… sudden like.'

'And has Willie been to see you about taking over the yard?' Eleanor said, thinking she probably knew the answer.

'He has, alright,' Maggie managed through gritted teeth. 'The afternoon that obituary came out, can you *believe* it? Like I would have given him a bean after that. And then you saw what Willie did at my John's funeral? Disgraceful! I don't know what to do with the yard, but I do know Willie had better never so much as set foot in it again.'

Back in the Rolls, Clifford held out a paper bag of boiled toffees to Eleanor before easing the car off down the lane.

'A little sweetener after another sour conversation, my lady?'

She popped one into her mouth and nodded. 'But at least we now know why Willie Green was so angry with Solemn Jon after he died. If he hadn't known the decision would pass to Mrs Jon, I imagine he might have thought the yard was his the very morning after the May Fair concluded. However, I have the feeling that that was only half of what Mrs Jon is holding back.' She sighed. 'Never mind. Having found out why Willie Green was so angry with Solemn Jon *after* he died, we now need to find out why he was so angry with Solemn Jon *before* he died.'

CHAPTER 37

Winsomes Tea Rooms were a particular favourite of Eleanor's for they served the most sublime fruit cake in healthy country proportions. As they settled down at a quiet corner table, she looked around at the decor so at odds with the murder investigation they had come here to pursue. The cream wall sconces, and the silver thistle relief of the vanilla damask wallpaper infused the place with a smart, but cosy, charm.

Gladstone took up his usual position in teashops – sitting under the table waiting for a tasty titbit to come his way – while Eleanor made herself comfortable and Clifford made himself as comfortable as he could be sitting in the presence of his employer.

'Which one do you think is Grace, Clifford?' Eleanor whispered, staring between the six smartly aproned waitresses.

'The young lady with the dark-chestnut hair and strikingly large brown eyes,' he replied without looking up from winding his pocket watch.

'How can you be sure? Ah, but of course.' She gave a mock tut. 'Silly question! Men are adept at guessing who other men might pick as their girlfriends.'

He sighed. 'Actually, the young lady's name is written on her badge. Hence my having placed our order with her while you were taking a seat to ensure it was she who attended to our table.'

'Of course. I, er, noticed too.'

A moment later, a waitress with chestnut locks tied in a neat bun appeared with a tray. Eleanor's eyes lit up at the sight of double rations of fruit cake.

'Sir. Madam. Shall I pour for you?'

Eleanor hid her smile as Clifford stiffly kept his hands by his sides, knowing he always struggled to be served, that being his meticulously executed province.

'Yes, thank you, ah, Grace, I see it is from your name badge,' she said, avoiding Clifford's eye. As the waitress set everything on the table, Eleanor wasted no time. 'Tell me, Grace, how do you like working at Winsomes?'

The young girl looked surprised. 'Er, very well, thank you. 'Tis nice to be busy so the day doesn't drag, but Thursdays can be a bit quiet, as you can see.'

'Still, saves your feet for more entertaining activities after work, perhaps. Like dancing?'

Grace's face clouded. 'Oh, no, Father doesn't like me dancing, madam.'

'Well, I'm sure he has good reason. Yes, milk, thank you. Still, even though it can be very quiet in the country, I'm sure you find something interesting to do with your young man in your spare time?'

The waitress swallowed hard, the knife in her hand trembling. 'Small slice, madam?'

Eleanor tutted. 'Absolutely not, a disgracefully large one, please.'

As the waitress cut the fruit cake, the tablecloth rustled as Gladstone caught the smell. He loved fruit cake, or at least, he imagined he did. He was never allowed to eat it as currants and the like were, apparently, no good for him, but he was ever hopeful.

Eleanor waited until Grace had finished serving.

'Do enlighten me, Grace, as I'm relatively new to the area. What do you young couples find to do here?'

'Um, I don't know. I don't have a young man, madam.'

Eleanor took her cup and looked the waitress in the eye. 'How strange, I was sure someone mentioned your name and Mr William Green together only this morning.'

Grace's face betrayed her panic. She glanced around the room and then back at Eleanor and away.

'How… how did you know?' she mumbled.

'It's alright,' Eleanor said gently. 'I didn't mean to scare you, Grace. Your secret is safe with us.'

'Really, madam? 'Cos Father would kill him if he found out.'

'Don't worry, I promise this will go no further than the three of us.'

The girl looked unconvinced, but nodded anyway. 'If you say so, madam.'

Eleanor took a bite of fruit cake and swallowed. 'Absolutely delicious!' She wiped her mouth with a napkin. 'Now, Grace, what I want to know is how Mr Green manages to tear himself away from his favourite hobby for long enough to spend time with you?'

'Hobby, madam?' Grace frowned. 'Willie doesn't do much aside from working for Solemn Jon. Well, afore he passed over that was, 'course. And, well' – she coloured – 'sometimes Willie likes the odd drink in the pub.'

Eleanor sipped her tea and regarded the young girl over the rim of her cup.

'But you see, now, isn't that the strangest thing, Grace? Clifford here thought he had seen him fishing recently?'

'Fishing! My Willie sitting on the bank for hours, mucking about with maggots and cold, wet fish? More likely the ducks will grow teeth than Willie will spend a minute fishing.' She clapped a hand over her mouth. 'If you'll forgive me contradicting your…?'

'Butler, Grace. This is Mr Clifford, my butler.'

The young woman looked at Clifford in confusion and then back at Eleanor. 'If you say so, madam.'

'I do, Grace. And are you sure Mr Green didn't go fishing? It was on the day of the May Fair.'

The girl stiffened but said nothing.

'It was really fun at first, wasn't it, Grace?'

The girl looked blank. 'What was, madam?'

'The fair. And the raft race. You would have been there with your parents, perhaps?'

She nodded, staring at her hands.

'Or perhaps you also feigned illness, so you could stay at home and meet up with Mr Green?'

The waitress' face turned so pale for a moment Eleanor was afraid the young girl was going to faint.

'Are you alright? Do you need to sit down?'

She shook her head. 'No… no thank you, madam, I'm fine.'

Eleanor put down her cup. 'Grace, I know you're just trying to protect him, but it's a terrible idea.'

A sudden sullenness hardened the girl's pretty features.

'You wouldn't say that if you knew my father.'

'I appreciate that, but Mr Green may be in trouble and we are trying to help him. Now, for his sake, please be honest. Were you with him during the afternoon of the raft race?'

The waitress kept her eyes down, but nodded. 'I was.' She turned to Clifford. 'So you can't have seen him fishing, sir, not that he would, anyhow.'

Clifford nodded back. 'True, Grace. Unless, of course, it was before or after he met up with you. What time did you meet him?'

The waitress thought for a moment. 'Willie met me at about two o'clock and left before four, it would have been. We daren't risk any longer 'case my parents came home early from the fair.'

'Just two more quick questions,' Eleanor jumped in as Grace bobbed a curtsey and made to leave. 'Why would Mr Green have written those obituaries published in the *County Herald*, do you suppose?'

'No idea, madam. I don't read things like that. All I know is, Willie is real mad about it. Been going on for days, he has. Especially with the police pestering him about them.'

'The first obituary was for Solemn Jon. Do you know why Mr Green had a falling out with him?'

The waitress shrugged. 'All Willie said was he was tired of always being the underdog. He'd finished his apprenticeship and wanted to do more. But Solemn Jon said as he'd never loosen the reins on the business, not until he had no choice because he'd moved on to the next world. But then' – she frowned as if remembering a difficult conversation – 'then Willie was furious when Solemn Jon did pass on.'

'Why?'

'I don't know if it were true, but he said as how Solemn Jon had promised to leave him his yard when he died, but Solemn Jon had double-crossed him, or summat. He was in such a fury. I didn't understand half of what he said.' She coloured again. 'But he can be like that after a few. I— Oh, sorry, madam, I've got to go.'

Over the young girl's shoulder, Eleanor could see the manageress waving at their table, a stern look on her face.

'One last quick question, Grace. You've told us why Mr Green was angry at Solemn Jon after he died. But the truth is, he was also angry about something Solemn Jon did *before* he died, wasn't he?'

The waitress tore her gaze away from her manageress. 'Yes, madam, he were. He said Solemn Jon had done summat wrong. But he never said what. Now, I really need to go or I'll get into trouble.'

Eleanor leaned back in her seat. 'Off you go, Grace, and please keep this conversation between you and me. I wouldn't even tell Mr Green, for his own good. And kindly inform your manageress I wouldn't let you go because I was praising how wonderful the food and service is.'

As Grace hurried off, Eleanor smiled at the manageress and waved. Under the table, Gladstone sighed and resigned himself to a fruit cake-less afternoon. Eleanor turned back to Clifford.

'Dash it, it seems we still don't know the one thing we came here for.'

He nodded. 'However, the young lady has confirmed what Mrs Jon told you earlier about why Mr Green believed he'd been double-crossed.'

'True.'

'And she has also confirmed Mr Green's statement that he was with her that afternoon.'

'Although he still had time to kill Solemn Jon afterwards, remember.'

'True, again, my lady. I would venture the opinion that what we've now learned clears, and at the same time, muddies the case against Mr Green.'

She reluctantly put down the piece of fruit cake she was about to eat.

'Go ahead.'

He cleared his throat. 'It seems there are two separate matters here. One, Mr Green believed Solemn Jon went back on his word, which would be a motive for murder. Except it seems Mr Green didn't learn of what he perceives as a breach of trust until *after* Solemn Jon's death.'

She nodded. 'And the second matter?'

'Mr Green seemed to be under the impression that he had some information that Solemn Jon would rather keep hidden. A secret which, if I remember correctly, even Mr Green found reprehensible, which *might* be a motive for murder as Mr Green learned of it *before* Solemn Jon died.'

'Mmm, except, even though Solemn Jon is now dead, Willie Green won't confess what that secret is.' She shook her head. 'It's totally ridiculous, but there's a part of me that wishes he was in the clear. But that's largely your fault, Clifford.'

He raised a questioning brow.

'Because of what you said about the probable reason Willie craves negative attention. You see, he suddenly feels rather tragic.'

He gave a discreet cough. 'Someone passing at the hand of another is perhaps a greater tragedy, my lady? If you will forgive my offering an opinion.'

'You're right, unquestionably. And there's no avoiding the fact that the timings Grace gave us would have given Willie Green time to dispatch poor Solemn Jon. We found his body just after four thirty and she said Willie Green left her around four.'

Clifford looked thoughtful.

'What have I missed?' she said.

'It merely struck me that Mr Green chose a peculiar window of opportunity to murder Solemn Jon, if indeed he did.'

She thought over what they'd talked about.

'Nope! I can't work out why.'

'Because, my lady, he could have fabricated a believable alibi, but didn't. He could have murdered him when no one was around, say at his yard. Then he could have gone to, perhaps, a public house. It would have been hard to determine exactly when Solemn Jon had died as there would have been no witnesses and Mr Green would have had an alibi, however imperfect. Instead he chose to commit the murder at a time when the body would inevitably be found almost immediately—'

'Having visited a lady he refuses to admit he is linked to—'

'And also one whom he failed to prime with a story in case she was interrogated that would place him at her house at the time of the killing.'

Eleanor nodded slowly. 'You're right. But' – she sighed and shook her head again – 'the fishing clothing, Clifford! We've just found them in his cabin. Why would a man who never fishes have stowed fishing gear in a hidden cabin in the woods?'

'True, but putting that aside for the moment, my lady, there is another conundrum. Why would Mr Green write an obituary that would almost certainly mean he would fail to inherit Solemn Jon's yard? There was no legal agreement in writing anyone has mentioned. Therefore the yard and business would automatically pass to Solemn Jon's wife on his death.'

'And Willie Green must have known that.'

'Precisely. So why do something that is guaranteed to enrage the only person who has the power to deny him what he believes is rightfully his?'

Eleanor groaned and rubbed her face with her hands.

'And there's the further conundrum of why then write another obituary?'

It was Clifford's turn to nod. 'Indeed, why write a second obituary for a person with whom it appears he cannot possibly have had a connection?'

'Exactly. Rankin was highly disparaging of anyone outside of his class. He was close to incensed that "commoners", as he referred to poor Solemn Jon, were even being discussed at the Langham luncheon. He would never have associated with the likes of Willie Green. So the answer to your question is the biggest mystery so far.'

'Although, my lady, having unwelcomely wandered into the mind of Mr Green while recalling his words a moment ago, the explanation may have hit me.'

'Explain.'

'He thrives on attention, albeit deliberately created negative attention. He believes no one has given him a chance since birth. Indeed, Mrs Jon told you that she believed he was tarred with the same brush as his father the minute he was born. At Chipstone Police Station, we witnessed Sergeant Brice's disgusted reaction when he confronted him over having written the obituary. Would it not be reasonable to expect that was only the tip of the iceberg in terms of the disapprobation Mr Green will have delighted in receiving after the second obituary?'

'So he seized on the opportunity of Rankin's death to court more attention and criticism, you mean? That sounds like the workings of a madman.'

Clifford let out a long breath. 'Or a man beseeching the world that he be noticed for something. Good or bad.'

'Maybe.' She picked up the last piece of fruit cake and chewed it thoughtfully and then sighed. 'But does that make him a killer?'

In the Rolls, Eleanor turned to Clifford. 'You know, I—'

'Sorry, my lady, a moment, please.'

She blinked as he halted the Rolls only yards from the tea rooms they'd just left. A few seconds later she realised why as Grace tapped on her window. She looked breathless.

'I'm so sorry, madam. I mean, m'lady. One of the other waitresses told me who you are.'

Eleanor smiled at the girl. 'That's alright, Grace. But I'm sure you didn't run out here and risk your manageress' wrath again just to apologise for that, did you?'

The girl glanced around and lowered her voice and eyes. 'I knows as how you aren't like the other… ladies and gentlemen, m'lady. You helps ordinary people. People like me, and… Willie. You see, I didn't want to say before, but Willie told me something about Solemn Jon's secret and I told him to keep his mouth shut. Told him people like him and me daren't go saying things 'bout titled folk.'

She glanced back at the tea rooms and Eleanor saw the manageress standing at the door glaring in her direction.

'Grace!' The young girl spun back round to face her. 'If Mr Green is innocent of any wrongdoing, then you need to tell me what you know. *Now*.'

The girl's words rushed out. 'Willie said that Solemn Jon had done something that if it was found out would turn folk against him. And send him to gaol. Or worse.'

Eleanor's brain raced. *What could Solemn Jon have done, Ellie, that would get him a prison sentence? Or the noose? And why would he do such a thing?*

'Grace, did Mr Green say why Solemn Jon did what he did? Was he… paid by someone?'

The girl nodded and half-turned towards the furiously beckoning manageress. Eleanor felt the opportunity slipping through her fingers.

She rapped on the Roll's door. 'Grace!' The girl stopped hesitantly. 'Who paid Solemn Jon to do such a terrible thing?'

The girl leaned in the window and whispered a name before hurrying off back to the tea room.

As they continued their interrupted journey home, Eleanor's brain whirled. *Why, Ellie? Why?*

CHAPTER 38

The earlier threat of rain had now materialised, adding a gloomy grey pall to the already overcast proceedings. Eleanor turned away from the entrance to the baroque, monolithic mansion that was Rankin Hall. It reminded her of a soulless garrison in desperate need of attention. Telltale patches of discoloured stone showed damp had taken hold and the once sharply detailed features of the carvings around the windows and gargoyles along the roofline looked rounded, even crumbling in parts.

Vehicles filled the extensive driveway, the entourage returning from Lord Rankin's funeral now stepping elegantly from the doors held open by a line of smartly suited servants. The ladies mounted the entrance steps, a sea of black. Feathered hats and velvet capes trimmed with ebony furs over long satin skirts, the gentlemen dressed in top hats and coats far too warm even for such a cloudy day.

She hung back, staring up at the imposing columned mausoleum on the hill opposite where she'd endured a singularly soulless and stilted hour's service. Clifford appeared, standing the respectful distance behind her that was de rigueur at such a formal event. She turned her head slightly and spoke in a low voice.

'I can't imagine living my whole life in the shadow of the place I would eventually be buried in. Why would you make that your view on rising and opening the curtains each morning?'

'I really couldn't say, my lady.'

'Well, thank goodness Uncle Byron didn't have the desire to build a similar eyesore.'

He gave a discreet cough. 'His lordship loved the view from Henley Hall just as it is. He never felt the need to mar it by ensuring every member of the population within thirty miles would remember his position in society even after his death.'

'Ah!' She smiled, understanding this was an oblique answer to her first question. She nodded to her good friends, Lord and Lady Fenwick-Langham, as they made their way up the entrance steps. As she did, a man with stiff grey hair and a thick sculpted beard climbing out of a black Rolls caught her eye.

'Clifford!' she hissed over her shoulder. 'See him? He was at Pendle's hound trailing meet.'

'That is Sir Gordon Tretheway, my lady. The gentleman is a wealthy, self-made banker.'

Hmm, rising to prominence in the financial world with no family connection, Ellie. Times are changing.

Clifford lowered his voice. 'Mr Tretheway is well known to gamble, my lady. Hence his being at the hound trailing event. In fact, I wonder if it was he who placed the not inconsiderable sum of two hundred and fifty pounds on one of Mr Pendle's dogs to win? Few others would have had the resources for such a wager.'

'Possibly.' She frowned. 'Didn't whoever place that bet lose, though?'

'Indeed. Solemn Jon's Patrick won.'

'Interesting. I wonder what sort of man he is? Maybe one to harbour a grudge?'

Clifford dropped his voice even lower. 'Sir Tretheway is known unofficially for having a predilection for what one might tactfully describe as "higher-risk investment options", my lady.'

Her brows rose. 'You mean crooked?' she whispered.

'That term has been mentioned in the same breath as his name on several occasions. However, he is far too shrewd for anything illegal to have been linked to him directly.'

'I see.' She watched him mount the steps and go inside. 'Well, I'd best mingle.'

'I shall await your return.'

'Dash it, Clifford. You mean you can't even come in and pay your respects from a suitable distance? I was rather hoping you could be my second pair of eyes and ears.'

'And so I shall. Among the staff, as is eminently more acceptable at such an event. And, I would suggest, more useful for our investigations.'

She nodded. 'Good call. I feel quite the cad in one way. I know I'm genuinely here to pay my respects, but it does feel wrong prying at the same time.'

'Not, my lady, when your "prying" could reveal that the person whose funeral it is, may, in fact, have been murdered.'

'Mmm. Well, let's not set off with a biased view. I'm keeping an open mind about Rankin's death, even though it was his name that Grace gave us.'

'Well said, my lady.'

She shook her head. 'I still can't believe that Solemn Jon was involved in some underhand business and that *Lord Rankin* paid him for it.'

'And yet, that is what we were told at the tea rooms – or just outside them.'

'I know. And I believe Grace.'

'As do I, although she was only recounting what Mr Green had told her, the veracity of which may be in doubt. Now, I had better make myself scarce, my lady.'

And with that, he started off around the back of the house to the servants' entrance while Eleanor took a deep breath and followed Sir Tretheway up the steps.

*

Inside the austere marbled floored and columned great hall, conversation seemed to have taken second preference to the genteel sipping of champagne and nibbling on canapés. Eleanor glanced around, noting gaps in the endless paintings on the oak-panelled walls and several unoccupied plinths. *Looks like someone has been selling off the family heirlooms, Ellie.* She looked for Tretheway, figuring that he might be just the sort to eat a few canapés and run.

'Marchioness, your chauffeur has delivered your stole as requested,' the butler said to a lady in her early to mid sixties to Eleanor's left.

Taking the fox fur without acknowledging him, she turned to Eleanor.

'Standing in the cold for such a long hour, I shall take forever to warm up.'

Eleanor hid a smile at the woman's lack of formal greeting.

'The breeze did get up rather, Lady Lambourne, but I suppose that's inevitable at the top of such a tall hill. But I think all funerals make one feel cold. Something to do with the mournful atmosphere of it all, perhaps?'

The marchioness eyed her wryly. 'Mournful? My dear girl, you must have attended a different service to the one I have just stood through. All I witnessed was the begrudging paying of insincere respects and a lot of crocodile tears.'

Eleanor contained her surprise at the woman's candour.

'These things are never easy. My sincere condolences, of course.'

'Thank you, but hardly necessary. I, like most, am here out of respect for the wonderful man who was Evander's father, God rest his soul.'

'I know you were a long-standing family friend, Lady Lambourne. You must have known Evander, I mean Lord Rankin, much better than I. We were fairly recent acquaintances.'

'I know, Lady Swift. A lucky escape on your part.'

Eleanor started. Before she could reply, she felt a bear paw on her shoulder and the tickle of a handlebar moustache against her cheek.

'Eleanor, old fruit!' Lord Langham's voice boomed in her ear, turning heads all round the room.

'Hello, Harold.' She was pleased to see him despite her eagerness for answers to the questions the marchioness' comment had thrown up. She hid a smile as she caught sight of his favourite plum cardigan poking out from the sombre funeral attire his wife had no doubt insisted he pour his portly frame into. 'Where's Augusta?'

Lord Langham flapped a hand.

'Oh, you know, effortlessly gliding around the room, doing and saying the right thing to all the right people. Sent me over here to stop me unwittingly stamping my size elevens into some poor family member's grief.' He scooped three champagne flutes from the tray of a hovering waiter, before handing them one each.

'A thin turn out,' the marchioness said.

He coughed through a glug of champagne. 'I'd noticed too. Bit of a bad show, old girl.'

He swept his glass in an arc, liberally spilling most of the contents. 'Not so much as a whiff of a close relly turned up. Poor old Rankin, what.'

'Oh, do try to keep up,' said the marchioness. 'Evander had no more close relatives after his father passed away in March.' Eleanor was burning to ask, but the woman pre-empted her. 'So, all of this' – she waved her champagne flute around the room as Lord Langham had – 'reverts to the crown. And to think of all that Evander's father did to keep it in the family! A disgraceful ending.'

Harold twirled his whiskers thoughtfully. 'Tricky with no heir, of course.'

Eleanor's thoughts whirled. *So no one inherits all this after Rankin's death, Ellie? If he was murdered, you'll have to look elsewhere for a motive. Maybe it was just an accident that killed him after all?* Then another thought struck her. *Maybe that's why he was in such a hurry to marry you, Ellie? He needed a wife to sire an heir.* Feeling quite unwell at the idea, she downed the rest of her glass in one gulp.

Lord Langham nodded approvingly and followed suit, placing his empty glass on the tray of a passing waiter.

'Excuse me, ladies, but I'd better check in with Augusta.' With an exaggerated bow, he ambled off.

Eleanor turned to the marchioness. 'So, excuse me asking but were you and… Evander close?'

You know they weren't, Ellie. Well, not on the surface, anyway. But at the Langhams' they both seemed to deny having heard of Solemn Jon, yet they both jumped at his name. Why?

The marchioness eyed her coldly. 'No, I wouldn't say "close". He was an acquired taste, as you no doubt discovered.'

For some reason, Eleanor felt she needed to stand up for the dead. 'Even the rarest of tastes have a few ardent fans, I usually find.'

The marchioness laughed drily. 'Look around. There are no friends here, not of Evander's, for a man like that has none. The old guard are here purely out of respect for the family name, as I am. Now, if you will excuse me.'

Eleanor stepped in front of her. The marchioness stopped in surprise.

'Just before you go, Lady Lambourne, what did you mean earlier by "I had a lucky escape?"'

'I thought that was obvious, Lady Swift. Evander had been spreading the "news" that you and he were courting.' At Eleanor's gasp, she held up a hand. 'I, for one, having heard of your… independent spirit, was not fooled for a moment. Obviously, he was trying to ensnare you into marriage.' She looked Eleanor up and down, an amused smile playing coldly around her lips. 'I assume, I was correct? That you had no intention of marrying a man like Evander?'

So she doesn't know about Rankin blackmailing you, Ellie! Just about the marriage, thank goodness.

At that moment Tretheway strode past and collared a slim younger man standing alone by the fireplace. She noted the marchioness' expression harden as he passed.

'Sir Graham Trethelman?' Eleanor asked, deliberately getting his name wrong.

'Gordon Tretheway. And definitely not one who deserves to be addressed as "sir" . Banker. New money,' she said as if that in itself was an insult.

'Oh, I see. A banker? Perhaps his twin is also here?' Eleanor pretended to look around the room.

The marchioness stared at her quizzically. 'Good grief, one Tretheway is one too many. Why on earth would you think he had a twin?'

'Only because I saw his exact double at a…' She glanced over her shoulder theatrically and lowered her voice. 'At a dog-racing event I inadvertently stumbled across on a walk. But it was most definitely a race where bets were being made. Not something Sir Tretheway would be at, I'm sure.'

'That is precisely why he would have been there.' Her tone dripped acid. 'Once a gambler, always one, however much one tries to legitimise oneself in the eyes of the world. Only if you are going to gamble, then make sure you win. The old fool always has been a loser. Hence' – she gestured over at the man Tretheway was talking earnestly to by the fireplace – 'he is always on the hunt for another fool to invest in his unscrupulous schemes.' She tutted and shook her head. 'Tretheway is one of the few here who knew Evander well, for one fool of a gambler can smell out another a mile away.'

'Evander used to gamble?' Eleanor said.

'Why wouldn't he? Like Tretheway, he has, or had, no moral fibre.' She locked her gaze on Eleanor's. 'When you're my age, trust me, you too will have long-tired of keeping quiet and saying the right thing.'

'I'm not sure I'm that good at it now.'

The marchioness smiled thinly. 'So I've heard.'

The Rankin's butler appeared at Eleanor's elbow. He held out a small silver tray.

'Please excuse me interrupting, but there is a note for you, m'lady.'

She took the folded note and opened it. Keeping her face neutral, she pocketed it and turned to the marchioness.

'It has been most enlightening meeting you again, Lady Lambourne, but now, I must go. I'm rather needed elsewhere.'

CHAPTER 39

'Ah, now this is a surprising way to introduce yourself.' Eleanor stepped into the small private drawing room and turned back to the butler. 'Please leave the door open, thank you.'

He nodded and left them alone, but the man leaning against the arm of the leather Chesterfield unfolded his arms and marched past her to close the door with his foot. Having done so, he spun on his heel to face her.

'Lady Swift, what a pleasure.'

Tretheway! What does he want, Ellie? She looked at the closed door and then back at him.

'Perhaps, it is, Sir Gordon. Although I confess to wondering why you would wish to make my acquaintance in a room away from the main gathering? And with the door closed? We ladies need to be careful with our reputation, you know.'

'Oh, but that is precisely why I have ensured we are not over-heard. Please take a seat.'

She stiffened. 'I'm fine, thank you. Whatever you wish to say will be sufficiently well received standing up.'

Tretheway laughed darkly, his thick moustache and beard masking that his mouth had even opened. 'And I thought Evander was mad, but it appears for once, I might have been wrong.' He resumed his pose against the arm of the settee. 'Shame he isn't with us any more to hear me say so.'

Enough of this, Ellie, who does he think he is?

'Sir Gordon, I understood that you were close with Evander, at least in business terms?'

'You really shouldn't listen to tattle, Lady Swift.' He cocked his head. 'Harriet Lambourne has hated me for years. Whatever venom she has just poured in your ears is all lies, I can assure you.'

'Perhaps, but I came here to pay my respects to Evander, not to become embroiled in whatever disagreements have passed between those who knew him.'

'Maybe. But I don't think that is the only reason you are here.'

What is he talking about, Ellie? 'Really? Well, to date, our conversation has not inspired me to stay and continue. Was there something particular you wished to discuss?'

'All in good time. I like to size up my investments.'

'Your what!?'

'You heard. Now, be a good girl and don't pull out the theatrical card, I have limited patience and female hysterics I find beyond the pale.'

Eleanor bit back a sharp retort and managed a dignified shake of the head instead.

'Then let me save you the trouble of explaining your latest investment scheme. I am not in the market for such a money matter presently. Thank you.'

There was that grim laugh again. 'Oh, but that's because you haven't heard what it is.'

'Does it involve dog racing, Sir Gordon?' His eyes betrayed his surprise. 'Because much as I was fond of Solemn Jon and still am of his wolfhound, Patrick, hound trailing isn't quite my scene. Perhaps Mr Pendle might be interested, however?'

'Pendle!' Tretheway spat. 'If he wasn't in my pocket, I'd swear he fixed that race with that bandy-legged outsider, Patrick.'

Eleanor nodded. 'Two hundred and fifty pounds is a lot for anyone to lose, I agree. It might make some men quite murderous.'

He opened his mouth to speak, but she carried on. 'Oh, don't worry, I'm sure Mr Pendle probably didn't mean to let slip how much you lost.'

Tretheway's eyes narrowed. 'That sounds like bluff, Lady Swift. Why would Pendle have told you that was me?'

'Actually, he didn't, Sir Gordon. But you just did. Evander did, however, inform me of his somewhat unorthodox financial dealings with you.'

'What did he tell you?' he snapped. 'The fool! And to think I believed he was immune to feminine guile.'

She shook her head. 'Evander had no interest in my guile. The only attraction he saw was in my money. Not that it is any of your business.'

He grinned and folded his arms. 'Perhaps it is, though?'

Where on earth is he going with this, Ellie? She racked her brain, then clicked her fingers.

'Evander owed you money, didn't he?'

'A great deal, yes.'

'And since his estate is to revert to the crown, you have no means of collecting on the debt?'

'Actually, that is not quite the case. You see, the secret you think is safe, unfortunately isn't.'

Eleanor's stomach filled with icy dread.

He laughed mirthlessly. 'That's right. I know that your precious uncle put a substantial sum into a highly *illegal* scheme.'

'That seems extremely unlikely,' she said through gritted teeth. 'Unless it was a scheme you initiated, of course.'

He let out a snort. 'My dear woman, Evander would have taken you as his wife, whatever your feelings on the matter. We men of the world get what we want, after all. So now I'm collecting his debt from *you*, his would-be widow.'

This is preposterous! It's time to call his bluff, Ellie.

'Sir Gordon, I have no intention of succumbing to your under-hand ways to redeem Evander's debt.' She turned and pulled open the door. 'If indeed he even had one with you.'

'Oh, he most definitely did. As do you now.' He smoothed his hand over his beard. 'It really would be such a shame for the world to learn what a financial rogue Byron Henley was. But that decision rests entirely with you, Lady Swift.'

Her heart quickened. *What does he know, Ellie? Probably nothing.* His next words, however, proved her wrong.

'I now have in my possession those very documents Evander was doubtlessly using to persuade you to be his wife. My requirements to keep your uncle's name out of the scandal sheets is much more palatable, though. You will simply pay me the money Evander owed me. In manageable monthly payments, of course. I'm not greedy.'

Without a word she closed the door behind her and bumped into Clifford who had just arrived outside. He looked her over in concern as he turned and kept pace with her angry march towards the main hall.

'My lady, Houghton, the butler, has just informed me where you were. Hence my hurrying to check on you. Especially after you noted Sir Tretheway had been with Mr Pendle. Mistakenly, I had assumed prudence would be your watchword.'

They rounded the last corner and Clifford nodded to the footman to open the double entrance doors. Eleanor paused outside on the top step.

'I might have invited Prudence along if she weren't such a hindrance, and we weren't deep in the mire of needing to extract information from a collection of unscrupulous brutes!'

'My lady, that is surely the very occasion to defer to caution and good sense.'

She sneezed as a line of dust drifted down onto the sleeve of her coat. 'Thank you for the lecture but I am still in one piece as you can—'

The crash of masonry hitting the ground next to her cut her short. In the stunned silence that followed, a cloud of dust filled the air. She was aware of several people running towards her and someone shouting, but she couldn't distinguish the words above the sound of her wildly beating heart. She looked around in shock. Pieces of stone gargoyle lay scattered over the front step. She felt her hands shaking. *Get a grip, Ellie. It missed you. But Clifford?*

A calm voice came through the dust.

'Are you alright, my lady?'

She breathed a sigh of relief.

CHAPTER 40

'Clifford, I really appreciate your solicitude, but it doesn't warrant this level of fussing. The gargoyle missed me – and you, thankfully – after all.'

'Counteracting the effects of shock and "fussing" are far from the same thing, my lady.' He scanned her face, then stepped back to close the door. While he did, she tried to gain an extra inch from the bulldog hogging most of the chaise longue, but Gladstone ignored her and pretended to be asleep.

'Master Gladstone. Down!' Clifford said, pointing to the thick pile rug. Getting nothing more than a mutinous look, he pulled a small tin from his pocket and shook it. With a leap that almost pushed Eleanor off as well, the bulldog launched himself at Clifford's feet, ready to receive his most favourite treat of all, liver biscuits.

'Lie down!'

'Me or Gladstone?' Eleanor said, trying to ease his concern with humour.

'Ideally both, my lady, but I fear one is more erroneously convinced of their physical resilience than the other.'

She pouted. 'Gladstone at least got an incentive.'

Clifford turned back towards the door and busied himself at the long, low mahogany table.

'Warmed brandy? Freshly baked Victoria rhubarb and pear turnovers?'

'That's more like it! Now, I can't deny the whole incident shook me up at the time, but—'

He turned and looked at her pointedly.

'Okay, maybe I am still a teensy bit shook up. But let's put the episode with the falling gargoyle to one side for the moment. Whether it was purely a case of shoddy masonry or a deliberate attempt to… well…' For a moment she had a flashback to standing on the front step and then the sound of crashing masonry and for a split second, the strange sensation of not knowing if she was still quite alive or not. She shook the memory out of her head. 'As I said, let's move on and go through what we both learned at Rankin Hall. Because, whatever else, it seems that we have found another link between Rankin and Solemn Jon, however tenuous.'

He hesitated, and then at her look nodded resignedly. 'As you wish, my lady. You are correct. Sir Tretheway.'

'Exactly! We saw him at Pendle's racecourse and we know Pendle was desperate to acquire Solemn Jon's dog Patrick to shore up his crumbling racing business. And he admitted that Rankin invested in his schemes…' She frowned. 'Although, that doesn't lead to any direct connection with Solemn Jon, does it?'

This time, Clifford shook his head. 'Not that springs to mind, my lady. However, it is a strong *indirect* association, and may become a *direct* one as our investigation progresses.'

'I hope so! That Tretheway character is one of the most odious creatures I've ever met. At least Rankin was just arrogant and manipulative. But somehow Tretheway using me on the back of Rankin's blackmailing scheme feels even worse. It's so—'

'Spineless, my lady. However, I once again beg that you rest and leave the investigation until at least tomorrow. Perhaps a quiet afternoon enjoying' – he gestured to the other item he had brought in – 'his lordship's birthday album.'

'Not a chance! I'm fine. I'll prove it to you by devouring all of these absolutely sublime pastries.'

'My lady, that will not prove anything to me. You have the most robust appetite I have ever come across, if you will forgive my observation.'

She flapped a hand. 'Better that than you tripping over a mistress who's forever fainting or having an attack of the vapours at the merest whiff of danger. So, no more talk of pausing our much-needed discussion. Admittedly, we are unfortunately back where we were when Rankin threatened to expose Uncle Byron's financial secret.'

He topped up her coffee with a quiet cough.

'Not exactly in the same position, my lady. Sir Tretheway merely requires money, albeit a large, but so far, undisclosed sum.'

She shook her head. 'You and I know very well that once a vulture like Tretheway gets his claws into me, he'll never let go. He'll bleed me dry.'

'Unfortunately, too true, my lady. But Lord Rankin required marriage. It is not my place to say, but I believe there is a particular gentleman who would think his death a vast improvement on the previous position.'

'Seldon, do you mean? Slow right down. In fact, no, stop, altogether. He isn't even speaking to me at the moment.'

'Most regrettable, as you need to ask for his help.'

She stopped mid-bite. 'What? Now look here, I absolutely do not.' She bit into the pastry and chewed indignantly. 'Besides, why would I ask for his help in trying to solve this case? He not only doesn't believe there is one, he also expressly forbade me to carry on investigating it on pain of...' She blushed. 'Well, he didn't state what in exact detail, but I got the message.'

'Undoubtedly, my lady. However, I repeat my belief that you need to seek Chief Inspector Seldon's help. Your safety was seriously threatened today. Almost with an end result I am unable to contemplate.'

She sighed. 'As I said, I appreciate your solicitude. And you could have been injured too, I'm very aware of that. But when Uncle Byron asked you to look after me, he knew you couldn't lock me in a box.' She winked. 'Much as I know you wish you could when I'm driving you mad.'

But he shook his head, clearly too concerned to join in with her teasing. 'My lady, we have been in these kinds of situations before. All too often, in fact. But no one has ever got so close before to… well, frankly, killing you. And never without my being alert to the threat.'

She scrunched her eyes tight. 'There's not just the teeniest chance it could have been an accident? I mean, Rankin's butler and the army of footmen who poured out all concluded it was an unfortunate, but blameless, case of falling masonry. A poorly maintained building is likely to let go of the odd gargoyle at limited notice, wouldn't you say?'

His silence was answer enough.

She sighed. 'Alright, I give in. I promise I'll think about calling Seldon. For now, let's focus again on how Tretheway could be linked to both deaths. And also what to do about his threat of blackmail. It's perhaps weighing more heavily on my mind than I'd care to admit.'

He bowed. 'Thank you, my lady. And on the matter of Sir Tretheway's attempted blackmailing, it occurs to me that I did not manage to ask at my butlers' club regarding information on Lord Rankin before his demise. However—'

Eleanor leaned forward eagerly. 'You might be able to ask there about Tretheway instead? Brilliant! Maybe you could uncover not only something that we can use to thwart his blackmailing, but also something concerning our investigation. Although tenuous, his is the only name we can link to both Solemn Jon and Rankin, as we said. Although in the case of Rankin's death, if Rankin *was* a source of income to him and still owed him money, as Tretheway said, why would Tretheway kill him? I mean, that's rather like killing the goose that lays the golden eggs, isn't it?'

'It is indeed, my lady. Also, as he was attempting to blackmail you in the place of Lord Rankin, why would he have someone drop several hundredweight of masonry on your head? Or even close by?'

'True, Clifford.'

'If I may ask, my lady, who else did you speak to at Rankin Hall?'

'Oh, yes, a most interesting fish. Lady Lambourne. We met before at the Langhams' luncheon.'

'Lady Lambourne, Marchioness of Wendlebury? Known for her sharp intellect and, ahem, tongue.'

'That's the one. She was certainly cutting about Rankin. And at his funeral, of all places. There was clearly no love lost between them. She was no better at the luncheon, actually. However, when I was talking to her, aside from constantly highlighting Rankin's faults compared to his father, she didn't reveal any motive she would have for murdering him. And she does rely on a walking cane so that might be rather a hindrance.'

Clifford gave a discreet cough. 'It is for show only, my lady. The elaborate silver handle is modelled on the foxhound in the Lambourne coat of arms.'

'Ah! I thought it was a spaniel. But that makes sense as she seemed as fit as a case of fiddles. She was also as sniffy about people outside of her class as Rankin. And she definitely despises Tretheway as much for his gambling habit as his audacity to rise above his station.' She smiled as her bulldog stared up at Clifford with imploring eyes.

He tutted. 'Yes, Master Gladstone. Her ladyship is sufficiently recovered to share, but not fight for, half the chaise longue.'

She waited while he helped up the bulldog. Gladstone turned in a circle and settled against her side.

'Clifford, what about your enquiries though? Maybe you discovered something that proves a link between Lady Lambourne and Solemn Jon?'

His hand strayed to his perfectly aligned black tie. 'As you say, my lady, any link would be highly unlikely.'

'Mind you, at the Langhams' lunch when Solemn Jon's name was first mentioned, she recoiled as if someone had bitten her. But then she acted as if she'd never heard the name before. Still, it might have been my imagination.'

'Possibly, my lady. Putting Lady Lambourne aside for the moment, which other line of thought might we pursue, do you suggest?'

'Well… I hadn't thought of it quite so clearly before. But after the matter of, erm, falling masonry on the front step at Rankin Hall, it feels a whole lot more likely that Rankin *was* murdered.'

He gave a reluctant nod. 'Hence my heightened concern for you, my lady. It occurred to me that since Lord Rankin died so soon after you left him that afternoon, the murderer was possibly shadowing you both.'

'You mean "probably", don't you? And I know what you said about William III and others who have died when their horse tripped over a molehill. But it feels horribly implausible that Rankin would have fallen from Arion. Even though he is the tallest, and haughtiest horse I've ever seen, in motion it was almost hard to tell where Rankin ended and Arion began. They were like one sleek, powerful, homogenous being, not rider and steed.'

'Hence the animal's name.' At her questioning look, he continued. 'In Greek mythology, Arion is a winged horse of unimaginable and unmatchable speed, who it was said could speak. Indeed, Homer referred to him in the *Iliad*, "No man thenceforth shall reach, or if he reach, shall pass thee by." In the legend, however, the horse is also immortal.'

'Unlike Rankin.'

'Unlike us all.'

'Yes, I hear you,' she said quietly. 'And one thing is for sure. Whoever we're looking for must know Rankin Hall and the estate well enough. At least to gain entrance.'

Clifford nodded slowly. 'Possibly, my lady. However, it is hard, as you know yourself, to keep intruders out of such a large estate. Especially as many walls on the Rankin estate are in disrepair. However, it is another matter entirely to gain access to the roof of Rankin Hall.'

She nodded. 'Absolutely. Which means it was probably one of the guests. Or servants. Unfortunately, that doesn't narrow the field that much! However, it seems unlikely Willie Green or Pendle could have gained access to the roof.'

'Although, my lady, Sir Gordon Tretheway obviously knows Rankin Hall and could have bribed a servant to allow Pendle access, seeing as we believe they are in cahoots, certainly in the matter of getting their hands on Patrick.'

'Well, whoever pushed that gargoyle off the roof, *if* it was pushed, must be the same person that killed Rankin. It's too much of a coincidence that I was there asking discreet questions about his death just before it happened.'

His inscrutable expression faltered almost imperceptibly.

'I was discreet! Well, as discreet as I'm able.'

Clifford frowned, then closed his eyes for a moment and rocked on his heels. On opening his eyes, he nodded to himself. 'On reflection, however, I'm of the mind that the falling masonry was not intended to injure, or kill you. I looked up at the roofline after the gargoyle had fallen but was too concerned for your safety at the time to comprehend what I saw.'

'Which was? Don't keep me in suspense.'

'Which was that the gargoyle that had fallen was not the central one, but one to the left. And as Rankin Hall is built symmetrically, the step directly outside the main door—'

'Is directly under the central gargoyle!'

He nodded. 'I suggest that whoever pushed it intended not to harm you, but to unnerve you. Unnerve you sufficiently to drop your investigation into these deaths.'

Her eyes glinted. 'I may have said this before, Clifford, but it's going to take more than a smidgeon of falling masonry to stop me finding out the truth.'

'Perhaps, my lady, but not that much more. Each gargoyle weighs, I deduce, several hundred pounds. Such a mass falling from a height of—'

She groaned. 'Alright, Clifford, I get the point. Anyway, whoever it is clearly doesn't realise I am at a total loss as to who they are. And—'

A soft knock at the door interrupted her.

'Come,' Clifford called out.

Mrs Butters peeped round. 'Sorry to disturb you, my lady, but I thought this might cheer you up.' She held out the afternoon copy of the *County Herald*. 'There's the most darling piece on Constable Fry and his three little triplets. The Women's Institute has knitted them little police outfits with helmets and everything to help with a fundraiser for the Orphaned Police Children's Charity. They are the cutest things you ever saw.'

Eleanor smiled. 'Thank you, Mrs Butters. That sounds like a very welcome distraction for a minute.'

''Tis page seventeen. Or was it nineteen? Oh, my memory, 'tis one or t'other.' She waited for Eleanor to finish the last morsel of pastry before collecting the empty plate and coffee cup and leaving. Clifford busied himself at the drinks table, pouring Eleanor another small brandy while she read the article. But at her sharp cry, he cleared the room in three quick strides and was by her side.

'My lady?'

'Clifford, no!' She breathed. 'It can't be!' She held out the newspaper, her hands shaking.

He took it and stared at the page.

'There is nothing about Constable Fry, my lady. Mrs Butters obviously has remembered the page wrong. I'll…' He looked up sharply. 'This… this is the obituaries page?'

She nodded. 'Yes. And my obituary is in it.'

CHAPTER 41

She rested the handset back on its cradle. It was the fourth call in the last twenty minutes. This time it was the Langhams.

'Poor Augusta and Harold, they were frantic. Such good friends. I tell you, Clifford, I'm positively livid. Honestly, the audacity of this person. At least the first two obituaries were for dead people, although that didn't quite come out the way I meant it to. Anyway, this third obituary has caused so many people so much upset.'

'I wholeheartedly agree, my lady. It is beyond acceptable. At least Sergeant Brice has now arrested Willie Green for publishing malicious gossip.'

Assuming it was him, Ellie.

Clifford fiddled with his neatly aligned cufflinks. 'My lady, did Sergeant Brice happen to mention how your... obituary was in fact delivered to the *County Herald* office?'

'Yes. The editor, Elijah Edwards, said the note was pushed through the letterbox, just the same as the other two were. And that reminds me. Brice has also warned Edwards for publishing the fake obituary in his newspaper.'

'Quite right! It was a shamelessly irresponsible act. Driven by an even more shameless lack of principles.'

Eleanor hid a fond smile. Since her obituary had published she'd seen first-hand just how much some people cared about her, Clifford being chief among them. Most would have thought by his manner that he was mildly annoyed by Eleanor's premature death being announced. She, however, recognised he was practically apoplectic with rage.

'Now calm down, Clifford. Apparently, Edwards told Brice that business is business and claimed he believed it was in the public interest to publish the obituary, given that he had no reason to believe it was unfounded and I'm a…' She blushed, still feeling the newness of her inherited position. 'A rather prominent member of the community.'

'An indubitable statement about yourself, my lady, but Mr Edwards was duty bound to check the details before publishing the words.'

'I agree, but Brice said Edwards is an old hand and knows the law better than many police, Brice included I imagine, although he obviously didn't say so. Anyway, all Brice can really do is caution Edwards as he hasn't actually broken any law.' She sighed. 'I hope Mrs Butters doesn't feel bad about showing me the paper?'

'I can't pretend that she doesn't, my lady, but like the rest of us, she is more concerned about you than herself. Even Joseph abandoned the gardens and appeared at the back door of the kitchen and is now being reassured by the ladies.'

'Oh, gracious, that is very thoughtful all round, but I really am fine.'

He gave a discreet cough.

'What now, Clifford?'

'My lady, recent events have shown that I am not the only one who has concluded you will not let this matter rest until you have discovered the truth.'

'Well, of course, I won't! Not only has someone murdered two men, but it also appears they may have tried to do the same to me or, at the least, are now taunting me with a fake obituary.' Two red spots appeared on her cheeks. 'I may seem the epitome of calm, Clifford, but inside I'm as furious as you are.'

The jangle of the front doorbell cut their conversation short. She wondered if it was another well-wisher. She was still wondering as she followed Clifford out to the hallway as he had mysteriously refused to say who it was.

She stopped in surprise at the sight of Seldon anxiously turning his bowler hat in his hands.

'Hugh!'

'Eleanor, thank goodness!'

She was vaguely aware of Clifford disappearing discreetly down the corridor.

'What brings you to Henley Hall today?' She blushed. 'I mean, it's unexpected but lovely to see you, of course.'

He stepped forward.

'I couldn't wait any longer for the blasted telephone line to be free, Eleanor. I needed to see for myself that you are alright.'

So it is another well-wisher, Ellie. And the best kind!

'I'm fine, thank you, Hugh. It's so nice of you to drive all this way to check I'm okay.'

He scanned her face. 'I called you immediately, or tried to, the minute I found out about this wretched obituary business. Brice rang me and asked me what I thought of it. I told him *exactly* what I thought and ordered him to arrest that William Green character immediately. He is obviously completely unhinged. I tell you, Eleanor, I'm glad it's Brice who has him locked up as I fear my temper would beat my professionalism by a very long chalk, likely all the way to my fists!'

She was stunned. She knew he had feelings for her, but she hadn't realised until now just how strong they were.

'Hugh, really, don't do anything you might regret.'

He held her gaze. 'I wouldn't have regretted it, Eleanor.' For a moment they stared into each other's eyes. Seldon cleared his throat and looked down at his hat. 'Anyway, I had another motive for coming here today. I wanted to apologise for the way I ended our last call.'

'No, Hugh, *I'm* sorry. I had no idea you had ever been married and…' She blanched. 'Widowed.'

'I know. And that was a poor way to tell you. But' – he nodded towards the telephone – 'nothing comes out the way I intend down that infernal apparatus.'

She laughed. 'I'm the same. Most people in Little Buckford still think the telephone is the work of the devil. Maybe they're right.'

He looked up and smiled, making her heart skip.

'Look, Eleanor, please be careful. William Green might be locked up for now but I can't keep him held forever. His idea of a sick joke might escalate after he is inevitably released. I'm pleased that at least you have given up investigating anything to do with this business.'

'Oh, right,' she mumbled.

He ran a hand through his chestnut curls as he stared down at her hands. For a moment, she thought he might reach out and scoop them in his. But after an awkward pause, he slapped his hat against his leg.

'Now, frustratingly, I've got to go. As I said, please take care.'

She bit her lip and stared after his retreating form as he hurried down the front steps and out to his car, hating herself for deceiving him.

Don't fool yourself, Ellie, you're committed. Ever since her parents' disappearance in the middle of the night when she was only nine, she'd always fought to know the truth. About everything. No matter the cost. And she never rested until she'd uncovered it. She sighed. *Maybe you're just trying to make up for the one truth you never managed to uncover, Ellie? What exactly happened that night.*

She watched his car recede down the driveway until it was lost from sight. Closing the door, she went in search of Clifford and a stiff drink.

She found him in the study, already having anticipated her need for a tipple and a run-through of their suspects so far.

'At the moment, Tretheway is uppermost in my mind, Clifford, and not only because he is the most loathsome.'

'Heartening news, my lady, since an unfavourable character is rarely sufficient for a judge's gavel to sentence him alone. But who else among our suspects might have a link with Solemn Jon *and* Lord Rankin aside from Sir Gordon Tretheway?'

Something about the way he phrased the question made her suspicious.

'I don't know, Clifford. But for some reason, I think you do.'

He nodded. 'The Marchioness of Wendlebury.'

She frowned. 'What? Lady Lambourne! But how?' She stared at him. 'But first, more to the point, how did you find out?'

'Forgive me, my lady. My information came to light whilst conversing with the other servants at Rankin Hall. But then the gargoyle incident occurred, followed by the publication of your obituary. It hardly seemed the time.'

'Fair enough, I think. But now, you absolute terror, tell me before I burst.'

'It was Houghton, the butler, who was also the one who alerted me that you were alone with Sir Gordon. Houghton struck me as a most reasonable fellow. Respectfully discreet but intelligent enough to know he could trust me to impart that he had overheard Lady Lambourne arguing vociferously with Lord Rankin when his father died.'

'Surprising! Mind you, maybe not. She was very blunt about not having liked Rankin. What were they arguing about?'

'Houghton overheard Lady Lambourne say, "Why is that man dealing with your father's arrangements? He's a troublemaker whose presence will bring disgrace on the family. If you don't do something about him, I will!"'

'Gracious! I wonder who she could have been referring to.'

'The gentleman she was referring to was none other than…
Solemn Jon.'

Eleanor's jaw fell. 'Really?'

He nodded. 'Indeed, my lady. The altercation was over the fact
that he was, at that moment, present at Rankin Hall.'

'Well, that certainly establishes a connection between Lady
Lambourne and Solemn Jon, but I really can't see her as the killer.
Hanging around a muddy riverbank dressed in fishing gear? Lying
in wait among the trees to ambush Rankin? If she is guilty, I think
it much more likely that she paid a third party. But why would
she? What had she to gain from either man's death?'

'Well, my lady, concentrating on Solemn Jon's murder, we
know now, like Mr Green, she harboured enmity towards him.
She considered him a "troublemaker" whose presence would "bring
disgrace on the family name". Why, we don't know at the moment,
but as she then promised to "do something about him" if Lord
Rankin would not, maybe that "something" included murder?' He
looked at her quizzically. 'My lady, are you alright?'

She shook her head. 'Sorry, but I just realised something. Solemn
Jon can only have been at Rankin Hall for one reason. Because
Rankin engaged him to bury his father! Grace told us it was Rankin
who paid Solemn Jon to do something, and now we know what
that something was.'

Clifford raised an eyebrow. 'Astutely deduced.'

'Thank you.' She rubbed her forehead so hard it left a pink mark.
'But Rankin hated "commoners" as he called everyone without a
title. Why would he have gone to Solemn Jon, a working-class
undertaker?'

'Why indeed?'

Eleanor's thoughts whirled back to the Langham luncheon.

'Rankin was so disparaging when the topic of Solemn Jon came
up. But at the time, it seemed purely out of snobbery. He didn't

give even a hint that he knew him, or indeed, had even heard of him. Lady Lambourne reacted the same way, as I mentioned before. Maybe Rankin had to engage Solemn Jon because he couldn't afford one of the usual undertakers for the high and mighty, and Lady Lambourne disapproved? If that is the case, then it would also explain why Rankin had a quick funeral with only a few people. He couldn't afford anything more.'

Clifford paced the floor in long strides, one hand tapping the palm of the other behind his back.

'But what possible explanation can there be for Solemn Jon having felt the need to keep secret the fact that he was dealing with Lord Rankin's father's funeral?'

'Maybe Rankin swore him to silence?'

Clifford steepled his fingers and thought for a moment.

'There may, however, be another, more sinister, explanation. Can you recall what Mrs Jon said to you at her husband's funeral about his having been acting differently?'

Eleanor scrunched her eyes shut. 'She said Solemn Jon had been acting strangely for a good few months like he was worried about something he couldn't shrug off.'

'Repeated verbatim, would you say?'

'Actually, I would. I remember that part very clearly.'

'A "good few months back" in villager speak would be early March which was—' He cocked a brow for her to finish his sentence.

'When Rankin's father was buried. We were away in Brighton. So that adds up.'

Clifford stopped pacing. 'It does. But what doesn't is that Solemn Jon should have been so agitated about having undertaken a funeral on the quiet to save a noble family embarrassment that his wife noticed. Not only noticed but felt that it was something that might just have got him murdered.'

Eleanor swallowed hard. 'You're right. There's only one possible explanation. That something was very off about how Lord Rankin's father died. Which means Solemn Jon might not have been an innocent victim. Maybe he helped cover it up?'

They stared at each other, the same thought registering.

She shook her head. 'For the first time, Clifford, I hope we're wrong. Because otherwise—'

He nodded. 'There will have been three murders, not two.'

CHAPTER 42

In the Rolls, Eleanor fidgeted all the way down into the village and out the other side. After ten miles, Clifford produced a bag of mint humbugs and politely suggested it was in fact still a fair distance to their destination.

'It's all this confusion that's making me itchy, Clifford,' she said, popping a sweet in her mouth. Ignoring Gladstone's insistence that he should have one too, she waited until the Rolls had navigated a particular sharp corner before continuing. 'Tretheway's close connection to Pendle and the fact he lost so much money over the two-hundred-and-fifty-pound bet on Patrick is definitely keeping him second on my suspect list for Solemn Jon's murder.'

'Not because he proved himself unscrupulous enough to blackmail you, my lady?'

'That too. Which we will need to address if he turns out not to be the murderer, by the way.' She shuddered. 'What a terrible wish I just made. Because Uncle Byron's secret will be safe if Tretheway…'

'Hangs? I apologise for my uncharacteristic directness my lady, but blackmail should carry the same penalty in my book. It ruins lives hardly any less than murder, if you will forgive my offering an opinion. But who is third on your list?'

'Lady Lambourne. After Houghton told you he heard her call Solemn Jon a troublemaker and that she would deal with him, if Rankin didn't.'

Clifford nodded along with her words, his eyes not leaving the road.

'And in number-four spot, my lady?'

She frowned. 'Pendle. He was losing too much money and face to Solemn Jon. When the rival hound races started up, Pendle could easily have panicked and decided he needed Patrick to secure his financial future.'

'Indeed. But as we now know the connection between Sir George Tretheway and Mr Pendle, might not our previous conjecture that they could have planned the murder together put them at the joint number-one spot?'

'Not quite. Despite everything, Willie Green is still up there.'

Clifford took one gloved hand from the wheel to cover his discreet cough. She gestured that he had the floor.

'Mr Green worked for Solemn Jon for many years. Thus he was certainly in his employ in March just gone.'

She clicked her fingers. 'Of course! Clifford, why didn't that strike us earlier? But do you think Solemn Jon could have arranged Lord Rankin's father's funeral without Willie Green knowing?'

'Categorically not. Apart from anything else, a new coffin would have had to be made given Lord Rankin's father's build. Even the largest among the line of coffins we saw in Solemn Jon's carpentry shop would not have entertained his measurements.'

'Wow! Taller even than Evander?'

'And even broader-shouldered, my lady. Being a close friend, your uncle affectionately called him Franken-Rankin after Mary Shelley's monster in her novel *Frankenstein*. It was a tribute to Lord Rankin's father's frame only, I hasten to add, not his facial features.'

She rolled her eyes. 'Boys! So unless Solemn Jon worked through the night and managed to hide the coffin—'

'And the body, my lady. If you will forgive my blunt mention of it. That too would have needed preparing.'

'Then Willie Green would *have* to have known. Especially if Rankin senior was such a large chap. Solemn Jon could never have handled his body alone. And I bet that's what Willie Green's girlfriend was talking about when she said Willie Green knew Solemn Jon's secret.'

'Although, my lady, I did believe her when she said Mr Green had not made her privy to any of the details.'

'Me too.'

'If Mr Green did know there was something off about Lord Rankin's father's death, and burial, it is no wonder he was disgusted with Solemn Jon for colluding with Lord Rankin in covering it up. If indeed, that is what happened.'

She nodded and wrinkled her nose. 'If this *is* all true, Clifford, how on earth am I going to tell Mrs Jon? I know we agreed we can only tell her the truth, but when we started, I never expected the truth to be something like this.'

'Which is why, if you will forgive me for saying, my lady, I quoted Mr Twain's caution before we commenced.'

She shook her head. 'I think I may have to disagree with him. You may learn some uniquely unwanted lessons if you swing a cat by its tail, but I think you may learn a lot more unpalatable lessons if you swing a murder investigation by its tail, if you know what I mean.' She pointed at the gatehouse in the near distance, fashioned like a miniature castle. 'Let's put that awful thought on hold and see what we can turn up about Rankin's death first.'

'Certainly, my lady. I do feel that we were right to conclude that events are moving too fast and the investigation is slipping away from us. With the possibility now of a third murder, the need to establish if the same modus operandi was used for all the murders is paramount. If we can establish this, then we will have a better chance of knowing if we are indeed dealing with just one killer.'

'Absolutely and, as we have nothing at the moment but speculation to go on with Lord Rankin's father's death, we'd better continue concentrating on Solemn Jon and Evander's first. On the surface, it seems they were not the same modus operandi, but there's a horrible similarity.'

'Indeed. In essence, both victims died from a blow to the back of the head, albeit one on water, one on land. And, of course, an obituary then followed each death.'

'Exactly.' She frowned. 'I assume there would have been an obituary published after Rankin senior died, but I'm sure it wasn't a disparaging one declaring it murder?'

He shook his head. 'Not to my knowledge, my lady. If there had been, I am sure we should have learned of it on our return from Brighton.' Clifford eased the Rolls to a stop just before the gatehouse to the Rankin estate. He held out a pristine handkerchief. 'For additional plausibility, my lady.'

She let out a quiet moan. 'I hate all this deception, Clifford.'

'Murder is the greatest deceit, my lady. Whoever is responsible is still walking and talking among the rest of us as if all was as it should be.'

He waited until she buried her face in the handkerchief then eased the car forward and opened his window. Gladstone shuffled across her and Clifford's lap and stuck his head out of the window in greeting. The gatekeeper tipped his cap.

'Good afternoon, m'lady. Mr Clifford. Master Gladstone.'

'Good afternoon, Mr Turnbull.' Clifford discreetly slid a slim bottle into the grey-haired gatekeeper's hand. 'This is most kind. Lady Swift will derive great comfort from visiting the spot of Lord Rankin's sadly fatal fall.' He lowered his voice. 'Her ladyship blames herself, since events might have turned out very differently had she not left their ride early that fateful afternoon.'

Mr Turnbull slid the bottle underneath his green woollen waist-coat and tapped his nose. 'Pleased to be of help, Mr Clifford. Guilt's a bad enough bedfellow without grief stealing in and hogging the quilt. 'Tis all clear for you to head on down to where I told you.'

Clifford gave him a grateful wave as the Rolls slid elegantly past.

Once out of view, and Gladstone re-seated, Eleanor emerged from her handkerchief and glanced backwards. The gatekeeper had turned away from the window and was showing the bottle to a square-shouldered man sitting at the table. She frowned. *Haven't you seen him somewhere before, Ellie?* She shook her head as the gatehouse was lost from sight by a swathe of trees as the Rolls swung along the twisting drive.

'Nicely set up, Clifford. But how?'

'Whilst you were inside on the day of Lord Rankin's funeral, I took the opportunity of ingratiating myself with a few key members of staff, just in case. It turns out Mr Turnbull is a considerable fan of chestnuts.'

'You didn't! That was a bottle of Mrs Trotman's chestnut liqueur you gave him, wasn't it? You know that stuff gives the worst hangover I've ever met.'

'Only when consumed after several bottles of parsnip perry and more so of her dandelion concoction, my lady.'

She waggled a finger. 'Well, when this is finally over, make sure you are prepared for exactly that by way of celebration. Last time, the ladies and I were forced to drink it all by ourselves.'

'So very noble of you.'

She hid a smile as they arrived at their destination.

Rather than proceeding to the main house, Clifford turned right when the driveway split into two. A few minutes later he parked and a short walk brought them to a large and peculiarly lumpy boulder, several feet across.

Eleanor glanced around. 'Are you sure this is the spot, Clifford?'

He nodded. 'Lord Rankin was found slumped against the puddingstone at the very point where the estate's eastern path to the mausoleum turns sharply right twenty yards before entering the yew forest.'

'Puddingstone?'

'A geological anomaly of the area, which runs in a line across the Chilterns through much of South Buckinghamshire. Formed millions of years ago, they consist of flint pebbles and sand, naturally cemented together with silica. They are known as "puddingstones", due to the shape resembling a traditional plum pudding.'

Her hand reached out to the boulder, her fingers tracing the unforgiving and jagged surface.

'And everyone has just accepted that Rankin died when he hit his head on this, I suppose?'

'Correct, my lady. After, that is, his horse apparently stumbled on a molehill.' He walked a few steps away from the stone and swept the ground with his eyes. 'Ah! Probably this one.'

She joined him and bent down. There were several molehills, one of which looked as if someone or something had tried to dig it up recently. She pursed her lips.

'I suppose it could have been a horse's hoof catching it?'

'Or a wanton bulldog, my lady?' He pointed to Gladstone who was furiously digging on an adjoining molehill.

She laughed. 'Possibly. Or the murderer's doing so it looked like a horse's hoof had caught on it and stumbled.'

Clifford marched back to the puddingstone and pulled a magnifying glass from his inside pocket, then looped his suit tails into his lap and dropped to his haunches. After a moment, he looked up.

'There is certainly no sign Lord Rankin's horse did indeed trip on that molehill over there. The hoof prints here are clear enough having been preserved in the chalk with the subsequent spell of dry weather.'

She was confused. 'Then how did Rankin end up out of the saddle, slumped against this stone?'

'Here.' With a leather-gloved finger, Clifford traced the outline of two longer, narrower imprints, closer together than the other marks. 'See how the rear of this print is cut out like a scallop? That is the front of the hoof digging in.'

She frowned. 'But how can the front of the hoof be at the back of the print?'

'Because Lord Rankin's Arion had fallen on his front knuckles. Or his pastern joint, as is the correct term. Arion must have tripped over something, but that molehill is too far away for it to have been the cause, in my estimation.'

She tapped her chin thoughtfully. 'Well, if it wasn't that molehill, perhaps someone put something across the path that neither Rankin or Arion could see?'

'Something invisible?'

She nodded. 'You take the left, Clifford, I'll take the right.'

Eleanor left the path and scoured the ground and base of the trees alongside. Gladstone, his nose still sporting a small mound of molehill, lumbered after her.

'Ouch! Wretched brambles!' She disentangled yet another one caught on her jacket sleeve.

From the undergrowth on the other side of the path Clifford called out, 'My lady, might I suggest—'

'No you may not,' she called back. 'Because' – she let out a long low whistle and beckoned him over – 'look what I've found!'

In two long strides he was beside her.

'Clifford, see there? Several lines of almost invisible cord wrapped round the base of this tree? And the long ends have all been cut. But that cord, peculiarly, looks rather familiar.'

Clifford hunched down next to her and ran the ends through his gloved hand before pulling out a penknife and snipping off a short section.

'This is in fact coarse fishing twine, my lady. Very strong and almost undetectable in the water. Or across a forest path.'

'That's it! That's exactly where I've seen some before. Wrapped around the back of Solemn Jon's raft with a bloodied fishing hook on the end!'

CHAPTER 43

As they motored back towards the gatehouse, Clifford turned to Eleanor.

'Perhaps I might enquire why you have not mentioned the twine and hook you noted on Solemn Jon's raft before, my lady?'

She shrugged. 'Two reasons. It seemed perfectly normal that a capsized raft would have caught some debris on its trip along the river. And secondly, Seldon dismissed it immediately, making the good point that the section of the bank we were standing on alone had several short sections of fishing twine trodden into the path, several with rusted hooks.'

'I see. All pretence aside, my lady, if visiting the scene of Lord Rankin's final moments has not caused you too much upset, perhaps you might show me the hook and twine?'

'Of course. And I'm fine, thank you for checking.'

'First I shall detour via Henley Hall that you might, ahem, swap your bramble-scarred attire for something more—'

She flapped a hand. 'No time for fussing about things like that. We— oh!' She stared down at her shredded stockings. 'Maybe a quick detour. Then we need to get to the river. We're on the right track, I can feel it. Pull up alongside the gatehouse for a moment first though. I want to test our theory.'

After Gladstone had been permitted to greet the gatekeeper again, Eleanor gave the man a wan smile. 'Mr Turnbull?'

He fidgeted, clearly unused to titled guests pausing to talk to him. 'Erm, everything alright, m'lady?'

'Certainly, much better now. Closure can take some odd forms, but seeing the actual place Lord Rankin met his unfortunate accident was more helpful than I can tell you. One question though, Mr Turnbull.' She ran her hand along the window ledge of the car, keeping her voice light. 'Has Henderson the groom mentioned to you how Arion is? I'm concerned that he might have been injured.'

'Not to worry 'bout him, m'lady. Mr Henderson said as how it would take a thunderbolt to injure one as strong as that beast. Mind, he's missing his lordship, for sure.'

'Off his food?'

'Not so much. More that he's bruised the front of his legs, just above his hooves. Silly fool must have spent that first night kicking at his stall, Mr Henderson said. Happens when they're grieving for their owners sometimes.'

'Thank you, Mr Turnbull.' She stole a sideways glance at Clifford who nodded in reply.

Unfortunately, by the time they reached the river, it seemed that the world and his wife had decided to take an afternoon's stroll there.

'How are we going to inspect the raft discreetly with so many people about, Clifford? This is hopeless.'

'Not to worry, my lady.' He snapped his pocket watch closed, then joined her in returning a series of cordial greetings and nods as a slow procession of summer-bonneted and cloth-capped couples passed them in the opposite direction. A moment later, he held up one finger as the bells of St Winifred's began to peal their sixteen-bar carillon that heralded the striking of each hour.

'Four o'clock, my lady.' He mimed folding a slice of bread in half. 'Jam and fold time.'

She watched everyone along the towpath pick up their pace and head off along the main path to the village.

'That was lucky timing.' She noted his expression and smiled. 'Nice timing, I should have said, Clifford.'

A few minutes later her mood turned sombre again. Solemn Jon's raft looked more forlorn than ever. Still moored to the spot it had been dragged to at the end of the May Fair, water lapped greedily up over the bow, flooding the deck where Solemn Jon must have stood just before… She shook the thought out of her head and helped Clifford haul the raft tight. While she held it and Gladstone, he carefully worked his way down the slippery bank to examine the rear.

'Clifford, please work your amazing magic and discover something about the twine and hook that will tell us who is responsible.'

It was said half in jest to lighten her mood, but she wasn't prepared for the response. He straightened up from inspecting the raft and shook his head.

'Would that I could, my lady, but I am struggling to see any twine or a hook attached anywhere.'

'What? No, that can't be!'

'Where exactly was the twine caught?'

'There!' She pointed. 'At the back. Round that sort of long wooden bar Solemn Jon was using to lean against when he was trying to steer.'

Clifford examined the bar but it remained stubbornly twine, and hook, free.

'Could it have fallen off, my lady?'

'Absolutely not. It was well tangled. I suppose it's possible Jack or Mew unwound it to use. Jack said he had no fishing gear and Mew obviously can't afford it. We could ask them.'

'Indeed we could. However, any of the village children could have taken it. Or our murderer.'

She frowned. 'But if it was our murderer, why remove it now?'

'You said it was bloodied, yes?'

She nodded slowly. 'Ah! So the murderer catches Solemn Jon's raft. Solemn Jon thinks he's got caught in the weeds or something. Our murderer, posing as a fisherman on the bank, maybe offers to untangle it and help push the raft back out. Then when Solemn Jon's looking the other way, bashes him on the head. Our murderer then tries to undo the hook and twine but in his hurry stabs himself with the hook and is forced to leave it. Or maybe he was disturbed before he could remove it fully. So—' She looked up. 'It's a shame the police can't tell whose blood it is. I suppose it could have been Solemn Jon's?'

'It would be a great help in cases such as these, my lady. I believe the police are actually working on such a system right now where they could identify which blood came from which body as it were. Rather like fingerprinting. But the actual application of such a system is, I understand, a way off yet.'

She shrugged. 'As our hook and the blood with it has disappeared, it wouldn't help us much even if it wasn't. Anyway, what I was trying to say was, if it *was* the murderer, I assume he gave up trying to unwind the hook and cut the twine, meaning to come back later and reclaim them.'

Clifford nodded. 'Which, it seems, he may now have done.'

He stared at her expectantly which made her groan.

'Alright, dash it! I agree we need to inform the police. But it can't be Seldon. I haven't the heart to tell him after he said how pleased he was that I wasn't investigating. And' – she felt her heart miss a beat – 'after the news about his wife.'

They rode back to Henley Hall in silence. Eleanor felt peculiarly dispirited, despite their discovery of the twine at the site where Rankin had been found dead. Gladstone seemed to pick up on the mood and spent the journey with his head out the window, his jowls flapping dispiritedly in the breeze.

'Hello, Sergeant Brice?' she said into the hallway telephone. 'Yes, it is Lady Swift. I wish to let you know something most important about the Rankin murder.'

'Accident, m'lady, if you'll excuse me correcting,' Brice's voice boomed in her ear.

'Not any more, Sergeant Brice. Please, you need to send some men up to the Rankin estate immediately…. well, I'll tell you why.' But several minutes later, she found herself still defending what she and Clifford had discovered. 'But I'm telling you, Sergeant, the twine is very similar or identical to that I saw caught on Solemn Jon's raft.'

Brice sounded respectfully weary. 'Lady Swift, there's only a couple of us here. We haven't time for going all the way out to the Rankin estate and be poking 'bout on the raft as well.'

'Well, actually the twine and hook have disappeared from the raft. What do you say to that?'

'Kids, m'lady. Folks without much is always on the watch for a free bit o' summat to fish with. Course, if there *was* twine and a hook to start with.'

'There was! And I'm not the only one who saw it.'

'Mr Clifford, was it?'

'No actually, it was, ah—' She bit back her words. 'That doesn't matter.'

If he rings Seldon to check, Ellie, you'll never get the chance to explain why you're still investigating. And then you couldn't blame Seldon for never speaking to you again.

'Alright, m'lady,' Brice's voice boomed down the line again, 'seeing as it's you, I'll send my only man up to the Rankin estate. And I'll see if we can also somehow manage to check the raft one more time and then give you a call back. But if you ask me, 'tis a hiding to nothing when both deaths was an accident, sure as cockerels shout 'bout the coming of dawn.'

It was almost two hours later that Brice rang back. Eleanor, having taken Gladstone for a short evening walk around the grounds, missed it. She entered the hall and handed Clifford Gladstone's lead.

'So, Clifford, what did Brice say? Did he send someone to the Rankin estate?'

Clifford nodded. 'Constable Lowe, as it happens.'

'Well, he's a very conscientious chap. We both know that of old.'

'Indeed he is. Regrettably, however, like that from Solemn Jon's raft, the twine around the two trees on the Rankin estate has… disappeared.'

'No!' She slumped down onto the arm of a chair. 'But how can that be… Unless…' She looked up sharply. 'Unless the murderer happened to go back in the intervening few hours to remove any evidence. But that's too much of a coincidence, surely?'

'Might I suggest it was no coincidence, my lady? The murderer knew they needed to act swiftly—'

'Because they followed you and I around the Rankin estate and high-tailed it to the raft before us?' She slapped her forehead. 'Blast! I should never have allowed you to persuade me to change my clothes!' She coloured. 'I say, Clifford, I'm sorry, that was uncalled for.'

He bowed. 'In fact, my lady, you are correct. And I am more convinced than ever that we need to engage the chief inspector's help now we categorically cannot go back to the local police.'

Eleanor winced. 'Brice wasn't too happy then?'

Clifford coughed. 'He expressed his displeasure rather vocally. The phrase "leading the local constabulary a merry dance" came into it, I recall. Although put rather more colourfully. My point is, the murderer has watched you on three separate occasions and got far too close with that falling gargoyle.'

'I know. But how can I go cap in hand to Seldon now that I have gone against his instructions and his wishes *again*?' She tugged at her red curls in frustration. 'I am suddenly so lost, Clifford. This time, we need a real-life wizard.'

For a moment she thought he hadn't heard her. But then he seemed to come to. 'Actually, my lady, rather fortuitously, I may be able to lay my hands on one.'

CHAPTER 44

As Eleanor stepped across the threshold with Clifford and Gladstone behind her, the ding of the doorbell brought forth a disembodied voice from behind a green calico curtain.

'Be with you in a moment, folks.'

She looked around in surprise. This was like no other shop she'd ever been in. There were no racks or shelves on the walls, just rows of stuffed fish. And spanning the worn wooden floor, no glass display cases or artfully arranged stands, just a hotchpotch of wooden tables heaped with products in no apparent order or logic.

Since she recognised very little, it looked rather like the contents of every shed and outbuilding in the county had been tipped onto whichever table had an inch of space left. Gladstone put his front paws up on one or two tables and had a good sniff. Deciding nothing was edible, he lost interest in the rest of the proceedings and sat down by the door until they were ready to leave.

'Clifford, this could pass as a ship's chandlery, a milliner's and a toy shop all rolled into one. What on earth do fisherman do with such myriad hooks, feathers, brass reels and miniature souvenirs of fish? And, what' – she pointed to a collection of contraptions not dissimilar to mini windmills with a central brass handle – 'are they? Yarn spinners?'

'Those are, in fact, fishing line winders, my lady. Even though recent innovations have allowed the modern angler to move on from horsehair to silkworm gut and now superior strength linen line, it still requires considerable care and maintenance. Indeed, the line needs to be carefully washed and methodically dried after each session to ensure it does not fall victim to mould, bacteria or the damaging effects of sunlight.'

She pulled a face. 'And I thought sitting on a bank in silence for hours was the epitome of boredom. But no, apparently, it carries on for hours when you get home too. I'd make a terrible fisherman.'

'Indeed, my lady. Fishing is the province of the patient, after all.'

She laughed. 'True enough. I've never exactly been the patient type. I can see why it is your chosen hobby, though.'

He cleared his throat. 'Tell me, how did you enjoy Mrs Trotman's baked trout and almond dinner yesterday, my lady?'

She rolled her eyes. 'Alright, I am exceptionally grateful that you and others fish on my behalf because in truth that was one of the most delicious suppers I have ever had.' She looked around the shop again. 'But I honestly didn't realise there was so much paraphernalia involved. How would you find anything you wanted in this topsy-turvy clutter?'

'By knowing one's art, my lady. Each table is in fact dedicated to the equipment required for a particular class of fish an angler would be keen to outwit.'

He led the way, threading in and out of the tables, pointing out the handmade nets and rods of every conceivable length in hazel, lancewood and, to his obvious preference, Indian bamboo. He paused at another table.

'These are lures, my lady.' He picked up an articulated model of a fish almost the length of his palm and wiggled its tail. 'An adaptation of Mr Allies' groundbreaking Archimedean Minnow of 1847. See how it appears to swim? And the left and right side fins are curved in opposition, one up, one down, to make the lure revolve as it is pulled through the water. All fatally tempting to the trout you enjoyed last night.'

She took it and ran her finger along its perfectly indented scales. 'Glass eyes too. It's actually a true work of art. I had no idea it was such a—'

'Science, my lady?'

She nodded. 'I see now why it appeals to you. And the fascinating manner in which you explained it all makes me tempted to join you on your next fishing excursion.' She chuckled as a flicker of horror crossed his face. 'Joke! Mind you, in all seriousness, do you think you could get Mr Allies to knock us up a similarly tempting lure for our killer?'

'Unfortunately, Mr Allies is no longer with us so we will have to make do with what we have found.' He slid his hand into his pocket and retrieved the two-inch piece of twine, together with a pair of what looked like slotted pliers. He slid the twine into the largest of the slots where it sat snugly. 'This is designed for coarse fishing, but specifically for the weightiest fish with the greatest fighting spirit such as giant carp and pike. Or even the illegally introduced catfish. Hence the twine having been strong enough to trip Lord Rankin's horse mid-gallop. Fish of a size and might requiring this strength of line are rare beasts, found not in rivers, but only certain lakes whose whereabouts are a closely guarded secret. The monsters that inhabit them are usually spoken about in hushed tones lest their reputation be spread too wide.'

'Sorry to have kept you, folks,' the genial voice called from back near the door. They turned to see a ruddy-faced man with wilful grey hair, dressed as if he had just stepped off a riverbank, his long green rubber boots flapping at his thighs. 'Oh, 'tis a lady, beg pardon, madam. And Mr Clifford! Haven't seen you in a long while.'

Clifford nodded. 'Indeed, Mr Bradenham. I have been rather caught up with other things since before last season and haven't made it out this way.'

Eleanor didn't miss how nonchalantly he had said this, clearly hoping she wouldn't notice. She remembered guiltily that he had, in fact, cancelled too many of his days off since she'd arrived at the Hall. She promised herself to make sure he had more free time in the future.

As Clifford engaged the man in conversation over the particular twine he was seeking, she snuck one of the shop's contact cards from the counter and slid it into her pocket.

At that moment, Mr Bradenham let out a long whistle. 'Now that's a gauge of line I don't sell from one quarter to the next. There's only two of us who even sell it within sixty miles.' He gave Clifford a nudge in the ribs. 'Where's the monster hiding at then? Jackson's quarry lake? Mallingford waters?'

'Actually, the same question is eating me up.' Clifford leaned in conspiratorially. 'I was rather hoping you might be able to tell me, seeing as you are known as the "Wizard of the Line"?'

Ah! So he's our wizard, Ellie!

The man chuckled. 'That I am, but I can't help you here. 'Taint many men brave enough to go after a beast needing this sort of line. I'm out of practice myself, I admit, what with being here at all hours. Even the breeding beds out back take up a goodly part of my day. Squatts are coming on a treat, though. Juicy and succulent fellows and no mistake.'

'Squatts?' Eleanor said, trying to join in. 'Perhaps we should purchase some for Mrs Trotman to work her culinary magic on for tomorrow's fish supper?'

Clifford shook his head. 'If you will forgive me, my lady, I doubt if even Mrs Trotman's culinary skills, great though they are, could make maggots a palatable meal. Although they are, in fact, quite nutritious.'

Eugh, Ellie! Eating spiders and locusts when needs must on travels abroad was one thing, but this is England!

Clifford turned back to the shopkeeper. 'The gentleman whose twine this is was apparently fishing the day of the May Fair.'

The shopkeeper frowned. 'But coarse fishing season is well over now, everyone knows that. Whoever he is, he needs a sharp word about sticking to the rules. 'Tis bad form.' He rubbed his chin. 'Can't have been old Jack Beale. Silly old stick spent the whole afternoon in here helping me while I was restocking, whining about folks with no idea 'bout angling. Had to steer him out the door when it came to evening so I could lock up.'

'What about Mr Banner?'

'Mac Banner? He did buy a reel of that line at the start of the season, spouting on about how he was going to be the one to snare' – he leaned in and spoke behind his hand – 'old Captain Shadow.'

Clifford turned to Eleanor. 'The most infamous pike in Buckinghamshire.' He winked at Mr Bradenham. 'If I were a betting man—'

'Too right, you'd be quids in. The captain made Mac look a fool alright. He'll be cursing having two-thirds of his pricey reel of twine left over since he lost half a finger. And a lot of face with the heckling he got at the pub afterwards.' He chuckled and ran his hand over his chin again. 'Brice Weldon? He bought a reel. When you've no wife calling you home for tea, 'taint no reason to leave the fishes afore dark is fully set in. So there you go, it's got to be Mac or Brice, I reckon, Mr Clifford.'

'Most helpful, thank you.' Clifford nodded and gestured to Eleanor that their work there was done. He tipped the brim of his hat. 'May they be biting well for you, Mr Bradenham.'

'Happy casting, Mr Clifford.'

Back in the Rolls, Eleanor accepted Clifford's judgement that neither of the two gentlemen mentioned were likely to be their prey. It seemed neither had any known connection to Solemn Jon or Lord Rankin that he knew of.

Eleanor sighed. 'Well, I've added their names to the bottom of our suspect list in my mind, anyway. How far did you say it was to the only other shop that sells this wretched twine?'

'Twenty miles, my lady.'

'Oh, well, if it's unlikely Mac Banner or Brice Weldon are our killer, I don't suppose we have any choice. Onwards!'

The only route to the other shop was through narrow country lanes, so it was a good three-quarters of an hour later when they finally arrived. Gladstone had nodded off, so they left him sprawled on the seat in the Rolls and walked up to the fishing shop.

'Gracious, chalk and cheese,' she whispered as they entered, everything being smartly laid out and labelled.

It was immediately apparent that the equally smartly turned-out owner was less interested in chatting than selling. As Clifford appeased him by buying something fishing related – *Thank goodness it isn't a bag of maggots, Ellie* – her gaze swept around the shop and back to the counter in record time. The only thing to vaguely catch her eye were three rows of newspaper clippings pinned to a green baize board behind the long glass counter. She shivered, remembering the last time she'd looked at a newspaper her own obituary had been in it.

Clifford's voice cut into her thoughts.

'The gentleman was very particular in his use of this very fishing line.' He placed it on the counter. 'So much so, that I am keen to ask him a few… insider questions as it were.'

The shopkeeper adjusted his bow tie and stared back dispassionately, clearly disinterested now the sale had been completed.

'Forgive me, it is not a popular line. I can't really remember the last time anyone bought a reel. With the season over, it must have been early March. Maybe even February?'

Eleanor felt frustrated at not being able to offer any assistance, having no knowledge of even the basics of angling. She cast about for something to keep the shopkeeper talking. Her eye fell on one of the newspaper clippings.

'I say, what a simply incredible fish in that photograph, Clifford. Look! Is that the sort of beast you need for such twine?'

Clifford pulled his pince-nez from his inside jacket pocket and peered at the photograph. 'That is a barbel, my lady, not a resident of our local river. You would certainly need some serious—' He frowned. She followed his gaze to the next clipping along. He raised an eyebrow to her and turned to the shopkeeper. Pointing to the photograph in the clipping he asked. 'Isn't this the South Buckinghamshire Golden Reel Championship?'

The man nodded. 'Yep. This year's.'

'I didn't realise you competed in fishing contests, Clifford?' she said.

He shook his head. 'I do not, my lady. As Henry David Thoreau noted, "Many men go fishing all of their lives without knowing that it is not fish they are after." Solitude has a pull as strong as any prize catch. However, I know many who do and' – he tapped the image of a man in the line of three holding a trophy – 'that, if I am not mistaken, is Charles Burgess.'

She stared at the man in the grainy photograph. 'Is he a friend of yours?'

He shook his head again. 'No, my lady. But I do know Mr Burgess as a fine fisherman. And the long-standing butler at the Rankin estate.'

She looked at the photograph again. Despite its graininess, the man's face was quite clear. Her brows met.

'But that's not the butler I met when I went riding with Evander. Or the one I saw at the funeral the other day. On both occasions it was the same chap. He must be, what, twenty years younger than the fellow in this photograph.'

'Indeed, my lady. The gentleman you refer to is a Mr Houghton. A recent appointment of Lord Rankin's.'

Of course, Ellie! When the butler brought Rankin his champagne he apologised for taking so long because he hadn't yet got the hang of something or other. Any butler that had been in service for any length of time would have known where everything was and how it worked.

The shopkeeper had started shuffling papers by way of a hint that he felt their business was concluded and they were now cluttering up his orderly shop. Eleanor ignored him. Something was tugging at her brain.

'You know, Clifford, I have the weirdest feeling that I've seen him before. And recently. How odd.'

Clifford snapped his fingers. 'My lady, do you still have the medallion on your person?'

She nodded and pulled it out of her pocket. He examined it with his mini magnifying glass again and shook his head. 'I really should have worked this out before, my lady. The "St… of…a" of this inscription are not part of the name "St Joseph of Arimathea", the patron saint of undertakers.'

'Then what do they stand for, Clifford?'

'They stand for "St Zita of Lucca", my lady. The patron saint of domestic servants… and butlers.'

The shopkeeper, clearly resigned to their continued presence, was now looking at the photograph too.

'You mean that man there?' He pointed to the grainy image of Burgess. 'No idea who he is. Only came in once, I think. Funnily enough, now I think about it, he was the one who bought the twine you showed me.'

CHAPTER 45

In the functional reception area of the *County Herald* newspaper office, Eleanor raised her voice to be heard above the boisterous clatter of the printing presses hidden by the office's whitewashed windows.

'Oh, but I think he definitely will. And Clifford here can vouch for my very limited patience, which I should mention will run out entirely in the next minute.'

Clifford grimaced at his pocket watch and nodded sympathetically at the bespectacled young man behind the low counter who was regarding them with dismay.

'But, begging your pardon, Mr Edwards really doesn't like being interrupted while he's deciding on what story to lead with on the front page.'

Eleanor cocked her head. 'I'm sure creating pernicious controversy must be very time consuming. Nevertheless, do tell him I am here.'

Sliding her calling card across the counter, she tapped her finger against her name. Up to now, she'd avoided having personal cards printed despite Clifford's insistence that they were de rigueur for a titled lady, believing them ostentatious. Recently, however, she'd given in, finding it more convenient than constantly having to explain why she didn't have any.

He stared at the card. 'L… Lady Swift. I had no idea.'

'About what? Who I am? Or my being alive and not deceased, as Mr Edwards libellously announced to the world in print?'

He gulped. 'One moment, please, m'lady. I'll try.'

'Thank you, but do tell him,' she called after his hurrying form, 'if he doesn't come out, I shall simply come in.'

No amount of machinery could cover up the snatches of angry conversation that erupted behind the whitewashed windows. Eleanor shared a look with Clifford and began counting down from ten, tapping her foot with each number.

'… don't care what she wants!' Edwards' voice carried out to them.

'Four… three…'

'Go tell her. Now, boy!'

'One.' Eleanor headed for the office door. As she reached it, she half-turned to Clifford and whispered, 'Let's hope our theory about Edwards is correct!' Turning back, she marched into the office and gave a cheery wave. 'Why, Mr Edwards, there you are.'

The newspaper owner begrudgingly acknowledged her presence with a frustrated nod before making a great show of finishing up his conversation with the three typesetters. Whooshing and clanking printing presses occupied the back wall, while the floor was filled with sack trolleys piled high with tightly strung bundles of newspapers. At four desks sat reporters, their fingers paused above their typewriters, their newshound senses tantalised by the air of scandal they'd detected at Eleanor's arrival.

Eleanor walked over to Edwards. He ran his hand slowly over his thick moustache before forcing a smile.

'Lady Swift. How nice of you to call, but perhaps you would like to make an appointment with my assistant here? I'm busy at the moment, as you can see.'

She stopped in front of him. 'A kind offer, but since you are here and so am I, and we are both exceptionally busy, let's do this now.'

'Do what?'

'Go through the photographs, of course.'

'What photographs?' Edwards shot a look at his assistant, who shrugged.

'The rest of these.'

Clifford passed her the previous week's edition of the newspaper and she tapped the article covering the May Fair. 'The photographs your chap took on the day that aren't published here. I saw him myself, busily capturing so much more than you had space to include.'

Edwards gave an exaggerated eye roll. 'Really, Lady Swift, if you would like to while away your afternoon checking which image shows your most flattering side as the fair's guest of honour, I suggest you wait until next May. Then your butler can follow you around with your own photographic apparatus. I am running an important news communication business, not a ladies' amusement hall.'

Eleanor's eyes narrowed. 'How peculiar, Mr Edwards, because I've come to realise what you are in fact doing is cunningly profiteering from the deaths of two people and the near death of another.'

Something flashed fleetingly across Edwards' face. He pointed to his assistant.

'Why aren't you out in reception?'

'Um, sir, yes, sir,' the young man stuttered, making for the door.

Edwards stepped closer to her, drawing up short as he registered that Clifford had done the same.

'That's rather an accusation, Lady Swift. I'm not quite sure what you are inferring.'

She smiled coldly. 'Oh, there is no inference, Mr Edwards. You deliberately wrote and published controversial obituaries for Solemn Jon and then Lord Rankin purely to sell more newspapers.' She was grimly satisfied to note how much that had made him jump. 'And then peculiarly one for me also. Yet' – she patted her hands down her front – 'as you can see I am perfectly well. So, would you like to make this easy and simply indulge my wish to view the photographs from the fair, or shall I take out a case against you?

You see, in law, as I am sure you know, you can't libel the dead, but you *can* libel the living. And I am, as we have established, very much alive.'

Edwards snorted. 'I had it on good authority that you had regrettably passed away, Lady Swift. Hence publishing your obituary which' – he waved an airy hand – 'arrived in the usual manner, through the letterbox. I'm afraid as I didn't write the article in question, merely published it—'

'Really, Mr Edwards? Then who did write it?'

'As you well know, Mr Green—'

Eleanor held up her hand. 'As well you know, Mr Edwards, Mr Green did not write any of those obituaries. And I can prove it.'

Okay, Ellie, that's a lie, but hopefully he'll swallow it.

Before Edwards could reply, Clifford stepped forward. 'So, Mr Edwards, unless you can prove otherwise in a court of law that you did not, in fact, write as well as publish, Lady Swift's obituary—'

Edwards held up his hands. 'I… now… Look here—'

Eleanor waved him down. 'Look here, nothing. For all the pain and worry you have caused through publishing not only my but also Solemn Jon and Lord Rankin's obituaries, I will take you to court, you know.'

Edwards' eyes flicked between them. Finally, he grunted and without a word, led them around one corner of the whitewashed windows to a row of long low wooden cabinets.

'All photographs are filed by date.'

Eleanor nodded. 'How very efficient. Please do feel free to leave us and continue running your newspaper.'

'Among other publications,' Edwards muttered as he turned on his heel.

She made sure Edwards had gone while Clifford slid out a large manilla envelope from one of the cabinet drawers marked "May Fair, May 1st 1921."

He tipped the contents onto the wooden top and spread the photographs out in five rows.

She stared at them. 'Clifford, it was a brilliant idea of yours to see if we could spot Burgess in any of these but this is going to take an age.'

'Perhaps not, my lady. They are in fact methodically organised in line with the schedule of the day. Starting with the opening of the fair and ending with' – he laid the last photograph down, lining it up precisely with its neighbour – 'the departure of the stretcher carrying Solemn Jon's body.'

She shuddered. 'Why on earth would you take a photograph of that?'

'Because it sells newspapers, sadly.'

Her eyes narrowed. 'Which we have realised is Edwards' sole purpose in life, irrespective of any moral considerations.'

Clifford nodded and ran a finger along the fourth row. 'These are all of the crowds watching the raft race. I'll start there.'

'And I'll start towards the end of the proceedings.'

She took the small leather case containing a fold-out magnifying glass he offered her. They worked in silence for a few minutes, stepping around each other as they scoured and re-scoured the lines of photographs.

'Dash it!' she muttered. 'It was such a good idea.'

'*Is* a good idea, my lady.' Clifford held up a photograph he'd scooped from the first row.

'Really! Where am I looking?'

He nudged her magnifying glass over to the top right.

'Behind the image of yourself trying valiantly to avoid Mr Prestwick-Peterson as we toured the fair at the start, my lady. The man turning away from the May basket stall with the hat pulled down low and thick scarf pulled up? There is no mistaking that nose the camera angle has fortunately caught him at.'

'That's him, Clifford! And that's why I recognised him in the fishing competition photograph. He bumped into me among the stalls while I was trying to make sure our ladies didn't see me so as not to spoil their fun.' She frowned. 'And I recognise him now as the man I saw at Solemn Jon's funeral at the back of the church.' She slapped her forehead. 'And he was the man sitting at the gatekeeper's table when we went back to the Rankin estate!' She scanned the rest of the photographs. 'Is this the only one, though? No, look! Now I know what we are looking for, this one has just leapt out at me. Here.' She picked up a photograph from the end of the second row. 'The person walking away from the procession I'm leading towards the river. It's Burgess again!'

Clifford nodded. 'Which means that we now have proof that not only did he purchase the very same fishing twine found at both murder scenes, but that he was also at the May Fair.'

Without a word, Clifford deftly slid both photographs into his jacket pocket. As they left, Eleanor bumped into Edwards emerging from his office.

'Ah, Mr Edwards. We're leaving, but you will be receiving some other visitors shortly. Do give his majesty's constabulary my regards, won't you?' She ignored the fear in his eyes and continued on her way.

CHAPTER 46

Outside on the pavement, Clifford cleared his throat.

'My lady, if Mr Burgess is responsible, I must remind you it would appear he is getting desperate. Consider, as I have constantly, the gargoyle incident again.'

She frowned. 'What do you mean?'

'I mean, despite what I may have said previously, I am now in significant doubt it was intended as a warning only.'

'Why?'

'Because it occurred to me that the culprit may have toppled that particular gargoyle simply because the one directly above you would not budge.'

She stopped abruptly. 'I hadn't considered that.' She thought for a moment and then shook her head. 'The only way to check would be to return to Rankin Hall and climb on the roof and try to budge the middle gargoyle, but we don't have time. We finally have a breakthrough. The killer, if we're right and my intuition is telling me we are, is no longer a faceless murderer. We know who he is. We know he was at the May Fair and we know he had knowledge of Rankin Hall and the estate. Therefore, he had the opportunity on both occasions. But why was he still hanging around the estate?'

Clifford nodded. 'That is a mystery, but he also had the means, having purchased especially strong fishing twine. Although, admittedly, the actual weapon he used to deliver the final blow to both men, we've yet to discover. And maybe never will. He may have thrown it in the river in the case of Solemn Jon's murder and thrown it in the ornamental lake in the case of Lord Rankin's. The lake is not far from where Lord Rankin died.'

She frowned. 'We still don't, however, have a motive.'

'Or know, my lady, where exactly Mr Burgess is. Or what his next move may be. He has killed twice already. And possibly tried to kill a third time.' He looked at her pointedly. 'I have to repeat my request from earlier that we contact Detective Chief Inspector Seldon urgently.'

Eleanor threw up her hands. 'I don't disagree in theory, Clifford, but how can I ask for his help, even with these photographs of Burgess and the twine? They won't convince Seldon the two deaths were not an accident, especially as the twine has disappeared from both murder scenes. And the hook. I don't think a worn medallion I found in the mud near the scene of Solemn Jon's death is going to convince him either. Even if he believed it himself, we both know he needs firmer evidence than that before he can act.'

'Reluctantly, I agree, my lady. However, let us not forget, we are also suspicious that Lord Rankin's father's death may not have been an innocent one. Which means Burgess, as he was in service as the head butler at that time, may in fact have killed three times already.'

It was her turn to nod. 'I understand that, Clifford. But there is only one way to get Seldon's help with this.'

He let out an uncharacteristic groan. 'Please tell me I'm wrong in what I think you are saying, my lady?'

'I can't. You know as well as I do, we have no choice but to find more evidence ourselves. And that means finding Burgess.' She turned and started walking towards the Rolls. Clifford hastened to catch her up. As they drew level with the car, he opened the door for her and she climbed in. 'The only problem is, Clifford, we have absolutely no idea where he is.'

He closed the door and made his way round to the driver's seat. Once he'd started the engine, he turned to her.

'*We* may have no idea where our killer is, my lady, but I know a man who might.'

Eleanor, having swiftly rung the bell, retreated to the third step, having no desire for a repeat of the falling gargoyle incident. Clifford stood beside the Rolls in the drive, scanning the roofline. As the door opened, he gave her the thumbs up and she darted past the startled butler. In the hallway, she turned to him.

'Good morning, Houghton.'

'Lady Swift, good morning.' He tried, and failed, to keep the surprise from his voice. 'Forgive me, did I, er, miss a message you were due to call?'

'Not at all. I never left one.' She had no intention of telling him why she hadn't rung ahead. In fact, Clifford had pointed out that, as Burgess' replacement, it was possible Houghton was in touch with Lord Rankin's ex-butler. And if that was the case, he might alert Burgess that they were on to him. 'But now I am here, I have a few questions.'

Houghton's expression registered confusion. 'I'm afraid all the guests from his lordship's funeral have left, my lady. The gentleman from the legal firm has retired back to Oxford until later this afternoon. It is just the staff making the initial preparations as per the lawyer's instructions for the passing on of the estate to the crown.'

'I know. However, it is you I've come to see.'

'As you wish, my lady.'

He showed her into a nearby drawing room with faded mustard wallpaper and a single stiff-backed upholstered settee. The blue patterned rug beneath her shoes gave off the air of having been stored in a locked and rather damp cupboard for some time. He clasped his hands behind his back and waited for her to begin.

'How long have you been here, Houghton?'

'Since March, my lady.'

'You seem to have taken things in your stride well enough. Besides, I'm sure your predecessor, Burgess, would have shown you everything pertinent before he left?'

He shook his head. 'I have not met the gentleman. He had... retired just before I joined.'

'Retired? Was that a decision of his own making, do you know?'

'I really couldn't say, my lady.'

Blast, Ellie! Why are all butlers so cagey?

'You haven't met him? That's strange. I assumed he would have called to pay his respects following Lord Rankin's passing. Given the news that Lord Rankin died intestate, it would be odd if he hadn't at least offered his sympathies to his former colleagues who will now need to seek alternative employment.'

'Mr Burgess has not had any contact with anyone at the house that I am aware of.' The butler's face registered his confusion. 'If you will forgive my speaking up, my lady, I am unsure why you have visited this morning to ask about my predecessor.'

She shrugged. 'Have you checked the soundness of the remaining gargoyles on the roof yet?'

His cheeks coloured. 'My humble apologies once again, Lady Swift. I do hope you were not too shaken. It was most regrettable.'

He replied so readily and genuinely, she had no doubt the event had horrified him as much as it had her. *Trust your intuition, Ellie.* She nodded to herself.

'Tell me, Houghton, do you know where I might find Burgess? It really is rather important that I speak to him.'

He shook his head. 'As I mentioned, I have never met the gentleman. But perhaps one of the more long-serving members of staff might be able to help. Would you like me to enquire on your behalf, my lady?'

'Very much so. And I appreciate your obvious discretion. I understand it must seem like a peculiar request.'

'Not at all, my lady.'

He gave a Clifford-worthy bow and stepped to the shortest of the bell sashes by the fireplace. A minute later, the housekeeper poked her head around the door.

'Did you ring, Mr Houghton? Oh, goodness, my apologies, m'lady.' She curtsied to Eleanor. 'I didn't realise there was company in the house. Most irregular,' she muttered. 'Er, will you take tea or coffee, my lady?'

Eleanor shook her head. 'Neither, thank you.'

'Mrs Frampton,' Houghton said. 'A question, please. Are you aware of Mr Burgess' location after he retired?'

She stared at him quizzically. 'No, Mr Houghton. Mr Burgess has no family in the area. Nor out of the area for that matter that I know of. Like the other staff, I suspect he has taken whatever lodgings wherever he could at short notice given his unexpected "retirement".'

'Perhaps another member of the staff might have been in touch with him?' Houghton said.

She threw him a sharp look. 'Before his lordship's death, we were all rather busy adjusting to his new appointments, as well as settling into his… new ways.' She sniffed. 'So different from his father. Anyway, we've had no time for chit-chat or goodbyes.' She shrugged. 'Although now his lordship is dead, we'll all be looking for new appointments, won't we?'

Houghton glanced at Eleanor who nodded, indicating there was no point pursuing the conversation. He turned back to the housekeeper. 'Thank you, Mrs Frampton. That will be all.'

With a curtsy to Eleanor, the housekeeper left.

Houghton escorted Eleanor back to the hallway and opened the front door.

'I am sorry you had a wasted trip, my lady.'

She smiled at him. 'Not to worry. At least nothing's fallen on me this time.' With a quick confirmation that Clifford was giving her the thumbs up, she darted out of the door and down the steps.

As they reached the gatehouse to the Rankin estate, Clifford slowed down the Rolls.

'I overheard Mr Houghton's parting remark to you, my lady. I take it none of the staff knows of Mr Burgess' whereabouts?'

She nodded. 'Correct, Clifford. Turn left, please.'

He looked at her quizzically. 'May I ask why left?'

She nodded. 'Because Houghton was wrong. It wasn't a wasted trip. The staff at Rankin Hall may not know where Burgess is, but I do.'

CHAPTER 47

'Willie's not here.' Mrs Trimble's sharp amber eyes bore into Eleanor's. She stopped running a bony hand over her rabbit's ears and pointed at her. 'Mind, if he was, I don't think as he'd appreciate you calling. Not after everything. You should leave.' She gripped both wheels of her adapted kitchen chair and spun round.

Eleanor stepped forward. The sun had already set and a cold breeze was blowing off the river. There were no street lights and the old mill loomed over them, a dark, ominous outline in the gathering dark.

'We aren't here to see Willie Green, Mrs Trimble, because I know he isn't here. He's locked up at Chipstone Police Station. I also know he's innocent of any wrongdoing.'

The landlady turned her chair back around, her expression suspicious. She looked at Clifford who was keeping a close eye on the front of the house. He nodded.

'It pains me to say, dear lady, that like many others, I grossly misjudged Mr Green.'

'Willie's got a lot of good in him despite what folk say,' she muttered.

'Unquestionably,' Clifford said.

Eleanor lowered her voice. 'Unlike your newest lodger, Mrs Trimble. It is him we've come to see. We believe that despite what Mr Green thinks, it is Mr Burgess who is responsible for much that Mr Green has been blamed for.'

Best not mention you were one of the ones doing the blaming, Ellie.
The landlady frowned and shook her head.

'Mr Burgess? But Willie found him for me when I was two lodgers short. Willie said he'd been cast out just like he had been and needed a place to stay till he was on his feet. Always paid regular, has Mr Burgess. And he helped me clear all the flints from the garden only today. So nice for Willie to have a friend.'

Exactly, Ellie! Thank goodness the housekeeper at Rankin Hall mentioned that Burgess had been forced to find any lodgings he could at short notice. We'd never have found him otherwise.

She looked over the landlady's face in concern. 'Mrs Trimble, you said last time we spoke that Willie Green had found you a lodger who had lost his job when his master had died. What better place for him to plan Solemn Jon's murder than in Little Buckford, right across the landing from Solemn Jon's assistant, Willie Green? The man who knew Solemn Jon's habits better than anyone.'

And the only man other than Solemn Jon and Evander who knew there was something fishy about Lord Rankin's father's death, Ellie!

'My dear lady,' Clifford's voice carried all the charm it had on their last visit. But now, also a sense of urgency. 'That is exactly why we need to find Mr Burgess before Mr Green is released from gaol. Mr Green's life may very well be in danger. Along with everyone else in this house.' Clifford looked directly into the landlady's eyes. 'We need to act quickly and get up to his room. Are there any other lodgers apart from Mr Burgess in at the moment?'

The suspicion in the landlady's eyes was now replaced by fear.

'No, there's… there's no one but … *him*, up there. Fourth floor. End of the landing.'

'Good.' Clifford glanced at the next house along. 'Can you go immediately and stay with a neighbour so we can be sure you aren't in any danger?'

She nodded, spun around and wheeled herself rapidly along the street to the next house. Clifford waited until he saw the door open and the landlady disappear inside before nodding at Eleanor.

Inside, in the unlit hallway, she pointed up the stairs. He blocked her path firmly with his arm. She shook her head vehemently and pointed up the stairs again. He hesitated, then resignedly removed his arm before sliding a pistol from inside his jacket and stepping noiselessly on up first.

As well as being near pitch-black, it was eerily quiet on the stairwell, except for the creaking of the steps as they reached the fourth-floor landing. Eleanor closed her eyes and calmed her heart. *Has anyone ever built stairs that don't creak, Ellie?*

Clifford stopped and pointed to a door at the furthest end of the landing, only just visible in the gloom. Burgess' room, according to the landlady. He gestured for her to wait. Watching him slide stealthily along the wall of the landing did nothing to keep her heart rate steady. At the door, he paused, his ear to it.

Eleanor couldn't stop her feet silently running to his side. 'Team,' she mouthed.

He went to argue but changed his mind and nodded. Focusing on the door, he inched his hand out to the handle. Slowly he turned it and let the door swing inwards.

Inside, the room was as black as the stairwell. Eleanor struggled to make out anything at all. Then the room was bathed in a shaft of moonlight. Through the window in the wall to her left she could make out the clouds peeling back from the moon. She realised the muted rushing noise she could hear outside was in fact the river directly four-storeys below.

In the ghostly light she could now make out a threadbare armchair with a coarse woollen blanket thrown on the seat as if someone had risen in a hurry. A half-drunk bottle of what she took to be brandy or gin stood on a rickety-looking table next to it. The room was bitterly cold despite the warmth of the day, an unlit fire sitting forlornly in the grate. The floor was unpolished wooden boards, bare except for a small, worn rug in the middle. At the other end of the room, only a few feet away from the armchair, was a single wooden bed and a small wash basin.

Clifford stepped silently into the room, swinging his pistol back and forth as he scoured it for any sign of life. Eleanor eyed the door, which had swung open until the wall had stopped it. *Perhaps he's hiding behind the door, Ellie?* She caught Clifford's eye and pointed to it. He nodded and slowly stepped around the armchair until he could see behind the door, his gun always in front of him. She held her breath but he shook his head.

He returned to the middle of the room, surveyed it one more time and then lowered his gun.

'It seems our prey has bolted, my lady.'

She nodded. 'It would seem so. I wonder if Houghton alerted him? Or perhaps he heard us talking to Mrs Trimble. Let's—'

A faint sound came from behind her. She was already turning when she felt the knife at her throat.

'I've been waiting for you.'

CHAPTER 48

She froze. Clifford spun round and trained his pistol just above her shoulder.

For a moment there was complete silence.

'Put your gun down, Mr Clifford.'

She could smell the man's breath on her neck. She frowned. *No alcohol, Ellie!* She looked across at Clifford. Had he guessed also, from the lack of slurred words, that the bottle had been placed on the table to subtly make them drop their guard? A man who'd consumed half a bottle wouldn't be much of a threat. In the wan light, she couldn't make out Clifford's features but his tone suggested he'd lost none of the calm he always exhibited in dangerous situations.

'I don't think so, Mr Burgess.'

Stalemate. *Don't move, Ellie! Just keep your cool. Breathe.* She slowly exhaled. She'd been in life-threatening situations before, here and abroad, but she'd never had a knife at her throat. The silence stretched on.

Burgess cracked first. 'I'm warning you. Put your gun down or—'

'Or what, Mr Burgess?' said Clifford, his voice as cool as if he were discussing a small matter of housekeeping, not her life. 'If you had intended to kill Lady Swift, you would have done it with that gargoyle while she was at Rankin Hall, not here, with a knife.'

What about his theory that Burgess meant to kill me but just couldn't shift the gargoyle directly above you, Ellie? She willed herself to say calm. He was just buying her time.

'I wasn't so desperate then, Mr Clifford.' Burgess' voice cracked. 'Desperation can lead a man to do things he wouldn't normally contemplate.'

'Like murder?'

'Like… murder. Now put down the gun and I give you my word as one butler to another I won't harm Lady Swift.'

It felt surreal to listen to two butlers discussing her life – and death – as if they were disagreeing over the correct way to carve the Sunday joint.

'Agreed, Mr Burgess. On the count of *three*, I will place the gun down and you will release Lady Swift.'

Three, Ellie! That's the signal.

'Agreed.'

'One… two… th—'

'Mr Burgess, do you like duck soup?'

Eleanor felt the hand holding the knife drop slightly as Burgess tried to make sense of her last remark.

Instantly, she grabbed his arm with her left hand and pulled it down to her chest, the knife now pointing away from her. At the same time, she stamped on his instep with her heel and bit down on his now trapped arm with all her might.

Burgess let out a howl, dropped the knife and leaped backwards. As it hit the ground Clifford was there scooping it up. Eleanor ran to his side and turned to face her attacker, Clifford's gun once again trained on him.

Now she was able to see that what she and Clifford had taken to be a solid wall behind where she'd been standing, was actually a small, concealed storage cupboard. She turned her attention back to Burgess who was nursing his arm and standing tentatively on his bruised foot staring at them in disbelief. *That's what you get for threatening a lady with a knife*, she thought with grim satisfaction. *It's time for some answers.*

'Why, Mr Burgess? Why?'

Burgess stared at her without speaking. Finally, he shook his head.

'Lord Rankin was a good man.'

She exchanged a confused glance with Clifford.

'*Lord Rankin?* The man you murdered?'

The old butler's weary tone turned to anger. 'Not that devil! His father. Like chalk and cheese, they were.'

'You didn't retire, did you, Mr Burgess? You were dismissed?'

He nodded slowly. 'He knew I loathed him for the way he'd deceived his father.'

Clifford lowered the pistol. 'You mean about the estate's finances?'

The old butler nodded again. 'After his first son was killed in the war, his lordship placed all his trust in his second son, Evander, who chose to repay him by bankrupting the estate and blackening the family name.'

'But that wasn't the only reason Lord Rankin dismissed you, was it?' said Eleanor.

He shook his head again. 'No, he realised I was the only one who might have been able to work out the truth of how his father died.'

Eleanor and Clifford exchanged another glance. *Of course, Ellie! He's telling the truth. You don't need your intuition to know that this time.*

Burgess' face twisted with disgust. 'Lord Rankin murdered his father! What monster poisons their father?'

Eleanor nodded slowly.

'But what about the Spanish flu story?'

'Made up. Entirely made up! His son simply poisoned him. Exactly how I don't know. But I know he then got old Doctor Crump to sign the death certificates quickly. Then he got that other devil to prepare and bury the body. And him, of all people, he should have been the one to speak up!' Burgess closed his eyes. 'I failed his lordship.'

'Even the strongest loyalty can't ensure we can always fulfil every duty we sincerely wish to, Mr Burgess,' Clifford said quietly. 'But no additional wrong can set another right.'

Eleanor nodded, but frowned at the same time. 'You said "he" of all people should have spoken up. Who did you mean?'

Burgess' eyes flashed. 'That scoundrel Solemn Jon, of course.'

'Solemn Jon? Why should he, of all people, have been the one to speak up?'

Burgess shook his head. 'I may have failed to protect his lordship's life, but I won't fail to protect his name. That will go to the grave with me. Ironic that the only one who guessed, no one would have believed. That's why he came to me.'

'You mean Willie Green?'

He nodded. 'That's right. Willie came to me the day before his lordship's funeral to tell me something was badly wrong, horribly, wrong. He'd tried to have it out with Solemn Jon but the devil just sent him off with a flea in his ear. Told him to keep his mouth shut or he'd never inherit his undertaker's business when he died. That's what made me look into finding out the truth.' He covered his face with his hands and spoke through his fingers. 'Lord Rankin and Solemn Jon covered the whole murder up between them.'

Oh, Ellie, why didn't you heed Twain's advice about swinging cats as Clifford cautioned before you began this? What are you going to tell Solemn Jon's wife now?

A noise outside the window away from the river caught her attention. Clifford motioned to Eleanor that they needed to keep Burgess talking.

'Why did you feel you couldn't go to the police with what you discovered?' she said quickly.

'Who would ever have believed me against the word of a lord? Justice doesn't work that way.'

That's the second time you've heard those words recently, Ellie. And you still can't disagree.

Clifford cleared his throat. 'Mr Burgess, you can still do one decent thing before this is over. Your guilt need not affect that of another erroneously. Tell me, how did you kill Solemn Jon?'

He ran a hand over his face. 'I'd been waiting for an opportunity, finding out what I could from Willie. Then he told me he was going to pretend to be ill on the day of the May Fair so he could see his girlfriend. That meant Solemn Jon would be alone and would struggle at the back, given that all the other rafts had teams of at least two. I snuck out and hid my fishing clothes and tackle and then simply waited.' His voice began to shake. 'I… I cast my line. It caught on the back of his raft and I reeled him in. He thought the current had caught him. Then I… I hit him on the head with a big flint I found on the bank and then threw it in the river. I tried to wrench the hook and line off but it ripped into my finger and I fled. Solemn Jon, though, I swear he didn't suffer. He was already dead when he hit the water, I'm sure of it.'

So it wouldn't have made any difference if you'd got there earlier, Ellie. She threw Clifford a grateful look.

'And you were watching her ladyship when she rode out with Lord Rankin?' said Clifford.

'Yes, but' – Burgess turned to Eleanor – 'I waited until you left before I killed him.'

She shrugged. 'Why bother, when you then tried to kill me with the gargoyle?'

He cast his eyes down. 'That was only supposed to scare you. Honestly. It was easy to secretly access the house after all my years in service there but I wasn't used to being on the roof and, stupidly, I slipped and the stonework fell far too close to you. Far, far too close. I'm so sorry. My head was all over the place by then. I was just trying to stop you finding out the truth because I knew of your reputation for investigating these things. But' – he shook his head wearily – 'at the same time I desperately wanted to be caught. To… to confess what I'd done. That's why I kept going back to the estate.'

Again, she believed him. After killing Rankin he could have quietly slipped away. Instead, he'd just been waiting here. *Waiting for you to come, Ellie. Then why did he hold a knife to your throat?*

Burgess started speaking again, as if he'd heard her thoughts.

'Somehow I found myself back where I'd killed that scoundrel Rankin. But then you turned up. The minute you'd gone, I cut the fishing twine from the base of the trees. I couldn't do it at the time because the gamekeeper interrupted me. I knew it was no use, though. I knew you'd find me in the end. And… in my heart I wanted you to.'

So it was kids taking the hook and line from Solemn Jon's raft, Ellie. You were wrong.

The low murmur of voices down below filtered up to Eleanor's ears. She caught the distinctive voice of Sergeant Brice. Clifford nodded to her. Someone had sent for the police. *Probably the landlady's neighbour, Ellie.* She stared at the sad figure Burgess cut. She had to be sure she was wrong about one more thing. She'd told Clifford if they found whoever wrote the obituaries, they'd find their killer. She now hoped she was as wrong about that as she believed she was.

'Mr Burgess, I don't think you wrote those obituaries, did you?'

He shook his head. 'No. I would never have put Willie's name on them. He didn't deserve that. And I've no idea who did write them. Willie was the only person who might have been suspicious about Solemn Jon's death, but no one believed anything he said after that first obituary. Something about it appearing in print was like some divine power aiding me, telling me I had to kill that devil Rankin as well. And then the second obituary came out and it was like that divine power telling me again I'd done the right thing. Only' – he shook his head – 'a part of me knew evil only begets more evil.'

'As Willie had come to you with his suspicions over Lord Rankin senior's death, were you not concerned he would suspect you?' Clifford said, holding up a discreet hand to halt the two forms who had appeared on the landing. 'Why did you not see fit to kill him as well? He was sleeping in the room here next to yours night after night, after all.'

Burgess shook his head. 'Willie was entirely innocent in Lord Rankin's father's death. They used him like a pawn. I'm not a saint, but I'm not a cold-blooded killer. I'm only an instrument of justice. Justice that would never have happened otherwise.'

Eleanor reached into her pocket and drew out the medallion. 'You mentioned saints, Mr Burgess. Did you lose this when you killed Solemn Jon, by any chance?'

He took it from her hand, Clifford training the gun on him as he did. He held it in his palm and nodded.

'My aunt gave this to me when I got my first job in service. She told me so long as I had it I'd always know the right thing to do. And now I've got it back—'

Clifford lowered his hand and Sergeant Brice followed by three other policemen entered the room.

Burgess glanced at them and then back at Eleanor. 'And now I've got it back and confessed my sins as best I can, it's time I did the right thing again.'

He turned and launched himself at the window. There was a horrible sound of splintering wood and glass and then silence.

The sound of his body hitting the water below galvanised Sergeant Brice into action. He rushed over and peered down into the inky river. He turned back, his face furious.

'Quick, lads, get down there! He won't get far afore—'

'Sergeant!'

Something in her tone, made Brice stop.

'Lady Swift, he's—'

'Going nowhere, Sergeant.' Suddenly wrung out, she dropped onto the edge of the armchair and looked to Clifford to explain.

Clifford nodded. 'I think you'll find, Sergeant Brice, that Mr Burgess jumped into the river with his pockets filled with flints from his landlady's garden.'

CHAPTER 49

Eleanor shuffled forward in the blue armchair, reaching out for the other woman's hand. 'Maggie, it's probably little consolation, but I believed Mr Burgess when he said Solemn Jon didn't suffer. It was over too quick for him to even realise.'

Patrick let out a soft whine and laid his head on his mistress' lap, which was already soaked through from the tears still pouring down her face. Maggie pulled another handkerchief from her pocket.

'Thank you, m'lady. I've been praying you'd come and tell me I'd been wrong to suspect someone did for my John, but I knew all along in here it were so.' She patted her heart. 'I never meant for you to be in danger though, nor Mr Clifford. To think you went and confronted the culprit. But thank you so much for getting him to own up to his terrible deeds.'

Eleanor squeezed the woman's hand. 'I can't take any credit for that, honestly. I truly believe Burgess felt completely wretched about what he did. Although it doesn't diminish his crime in any way, in his mind he is convinced he was an instrument of justice.'

Her heart stopped as her last words came out. *Ellie, no! She hasn't asked why Burgess killed Solemn Jon. That will surely have put the idea into her head!* She held her breath, dreading what she would hear next.

'Nothing'll ever make what that man did to my John right,' Maggie said. 'But 'tis done. I can't change time and bring him back.'

Confused but relieved she hadn't been asked the dreaded question, Eleanor struggled for a few final words of comfort, wishing Clifford was there, not waiting for her in the Rolls.

'I hope that very soon you can focus only on all the happy memories you have of Solemn Jon. With Patrick's help, of course.' She ran her hand along the wolfhound's back.

Maggie glanced over at the corner of the room and paused. With a quiet decisive nod, she lifted Patrick's head from her lap, kissed his long nose and then rose from the armchair. 'M'lady, I'm so grateful for all you've done.'

'Oh, yes.' Eleanor stood up hurriedly. 'Of course, it's time I let you be.'

'No, my lady.' Maggie looked down at her hands. 'I never told you quite… everything. 'Tis me who's to be sorry.'

Eleanor flapped a hand. 'Please don't apologise, Maggie. Nothing else need be said.'

Maggie shook her head. 'Nope, 'tis one more thing that must be done, m'lady. Begging your pardon for saying different to you, mind.'

Eleanor followed her over to the far corner where she paused at the roll-top desk. 'My John built this himself, m'lady. He could have been a cabinet maker, but he felt such a compassion for the deceased, he followed in the family footsteps.' She hesitated again. 'The thing is, m'lady, I can tell he's hurting badly at the thought we don't know summat. I can hear him calling me. You see, I was tidying John's things as is only right the day after the funeral and I found this.' Maggie lifted the roll-top section of the desk. 'My John led me to it.'

Eleanor leaned over and gasped. 'There's a secret drawer!' She looked anxiously at the other woman. 'Maggie, are you sure you want me here?'

'My John wants us both here, m'lady. Afore when I realised there was summat, I knew right away not to look inside, especially until the man that did for him was locked up. But now he's asking me to.'

Eleanor nodded and watched as Maggie slid the drawer aside. They both bent down. ''Tis some papers, m'lady.'

Back in the armchairs, Eleanor poured Maggie another cup of tea and placed it gently by her hand while the woman read through the letters and documents. The tea cooled as the woman gasped and shook her head repeatedly. Finally, she looked up.

'Well, it's hard to credit, but 'tis quite clear from this, m'lady. My John's real father was Lord Rankin senior.'

It was Eleanor's turn to gasp. 'What? I mean, how?'

''Tis all written here. I knew my John was adopted, but he always told me his parents said as how the orphanage never told them who the real parents were. It seems he was a mistake baby, born out of illicit passion with a woman below his father's station. He was given away to a couple who were moving into the area. Lord Rankin's father paid for them to start an undertaker's here in Little Buckford as the previous undertaker had just passed away and had no successor.'

It was Eleanor's turn to shake her head. *So that's what Lady Lambourne meant when she said Solemn Jon's presence at Rankin Hall would bring shame on the family name, Ellie. She knew about Lord Rankin's father's affair and that Solemn Jon was his illegitimate child.*

Maggie waved another paper at Eleanor. 'And it says here, my John found out about his father when he was twenty-three. He went up to Rankin Hall to meet him. Told old Rankin that he didn't hold any grudges and was happy with his lot and wouldn't change it for the world. It seems they even met up on the odd occasion after too. In secret, of course.'

She passed Eleanor another of the letters. Eleanor bit her lip as she read it. It was from Evander to Solemn Jon claiming their father had committed suicide due to insurmountable debts. It called for his help in burying him quickly to save their father's good name and the family a scandal.

Oh, Ellie, I knew Solemn Jon was a good man after all. Evander tricked him! If only Burgess had known the truth about what Solemn Jon believed he was doing.

'Financial, what was it?' Maggie cut into her thoughts as Eleanor scoured the letter in her hand again.

'Irregularities,' Eleanor said quietly. 'The Rankin estate was in financial difficulty, that part is true. But only because Lord Rankin the younger was bleeding it dry to pay for Tretheway's illegal schemes.' She remembered Tretheway's threats, but shook them out of her head. 'And Lord Rankin's father didn't take his own life. Lord Rankin lied.'

Maggie frowned. 'How did he die then?'

'Lord Rankin poisoned him.'

Maggie gasped. 'I can't believe a son would do that to his father. It beggars belief.'

Eleanor nodded. 'Maggie, Solemn Jon genuinely imagined he was saving his real father from disgrace by helping Evander bury him quickly under the guise of Spanish flu.'

Maggie managed a half smile. 'I won't say as there'll never be another like my John, but there's not many who'd have done what he did. I see now that Burgess fellow mistook what my John did. And God bless you for having the courage to come and tell me.' Before Eleanor could reply, Maggie picked up her now cold tea. 'Now, you know how my John felt, m'lady. Always said we should celebrate a person's life, not mourn their passing.'

They raised their teacups to Solemn Jon.

Maggie placed her cup down and shook her head once again.

'I can't believe though that the newspaperman wrote those obituaries and published them himself, m'lady. What on earth made him do that?'

Eleanor nodded. 'I didn't believe it at first, either, Maggie. It seems Elijah Edwards' business was in serious trouble as circulation had dropped badly on all his publications. He didn't have the money to invest in turning over to the more modern magazine style that people want now. So, disgracefully, he had the idea of publishing a controversial obituary for Solemn Jon, knowing it would sell papers because he was such a popular character in the area. Everyone bought a copy out of disbelief and uproar, just as Edwards reckoned they would. And he hit on the idea of signing it 'William Green' because he knew Mr Green was about the least respected member of the community. Therefore, everyone would readily believe he was capable of such an act, and would also disbelieve his denials.'

Maggie's lips met in a thin line. 'And he done the same for young Lord Rankin too, then?'

Eleanor nodded. 'With Lord Rankin's obituary, it was doubly personal because he'd insulted Edwards publicly. I was there, actually, at a lunch at Langham Manor. It was unforgivably rude of Lord Rankin. I imagine Edwards took extra delight in writing and publishing that one.'

'But the obituary for yourself, m'lady. That must have given you the shock of your life.'

Eleanor nodded again. 'That's a longer story. Suffice to say, Edwards had informants all round the area who would feed him juicy titbits in exchange for cash. One of them worked at Rankin Hall and was there when I… when some stonework fell from the roof. Edwards deliberately ignored the fact that I was fine, if a little shaken, and printed an obituary for me, again falsely signing it "William Green". Again, it was designed to sell more of his wretched newspapers.'

And to think that you came to that man's defence at the Langham lunch, Ellie!

'Well, thank the stars you're alright, m'lady. And so bright at these things. You and Mr Clifford are quite the team, mind. But how did you know it was the newspaperman as what wrote the obituaries?'

'Edwards tried to be clever. He misspelled the notes he posted through the letterbox of his office to make it look like Mr Green had written them. And, of course, the typesetter would innocently back up the story that they must have been written by someone less educated because he had to correct most of the words. But Edwards made one simple mistake. He signed the obituaries "William Green" and Willie hates being called William. I saw that myself.'

Maggie thought for a moment.

'When you was telling me about how you worked out the fisherman on the bank was this Burgess man, you said at first you suspected it was Willie. On account, you know, of finding the fishing hacksters in his cabin.'

Eleanor tried to be tactful. 'Mr Green was very honest about them. He found them hidden in the woods on the way back from meeting his g— on the way back from somewhere. He hoped he could sell them, seeing as they must have been, you know, abandoned, as it were. He'd have been horrified if he'd known who wore them and why.' She cleared her throat. 'Anyway, Maggie, one last thing, and forgive me I don't wish to pry at all, but will you be alright?'

Maggie patted Eleanor's hand. 'I understand as you mean for money, and thank you for being so kind but, yes, m'lady. I did Willie wrong by refusing to let him have the yard when I thought he'd written that awful obituary about my John. I've told him since as how I'd like the business to be a partnership. I'll deal with the accounts as I did for my John. And also with folks as come to agree the arrangements for their loved ones. Willie was very happy about that as he's not so good with folks, as you know. And he'll deal with the coffins and headstones, prepare the bodies and drive the funeral coach. 'Twill keep me busy and' – she stroked the wolfhound's ear – 'let Patrick be where he's spent all his best days, in his bed in John's woodworking shop.'

'Maggie, that's wonderful!'

She nodded. 'Folks was wrong about Willie. Me too. He tried to go to the police when he suspected it was no accident that took my John even though he believed my John did summat bad in burying Lord Rankin's father secretly, like.' She tilted her head. 'And his father too, we know now. But Willie never told the village, nor the police. In his way, he stood by my John, and tried to get justice for him, despite what he thought he'd done. And that makes him alright by me, and' – she patted the wolfhound's head that lay in her lap – 'Patrick.'

As Eleanor closed the garden gate behind her and turned to walk to the Rolls, a voice called out.

'So, still spying on me are you, Lady Swift?'

She spun round. It was Willie Green, except the usual fixed scowl on his face had been replaced by something close to a smug grin. She laughed.

'No, Mr Green, I'm not spying on you. Maybe you are spying on me?'

He shrugged. 'Can't have been spying on you and your fancy man though, can I? I've only just got out of gaol. Now –' he doffed an imaginary cap – 'you'll have to excuse me. I've got a business appointment with my new partner.' He pointed to Maggie standing on the doorstep of the cottage. Eleanor moved aside so he could pass. At the gate, he swung round. 'I still don't get you at all. But' – he grinned – 'thanks for believing in me. Finally!' He sauntered away down the path.

Eleanor slid gratefully into the Rolls.

'Where to, my lady?'

She sank back into the seat and closed her eyes.

'I thought you were a wizard. Guess!'

CHAPTER 50

'It's so kind of you to call, Hugh.'

On the hallway settle, with the handset of the telephone tucked against her shoulder, Eleanor hugged her drawn-up knees.

'And I'm still sorry. It wasn't that I wanted to deceive you about my continuing to investigate the two deaths, it's just that—'

'Don't worry, I understand what drove you to carry on. You made a promise to Solemn Jon's wife, not to me. In truth, it was very presumptuous of me to assume you'd break your promise. Although' – a short rich chuckle tickled her ear – 'now, you're lost.'

She frowned. 'How so?'

'Because, Eleanor, in future if this situation arises, I'll make you swear an oath to me personally. That should do it. After all, as you've proved again, you're a woman of your word.'

'Dash it! That's not fair!'

'No, but at least it might keep you safe.'

She laughed. 'But in all seriousness, how can I ever thank you enough for dealing with that leech, Tretheway? I thought he'd well and truly got his claws into me.'

Another chuckle came down the earpiece. 'It was my pleasure, Eleanor. I merely advised him, as a senior police detective, that a most incriminating file on certain of his more "exotic" business dealings was on my desk. If he didn't play ball and hand over to you all papers relating to Lord Henley's completely innocent part in his confounded illegal scheme, I'd be forced to pass it to my superiors.'

'And do you have such a file?'

'I do. Sir Tretheway is well known to us. Unfortunately, he's also been far too smart, so far, for us to have gathered any real evidence against him. But Tretheway doesn't know that and couldn't risk it. He was very contrite indeed. You have nothing to fear from him.'

'Well, thank you so much again. And for feeling you didn't need to investigate Uncle Byron's part in the whole affair.'

'I know both you and your uncle are beyond reproach, Eleanor. I have no trouble accepting your word.'

She laughed again. 'That's just as well, because Clifford has just finished burning the papers Tretheway sent over!' *You see, Ellie, Clifford was right. You could have asked for help earlier.* 'Now, I was serious. How can I thank you?'

'Ah, yes, how can you thank me?' There was a pause before he replied. 'How about we go for tea together again? But I insist there will be no talk of murder or other assorted mayhem. Agreed?'

'Agreed!'

'And maybe this time, Eleanor, we'll take a window seat.'

As she put down the receiver, Clifford materialised at her side.

'I believe, my lady, your presence is required in the kitchen.' Intrigued, she followed him. 'Ladies,' he announced as he held the door open for Eleanor to enter, 'it is time!'

Mrs Trotman bumped hips with Mrs Butters and Polly clapped her hands. Gladstone's ears pricked up and he woofed excitedly from his bed by the range.

Eleanor looked enquiringly at her staff. 'What time?'

The sound of a trumpet echoed brightly from the hallway. She spun round in surprise as Clifford marched back into the kitchen playing a fanfare.

'Clifford! How is it that you know how to play every instrument you pick up? And *what* time is it?'

He lowered the trumpet and took up a silver tray with five filled glasses.

'It is, in fact, my lady, the end of spring cleaning. We are done for another year.'

'Hurrah!' Eleanor said with heartfelt feeling. 'Thank you all so much. Now, I have a little surprise for you.'

She hurried upstairs to her room and returned a few moments later with her arms full.

'They're just a small token of my thanks.'

She motioned them all to the table where Clifford set a glass in front of each of them, Polly's being filled with non-alcoholic cordial with fruit pieces and a striped straw.

'Oh, my stars!' Mrs Trotman held up her box of scented hand cream. 'Thank you, my lady. No dishwater hands for me from now on, though 'tis too beautiful to use.'

'Trotters, look, there's matching soap too,' Mrs Butters said. 'My lady, you shouldn't have.'

'And a snuggly hot-water bottle,' Polly breathed, running her hand over its soft-knit jacket. 'Thank you kindly, your ladyship.'

Eleanor stole a peep at Clifford as he unwrapped his first gift. 'My lady, this is beyond thoughtful,' he murmured, his eyes shining. 'Voltaire's *Essay on Universal History, the Manners and Spirit of Nations*. An unimaginable treat.'

She couldn't keep the smile from her face. 'There's one more for you, ladies. And one for you too, Clifford.' She pointed to a catalogue she'd brought down with the presents. 'I have ordered us an electric washing machine with a built-in mangle to trial. What do you think?'

The ladies all cheered, causing Clifford to wince.

'I've never seen one of them afore,' said Polly.

'What'll we call her, my lady?' said Mrs Butters.

Eleanor tutted. 'Her? Why would the machine be a *she*? You've all named the vacuum cleaner Victor, after all? What about Walter, William or Wilfred?'

Mrs Trotman shook her head vehemently, looking mischievously at Clifford. 'We're not putting our underthings in anything called Wilfred, my lady! Lummy, how would that be for decorum, Mr Clifford?'

He ran a finger round his collar. 'I really couldn't say. If, however, I might claim the honour of naming the new washing machine, I propose "Hygeia", after the Greek goddess of hygiene.' He glanced at Eleanor. 'To save too much bawdy hilarity every Monday washday.'

Mrs Trotman frowned. 'But it don't, what's the word, Mr Clifford?'

'Alliterate?'

'That's it. It's got to alliterate.'

Eleanor and the ladies all nodded.

Clifford sighed. 'There are no Greek or Roman gods beginning with "w". How about "Wepwawet", the Egyptian god of water?'

Polly giggled. 'Wepwawet the Washing Machine!'

'That's decided then,' said Eleanor.

'Cake, Trotters!' Mrs Butters said.

As the three ladies scurried about getting plates and cake tins, Eleanor pushed an envelope towards Clifford.

'I know it's breaking the rules to apologise, but I am sorry that since I arrived I've unwittingly stolen so many of your days off. And before you even try and refuse, the voucher inside cannot be returned, only spent on fishing gubbins.'

'It is a shocking disregard for the rules, my lady, but I shall overlook it this once.' The corners of his mouth twitched. 'And I shall most gratefully go "gubbins" shopping. Although I might actually return with "fishing tackle".'

'As you wish.' She leaned across the table and whispered, 'Wepwawet isn't really the Egyptian god of water, is he?'

He shook his head. 'No, my lady. But I think we will be safe from his wrath. And, on the note of gifts, may I congratulate you on your choice of gift to the village?'

'Well, it was entirely your idea.' She turned to the ladies. 'I've bought a plot of land to be made into allotments for the villagers. I can't wait to see it all set up once the final permission is through.'

'Actually, it came through from Chipstone Town Hall half an hour ago, my lady. However, I did not want to overshadow your telephone call with a certain gentleman with the news.'

'So, it's official?'

'Indeed. So many families, Jack and Mews' included, will be able to grow fruit and vegetables at next to no cost. Especially with your generous stipend of an assortment of seeds to accompany each peppercorn subscription. We also secured a licence for hen houses to be allowed.'

'And how did Mr Mayhew take our offer of a remuneration for being the one to manage the plots and check on the welfare of the chickens?'

'With uncharacteristic gusto, my lady. You pitched the suggestion exactly right.'

'Excellent. And on an unrelated, but equally cheering note, I can't believe Mr Prestwick-Peterson has agreed to have look-out marshals along the riverbank at next year's May Fair raft race. Frankly, I was amazed.'

'Quite so. Perhaps your generous and, ahem, long-winded praise of his organisational skills helped? Could it be that you're finally learning the art of diplomacy, my lady?'

She hid a smile. 'I really couldn't say, Clifford.'

His eyes twinkled. 'Actually, before we partake of tea and cake, I believe Polly wants to speak with you.'

The ladies stopped laying the table and Mrs Butters gently pushed the nervous young girl forward. She looked back at Mrs Butters and then at the floor in front of Eleanor.

Eleanor smiled. 'Don't be shy, Polly. What is it?'

The young girl hesitated and then took the plunge. 'This evening, your ladyship is invited to the garden drawing room at… at…' She glanced back at Mrs Butters, who mouthed 'seven o'clock'. 'Oh, yes. Seven o'clock, your ladyship, for' – she ran her fingers up and down the table – 'for an evening of Sunday frocks and singing at the baby grand piano.'

Eleanor cocked an enquiring eyebrow at Clifford.

He cleared his throat. 'I hope, my lady, you do not take it as a liberty being invited to an evening function in your own house by your staff? You see, it is a tradition insisted upon by his late lordship to thank everyone for the extra work entailed during spring cleaning. And I know how insistent you are on keeping his lordship's traditions.'

She nodded. 'Absolutely. So what exactly *is* this particular tradition?'

'As you know, my lady, his lordship was never here when spring cleaning finished, not returning until the following day. Therefore he insisted all the staff had an evening's entertainment in any room in the Hall they wished the day spring cleaning finished. Excluding his study, of course. But as you have not left, young Polly asked if she could invite you to tonight's end-of-spring-cleaning celebration.'

She shook her head in amusement and turned to her maid. 'Thank you for the invitation, Polly. I would absolutely love to come.'

'Good job!' Mrs Trotman said. 'I've plenty of my cherry brandy.'

'And chestnut liqueur, I hope.' Eleanor laughed at Clifford's look of mock horror. 'Don't worry. I know what I'm letting myself in for, now.' She turned back to her housekeeper. 'Will Joseph join us, do you think?'

'I'll drag old muddy boots in myself,' Mrs Butters said. 'Joseph's got a beautiful voice. He sings to the plants in the greenhouses. Reckons it makes them grow. If we pour enough of Trotters' liqueur in him, he'll serenade us for hours.'

As they sat down at the table, Clifford checked his notebook.

'Ah! Perhaps before our musical soirée this evening, you might like to start on planning the afternoon tea you invited Miss Green, the postmistress, and her mother to? And then, perhaps, the event for Solemn Jon, my lady?'

She took her eyes off the enormous walnut, plum and chocolate cake Mrs Trotman was dividing up.

'Oh, yes, please. To both! I must say, I wasn't sure Maggie would take up my offer when I suggested she give the villagers a chance to join her in celebrating Solemn Jon's life.'

'Why not, my lady? It is a wonderful idea. And it was very generous of you to offer to provide everything needed to do so in the ballroom at Henley Hall. I believe Mrs Trimble, Mr Green's landlady, will be attending, along with Mr Green himself. And, I hear, he will not be coming alone.'

'Really? Who's he bringing along?'

'His now official girlfriend, Grace Padgett, my lady. I passed them walking out together in the high street earlier.'

A LETTER FROM VERITY

Dear reader,

I want to say a huge thank you for choosing to read *Murder at the Fair*. If you did enjoy it, and want to keep up to date with all my latest releases, just sign up at the following link. Your email address will never be shared and you can unsubscribe at any time.

www.bookouture.com/verity-bright

I hope you loved *Murder at the Fair* and if you did I would be very grateful if you could write a review. I'd love to hear what you think, and it makes such a difference helping new readers to discover one of my books for the first time.

I love hearing from my readers – you can get in touch on my Facebook page, through Twitter, Goodreads or my website.

Thanks,
Verity

@BrightVerity
veritybrightauthor
veritybright.com

ACKNOWLEDGEMENTS

My thanks go to our wonderful in-house support team (you know who you are) as well as to the amazing team at Bookouture for helping this book be way more than it had the right to be :)

HISTORICAL NOTES

May Fair

May Fairs or 'Fayres' like the one Eleanor is guest of honour at have their roots in the ancient Celtic festival of Beltane. Villagers would cavort around the maypole, often in drunken revelry with Jack-in-the-Green leading the festivities. (Often seen on public house signs nowadays as the 'Green Man'.)

When the established Church tried to ban May Day celebrations in Henry VIII's time, due to their pagan roots, there was widespread rioting. Oliver Cromwell's Puritans called maypole dancing a 'heathenish vanity generally abused to superstition and wickedness'. It wasn't until Charles II and the monarchy was restored, that May Day and maypole dancing was once again allowed.

Maypoles

The first mention of the maypole itself is in a poem attributed to Chaucer, 'Chaunce of the Dice'. Originally maypoles were a permanent fixture and thought to bring good luck, which resulted in rival villages stealing each other's maypoles and sometimes all-out pitched battles. Until Victorian times, adults as well as children danced around the maypole. I remember doing so as a child, although obviously not in Victorian times :). So Clifford's excuse that he is too old to dance around Little Buckford's maypole is unfortunately true.

Morris Dancers

The first reference to morris dancing was in 1448. The name originally meant 'Moorish dance', although there's very little in modern-day morris dancing to link it to the Moors. Often the dancers would blacken their faces, one supposes to look more like Moors, one tradition which, thankfully, is no longer continued.

Aunt Sally

This is a genuine game originating around the seventeenth century in Oxfordshire and still played throughout the Chilterns and Cotswolds. There's even an Aunt Sally World Championship, although it's doubtful if many teams from abroad have ever entered. There is, however, a French version of the game called 'jeu de Massacre' or 'The Killing Game'.

Raft Race

There have always been fun races in village fairs where villagers compete against each other or against rival villages whether on land or water. In recent years raft races have become widespread in British festivals, so I have borrowed some of the more familiar elements and included them in Little Buckford's raft race. After all, it was instigated by Eleanor's uncle, Lord Henley, a man ahead of his time.

Thornton's Bookshop

While in Oxford, Eleanor buys Clifford a copy of Voltaire's *An Essay on Universal History, the Manners, and Spirit of Nations* at Thornton's, the oldest university bookshop in the town. Founded in 1835, it sadly closed its doors in 2001 and became mail-order only. While it was running, it was used for TV series such as *Brideshead Revisited* and *Inspector Morse*.

Queen's Lane Coffee House

The coffee house Seldon takes Eleanor to in Oxford still serves a good cup of coffee, I can vouch for that. It's been there a long time, since 1645. Coffee was originally seen by the Puritans as the 'great soberer' and was praised for the way it 'heals the stomach, makes the genius quicker, relieves the memory, revives the sad, and cheers the spirits, without making mad.'

Unfortunately, politicians disagreed as, for the price of a penny entrance fee, anyone could grab a cup and sit and discuss politics freely. They tried to ban them in 1675, aided by 'The Women's Petition Against Coffee' that complained that coffee houses were turning their once virile, hardworking men into gossiping layabouts. The Queen's Lane Coffee House survived along with others and they became a centre for science as well as popular culture, Isaac Newton even dissected a dolphin on the table of one.

Blood Typing

The blood Eleanor notices on the hook in Solemn Jon's boat was indeed from Burgess. However, at the time, there was no way of matching blood types. It wasn't until 1923 a method was found of checking different blood types using small samples taken from the scene of a crime and it was many years before it became commonplace to use this as an aid to conviction.

Hound Trailing

Dating back to the eighteenth century, hound trailing originally came from Cumbria where it's still very popular. I've taken the liberty of having a Yorkshireman introduce the sport to Buckinghamshire, so I hope I'll be forgiven. There are often fifty to sixty dogs racing in a single event and the 'Trail Hounds', as they are called, are usually specially bred foxhounds.

Horse Riding and Hats

One of the reasons it would not have been suspicious for Lord Rankin to have struck his head and died when falling from his horse was that riding hats weren't commonly worn in the 1920s. Foxhunters often wore top hats or bowlers purely for style. If Lord Rankin had been wearing a bowler hat, it would have offered him little protection from something as hard as a puddingstone.

Sir George Tretheway's Illegal Scheme

At the time, illegal schemes such as Tretheway's were hitting the news, often across the water in the U.S. The most famous, which gave its name to all others of its kind, was instigated by Charles Ponzi in 1920. He promised to double his investors' money in a mere ninety days by buying and reselling international postal-reply coupons, even though the U.S. Postal Service itself stated they could not be redeemed for cash. Nevertheless the scheme netted Ponzi a cool eight million dollars (the equivalent of around one hundred million dollars today).

Wepwawet

Wepwawet is an actual Egyptian god, although as Eleanor rightly guesses, not of water. The half-wolf god actually helps the dead navigate the dangerous waters of the afterlife so they may reach the final judgement of the dead.

The Strange Case of Mr Challoner by Herbert George Jenkins

One of the books Eleanor buys for herself in Oxford was actually published in 1921 and featured a crime story where the butler was the culprit, a most unusual occurrence. Sherlock Holmes had dabbled with the idea before and Agatha Christie in *The Murder of Roger Ackroyd* published five years later cast the butler as a suspect, but he was later proved innocent.

The reason it was so unusual at the time was that it was de rigueur in crime novels to have the guilty party as someone the reader would least suspect. However, at the time, servants were believed to have so little moral fibre, that it would be too obvious if you cast one as the villain!

The well-known phrase 'the butler did it' is actually attributed to the playwright Mary Roberts Reinhart, known as the 'American Agatha Christie' who wrote the play, *The Bat*, that Eleanor stars in in the Little Buckford Amateur Dramatics Society production in book two of the Lady Swift series, *Death at the Dance*.